Deaf Wish

Geoff Cook

Rotercracker Copyrights- ©2019

Published by Rotercracker Copyrights, 2019

Copyright © Geoff Cook, 2019

Geoff Cook has asserted his right under the Copyright, Designs and Patents Act 1988

to be identified as the author of this work

This novel is a work of fiction. Names and characters are the product of the author's imagination and any resemblance to persons living or dead is entirely coincidental

This book is sold subject to the condition that it shall not, by way of trade or otherwise, be lent, resold, hired out, or otherwise circulated without the publisher's prior consent in any form of binding or cover other than that in which it is published and without a similar condition, including this condition, being imposed on the subsequent purchaser

First published in Great Britain in 2019 by Rotercracker Copyrights

Pacific Heights South, 16 Golden Gate Way, Eastbourne,

East Sussex, BN23 5PU

Paperback ISBN 9789899730045

A CIP catalogue record for this book

is available from the British Library

For more information on Geoff Cook, his books and plays, please visit

www.geoff-cook.com

https://www.facebook.com/novelgeoffcook/

Deaf Wish is a work of fiction and comes with the standard health warning that all the characters along with the towns of Cavalla in Portugal and Sanlazer in Spain are but guests in my imagination.
Personal experiences and relationships may shape
and influence this fictional world, but as distorted
and exaggerated from reality as they may be portrayed,
one or other of the characters in these pages
might possibly seem familiar.
You may well think this, but I could not possibly comment.
I can only say to all of the people who have helped to shape this novel that
for any hurt I may once have caused,
I most sincerely apologise. I dedicate this work to you.

In producing this novel, I extend my thanks for their
invaluable support, wisdom and guidance to
Brett Hardman, Nicky Taylor and Andrea Orlic.

"These violent delights have violent ends
And in their triumph die, like fire and powder,
Which as they kiss consume: the sweetest honey
Is loathsome in his own deliciousness
And in the taste confounds the appetite:
Therefore love moderately; long love doth so;
Too swift arrives as tardy as too slow."

Romeo and Juliet
Shakespeare

THE END
Madrid – 2019

He had sat in the car since four that morning. The fake Rolex showed it was now almost ten. That would make it eleven Spanish time. He adjusted the dial. It would always be Spanish time from hereon in. After today, he doubted he would ever need to turn it back to Portuguese or UK time. They would never release him. They would take the watch. Just as well. It was a miracle the fucking thing hadn't stopped working years ago. What kind of fake keeps going? Him, perhaps?

He had kept the windows closed whilst the early morning chill in the city persisted. His stale breath had misted up the windscreen. The interior of the ageing Astra carried the faint smell unique to the aftermath of a takeaway McDonald's hamburger meal and tinged with an aroma of ground coffee beans from the *café con leche* to accompany it.

He clasped his fingers around the cuff of his jacket, moving forward in his seat to clean the windscreen with his arm. The finished result was worse than when he started. Leave it. As soon as he saw them, he would start the engine and put on the heater blower. That would clear it. No point in drawing attention to a parked car with the engine running, especially one with UK plates and no road tax or insurance, and a driver with no licence.

It hadn't rained overnight, so the car was still clean from yesterday's car wash. It had taken a mix of Castellano and sign language to convince the attendant he wanted the super-duper wash with the wheel polish, special waxing and underbody sealant treatment. The man had looked bemused. The paintwork on the car was faded and pitted with age, rusting in points where it had been standing for too long. The wheels were encrusted with dirt and burred where they had been scraped against kerbs.

'*¿Estás seguro?*' the man had asked, looking at his colleague with a sardonic smile on his lips. Crazy English. More money than sense.

'Perfectly sure,' he replied. '*Sí.*'

He couldn't be angry. The attendant had his best interests at heart. He wasn't to know.

He half-opened the window and brushed the remains of a cobweb off the wing mirror. Tenacious things, cobwebs. With all those whirring brushes, streams of water and hot air to contend with, they still hung around, seemingly indestructible. Lucky humans weren't built that way.

He felt he owed the couple that much. If he was going to accelerate into two people and get blood and twisted limbs all over the paintwork, at least he would show them the courtesy of making sure they were killed by a clean car. It was the decent thing to do.

The front door of the apartment block opened. These people were creatures of habit. The man checked he had the keys in his pocket, ushered the woman down the steps and closed the door.

He started the engine, turning the screen heater to maximum as he did so. The car spluttered into life. Traffic was light along this residential street. He knew exactly how long it would take him to reach the crossing. Two days of watching and practice. You know what they say: practice makes perfect. The car rolled forward.

Some people never did the sensible thing. Ridiculous! The *pastelería* was on the other side of the road, twenty metres before the marked crossing. The sensible thing to do was walk further along, cross the road safely and stroll back to the café for their morning *solos y pasteles*. But no, they crossed as soon as they were directly opposite. What would they save? Two minutes? Lazy. Plain lazy.

Why was he getting uptight? On or off the crossing, he was going to kill them anyway.

He pushed down on the accelerator, his arm accidentally jerking on the windscreen wipers. He slowed slightly as he looked to cancel them. Shit! The windscreen was all smeary on the outside now. Damn! He fumbled to locate the screen washer control. At the very last moment, they had to be able to see him, to recognise their executioner.

They were looking around to see if it was safe to cross. Give me another few seconds, he said under his breath.

The car was doing sixty. That was miles per hour, not kilometres. He didn't need to look at the speedometer. The tracking wobble began at sixty, the steering wheel trembling under his unyielding grip.

They had started to cross and he was closing fast.

They were in the middle of the road, no man's land. Not far enough across;

too far to turn back.

One thing he hadn't foreseen. As they saw the car advancing, they halted, unsure of whether to continue. He was fifty metres away.

A car was approaching in the other direction. Hurry on or turn back? What would they do? He pushed the accelerator to the floor.

They began to turn back, all the time looking straight at the Astra. Had they seen him? Did they recognise him? It wasn't just terrorists who drove vehicles at innocent people; not that these evil bastards could be described as innocent.

The oncoming car began to slow down, giving them the opportunity to turn and walk back.

It was now or never. He swerved across the road, picturing in his mind the moment of impact. With any luck, once he hit them they would be propelled backwards into the air and crash into the other car. Thankfully, the other car looked fairly clean.

He aimed and closed his eyes tight. He could not look. 'Here I come. Die, you treacherous bastards!

'For God's sake, someone, tell me,' he screamed. 'How has it come to this?'

PART ONE – GILBERT – REAWAKENING

CHAPTER ONE
Chepstow, South Wales – 2008

The envelope is gathering dust on the mantelpiece, propped up exactly where I put it the day it arrived.

In retrospect, it was a futile act with only one possible outcome. Every time I walk into the lounge, I force myself to look straight ahead, as if to ignore the fact that not opening the letter would somehow postpone the inevitable. Why am I giving it such prominence if I have no intention of reading the contents?

I try to analyse my motives. There is no reason to be apprehensive. In today's digital world, the only bad news that arrives by letter is in a franked envelope and comes from the taxman. But what possesses me is a sense of foreboding, a prescient warning that by acknowledging this unwanted intrusion, I will be faced with the consequences of opening doors to a family life long since locked shut.

From the Portuguese postmark, I know who sent the letter, although the hand that penned the name and address is not my son's. When Albert was young, I often used to tell him jokingly he should follow a career as a GP, for no one would be able to read the spider-like scrawl that passed as handwriting. 'I know, Dad,' Albert would say wearily, with a gravitas which belied his tender age. 'I write like your doctor. You've told me a hundred times.'

It was true. I had, but my adolescent son said it in such an endearing way that I went on repeating it until ...

Until? There I go again. That's exactly why opening the letter will do no good. The past is in the past and I should know better than anyone I must leave it there. To face the contents of the envelope risks propelling all those traumas from another life into the present, wrenching slits into the delicate threads that have woven the last sixteen years into the fabric of another existence.

So, decision made. No longer do I need to treat the envelope as if it's dusted with some deadly nerve agent. My mind is made up, isn't it? Just pick up the damn thing and throw it away.

I hold the four corners between my fingertips. The name and address are written in a rounded hand, delicate and feminine, suggesting a purposeful yet sensitive personality; the use of a fountain pen and not a biro, a certain traditional refinement. The writer has put *Senhor Engenheiro* and not just plain 'Mr'. The literal translation into English of 'Mr Engineer' really doesn't do the title justice. The British afford lowly status to the term 'engineer', little better than the man who fixes the boiler. In Continental Europe it is a respected professional qualification akin to a degree, and I rather relish the idea of this new status. Senhor Engenheiro Gilbert Hart. I can see myself as a member of the Portuguese social elite, warmly known to friends and associates as 'Engenheiro Gilbert, partner in a leading firm of civil engineers with offices in Lisbon and Porto'. It is much more me than 'Hartless', the nickname I gained for making the regulars pay their tabs on time at the seedy bar in Spain that was the final stop in my chequered career.

That misery dwells alongside the many others I can now lock into the compartment labelled 'MISTAKES'. Two years ago, having turned sixty-three and outrun another stormy relationship – the third since Rosita died – it was time for me to wait for nightfall, lock the door of the bar for the last time and return to the UK before the creditors appeared.

I wasn't just 'Hartless' any more. Now, I was 'Potless', or I would have been, were it not for the good old British welfare system. I may have avoided paying social security for half of my working life, but by brandishing my passport and sounding suitably contrite, I was swept into a benefit support arrangement that also provides the one-bedroom flat in Chepstow I now call home.

There is an upside to being one of life's dismal failures. Finally, by accident, I have achieved the one thing I never experienced in all those years of wasted effort and spent emotion. I now know what peace is, not only in the cessation of hostilities with the trail of women who first adored then came to despise me, but from the pressure of constantly fighting to survive and improve, only to see my prospects extinguished every time the bank called in its loan or some money-grabbing landlord tried to chop my legs from under me.

It has taken two years but, finally, I have begun to understand what peace of mind is. No longer do I wait apprehensively for the next argument to blossom, or the final demand to fall on the mat, or the knock on the door, or the ring of the phone. Today, and every day from hereon in, I can step outside the front door and take a deep breath without peering tentatively around the corner to see if some debt collector is waiting to accost me.

That get-out-of-jail-free card is worth everything, and I am damn sure I'm not going to exchange it for some lousy letter from Portugal destined to wreck my precious peace.

The words begin to blur. I wipe a hand rapidly across damp eyes as if caught in the act of displaying my frailty. The envelope is back on the mantelpiece.

Tears come too frequently these days. Self-pity? Regrets? Whatever it is, the descent into sentimentality offends me. The answer is still no.

The ping of the microwave breaks the silence. I push last night's dirty crockery across the melamine surface of the kitchen table to make room for my toad-in-the-hole meal for one. The apartment has a conventional gas oven but I've only half-heartedly contemplated using it once or twice, just to put my head in, certainly never to cook anything. On the other hand, those waves in the magic box standing on the fridge are a source of both wonderment and mystery. I remember sitting one afternoon for hours with the window ajar, listening to the world go by and trying to fathom out why the microwave instructions on the pilau rice pack insist the food needs to rest for a minute after cooking. Is it tired?

The sensation on my wrist is more like a mild electric shock than a vibration. It really is time to invest a few quid in a new watch to replace the fake Rolex I bought from the Somalian hawker. He looked imposing, dressed in flowing robes, as he cornered me in the bar – must have been ten years or more ago now. My genuine Oyster had been stolen and – okay, it was a weakness, I knew – I could see the man was desperate to make a sale, and I was in a good mood. I recognised the scam but the watch looked the part, the till reflected a healthy day's take and I enjoyed the sob story about his sick mother back in Mogadishu. It was a comforting thought that my eighty euros would keep this frail figment of his imagination alive until he sounded out the next punter. After all these years, the watch is still just about working and tells me the time is two thirty: half an hour to go before kick-off.

Every second Saturday during the season, I walk the mile or so to watch Trefil Wanderers play a soccer match in some obscure Welsh league sponsored by a chain of local fish and chip shops. The most attractive aspect of the Wanderers' game is the bright red shirts with the fish skeleton emblem. It's certainly not their ball skills, but that's not the reason I stand in line at the turnstile.

If the quality of football rarely merits the five pounds handed over by the two hundred or so stalwarts spread around the terraces, it is the opportunity to pass a comment about life or share some harmless banter with a group of regulars whom I can loosely describe as friends. At every match, we congregate in our regular spot with a silent nod of recognition, a comment or two about the weather or somebody's absence, and wait for the referee to blow the whistle. That's our motivation. Out come all those well-worn clichés, shouted rejoinders to the centre forward about barn doors or questioning the birthright of an opposition player.

At the interval, a cup of tea in hand, we run through the events of the first half, compare the two sides or discuss the merits of the managers. The conversation is animated and expansive but never sufficiently contentious or intrusive to challenge our frail relationships. I can only recall one occasion when a member of our group, an ex-marine who had fought in the Falklands, lost his temper with the acne-ridden young lad and his two mates who appear at every match and take turns to pound on a drum throughout the entire ninety minutes. I had never seen him angry. It must have been a terrifying sight watching him in action, charging towards you, bayonet in hand. He never talks about how he came to suffer the injury which cost him the lower part of his leg,

The match resumes in much the same fashion as the first half. At the final whistle, we exchange a smile and another nod before we retreat back into the real world and, in my case, fast food and the babble of a radio programme in the background.

The truth is, sad to say, apart from a couple of hellos to neighbours, I have not exchanged more than a few words with another living soul for four days, and then it was only to a tele-salesman who wanted me to subscribe to a satellite television network. I kept him on the phone for twenty minutes before I dropped the bombshell. Not only was I amongst that dwindling minority who did not need or want broadband, but, by my calculations, if I took advantage of the sensational special offer, I could certainly watch television for seven days a week but eat for only two.

'Hello, Gil.'

I recognise Madeleine's voice at once. Whenever there's a break-up, friends and acquaintances tend to end up in 'them' and 'us' camps. She was definitely in the 'them' camp. I don't look around, my eyes glued to the pitch. I hope she finds it disconcerting.

'Your neighbour told me you would probably be here,' she says. 'You always go to the home matches.' She pauses, waiting for a reaction. 'You might at least acknowledge my presence, Gil. We've known each other long enough.'

My attention remains steadfastly focused on the match. 'My neighbour is a nosey old cow who has nothing better to do than spy on the other residents. Lucky you didn't ask to see the man in fourteen. She'd have put you down as another one of his special lady friends.'

'Is it a good game?'

Directly behind us, the drumbeat starts up. The three lads are pushing their luck. Bravado, I reckon; the ex-marine is standing just yards away. 'SPE-shill TRE-fill' they begin to chant repeatedly to the incessant beat.

I grab Madeleine's arm, leading her to the back of the stand, away from the noise and the drumbeat, ushering her across in front of me so that she ends up standing to my right.

'I'm deaf in my left ear,' I say. 'Stone deaf. Only if you stand as you are can I hear what you're saying.'

'I didn't know. I'm sorry,' she says. 'I asked you if it was a good game?'

I shrug. '"Good game" and "Trefil Wanderers" are not words you ever use together in the same sentence.'

'You could say, "How are you, Madeleine? Nice to see you again after such a long time, and sorry I was rude to you the last time we met."'

She's a few years younger than me and carries her age well. The wind swirls the fine blonde hairs loose around the bun she has tied severely atop her head. There is an appeal to a smile in those soft olive-green eyes and an evocative recall in that sixties-style 'kiss me quick' lipstick bow design applied lavishly to naturally pouting lips. I have known her since our secondary school days in South London, when I was first attracted to the slim waist and the firm bust she has preserved remarkably well into old age.

Most of the sixth form had her on their radar, but for some reason lost to me now, we never dated. I had the distinct recollection of wanking off one night, clutching an end-of-term class photo in which she featured. The memory must have brought a smile to my face.

'What do you find so funny, Gil? You were damn well rude to me, and I am still waiting for an apology.'

'No, it isn't that. I was thinking of something else.'

'And?'

I feign being distracted by something on the pitch as I frame a reply.

'I don't recall offending you but I won't vouch for my memory. If I did, I apologise.'

'Sounds a little hollow.' She stamps her feet on the ground and exhales loudly. 'If you're not going to talk to me ...'

'You feeling the cold?'

'For God's sake, Gil. I didn't come here to talk about the bloody weather.' Her eyes close for a few seconds. 'Listen. I put your reaction to me down to the fact that you see me simply as Sandra's friend, and you think of me as a conduit for passing information back to her.'

I give a non-committal grunt. My ex-wife is not a topic I am prepared to be drawn on.

'Just so you know, Gil, I am my own woman and in no way attached to Sandra's umbilical. It's important for you to understand that.'

Any chance of developing the conversation is lost as the referee blows the half-time whistle and the mud-splattered teams make their way from the pitch. I take off my leather gloves, feeding her wind-chafed fingers into the fleece interior. They are a good fit. 'Fancy a drink?' I say.

'I didn't realise they had a bar here.'

I can't help but laugh.

'Did I say something funny?'

As we join the queue shuffling towards the hole in the wall, she squeezes my arm. It's a gesture of solidarity I guess she wants reciprocated, but I don't.

The old man directly in front of us, dressed in clothes two sizes too big for him that smell stale and unwashed, starts a phlegmy coughing session. He takes the plastic cup and paper cone full of wedge-style chips from the woman behind the counter. His hands tremble as he coughs, sending him stumbling forward and dislodging half the chips onto the floor. Madeleine bends to support him but I pull her back.

'Don't draw attention to him,' I say. 'Just pretend it hasn't happened. Most here are down-and-outs who need a helping hand. They just don't like to admit it.'

'Is that the way you feel?' Sadness tinged with pity; two emotions I try hard to avoid.

I ignore the question. We are reaching the front of the queue. 'Pimms Number One or Tequila Sunrise?'

There is little within view on the Formica counter other than a few assorted packets of crisps and some rather dubious-looking sausage rolls. In the background is a bubbling fat fryer, hot water urn, tea bags and a jar of instant coffee.

There is a questioning glance. 'I don't know what to have,' she replies. 'You choose.'

I look up at Charlie. He is having a hard job keeping a straight face. 'What do you recommend?' I ask.

He turns and starts to pour tea from the urn. 'I'd go for the smoked salmon and a glass of Prosecco if I were you.' The female assistant digs him sharply in the ribs.

'There you are,' I say, handing Madeleine a steaming plastic cup of tea and a packet of salt and vinegar crisps. 'Cheers.'

'You are a sod, Gil.' She squeezes my arm again. 'You were just trying to embarrass me.'

We thread our way back to our place on the terrace as the teams re-emerge. I lean against a metal crowd barrier, balancing in one hand the packet of crisps into which she delicately fishes, removing one crisp at a time for careful examination before eating it. I hold the packet up to my mouth and shake a few into the void. She pretends not to notice.

The match resumes to the now-distant beat of the drum and the 'SPE-shill TRE-fill' chant.

'I've never been to a football match before,' she says. 'Henry was a rugby man. I didn't enjoy the physicality—' She hesitates. 'Of the game, I mean.'

'I remember him. He was a giant of a man. Second row, wasn't he?'

'No idea. He always came home with shirts ripped and caked in mud.' She shakes her head.

'I am sorry for your loss. Heart attack, wasn't it?'

'He was standing talking to me one minute and, then ... he just crumpled onto the floor like a piece of burning paper.' She shakes her head again, this time violently, and is silent for a moment. 'Five years ago now. Let's not go back.'

'You still haven't said why you came to seek me out at this unlikely venue?'

'I thought I'd have trouble spotting you in the crowd. Look out for the old suede jacket with the imitation fur collar, your neighbour volunteered.' She raises her eyebrows. 'She certainly takes an interest in your dress code.' There is the flash of a smile. 'The years have been kind to you.'

'Kind isn't a word I'd choose. Come on, now, you're avoiding my question.'

'Are you going?'

'Am I going where?'

'To the wedding, of course. You must have received the invitation.'

'So that's what it is?' I know I sound flat, resigned to this new information. 'I haven't opened the letter and I don't intend to.'

'Albert is relying on you. Please say you'll go.'

I close my eyes and slowly shake my head. 'The last thing Albert is relying on or wants is my presence in his life. He is thirty and his way in the world has been shaped without me. My going would achieve nothing. On the contrary, it would just open up wounds that have long since bled out.'

She tugs fiercely at my sleeve. 'You're wrong. Please listen to what I have to say.' She prises away the plastic cup I have squeezed tight, letting it fall to the ground.

'Look at me,' she demands. Her eyes are transfixed as if she is actually living within the memory. 'When Henry died, everybody expected me to be beside myself with grief. I have to tell you, as devastated as I felt at having lost the only man I ever really cared for, I could not bring myself to cry. Even at the cremation, I didn't feel any emotion. Everybody must have thought what a hard bitch he married! I couldn't blame them.

'Only a few days after the funeral, I met a neighbour. You know what it's like; everybody is full of all the clichés and platitudes heaped on the bereaved.

But she said something that opened the floodgates.'

She stops for a few seconds, seemingly holding back the memory and the tears that are close. 'It was just one of those famous one-liners people repeat almost without thinking. This woman said, "Still, at least he died knowing you loved him".' She produces a tissue and blows her nose. 'The trouble is, he didn't.'

Neither of us speak while she composes herself.

'Not a day passed that Henry failed to lavish some compliment or expression of love upon me. And what did I do? I just smiled back. I adored the ground he walked on, but I couldn't remember the last time I said I loved him. And then, I began to think of all the other things I wished I'd said to him. Not just smarmy, lovey-dovey things, but my intimate feelings about our life together. The regrets, not the recriminations, about not having children. The dreams I had for us both for the future, when he retired. A hundred things I chide myself for never saying and for which I have not stopped crying all these years later.'

She squeezes my hand tighter still. 'Please don't let that happen to you, Gil. Make peace with your boys and admit you're sorry, because I know you are. Let them get to know their father again, warts and all, before the chance has gone.' She peers at me. 'You're crying, Gil, you're crying!' I tug my hand away like a petulant schoolboy, stand upright and stretch my arms out sideways in a gesture that says I don't care.

A collective groan rises from the crowd as the home side ships in another goal.

'Trefil Wanderers and Gilbert Hart have one thing in common,' I say, with a sardonic laugh that is not a laugh at all. 'We are both losers.' I shake my head, more to clear it than to deny her request. 'My boys don't give a monkey's toss about me, and who can blame them? Besides, what does Sandra think about this initiative of yours? She doesn't want me at the wedding, surely.'

'I don't know what Sandra wants, but you are probably right. She would rather you didn't go but that's to be expected. She has never learned to accept, let alone forgive you for deserting them in the way you did. But I didn't come here today because of Sandra, and I have no intention of telling her I have seen you unless she asks.'

'I assumed ... Then why are you here? To make Madeleine feel better?'

I can sense by the put-down stare she gives me I have gone too far. It reminds me that as a young woman, she had a feisty and quick-tempered nature.

'That is unkind, Gil. Don't take your angst out on the messenger.'

'Messenger for whom?'

'I think Albert sometimes finds his mother a little too full on and uses me as a sounding board.' The palms of her hands come together as if she is about to pray. 'When he phoned me last week, he said he expected you to say no. We've kept in touch since I was out in Portugal with Sandra and Roger last summer.' She interlocks her fingers, her knuckles white. 'He asked me to try and convince you to come.

'Albert is still very committed to the Buddhist faith. His working life is tied up with Buddhism, practically as well as spiritually. He says he really wants you to figure in his world, not simply be the stranger who brought him into it.'

I ease my shoulders around inside my coat. Her conversation is making me feel uncomfortable, images of family life still so vivid.

'His interest seemed to develop from nowhere. From one day to the next, as he approached adolescence, Albert began to take an interest in Buddhism.' I hesitate, shuffling my memories. 'You wouldn't have believed they were brothers. Vernon had his bedroom wall plastered with posters of heavy rock bands and violent video games. Albert had pictures of the Dalai Lama, and burned incense that stank like those lettuce cigarettes my mother once took up when trying to quit smoking.'

A cheer comes from the crowd as I go to carry on. An opposition player has been shown a red card and is trudging from the pitch. The chant of 'SPE-shill TRE-fill' is temporarily substituted by a barrage of drum-beating and 'Who are YER? Who are YER? Whoever you are, yer OFFFFFF!'

I lean closer to make myself heard. 'I'm not surprised Albert is that way inclined. He was always remarkably single-minded.'

She nods. 'His words to me were, "Tell Dad I don't *want* him to come to the wedding".' She seems to stop for effect, like a bad actress in a bad play. '"I *need* him to be there."' There is another dramatic pause as if she is waiting for the applause before continuing. 'And it's not just Albert who wants to see you.'

I raise my eyebrows. 'Vernon?' It's more in hope than expectation.

'Sorry. I'm afraid your elder son is very much hardcore anti-Gil. He still blames you for the breakdown Sandra suffered all those years ago when she first heard about the baby. I don't think she'll ever encourage him to seek a reconciliation with you, but Vernon is not a man who needs much of an excuse to blame anybody for the cards he considers life has dealt him.'

I can feel the pulse beating in my neck. 'After all this time, I had hoped …'

She shakes her head. 'It's not just you. Sandra won't admit it, but Vernon has a problem. He experiences violent mood changes. One minute, he can be smiling and pleasant, and then, for no reason, sullen and moody the next. Worst of all, he has a very violent temper.'

I have memories of a teenager with a radiant smile and an unpredictable temperament. The vandalised traffic lights, the 'devil worshipper' in spray paint across the vicar's car and many more signs of a disturbed adolescence I had conveniently dismissed as growing pains, rather than face the reality of a parental issue needing to be resolved. Back then, I was totally wrapped up in my own little purposeless world, seemingly indifferent to the challenges of a family life with which I was rapidly becoming disenchanted.

'So, if not Vernon?' I try to sound mildly curious rather than interested in the answer.

'Albert is marrying a lovely lady called Jasmin. She is the local vet and anxious to meet and know Albert's natural father. You must not let her down.'

'These are just platitudes, Maddie, and you know it. What possible interest can she have in me? She has met Roger. He's Sandra's husband and the father-in-law now. I don't see the point.'

'Because she wants you to get to know your grandson.'

'They have a child?' It isn't confirmation I need, just the privacy of the moment to process the realisation. I am a grandfather.

'Francisco. He's three years old. A wonderful little boy, so full of energy and so inquisitive, you would not believe it. You'll adore him, Gil.'

'I didn't know, did I?' Of course I didn't. Why am I asking stupid questions? 'I can't go,' I say, more in desperation than denial.

'Of course, you can. What could stop you?'

The final whistle blows and the players tramp slowly off the pitch, looking as lifeless as the emblems on their shirts. The hardy supporters who have suffered to the end are making their way to the exit.

As the remnants of the crowd filter through the exit, we stand facing each other on the narrow pavement, forcing people to step onto the road in order to skirt around us. Some glance across, mumbling, probably complaining at our insensitivity, but neither of us move. I have no intention of prolonging the conversation in some other location, inviting her back to the flat or sitting in her car. I guess she feels the same way.

Suddenly we're alone, standing in the failing light, searching for words and finding none. She is fiddling with a silver four-leaf clover pendant on a gold chain around her neck. I remember she once told Sandra it had been her grandmother's. Sandra said it betrayed her mood, that she would play nervously with it whenever she was uncomfortable or embarrassed, just as she is now.

'Please don't be stubborn, Gil,' she says finally. 'You must meet him.' She smiles, as if holding a memory. 'And they need to see you.'

The one thing I am certain of is the knowledge I have a grandson changes everything, not only weakening my resolve but scuppering any objections I might raise. Even so, there is a voice in my head saying it's wrong, it won't work out for the best; all those reasons I lined up for not opening the damn invitation in the first place. But come on, I didn't count on there being a grandson, did I?

'I live on pension support.' I hold my hands outstretched. 'Even if I wanted to go, I simply couldn't. I don't have the spare cash to fund a trip to Portugal.' I follow up quickly with the clincher to forestall what I guess might be her reply. 'And I am definitely not prepared to accept charity from anybody to get there. That is cast in stone.'

A smile crosses her lips which smacks of the victor who has expected me to parry and can now counter with the coup de grâce.

'I don't think anybody would offer you charity, Gil. But, as it happens, it did cross my mind finances might play a part in your decision. I have a proposal for you.'

You calculating bitch is what I'm thinking.

'I never did get around to selling Henry's Astra. It's a diesel and very economic. I've also got a loyalty voucher from the ferry company for a five pound trip to Bilbao. You have to depart in the middle of the night and there's no cabin, but the reclining seats are quite comfortable. You're supposed to sail back within twenty-four hours, so they can get you to spend all your spare cash on board, but you just don't turn up for the return leg. You're welcome to use both to solve the problem.'

'There's still the fuel, tolls and return ferry costs. How am I supposed to deal with those?'

'Don't sound so pathetic. That's not like the Gil I remember who enjoyed a challenge. I'll have you know I've given this a great deal of thought on your behalf.' There's a smug look of self-satisfaction on her face. 'Look, from Bilbao to Northern Portugal is less than a day's run. Take the non-toll route back to Dieppe or Calais; you can do the whole thing for a couple of hundred pounds, max. Apply for a credit card. The wedding is not until July. Even as a pensioner, they are bound to give you a basic credit limit. Lie on the application form if you have to. You don't have any debts here to count against your credit score, do you?'

I shake my head. There is little I can do other than admit defeat gracefully. I say nothing, just hold her shoulders and kiss her on both cheeks as they do on the Continent. 'I may have serious doubts, but I appreciate your concern.'

She clenches my hand. 'I'll tell Albert you'll be going. By the way, what was the final score?'

'I don't know. We lost, I expect.'

CHAPTER TWO
En route to Cavalla, Portugal – 2008

The Basque country might be bathing in a sun shining out of a classic blue sky, with not a trace of wind to ruffle the leaves on the trees, but this scene of tranquillity flatters to deceive the torment taking place offshore.

After the most miserable twenty-four hours of my life, I have reached the conclusion the Bay of Biscay is one of the most hostile sea passages the unsuspecting traveller can possibly encounter. The crashing of the waves against the hull is not only frightening in its severity, sufficient on two occasions to eject me from my seat onto the floor, but the swaying rise and fall of the ferry, so constant and inevitable, tells me there will be no let-up to my stomach-churning nausea.

Once beyond the choppy swell of the English Channel, the vessel steers into calmer waters as it follows the shoreline around the Brest peninsular. The crew look on with a maliciously sanguine appreciation of what is to come, as their human cargo takes heart from the improving conditions and tucks into a breakfast of full English. Those smug bastards know we will soon be disgorging our stomachs, ashen-faced and staggering around the vessel like drunks in a hurricane, praying for a release from our misery.

And so it is, early the following morning, I find myself six kilometres from the port of Bilbao, parked in a lay-by. My mouth is bone dry, my breath caked in the stench of the vomit dried to a crust on the front of my Status Quo T-shirt. With no air conditioning, the heat in the Astra is oppressive. Exhausted not only from the lack of sleep but from the torment of my recent ordeal, and still experiencing the effect of the vessel's undulating motion, my legs singularly fail to respond to my brain's command to exit the car.

My plan was to benefit from the ferry's early arrival by driving non-stop south-west through Burgos and Salamanca before turning west and across the border into Portugal, where I would check in with Albert for final directions to his home in the town of Cavalla. There is no way now I can maintain this timetable.

With what feels to be a superhuman feat of willpower over lethargy, I drag myself out of the car and, like an overgrown child with a security issue, pull my sweat-stained pillow and blanket behind me. Madeleine counselled bringing the bedding to make the sea crossing 'more palatable', as she phrased it. Only twenty-four-hour knockout drops could have achieved that objective.

I arrange the blanket to cover the bird droppings on the long wooden picnic table, turn the pillow to its less offensive side and lay down. At the time, it seemed like a perfectly logical thing to do. In retrospect, I realise I must have looked like a corpse on a mortuary slab.

All I need is forty winks.

It didn't make sense. The tide was definitely coming in, but the rowing boat was bobbing up and down in the swell and moving farther away as it did so. Rosita was sitting there, dressed in that low-cut blue floral dress which she loved and I detested. I thought it made her look like a flirt, connotations of the persona I felt she adopted whenever she wore it.

She was waving at me, smiling, turning her head so I could see the flower, a small red rose, its petals closed tight, caught in her hair above those delicate and beautiful ears I loved to kiss. In those heady early days, I could make her react by playing around her ear lobes with my fingers or gently nibbling with my teeth, sometimes flicking the tip of my tongue inside in a rapid penetrating movement, her legs wrapping around me as the simulation fed her imagination.

I could see something wedged between her outstretched legs, pressed tight to her crotch. It seemed like – it was – a baby in a white christening dress, one tiny hand rising and falling. I waved back, beckoning them closer to the shore, nearer to where I could wade in and pull them to safety.

But the swell was rising; the boat pitched and tossed on the waves. It must be leaking. Rosita stopped waving and began to bail out water with a teacup. She dipped her hand in front of the baby and filled the cup, tossing its meagre contents into the sea. I could see now. It was not water she was ejecting. It was red, blood red.

I heard the motor start up. If she had an engine on board, why didn't she turn the rudder and head back towards the beach and safety? But as the noise increased, the boat slipped further and further away until it became just a dot on the horizon.

The image has passed. I am sweating, momentarily unaware of my whereabouts, confused by the sunlight warming my eyelids and the stench of the exhaust from a two-stroke engine. The clutch engages with a clunk, followed immediately by the sound of gravel spitting out from underneath tyres. The pillion passenger turns to give me the middle-finger salute and the motorcycle races away.

In those initial seconds, hazy with sleep, I'm confused by my surroundings and the scene confronting me. All the car doors are open and my suitcase lies upside down, the contents strewn around in the dirt.

I stagger to my feet. How stupid could I have been? The sensible thing was to lock the car, not invite some chance thieves to help themselves to my paltry assortment of belongings.

My wallet? Passport? Money? The sensation of dread passes with the lungful of air exhaled in relief as I touch the bumbag clipped to my waist. But the slot for my mobile is empty. I threw it onto the passenger seat after checking the route map. Of course, it's gone, along with the cut-glass decanter I bought as a wedding present and the motorised toy tractor for my grandson, a special buy from the charity shop in the high street.

As far as I can tell, apart from an old electric shaver the thieves did not consider the rest of my possessions worth stealing. And it could have been worse. I was not physically harmed. Panic. Car keys? I scramble around inside the car. Thank God. They are nestling in the pocket of the driver's door.

I shake my head to rid it of the malaise. After a rinse and change of shirt at a service station, memories of the ferry crossing start to recede. It could have been worse. I'm beginning to feel like my old self and keen to make progress.

I drive slowly, remembering the rules for handling a right-hand-drive car on the wrong side of the road: ensure the driver's position alongside the kerb and bear right at roundabouts. My technique is far removed from that confident expatriate beginning a new life in the sun all those years ago, weaving confidently through the traffic on the highway from Malaga to Marbella. That same man is now crouched earnestly over the wheel of an ageing Astra, unwilling to see the needle on the speedometer pass the sixty mark.

Perhaps both these images of Gilbert Hart are reflections of my passage through life. Back then, a fresh start – the new man – a false optimism, racing forward to shroud the past. And now, I head cautiously towards the endgame, fearful the prospect of reconciliation will be dashed and replaced by a return to rejection and solitude. What I crave is one last curtain call where the players hold each other close, shoulder to shoulder, smiling, happy and united. What I harbour is the death scene from a Shakespearian tragedy.

My body aches as fatigue sets in. The dashboard clock indicates twenty minutes past midnight as the streetlights of Cavalla finally come into view.

The address and contact number for Albert are safely and exclusively recorded on my stolen mobile. The best thing I can do is to enquire at the local police station. Signs at the intersection lead me to a small retail park and a double-fronted red brick building with a shallow V-shaped roof. The light from a single, low-wattage light bulb barely illuminates the recessed entrance door framed around a sheet of frosted glass.

A half dozen rickety, straight-backed wooden chairs are set around the sides of the room, leaving space for two doors: one from the entrance; the other, to the internal offices. In the centre, there is a sliding glass partition with a counter panel either side. The image is something between a doctor's waiting room in some Third World backwater and a ticket office at a lonely station outpost. There is nobody about, just raised voices coming from the inner recesses.

As I go to knock on the counter for a second time, the internal door is flung open, striking the partition wall. An unseen hand ejects two individuals into the reception area with a grunted instruction I don't understand. They are both young men, swarthy with the North African features I remember so well from my years in southern Spain. The one with the dark beard shaped to a point looks at me with hollow, suspicious eyes. The second man, shorter, with dirty stubble, is slightly younger and has been in a fight. A purple swelling around his left eye, coagulated blood under his nostrils. A damaged right arm hangs limply to one side of his torn and bloodstained T-shirt.

I merit no more than a cursory glance as they slouch onto chairs, heads bent towards the floor. The one with the beard speaks in a coarse, guttural voice. Schoolboy French and a moderate grasp of Spanish are all I can harness, but cursing sounds much the same in any language.

Before I can knock on the counter for the third time, I watch and wait as a man I take to be a plain clothes detective ambles along the corridor towards the reception area. He catches my eye, stopping in his tracks.

'Dad?' he exclaims in astonishment. 'Gilbert?'

I don't recognise him at first. The wiry black hair swept back, collected into a stubby ponytail; his height, well over six foot – he was just a gangly boy when I last saw him. But his mulatto skin, those sensuous, full Caribbean lips and the piercing blue-grey eyes Sandra said were from her mother's side of the family, they are unmistakeable.

'Albert? I didn't realise you were a policeman.'

The man with the beard looks up in amazement.

'I'm not,' he replies emphatically. 'Give me a moment while I speak to these two, would you? Then, fill me in on what on earth you're doing here. I expected you to go direct to the house. Jasmin is waiting for you.'

Before I have the chance to reply, he goes into a huddle with the two men. The conversation is whispered but with undertones of anger and hostility. After a few minutes, there is a cursory shake of the hands and a sideways glance towards me before Albert ushers them out.

My son is a good three inches taller than I, broad-shouldered but with a torso tapering to a slim waistline that accentuates his height. The slightly protruding chin, a feature inherited from my grandfather, the high cheek bones; both features suggest to me a resolute yet sensitive individual. All in all, he has grown into a handsome man that says everything good about the product of a mixed marriage. Yet, there is something about the guarded smile, the difficulty in making eye contact that makes me feel a little ill at ease.

'So?' he asks, putting his hands gently on my shoulders.

I give him a potted version of the ferry crossing experience, exaggerated to excuse the obvious failings in protecting my property.

'Lucky I'm here, then, isn't it? You may not believe this, but until tonight I had not met our local police chief, so I doubt he could have pointed you in the right direction.'

'Perhaps he would have put me up for the night.'

His laugh erupts into a cough, but I sense concern my sudden appearance may have created a dilemma for him.

'From what I've seen, the accommodation is nothing to write home about,' he jokes.

'You seem to be well acquainted with the place. Begs the question of what you are doing here.' I really don't mean to sound like the censorial father, but old habits die hard. I must learn to keep my own counsel.

For a split second, I'm afraid he's reacted by turning away without saying a word and leaving me in reception, but I have misjudged him.

'Look, to be honest, your turning up here is an embarrassment. Can I ask you to do something for me?'

'Of course.'

'If I tell you what's happened, can you do me a favour and go and sit in your car for ten or fifteen minutes until I come to collect you? Do you mind?'

What can I say? I wait for the explanation.

'I want to avoid another confrontation,' he says.

I begin to understand. 'Vernon?'

'He was involved in a fracas in one of the local bars with the two men you saw me speaking to. He was drunk. He's staying with Mum and Roger at a country hotel in the valley. It's quiet. He came into town for a little nightlife and got into a fight.'

'Over what?'

'Don't know.' As a kid, it was always easy to tell when Albert was lying, but I don't want to press it.

'It's almost sorted. It was a close-run thing. The guys were going to make a complaint but I convinced them to back off. The police chief here, Lannier, doesn't want the aggro and will probably let him off with a caution. My main concern is to make sure Mum doesn't get to hear about all this. She will go ballistic. It's the wedding tomorrow.' He glances at the clock. 'Later today,' he corrects, 'and we could all do without the hassle.'

From somewhere inside, I hear a series of profanities in English and the sound of hurried footsteps approaching. I turn to face the wall, fearing the worst. I don't want to confront Vernon here and now.

Albert speaks in Portuguese. I turn back, breathing a sigh of relief.

The man could have easily been Albert's father. His skin is the colour of ebony, naturally brilliant; his face, classic features with deep-set green eyes. And he is tall. Six-four at least, I guess, and an impressive physique that points to daily sessions in the gym. He says nothing, just stares me down.

'I was explaining to Sargento Lannier that I was giving you directions to your accommodation.' Albert's eyes are pleading. 'I think you know where to go now, yes?'

Nodding my thanks, I walk back out into the clammy night air. The scent of honeysuckle hangs heavy in the soft breeze. I climb into the driver's seat and wait.

From where I'm parked, and with only hazy moonlight to illuminate the scene, it is difficult to make out the features of the man supported around the shoulders by Albert as they make their way to an old blue Peugeot estate. He is a good deal shorter than his brother and clutches an ice pack to the bridge of his nose and forehead. His slow, cautious gait suggests he has received a severe kick in the groin. If anything, he is a little darker-skinned than Albert, although this could have been accentuated by his shaven head which is dotted with small white squares of dressing. In spite of his brother's vain attempts to quieten him, Vernon roars a litany of abuse directed at the Portuguese. Fortunately, there is nobody around to hear his slurred Welsh accent and gutter vocabulary.

I watch the tail lights disappear into the distance.

The silence is oppressive. Nothing stirs. I am alone, but much more. I cannot recall having ever felt so lonely as I do at that moment. No longer am I central to anybody's life; just somebody who exists in the margins, an afterthought, a throwaway name in someone's tale about the past. The pulse throbbing in my stomach tells me there is no one left to cuddle me, to tell me that the pain will go away, to assure me everything will be all right.

I reach down, feeling for the pre-programmed buttons on the car radio. I need to discard this isolation. Nothing. Silence. Of course not, you idiot! They're set for UK radio stations. My fingers fumble with the tuner.

The sound of the sea crashing against the shore fills the space. A man's voice, soft and comforting, rolls in behind the waves. *'O seu rádio: Oceano Pacífico. O som de um novo dia.'* My knowledge of Spanish gives me a sense of the Portuguese and his introduction to the sound of a new day. The perfect timbre of Benny Goodman's clarinet picks up the opening refrain as Peggy Lee's lazily sensuous voice glides into the lyrics. Smoke may get in your eyes, I thought, but the quest to define love is never-ending.

How *do* you know when love is true? Sandra had asked me the very same question the day after we had announced our intention to get engaged.

At the time I had an old Ford with a bench seat across the front, ideal for courting couples who wanted both privacy and intimacy without having to perform major gymnastic feats across the handbrake void between the usual bucket seats. For the over-energetic, the Ford's ivory-coloured, wobbly column gear shift could have damaged a lot more than just pride, but neither the bench seat nor the shift was a factor in our developing relationship.

It wasn't that Sandra felt restrained sexually; we were as intimate as you can be without fumbling into intercourse, but she needed to be loved and to feel love in a way so that our physical engagement would follow naturally and completely – her words, not mine. Above all, Sandra could not conceive that everything she had to offer should be constantly challenged by the sideways glances or disingenuous comments from members of a closely-knit immigrant Caribbean community who lived in each other's pockets and, it seemed to me, congregated daily around her family home. I could only imagine just how much her attitude must have been influenced by her parents' view, as forcibly expressed by her outspoken brother: that 'Whitey' was only interested in one thing and would bugger off when he got it. Even so, I never criticised her family, never a sign of the resentment I felt towards the countless aunts and uncles, nephews and nieces whose hands I shook and whose eyes prejudged me. That would have been taboo, but the frustration lingered all the same.

There was nobody to talk to about my pent-up feelings. Whatever expressions of solidarity I might have received from my small group of friends, the truth, I knew, was that they all secretly felt my motives were much as Sandra's brother described. So, I said nothing. As for my parents, Mum believed the panacea for any emotional discomfort was the offer of a steaming mug of tea, and my stepdad … I did try talking to him on one occasion. He actually let the *Daily Mirror* slip into his lap and listened. He said he'd never understood me. How any child could run the bath so hot that they knew when they put their toe in, they would have to immediately take it out, he could never fathom. 'Most people put cold in, but not you,' he said. 'You wait until it's cooled down just enough and then you chance it. The water's still too hot but you get in. You're doing just that with this black bird.' And as for his take on Sandra's romantic attitude to our relationship: 'Sounds to me your tart's got her head stuck in the agony aunt columns of *Woman's Own*. She'll be so concerned with worrying over whether you still love her or not, she'll forget to cook your supper or wash your undies.'

I was definitely on my own, but I didn't care.

Sandra would lay along the bench seat, her feet dangling out of the passenger window into the darkness, her head resting on my lap. She must have realised from the rigidity of my erection just how uncomfortable it was for me, but there was no concession to my discomfort and no attempt on my part to move her head. She would talk and I would listen. Story after story, retold from her mother and the circle of female relatives who had once experienced life on a small Caribbean island before embarking on a new life in the suburbs of London. Sandra's voice would assume more of those lilting black tones as she talked of life in a strange world where Evangelical Christianity meets black magic, where one God meets the deities of Kalfu, the moon god, the foul-mouthed goddess Maman Brigitte, who watches over the cemeteries and, Sandra's favourite, Erzulie, the goddess of love, beauty and passion.

How silly we were. I recall feeling stupidly disheartened for the entire precious hour we spent together on one occasion, when she insisted just how she wanted to be like Erzulie. As crazy as it seems, I got angry. Why did she admire so much somebody who spent most of her time drinking champagne, wore three wedding rings – one for each husband – made love freely with other gods, yet refused Nibo because he was black? Did she really want to be like that? She just laughed. You're silly, she told me. Erzulie isn't real. But, for me, right there and then, she was.

Smoke gets in your eyes. I never did get around to answering her question. Just as well; I didn't know the answer. Still don't.

Headlights are approaching in the distance. Albert will shortly be taking me into his world, introducing me to his family. What a mess I have made of it all! How can I possibly hope to make things right again?

CHAPTER THREE
Cavalla – 2008

A Buddhist educational centre set in the rolling countryside of Northern Portugal is an unlikely setting for a wedding reception, but once you put convention to one side, the choice struck me as a sensible option for a couple with a limited budget.

Quite how difficult finances are for Albert, his wife-to-be and child becomes apparent early the next morning when I am given the obligatory, albeit brief, guided tour around their house.

There is neither the opportunity nor the inclination to appreciate the surroundings when we arrive in the early hours. Our whispered conversation in the light of a single candle is limited to ensure we do not disturb Jasmin and Francisco and to point me in the direction of the sofa bed in the lounge. With an offer of a bottle of mineral water and a string of instructions as to where the bathroom is situated, the location of the light pull cord, removal of the baby's fit-on toilet seat before using the loo and a request not to press the flush, Albert mouths a silent goodnight and disappears into the darkness. That's fine by me. I'm so physically exhausted and emotionally drained that despite the ping of some uncomfortably loose springs as I settle down on the mattress, sleep comes quickly.

I suppose you have to get used to a universe of bugs and creepy crawlies when you live in the country, but the little devil tickling the hairs in my nose is both persistent and noisy. Fortunately, I open my eyes just as I bring up my hand to swat the offending intruder. The tiny fingers poking in my nostrils are attached to a small figure lying stomach down on my bedclothes. A head of curly brown hair rocks from side to side as he begins to giggle uncontrollably at the discomfort he is causing me.

As I move my head, he jumps up and scampers to the end of the sofa. The flannelette dressing gown splays open to reveal a pair of pyjamas with a Thomas the Tank Engine design I haven't seen since my boys were his age. There is no fear or wariness of a stranger in his demeanour. He is just out for fun. As he stands at the foot of the bed, those tiny hands gripping tight onto the arm of the sofa, he begins to shake it with all the strength he can muster.

He giggles again, and as I pretend to be scared, he giggles even more until the effort of laughing eclipses his physical strength and he falls onto the floor, out of breath and lost in his humour.

'Francisco!'

He reacts as if he has received an electric shock, climbing immediately to his feet and looking warily in the direction of the voice.

She is dressed in a one-piece dark-blue overall outfit with an apron cross-strapped over her shoulder. Her features are heavy yet beautiful; full lips with creases in the corners to suggest a permanent smile and slightly slanted eyes that give an oriental appeal. She runs long, delicate fingers through a thatch of straw-coloured hair.

'Leave your grandpapa alone. He is tired from his journey and needs to rest.' She speaks in English.

I can't remember which of my employees used to say, 'Don't get me wrong,' before making a controversial statement, but don't get me wrong when I say I do not know or have ever known anything as sensually arousing as an attractive woman speaking in English with a wonderfully accented Latin tang to her voice.

'You're awake.' Albert stands in the background.

I'm blushing, ashamed and randy all at the same time. I manage a weak smile and a rather stupid wave.

'I see you've already met Jasmin and Francisco.'

I sit up and offer my hand to Jasmin with a welcoming greeting and a plea not to worry about the child. He is not disturbing me. I remain firmly tucked into the bed covers. My packing didn't extend to a dressing gown and I've got a hard-on.

Albert appears to be appraising me. 'We'll give you a chance to get washed and dressed. It looks like it is going to be a lovely day, so we thought breakfast outside. You okay with that? There are some fresh croissants and local honey.'

Today there is something distant in his attitude, impersonal, as though he is simply extending a courtesy to a stranger. In a way, I suppose he is. Natural enough, I tell myself. What with concern for his brother and the prospect of getting married at five that very afternoon, he is bound to have a lot on his mind. If I had expected a fairy tale reunion with tears and hugs, expressions of remorse and forgiveness, I can forget it. The stony expression, the sideways glances are telling me there is a mountain to climb.

Thirty minutes later, we are sitting in white plastic chairs around a rickety matching table. At least the simple fare is delicious and the coffee, strong and black; just how I like it.

Francisco continues his obsession with my facial hair and has now turned his attention to balancing on my knee and reaching out to touch the strands in my ears as if he were stroking a cat. I override the parental objections with a plea not to stop him. Playing with my grandson is a novelty for me and something I cherish.

'Are you going to answer the question?' Albert asks.

'Sorry?'

'Jasmin asked you a question.'

I turn my head to the left and recognise the quizzical expression. 'I didn't hear you, I'm sorry.' I smile. 'I forgot to mention. I am stone deaf in this ear and often miss what people are saying. Don't be offended.'

'How did it happen?' she asks.

'Not sure. Neither is the doctor. Most likely the result of an infection, a side-effect from the drugs I take for high blood pressure, or a mini-stroke. Nobody can be certain but, apparently, it's irreversible.'

I recall Madeleine telling me Jasmin was a vet by profession, and the look she gives me fits my idea of the portfolio of expressions to adopt when about to put a client's pet dog to sleep.

'What was the question you asked me?'

Albert responds. 'She wants to know if you need any clothes pressing for the wedding.'

My one and only suit has survived the journey relatively uncreased, and as nobody will care what I look like, I shake my head. 'You were going to show me around the house.'

As Jasmin clears away the breakfast things, Albert appears relieved with the distraction from whatever is going on inside his head.

His aim, he tells me, is to improve the garden with a pond, a playground for Francisco and an orchard of various fruit trees. The proposed transformation from what Albert calls a lawn but can only be described as a field with intermittent patches of grass is a leap of faith to tax any practical person's imagination. With a fence separating it from the adjoining farmland on two sides and a border marked by bushes and shrubs beyond which is a small copse, it's certainly large enough, but his ambitions are asking a lot of one man's spare time.

To the west, there is nothing to see for miles but the undulating hilltops and neatly defined woodlands; to the east, houses are dotted along the road leading into town, increasing in density as I look into the distance.

The house itself is a simple single-storey, detached building on a corner site at the perimeter of the urban limits. To the front, a large area of dirt has been beaten to provide a stand which, I guess, would do for six vehicles. Today, there are just the Astra and Albert's ageing Peugeot estate.

The internal layout of the house is an unusual design, in that there is no entrance hall or corridor; you walk straight into the lounge, from where each of the bedrooms, kitchen and bathroom are accessed. Consequently, there are doors everywhere and, except for the wall to the rear which is divided by French windows leading to the garden, there is barely space to hang a picture. Although the lounge contains the sofa bed, two casual chairs, a flimsy bookcase and TV, it is as much a transit route from one room to another as a place to relax.

As we move around the house, Albert's perfunctory recital of past achievements and future projects are rendered in an unenthusiastic monotone. The overriding impression I gain is of a neglected property renovated by an unsupervised DIY amateur on a strictly limited budget. Nothing started has been completely finished. The double-glazed windows have been fitted, but the surrounds neither rendered nor painted. The odd wall is still brickwork awaiting plaster. And when it comes to the small utility room and the gas boiler and hot water installation, memories of my former trade in the UK come flooding back.

'This needs serious attention, son.' I take a chance with the word but he doesn't react one way or the other. 'The way this has been done is dangerous. Look, the pipework's loose, placing a strain on the fittings. The electrical connections need insulation. There's no failsafe. I could name a dozen problems. Don't you need a safety certification in Portugal like we do at home?'

'I don't know,' he says. 'Hugo and I put it in. We googled how to do it.'

'Get an expert to put it right.'

'Maybe you could write down a list of what needs doing? It would be a great help.'

At last, I can contribute. I'm needed. 'Of course. I'd offer to fix it for you but you need somebody who understands all the local requirements. Anyway, I've forgotten most of it.'

'A list will be fine.'

Jasmin coughs to attract our attention. She is going to meet up with colleagues from the veterinary practice to help her put the finishing touches to the room reserved for the wedding reception. In an oblique gesture, she hands Francisco to me rather than to his father with the comment, 'He seems to have taken rather a shine – is that what you say in England?' spoken with an assurance that suggests she does know, 'to his grandpapa.'

The child is sucking hard on a soother and I can feel the warm dribble running down my neck as he clings tightly to me.

Albert opens the door to what was once a garage but is now part storage, part workshop. We are nearing the end of the tour.

'How did you get on with Vernon last night?' I ask.

'Okay,' he replies, equivocally.

'Anybody up when you got back to the hotel?'

He turns around. I expect Francisco to hold his arms out, anxious to be taken, but neither he nor Albert react.

'Mum and Roger had already gone to bed. Madeleine was waiting to let him in. It's a small, country hotel – a *pousada*, as they are known. Mum calls it an exclusive boutique destination.' He laughs. 'Whatever, they don't expect guests to be out after midnight, so the doors are locked. Madeleine assumed he would come back the worse for wear, but not quite in the way he did turn up. She saw him off to bed.'

'Why didn't you want Vernon to come face-to-face with me?'

He turns back to face the front, avoiding my questioning gaze.

'You saw him. He gets violent when he's drunk. Chances are he would have found a reason to hit you.'

'Does he hate me that much?'

He hesitates. 'You've earned the right,' he says, eventually.

That hurts. The truth always does, they say. I should have pressed on but like a coward afraid of the outcome, I change the subject. 'What's this for?' I ask, pointing at an industrial sewing machine sitting on a large square table.

'Cushions,' he says. 'I make prayer cushions and artefacts for Buddhists and followers of the faith. We sell them on the internet.'

'Does it give you enough to live on?'

'Just about. But I do other work, as well: labouring for friends, seasonal work in local farms and helping out in the *adegas*.'

There is a large pile of rectangular-shaped cushions in the corner of the garage. 'Are these they?' I ask.

'Yep. All made to order, ready to be shipped. Jas and Adele help out when I'm busy.'

'Adele?'

'A friend from way back when. She's the local pharmacist.'

Through late morning into early afternoon, I become the surrogate babysitter. Jasmin returns with the announcement they have forgotten to make a table plan, provoking a flurry of activity as she and Albert make numerous telephone calls before huddling together over a large sheet of paper and a list of guests' names.

Francisco and I watch on but after three hours of amusing each other, we are both in need of a nap. As soon as he is bedded down on the sofa, I try to doze in one of the casual chairs.

An issue preys on my mind as I drift in and out of sleep.

Why has Albert gone out on a limb to invite me, blatantly contrary to the express wishes of the rest of the family? Is he trying to make a gesture intended only for the day and laying no foundation for the future? I try to convince myself there is a simple explanation for his apparent failure to come to terms with my presence, but the nagging doubt gives me a sense of total isolation. I am starting to feel unwelcome. The opening to talk about our relationship and my misgivings was lost at the mention of Vernon's name, when he put me firmly in my place. I bottled it but the opportunity will present itself after the wedding, when the time is right.

I awake with a start. Think positive. I have to get ready for a wedding.

The car horn blares impatiently. I check my appearance in the mirror one last time, praying the jacket button around my midriff will hold out. My concerns will wait. It has to be all down to a simple question of timing and will be happily resolved. I have nothing to fear, do I?

CHAPTER FOUR
Cavalla – 2008

The civil ceremony at the Conservatório, the registry office, is quick and simple, officiated in a dark, wood-panelled anteroom by a stern-looking lady in heavy-framed glasses who has an abrupt manner. Only the immediate families are present, and I get a cursory nod of recognition from Roger and a warm smile from Madeleine. As I expect, neither Sandra nor Vernon acknowledge my presence. In the circumstances, just as well. Someone has done a remarkably good patch-up job on Vernon who, apart from a slight swelling under his left eye, looks nothing like the wounded figure I watched stagger to the car the previous night.

Although Jasmin comes from a large family of Anglo-Portuguese extraction with its roots in the wine trade, only two members are present, she tells me. Her mother, a matronly woman whom I subsequently learn runs the local primary school, wears a permanently censorious frown as she looks over her glasses at me as if I have an infectious disease. She has a cigarette, sometimes lit, sometimes on hold, permanently wedged between her lips. Hugo, Jasmin's brother, is taking the job of best man extremely seriously, herding the guests around as if he were tending to an unruly flock at a sheepdog trial.

An elderly couple, heads bent in apology, shuffle into the room as the proceedings get underway. Looking uncomfortable in clothes lined with creases, suggesting special occasion wear only, they acknowledge Jasmin and her mother with embarrassed smiles and receive a glare of admonishment from the registrar.

Freed from Jasmin's control, Francisco amuses himself by darting intermittently in between the legs of the guests to emerge holding his hands up for me to lift him into my arms, where he rests for a minute or two, only to wriggle to the ground once more to repeat the antic.

Although Sandra deliberately pretends not to notice, this ritual does not go unseen; a mini triumph which gives me a surge of pleasurable one-upmanship. It is short-lived and fades as I realise just how meaningless it is.

Can she sense I am standing directly behind her? Is that gesture of gently running her fingers along the spine of Roger's jacket an unspoken comment for my benefit? Look at what you sacrificed. And I did – look, that is.

The years have treated Sandra kindly. I like to think today she dressed just to impress me, to prove her point; that snappy lemon-coloured two-piece showing off her statuesque yet voluptuous figure; the matching blouse, low-cut and tailored tight in at the waist, designed to enhance both a patch of dark-brown skin with a brilliant sheen and the contours of a skimpy lace bra that accentuate the line of her breasts. She has lost none of the allure which once captivated me. No doubt over the years we were together, I allowed it to become tarnished in my eyes by familiarity, neglect and pressures of family life, but now, as she stands proudly alongside her husband, for the first time I can remember I feel pangs of jealousy.

Her face is unlined. She never bothered or needed to use much make-up. Somewhere back along the line there must have been cross-breeding, because her features have a thin and precise definition so characteristic of an Indian or Asian appearance. She has always carried off her natural beauty with an air of naivety mixed with self-confidence. But I remember another Sandra. On a bad day, the tightness of her lips, the dispassionate, unblinking stare from those exotic sea-blue eyes, and a haughty and self-assured look that shuns attention, all precursors to the severe bouts of depression from which she regularly suffered, at least in the early years of our marriage.

With the formalities complete, we assemble outside the imposing entrance to the registry office to allow Hugo to take some impromptu photographs of the newly-weds on his Blackberry. Madeleine and Roger follow suit and I feel obliged to join in, carefully shielding from public view the ancient Nokia which Albert has loaned me. As we click away, Hugo begins to usher the group towards their respective vehicles for the twenty-minute drive from Cavalla to the venue for the reception.

The four-car convoy sees Jasmin a passenger in the lead car, driven by her mother, with Francisco alone in a child seat in the back. Albert follows in the old Peugeot with Madeleine, his parents and brother, and I sit alongside Hugo in the third car, the rear seats of which are occupied by the elderly morose couple who arrived late and whom Hugo introduces as grandparents on his father's side. Unfortunately, they speak no English. The final car contains the three maids of honour.

After craning my neck around to give a smiling welcome in my best Spanish and receiving a tepid smile from the old man and a look of incomprehension from his wife, I turn my attention back to Hugo.

It's the first of many occasions when I compliment somebody on their command of English and apologise on behalf of the entire Anglo-Saxon race, probably unreasonably, for its own linguistic failings.

'My maternal grandmother was from the north of England,' Hugo explains. 'She died some years ago, but she was always adamant that the family spoke only English every night at dinner. Sometimes we would curse her stubbornness under our breath but she was right to insist. It made my life easier when I lived for two years in Brighton.'

'Working?'

'Well, yes and no,' he replies. 'I opted out of further education, preferring to start earning a wage. I didn't fancy staying in Porto, so I was faced with the choice of one of the two things that you can do in Cavalla if winemaking' – he indicated with a nod the couple in the back – 'is not for you. It's either the pharmaceutical industry or commercial paints.'

'You don't look like the decorating type to me.' Hugo is tall and wiry, not an ounce of excess fat on his body, yet he doesn't have the appearance of somebody who works out. It's more a natural physique, not in any way muscular. His features are soft yet given a masculine appeal by the pencil moustache and goatee – I hesitate to say beard, more cultivated stubble – following the line of his cheekbone.

'And the connection with Brighton?' I press.

'I joined SantaCavalla as a trainee representative in the MRCW division. It's selling to chemists and wholesalers. The industry is full of technical language, mostly in English, so as soon as I joined, they packed me off to Brighton on a degree course to master the detail.'

He steers the car off onto a minor road. The scenery changes dramatically. One minute we are following the sweeping path of the River Douro towards its source, another five hundred miles away in the depths of northern Spain; the next, we are climbing the sloping uplands away from the river. Traffic is light, the road twisting and turning between acre upon acre of neatly tethered rows of vines, the intense green leaves cloaking bunches of grapes ready to be harvested. Sunlight flickers between the shadows cast by the tall stone pines that line the narrow strip of asphalt.

Suddenly we emerge into bright sunlight and our first view of the Dharma Meditation Centre. It looks about the size of a small village school, but as the road dips into a hollow, I can see this first impression is deceptive. What I had assumed was a view of the entire building is merely the first and second floors set above a ground-floor complex easily three times the size. The structure is typical of seventies functional office architecture, red brick with single-glazed windows encased in green painted metal frames.

'Who stuck this place in the middle of nowhere?' I ask.

Hugo laughs. 'Believe it or not, it was built with Russian money shortly after the Revolution of 1975. It was supposed to be a Luso–Soviet social integration facility, where we Portuguese, oppressed by decades of dictatorship, could learn all about the utopia of communism. Needless to say, it didn't last. Mc Donald's ruled and the Soviets went home. The Buddhists took it over. They love the place, come from all around the world.'

Distracted by my question, he brakes late. As the tyres bite into the gravel, loose stones career up to rattle against the panes of glass of a double full-length window, behind which a group of people are standing, arms folded, facing towards a blackboard and a thickset man in grey-coloured robes. Nobody inside reacts, their heads remaining steadfastly pointed towards the front, intent on whatever the robed man is saying.

Hugo registers my look of surprise. 'Bonkers, if you ask me,' he proffers. 'The lot of them.'

I cannot get the image out of my mind. The noise inside must have sounded like the rattle of a machine gun, yet not one head turned nor a single expression changed.

'Albert's just the same,' he continues. 'It's annoying, as if he goes into a sort of self-induced trance to cut himself off from reality if he doesn't like what you're talking about or feels threatened. Drives me crazy sometimes.'

'You've got to know him very well.' It's just a throwaway line, something to say, but his eyes narrow and he studies my face.

'Married my sister, hasn't he? Best I understand what's going on in my brother-in-law's head, don't you think?' He sounds as if he's challenging me to disagree.

The remaining cars park. 'You had best follow me,' Hugo announces. 'We are in the main prayer room. It's a complicated layout. You can easily lose yourselves.'

Like Indian bearers penetrating deep into the jungle, we make our way single file along a maze of corridors, threading a path amongst a throng of people moving between various study rooms.

The main prayer room is situated in the middle of the building, from where all the ancillary facilities fan out. There is no natural light. It is a large rectangular room which appears to have been hurriedly converted into a venue for a no-frills wedding reception.

In one corner, heaped together, lay a pile of prayer cushions, several ornate, gold-veneered pieces of furniture featuring cross-legged figures, and various lengths of material with highly decorative tassels at either end. Around the walls are hung a series of equally ornate tapestry carpets from which there permeates an unpleasant odour of stale incense.

At the far end of the room, forty or so guests hover in small groups in front of six trellis tables on which are laid out small plates of appetisers, jugs of red and white wine and a variety of soft drinks.

Hugo is off, hands waving, on best man duties, leaving me on my own, smiling and nodding as I edge towards a spare glass, the jug of red wine and a handful of filled cocktail sticks from a cheese and pineapple arrangement which went out of fashion on the canapé scene decades ago.

A lone bystander at a party can often be a sorry sight, ignored and banished unnoticed to the perimeters. But I'm not alone. No sooner do I devour a mouthful of bland cheese mixed with overripe pineapple and have one hand free, than my social integrator, in the form of Francisco, is upon me, nestling his bottom in the crook of my arm, his hands clasped around my neck. '*Avô,*' he exclaims.

Immediately I am no longer an outcast. People appear alongside me, reaching to stroke those little arms, talking at him in cartoon accents and acknowledging me with a smile and sideways glances that categorise me as a stranger with apparent family credentials.

I find myself back on to Sandra as she converses with the elderly couple who were sitting behind me in the car. Roger is ostensibly in attendance but is paying little attention to his wife. The grouping intrigues me as, to the best of my recollection, Sandra knows no Portuguese.

'... although we didn't need the extra two bedrooms – after all, four is enough for anybody.' Sandra barely stops for breath. 'The fact that the lounge was so spacious with such a commanding view – and the conservatory, of course – well, that convinced us to go the extra two hundred thousand. Didn't it, darling?'

Darling is busy looking over at the three bridesmaids who have just walked into the room, barely clad in matching light-green chiffon dresses. Roger is like a caricature of the English country gentleman, with the flamboyant silk cravat tucked into a large check shirt and a Burberry-style waistcoat that boasts a gold chain and pocket watch.

'Roger!' she prompts.

He turns back sharply as if caught with his hand in the cookie jar, but he remains impassive, composure intact. '*Sim, sim,*' he says with a broad smile, prompting her to continue.

'Of course, Roger was sold on the grounds with the lake.' She waits momentarily for a reaction that does not come. 'We will have to make sure it's out of bounds when Albert brings young Francisco to stay, won't we?' I don't believe she's aware of our presence directly behind her.

'As I was saying, Roger thought he might turn the second field into a pitch and putt course but it didn't happen, so we let it out to a local farmer for grazing.'

I can hear Hugo's voice interrupting. He introduces the couple to whom Sandra is talking as his grandparents.

Sandra says, 'Pleased to meet you,'; Roger, an exaggerated '*Prazer*'.

Hugo explains the couple run a farm and vineyard on the outskirts of town. 'Unfortunately,' he says with regret, 'neither of them speaks any English.'

I stifle a snort of laughter. It's right at this point I realise I desperately need to go to the toilet before we sit down to dinner. As I move away, signalling to Jasmin I need to hand over my charge, I catch the tail-end of the conversation.

'I am sorry.' Sandra turns to Hugo, breathing hurriedly as she speaks. 'And here I am, babbling on. What must they think of me? They appeared to understand everything, smiling and laughing. Silly me.'

Roger looks around, out of her earshot. 'They must have learned the technique from her friends.' His aside is not directed at anyone in particular but he gives a conspiratorial wink and nods at me.

Lost in a maze of corridors and sweating with the exertion of trying to keep my bladder in check, there is no other option than to burst into one of the study rooms and ask for directions. A man in a deep-red robe stretches out his arms and rests his hands on my shoulders. Miraculously, the urge to pee is stilled. In somnolent tone he assures me someone will accompany me, and asks will I promise to return to the room for five minutes afterwards? How can I refuse? At that precise moment, I would have sold my mother, God rest her soul, to avoid the embarrassment.

In my haste, I must have passed the toilet block shortly after leaving the reception.

'Don't forget to come back and see the master,' the anxious young man says as he points at the sign on the door and scurries away. I'm standing at the urinal, voicing my relief into the empty void as the outer door creaks on its hinges and a draught of cold air tells me I have company. The figure stands at the urinal next to me; not the customary 'leave one between us' unwritten rule common to normal male cloakroom behaviour. A hand the shade of milky coffee fumbles with his fly. I look around.

'Hello, Vernon.'

He neither looks at me nor speaks, his eyes riveted on white porcelain.

I finish and go to step back but his free arm presses against me, holding me in check. 'What is it?' I say, flustered. 'I didn't come here to cause a problem. I was invited. Let me go, please.'

'Glad you didn't say "son".' His voice was rasping, an undercurrent of hostility.

'What?'

'Glad you didn't say, "Let me go, please, son." I don't have a father. He died; as good as. I've got a mum to look after. That's enough.' The material of my jacket is twisted around his hand. He's a lot stronger than his frame suggests. There's the strong scent of vinegar ammonia on his breath, like the smell of paint cleaner.

'As I said, your brother invited me and I accepted. If that offends you, I'm sorry. Things need to be said.'

'They certainly do. How right you are. Things both need to be said and to be done. That's fine by me.' The blank expression on his face suggests otherwise.

'It is?' I am momentarily lost for breath. 'Is it really fine?'

'Mum doesn't want you here. It's upsetting her, making her agitated, and I can't have that.' Another turn of the material. My head is being pushed close to the tiled wall.

'What do you suggest I do to avoid any embarrassment?' I push back as I say it. 'Do you have to use force to make your point?'

'Like I say, things have to be said and actions taken.' All of a sudden, he releases my jacket and begins to wipe at it with the palm of his hand, stroking the creases as if trying to remove them. 'I'm not sorry you came. Everything can be sorted out.' He gives me a forced smile. 'I saw you standing close to Mum. Just keep away from her, all right? I don't want her getting all tearful again. We've told her you're a piece of worthless shit' – he looks down at my shoes – 'who can't even piss straight. You bring back painful memories for her and I can't have that, can I?' He turns on his heels and strides out of the door.

I need a few minutes to try to understand just what that thirty-second confrontation is supposed to mean. Is the intention to try and find a modus vivendi to suit us all, or to provide some form of closure for Sandra? Still confused, but conscious of my promise to return and speak with the master, I make my way back to the room in which I sought directions.

Ten minutes have passed and I need a breathing space, fresh air and some time to dwell on the significance of my two very contrasting experiences since I left the wedding reception.

The steel-blue sports car with the Mercedes logo on the grill comes to a stop in the cross-hatched space marked for disabled drivers. The driver emerges in a rush, fiddling frantically with the remote key fob to lock the car. With severe swept-back black hair, heavily greased, tanned features and an immaculate light-grey suit, he looks as if he has just walked off the set of *The Godfather*. As it is, he must have taken me for a janitor, firing several sentences in Portuguese in a voice obviously used to ordering people around.

'I'm sorry. I don't understand.' I'm tempted to add, 'I'm English,' but it seems superfluous.

His expression changes as if the sun has suddenly appeared from behind a rain cloud. 'Do forgive me. I am terribly late for my niece's wedding and my sister will be most angry. You don't know where it is, do you?'

'We're at the same event. I'm Gilbert, but everybody calls me Gil.' I hold out my hand.

Smooth, tanned skin and polished, manicured nails are on show as I feel his firm grip. 'Lino. Lino Reyes. I'm Jasmin's uncle. And you would be?'

'Albert's father,' I reply, hesitantly.

He stops to look me over. 'I remember you as a taller man,' he queries.

I give a knowing smile. 'You must have met Roger, Albert's stepfather. Sandra and I are divorced. I'm ...' I'm searching for the words.

'The biological father?'

'Yes. No. I was about to say I'm returning to the fold after a lifetime in the wilderness.'

'How terribly biblical,' he says, as we enter the room, his head suddenly bowed in apparent contrition and his attention directed towards Jasmin's mother who reacts by beckoning anxiously for him to greet the newly-weds.

All the guests are now seated at three large rectangular trellis tables covered in paper tablecloths and casually sprinkled with confetti. Vases of garden flowers and jugs of wine and water are interspersed along the centre of each table. Each place setting consists of a piece of folded paper with a handwritten name on it, a lonely bread roll on a side plate, a wine glass and an empty main course plate. The buffet is being arranged on the tables behind us by three serious-looking, bald oriental men wearing starched white aprons.

In the middle of the central table sit Albert and Jasmin, with Hugo to the groom's left, and Francisco, in a high chair, next to his mother. Around this group are Albert's immediate family, a Buddhist monk whom I have not seen before and the old couple from the car.

Lino pulls at my arm, directing me towards the only vacant places on the second table. 'We appear to be sitting together,' he says.

The guests at the remaining tables are either friends or relatives of the bride's family, and Lino spends a good few minutes shaking hands and exchanging exaggerated air kisses and brief comments, few of which I understand. He is apparently well known and well liked.

He resumes his seat and says something to me which obliges me to turn my head towards him with a request to say it again. I explain the deafness on my left side.

'I was saying that the seating plan must have been arranged so that you do not feel lost amongst all these newly acquired friends.'

I watch Vernon, head bowed, deep in conversation with Madeleine on the main table. She looks earnestly towards me with a half-hearted smile that says keep your distance.

If I could not address my family directly, I can still feel the inspiration from the teacher of the study group, the man in robes who had asked me to step back into his class. The adrenalin is pumping. I need to make my position clear. I stand up and tap a fork on my empty glass. The room falls silent. It's my opportunity. No turning back.

'Sorry, I cannot speak to you in Portuguese. Can I ask those who understand to roughly translate for those who do not speak English? I'd just like to say a few words before the food is served.'

People look quizzically at each other. Sandra wheels around in her chair as if someone has pinched her bottom. Her half-whisper is well within my earshot. 'What the hell! He turns up out of the blue and starts acting as if he owns the place. If anybody is taking the role of the groom's father, it's you, Roger.'

Roger shrugs. 'Let him have his five minutes of fame.'

I look around at the expectant faces. I feel empowered. 'Thank you for your attention. If I don't say what I feel at this moment, I will not have the courage to speak up later.' I take a deep breath. 'Some minutes ago, I went off to look for a toilet and ended up in a room where a group of people were sitting cross-legged on the floor in meditation.' I indicate the robed man sitting on the main table. 'A man dressed like this gentleman grasped my hands, smiled and welcomed me. I said I was amongst strangers and felt lost. He looked deep into my eyes and told me that I could not possibly be lost because we had just found each other. To take the time to learn just a little about each other would make life richer for both of us. And, we did.'

A few people are actually bothering to translate, so I hold fire for a few seconds.

'That simple statement made me realise just what today and the marriage of my son, with whom I have had little contact during his adult life, to the lovely and beautiful Jasmin, really means to me. When I entered this room today, I felt totally alone. For years, for many reasons, I have been lost; and now, I have found you all and ask, in turn, that through the joining of our two families, you search your hearts and find me.' There may be nothing in my glass, but I hold it aloft all the same. 'Thank you for inviting me; and to my son, his wonderful wife and child, I toast your health, happiness and long life. Thank you.'

I sit down to a smattering of applause and Sandra's voice, part laughing, part contemptuous. 'Wasn't that just cringe-making?' She looks around for support.

'Sounds like he's trying to find some Facebook friends,' Roger adds.

Hugo is on his feet, explaining the programme for the rest of the evening. Lino looks askew at me. 'What was all that about?'

The adrenalin that inspired me is now draining rapidly from my system and I am beginning to regret my precipitous action.

'It seemed like the right thing to do. A cry for help, perhaps.'

He slaps me on the back and ruffles my hair as if we are old friends. 'All you have achieved is to embarrass yourself and the people you are anxious to convince.'

'I take it you don't approve.'

He shrugs. 'You sounded like the man who murders his parents and then asks the judge for leniency on the grounds he is now an orphan.' He stands up. 'Shall we try the buffet?'

There is a restraining hand and I turn to face the woman sitting to my right.

I was so obsessed with my new vision, which is now beginning to feel fanciful and vacuous, I have not even acknowledged her presence. As I recall, I first noticed her shortly after my arrival. Conspicuous because she was standing apart from the other guests and permanently engaged on her mobile, her demeanour seemed to say leave me alone. Now, she gives me a welcoming smile to hold my attention.

With an air of worldliness and depth of experience in her eyes and facial expressions, I guess she is in her mid forties, whilst her looks and slender figure say she could easily pass as ten years younger. There is something demur, cherub-like about that round face, framed by a haircut I associate with the sixties style introduced by Vidal Sassoon where the locks curve around the contours of the face. The subtle way she looks at me conjures up an image of Lolita, the appeal of the temptress combined with the deceptive look of compromised innocence.

She glances at Lino who remains standing, waiting for me to join him. 'Don't pay any attention to my brother, Gilbert. He's a pretentious prick.' She gives him a brief hot tap–cold tap smile. 'Isn't that right, Lino?'

He proffers a cynical bow of his head in acknowledgement. 'Gilbert, let me introduce you to my headstrong younger sister.'

She ignores my extended hand. 'I am Brigitte. Please, never abbreviate it as he does. I was not named to be known as the structure that facilitates your passage from one side of the river to the other. Shall we eat?'

We pick at our plates of a vegetarian mishmash.

'I'm a meat eater,' she announces. 'You can't just have the accompaniment without the main event.'

Lino stops in mid-sentence a conversation he is conducting with an admiring audience and turns towards Brigitte, raises a knowing eyebrow and winks at me.

'Don't be taken in by my loan-sharking sister,' he whispers loudly, as if pretending to take me in to his confidence. 'She preys on the weak and helpless.' He blows her a kiss.

'That is your prerogative, is it not, Lino? By overcharging for your fancy potions, the pharmaceutical industry keeps its fat-cat executives in TAG Heuer watches and flashy cars.'

'At least I don't charge destitute old ladies interest upon interest so I can afford a chauffeur.'

They are talking across me as if I'm not there. How do they see me; the weak and helpless – they were the words he used – vagrant, taken in off the street and given a free meal?

'Bollocks, Lino!' she fires back at him.

He senses the advantage and addresses me. 'You know my sister is always on the phone? It's a ruse. There is no one on the other end, if you don't count Eros Ramazzotti or some other Italian pop star growling in her ear. She thinks by pretending to be part of an animated conversation, it keeps people from approaching and intruding into her space; just the way she likes it.'

'Most people respect your privacy,' she retorts. 'That excludes Lino, who is about as sensitive as a frostbitten toe and delights in embarrassing his younger sister.'

I turn my head like a spectator at a tennis match, waiting for Lino's rebuttal, but he just smiles.

'I read somewhere your corporate strings are now being pulled by some Third World dictator.' I recognise she is trying to penetrate his thick skin, but I sense he is used to coming out the victor in their skirmishes.

'If you are referring to the acquisition of Industrias Quimicas SantaCavalla by a Brazilian conglomerate headed-up by an inspired entrepreneur who seeks nothing less than global domination of one small corner of the pharmaceutical market, then you would be correct. And of its Portuguese outpost, I am pleased to say that I am its esteemed commercial director.' He gives an exaggerated bow of the head.

'I am pleased things are going well for you.'

The jousting nature of their exchanges has passed. 'To be brutally honest, these are exciting times and rather cast our previous existence in a poor light. The Brazilian management is totally on the ball and incredibly demanding. It's sixteen hours a day full on at the moment.' He nods towards a man at the other end of the table. 'Same for the people on the technical side.'

I finally see an opening to join the conversation. 'Rather destroys the myth that Brazilians spend their days in the sun and the nights dancing samba, never doing today what they can leave until tomorrow.'

'Nothing like it,' he retorts. 'The corporate culture comes from the big US multinationals where there is intense competition amongst a breed of executives who have sold their souls to the corporation. The locals have taken this on board and do not stop pushing. I sometimes think it is we, the Europeans, who are doing the samba as we watch our continent start to disintegrate around us.'

A mobile begins to ring to the tune I recall won this year's Eurovision contest.

'Time for another Brigitte musical interlude,' Lino says sarcastically, his attention switching to the other end of the table.

Brigitte turns her head towards me, the mobile to one ear and a hand shielding her mouth to avoid anyone around the table other than me overhearing what she is saying.

The only things I pick up are the caller's name, Claudio, and his failure to collect money from a client. By the tone of her voice, I guess he must be an employee. As her frustration grows, the speed of the conversation accelerates and I understand nothing, save her last remark, spoken finally in a measured voice, to advise that she will be returning to Porto that evening and they will meet.

As the call ends, she downplays her annoyance. 'Getting people to work for you is one thing; getting them to do their job properly, something else. I think hell must be having to meet up for eternity with all those people you couldn't stand on earth.' She shakes her head as if to rid herself of the thought. 'Anyway, contrary to what my brother says, I enjoyed your spontaneous outpouring. You have enlivened what was shaping up to be a very tedious event.'

'Is that what it sounded like – a spontaneous outpouring?'

'I guess so, but as you can see, your plea has fallen on deaf ears. How can I put it?' She pinches the ends of her hair between her thumb and index finger, playing the strands into the corner of her mouth as she works on a metaphor. With a flick, the hair falls back into place. 'Knowing my family as well as I do, it's like a doe approaching a pack of hyenas and asking, if she lies on her back, will they rub her stomach?'

'I thought hyenas only approached when their prey was weak and dying.'

She tuts. 'What naivety in such an experienced man! There is always at least one behind the false laughter who will attack the defenceless. When he does, they all join in.'

'And who would the aggressor be in your family?'

'I couldn't possibly spoil your fun and tell you. You must find out for yourself. After all, it could be me.'

'You don't look as if you could tear me to pieces.' The second the words leave my mouth I realise she might read some unintended sexual connotation into the remark. By the expression on her face, I'm right. I change tack with my stock line on linguistic ability. 'Your family is giving me a distinct inferiority complex. You, Hugo, Lino – your English is impeccable.'

She is enjoying my awkwardness. 'Mother's influence, plus husband number two in my case, an impoverished Canadian poet with some unusual predilections.'

'Are you still married?'

'Good Lord, no! Gone through three since him. We only lasted two years but he taught me a couple of invaluable lessons.'

She turns to deflect a comment from someone to her right, at the same time delicately cleaning the French dressing from her bottom lip with a paper napkin.

'Sorry, you were saying,' I prompt as she turns back.

'My poet? Yes. You know, Gilbert, poetry is like the phases of physical appeal in a long-term relationship. At first, it is like an aphrodisiac, stimulating the senses and bringing you to the heights so quickly and so intensely, it is almost too much to bear. Next, it mellows and sustains you for some time. In the next phase of your appreciation, you become extremely selective, sometimes critical. Finally, it starts to bore the hell out of you.'

I laugh. 'You said a couple of lessons?'

'Ah!' She points her index finger at me. 'Most important of all is the well-trodden advice that after one shot of marriage for love, any woman with a modicum of good sense should stick single-mindedly to marrying for money.'

'You have a very avant-garde approach to life.'

'There you are, you see. You have to use a cliché. I've always found with you Anglo-Saxons you feel more at ease when you can pigeon-hole people. The need to put everybody in a compartment, it avoids dealing with the complexities of the individual.'

Have I offended her? It's difficult to tell. 'I suppose I see a woman with a liberated attitude to life. Is that classifying you?'

She heaves an extended sigh. 'Liberated attitude, avant-garde; just silly labels. You will probably go away from this conversation believing that I am some progressive, strong-willed feminist who likes to dictate in the bedroom. True or not, it may never cross your mind to wonder whether I have a comfortable pair of dog-faced slippers, striped winceyette pyjamas and a paperback romance in large print on my bedside table.'

'Do you?'

She reaches inside a small, expensive-looking handbag. 'The allure of a woman is to have those small intimate secrets. Listen. I expect now you have made contact with your son, you will return to see him. If you are ever in Porto, look me up. My private number is on the card. I'll lend you a book to while away those lonely nights.'

'Brigitte Cousteau.' I place the card carefully in my barren wallet. 'The name rings a bell.'

Hugo stands in preparation for the speeches. The noise of the guests subsides.

'No relation, I regret,' she says above the silence. 'You are thinking of Jacques, the seafarer. My Cousteau was no diver; not in that sense, anyway. Mine was a diamond merchant with a bad heart.'

'*Senhoras e senhores,* Ladies and Gentlemen ...'

CHAPTER FIVE
Cavalla – 2008

The sun is about an hour away from setting as I sit on a bench at the edge of the car park, where a corner of the adjoining lawn has been turned into a small children's playground. I'm taking my job as babysitter seriously, concentrating on Francisco's every move, standing the instant I feel disaster is imminent and amazed every time the boy somehow manages to sidestep my worst fears and career on to the next distraction.

All in all, I am grateful for the godsend of having found an excuse to escape the rigours of polite social intercourse with only one good ear. My stereo function of locating and identifying individual sound sources has long since left me and, in my monophonic existence, all the noises blend into one, making a normal one-to-one conversation difficult. One or two interruptions with 'excuse me, would you mind repeating' are acceptable. The constant need to have everything said twice or more is as infuriating for the speaker as it is for me. In the end, I just try to lip-read or smile and nod as I guess the comment merits.

The parade of speeches from Hugo, as best man, and my son, followed by a random assortment of friends and relatives, is predictable and suitably clichéd – or, at least, the bits I understand. Roger provides an amusing interlude by cheering loudly as Hugo gives the customary thanks to the bridesmaids. Ten minutes later, his voice can be heard again as it rises in anger to Sandra's provocation. 'No. I will not make a speech and that's final. Now shut up!' He smiles limply as heads turn towards him.

I didn't have the opportunity to speak with Madeleine, whose sole role appears to be entertaining Vernon as far away from me as possible. I looked over at him on a few occasions, smiling recognition, only to receive back a stony stare.

Background music from a portable home entertainment centre encourages guests to gather into small groups or jig around on the makeshift dancefloor. With Jasmin's blessing, I take Francisco and we make our way out of the room. As I watch him play, I recognise my grandson and I have a mutual interest, based on different needs, bringing us closer together to the exclusion of other people.

I spoke to myself too soon. The sound of high heels tottering unsteadily on the paving stones behind my back goes unnoticed by Francisco as he attempts to mount a plastic horse set on a large spring, but brings a dull ache to my stomach. My peace is about to be disturbed. Although my hearing may be deficient, my sense of smell is acute enough to recognise the scent of a distinctive perfume curdled with a hint of gin.

'Hello, Sandra.'

She walks around in front of me, hovering, a little unsteady on her feet. A sort of cock-eyed smile splits her face. Her eyes are blinking fast. Surprisingly, she is wearing fresh make-up.

'Enjoying yourself?' she says, taking an involuntary step to one side and blocking my view of Francisco. I wave her away from my line of sight before she has the opportunity for a follow-up line.

'All good, thank you,' I reply.

She moves back, grinding one of the stiletto heels deep into the grass. 'Thought I recognised the receding hairline and hunched shoulders from a distance.'

Is there a faint hope I can neutralise the conversation? 'A happy occasion, today, eh?'

'Let's forget the small talk, Gil. Why don't you tell me just what the fuck you think you're doing here?'

I know if I laugh, it will make her angry, so, stupidly, I do. 'Why don't you come straight to the point, Sandra?'

'Don't try to wind me up, Gil. I asked you a question.'

'I had an invitation. By the way, I can't remember if I used to tell you how sexy you are whenever you get mad at me. It's quite a turn-on.'

She moves her free leg back theatrically, at the same time forcing her head forward with an expression as if she is studying a distasteful foreign object. 'Good God,' she says, the contempt heightened. 'I don't believe it. After more than forty years as boyfriend, lover, husband, father and, above all, total bastard – finally, a compliment.'

She is teetering on the brink of losing her temper and I am trying to goad her – what am I playing at? Trying to score points. The relationship was always competitive. Surely by now, I have learned my lesson. 'I'm sure I must have lavished praise on you many times. They say love is blind. Maybe it is. When it all goes bad, you can't allow yourself to remember the good bits.'

She shakes her head. 'What good bits? And now, the prodigal father decides to return. What do you think is gained by coming here, just to stand up and make that ridiculous speech like a beggar pleading for an emotional handout?' There is a caustic laugh. 'By the way, whatever you think, I was sorry to hear about Rosita. Drunk, was she? You drive all your women to drink, Gil?' She looks around, but the glass in her hand is empty. 'The simple facts are you abandon your wife and family, destroy the lives of the other women you dig up to shag and disappear into the wilderness for the best part of God knows how long.'

'I'd hardly call Spain the wilderness.'

She waves a hand to dismiss the comment. 'It's as good as, if you can't be bothered to keep in touch with your own flesh and blood. Then, out of the blue, like the proverbial bad penny, you reappear to prey upon the fragile emotions of the son you discarded and his new family.'

Francisco stops playing and stands still, holding the rope of the swing, studying the two of us.

'That's hardly fair. When the business failed and I was forced into retirement, it took me time to reorganise my life. I wasn't thinking much about anybody else. And the last word I would use to describe Albert is fragile. After being around him for a while, I would say that your stabilising influence and his life, built around the Buddhist faith, have turned him into very much the well-balanced individual.'

There is a slight tremor of her left hand which she quickly holds with her right.

'All credit to you and Gordon's,' I mumble. I know. Don't tell me! There's a demon inside me and I immediately kick myself for saying it. Thankfully, she misunderstands.

'His name is Roger, not Gordon, as you know full well.'

If my compliment momentarily softened her tone, the introduction of her husband into the conversation hardens the mood.

'Don't try and belittle him,' she says. 'He's twice the man you are or will ever be, Gil; a real husband and lover, not a part-time self-satisfier. Thank God, he came along at the right time. Me, cast adrift, with two young boys to fend for.'

I can't resist it. 'Yes. Poor you. Cast adrift with a thriving business, the house, most of our savings and a good slug of maintenance every month. Some shipwreck! And as for Roger, as I recall he didn't just come around, as you put it. He'd been there, sniffing around you for years. I never realised just how close he must have got.'

She feigns indignation. 'You are a cruel man, Gil. At least he knows how to treat a woman.'

'He's had plenty of practice.' It is hurtful, provocative and uncalled for. I desperately need to reassess a reunion that is going nowhere but downhill. 'Look. Let's stop this sniping. It's all water under the bridge.' I smile, more at the mixed clichés than at her, but she holds a tight-lipped expression.

'If there is one thing I've learned today,' I go on, 'from the aura that surrounds this place, it is that whilst we might like to turn back the clock and do things differently, the only useful thing about the past is to learn from it. What's important is the here and now. I think the Buddhist term for it is to declutter. So, why don't we?'

If I could just stall the conversation. 'If you look after Francisco for five minutes, I'll go and get us a drink.'

She shakes her head. 'You always were a hopeless dreamer. You might be mesmerised by all this bell-ringing, incense and chanting, but I'm the one who is living in the here and now. Your presence after all this time is disruptive. I don't want you around. Vernon is at boiling point. It's all Maddie can do to restrain him.'

'How is the boy?'

'Boy? Yes, he was a teenager when you walked out. He's into his thirties now, and he still can't stand to hear your name mentioned.'

'I'd like to think I could change that.'

'Forget it! You'd end up with a bloody nose.'

She is still spoiling for a fight, to make it right for her. The hurt I caused all those years ago is still alive in those eyes.

'Anyway, tell me, Gil, how does somebody who claims he hasn't got a pot to piss in, who Madeleine informs me relies on pension credits and housing benefit – how does he manage to afford to come on this jolly?'

'I'll admit it wasn't easy.'

'Don't tell me the government is now dishing out all the taxes I pay as grants to old farts for foreign travel.'

'Regrettably not. Benefits and a bus pass don't get me much further than Newport.'

'So, did you rob a bank?'

Francisco comes over to stand between my legs as if in moral support. He looks up searchingly at Sandra, who takes no notice.

'In a way,' I reply, gently squeezing the bony little shoulder, 'Foolishly, they offered me a credit card – derisory limit, but just enough to get me here and back.'

'Just one more debt you can't pay back, is it, Gil?' she hisses. 'Or do you still have a secret hoard?'

'Don't start on that, Sandra. It was never my intention to keep it a secret from you. Nobody knew. It was safer that way; safer for all concerned. I was wrong. Just how many times do I have to say I'm sorry?'

Francisco looks up at the sound of someone approaching, a smile breaking out on his face.

Sandra presses on regardless. 'Roger said it showed a weakness of character. You've been a pathetic failure all your life.'

I can't disagree. The reality speaks for itself.

Sandra prises the stiletto heel out of the grass. 'Hello, Jasmin,' she says, unsmiling, the emotion still simmering. Francisco jumps into his mother's arms. 'Did I say how lovely you look? Pity Roger and I didn't get a mention in Albert's speech, but don't say I said anything. I wouldn't want him to be upset. Have you seen my handsome husband, by the way? I've finished here.' She lets loose the remark as if she's tossing a bin bag onto the rubbish dump.

'He was saying goodbye to a few guests in the car park,' Jasmin answers.

'Guests?'

'Some of the girls from work,' comes the innocent reply, but Sandra has already turned and is hurrying away.

'Was it something I said?' Jasmin looks perplexed.

I laugh. 'No. Nothing to do with you. She's concerned about myxomatosis.'

'I do not understand.'

'She wants to catch Roger the rabbit before he can infect any other little bunnies.'

She looks blank.

'Don't worry.' I say. 'Private joke.'

After entertaining Francisco in the play area for five minutes, Jasmin returns him into my charge with an invitation to come back inside when we are ready to enjoy the music. A friend is acting as an amateur DJ with a selection of country-style music for dancing. I have no idea what that means, but it sounds like something I will hate. Thankfully, my grandson is soon to team up with two other youngsters in a makeshift game of kick the ball and chase, which gives me the opportunity to find a seat and relax. When the game finishes, he climbs into my arms and is asleep in a matter of seconds. I must have dozed off as well because day has turned to dusk and there is a chill in the air when I open my eyes.

By the time we make it back to the reception, most of the guests are filtering towards the exit and the DJ is stashing his equipment. A few people are stood around talking to Jasmin, who catches my eye and motions for me to put Francisco, still asleep in my arms, into his pushchair. As I do so, I notice Sandra in animated conversation with Albert, her hand pointing from time to time in staccato fashion towards the recumbent figure of Roger, slumped in a chair, his face blotched red, his gaze fixed firmly on the floor. He looks totally deflated.

All is not well. Not wishing to exacerbate Sandra's fragile mood, I decide to seek out Hugo to find out when we are leaving. The route takes me back along the now deserted corridor towards the main entrance, when I hear someone whisper my name; or, at least, that's what I think it sounds like. I stop and turn in the direction of the voice.

A hand briefly touches the sleeve of my jacket, feels for my wrist, grips tightly and yanks me sideways. I find myself staring into the dark and musty confines of a small storeroom. My first reaction is to pull away, but fingernails dig into the flesh on the back of my hand, prising me forward into the room.

'Gil. It's me!'

'Madeleine? What's wrong?'

We have done little more throughout the reception than exchange a nod, a supportive smile across the room. She has looked preoccupied. Now, her face is drawn and pale, her eyes pinched and moist. She pulls me close to her, not out of affection but to enable her to look over my shoulder towards the corridor.

'He didn't see you, did he?'

'Who?' I grab her hands, pulling them down straight between my legs, bringing us closer still so I can look into her eyes. 'You're not making any sense. What's going on?'

'I'm sorry, Gil. I've made a terrible mistake.' She releases her hands from my grip and begins to stroke the sleeves of my jacket.

'What is it?' I press.

'You must do something for me. Promise? Directly you get back to the car. It's dangerous to stay.'

'Why?'

'He came back to the hotel drunk. He'd been in a fight. Thank God everybody had gone to bed. He was cursing, rambling on about revenge. He's out of control, Gil.' Her fingers grip the material of my sleeve. 'He said terrible things; things I wasn't supposed to hear.'

'This is Vernon you're talking about?'

She starts at the sound of a group of men talking in the corridor as they stroll past. 'That's not him, is it?'

'Calm down, Maddie. He's—'

'Listen, get your things together – your money, passport – and leave.' Her eyes are pleading with me. 'Promise me you'll go. I should never have convinced you to come. I tell you, Gil, he's evil. He'll stop at nothing.'

'You've let him get to you.' Tears well in her eyes. 'I understand the bitterness, the anger ...'

'You don't! You don't! He's obsessed with you. Nobody is on your side. You can't trust anybody.' She sounds like the bad actress again.

'I feel I will be able to get through to him.'

She shakes her head violently. Tears splatter onto my face.

'Madeleine!' Sandra's call echoes along the corridor. There is no response. 'Oh, it's you,' she says, as footsteps stop close by. 'Have you seen Madeleine? We're all about to go and she's gone missing.'

Madeleine tenses as the reply comes. He can be no more than ten metres from where we're standing. 'I'm looking for her too.' Vernon's voice is hoarse and slurred.

'I'll check the loo. You go and fetch Roger. He's sulking from my tongue-lashing.'

'I heard. Hard not to, the way you were screaming at him.'

'I'll teach your stepfather to show me up in public.'

My face is impassive but I'm smiling inside, remembering Sandra's hurt but self-righteous tone.

'Don't call him that! He's just Roger, that's fucking all! Got it?'

'Please don't swear. You know I hate it.'

'I don't have a father and I don't have a stepfather. Just remember that and I'll keep my cool. I really need to find Madeleine. Meet up in the car park.'

Footsteps recede along the corridor.

Madeleine pulls away from me. 'I must go. He watches my every move. Please, don't hang around. I'll explain everything back in Chepstow.' With that, she is gone.

As I travel back in the car with Hugo, I think about what she said. But everything seems so normal once back at the house. Francisco has stayed asleep and Jasmin and Albert are exhausted, retiring directly to their bedroom.

I lie awake for a while thinking things over. Surely Madeleine was being neurotic. It seems drastic and over the top to just get up and leave. Anyway, I am hoping the opportunity will present itself to speak frankly to all the family. I might not be able to handle Vernon physically, but if nature and nurture count for anything, the father–son relationship still exists somewhere deep inside us and I desperately want to explain my actions, accept the blame and move on.

CHAPTER SIX
Cavalla – 2008

Nobody is on your side.

The words pitch around in my head like a sailing boat in a storm. I can feel the pulse in my stomach. I want to be sick. The acid rises in my throat and reflects into my mouth. I make it to the toilet just in time. The only sound is of me retching. Everything else is still, a sense that the world has come to an end and I am alone. I stumble back to the couch and close my eyes.

I must have slept deeply, because the sun is streaming in through the gap in the curtains when I finally awake. It's nearly ten; there's nobody around and I shudder as the memories return.

I recall people earlier, shuffling around in the dark, some muttered phrases and a car door slamming but not loud enough to wake me. Now, dehydration has kicked in and I have a thumping headache, a reminder of those last twenty minutes at the reception.

Perplexed by Madeleine's outburst, I had returned to the main room hoping to find Vernon and confront him. The place was deserted. A tray of half-finished drinks was on one of the tables. Somebody had extinguished a cigarette butt on a slice of lemon in the bottom of a tumbler. There were two brandy glasses, each with a couple of shots left. I downed them both. One of the glasses tasted of lipstick, and what I was drinking wasn't brandy. Hugo's voice came from behind. He was irritated. Was I coming? Everybody else had left.

There is a stale-looking piece of cheese in the fridge and two lonely bottles of mineral water in the shelf compartment. I drink greedily, finishing both. The headache mellows to a dull thud, but I feel light-headed and uncoordinated. Another ten minutes laying down and I begin to feel human again.

Cleaning my teeth thoroughly has always seemed a necessary act when trying to exorcise a prior day's booze session, and I give it a good five minutes.

I put on a pair of creased, lightweight trousers and a cotton polo with the embroidered emblem of the plumbing and heating firm which I once owned.

Albert had found it in a trunk, he said, and insisted I wear it. The thought was touching, especially as I have food and drink stains on the only shirt I brought. The comment as he handed it over I found especially heartening.

Hugo ran a taxi service for some other guests before dropping me at the house. I was feeling a little tipsy which Albert chose to ignore. Jasmin and Francisco have gone straight to bed, he told me, although he made no concession to them by lowering his voice. He held out the polo.

'You look a state,' he said. 'Mum has about a dozen of these stored away. She suggested we use them as dusters; otherwise, she'd burn them. I couldn't do that.' He gave me a weak smile.

Was this the breakthrough? Ever since I'd been at the house, he had barely looked at me; not as if I wasn't there, but addressing me either with his eyes cast to one side or seeming to stare through me, glazed and distant. At that moment, he held my gaze.

'Wear it tomorrow,' he said. 'It will remind us all of the way things were and just why we are all here.'

That was both touching and encouraging. Not only was it tinged with emotion, but the 'us all' and the 'we' suggest there will be some kind of family reunion.

As my head clears, my mood improves. Maybe things are about to change for the better. I strip and stow the sofa bed. I think about checking the oil, water and tyres on the Astra, ready for the trip home, but decide to bring a more rigorous examination to a summary conclusion when I can't find the bonnet release. Kicking the front tyre tells me everything is fine in that direction.

Children are blessed for having curious minds; old women peeking out from behind lace curtains condemned as nosy. Yet the distinction between the two words, one a virtue, the other bordering on sinful, is, in reality, fine. I suppose what I was doing could be described as either. I really know nothing about my son or his wife and child. Maybe looking at their possessions will give me some clues.

The larger of the two bedrooms, like the rest of the house, has unevenly plastered walls painted in a flat magnolia hue, with no skirting boards or ceiling coving. A single lightbulb hangs in the centre of the room, swaying gently on a bare wire in the breeze from the partially open window.

A low-tog duvet with no slip covers the simple double futon. Alongside is a cot-sized mattress with a blanket and matching pillow decorated in Disney characters. The wardrobe is an alcove in the wall to which a rail and makeshift curtain have been fitted to hide a pine chest of drawers and an untidy rack of clothes. The rail sags in the middle under the weight of so many garments – suits, trousers, shirts – but not one single piece of female or child's attire.

I look around for another wardrobe and, not seeing one, assume it's in the second bedroom. Albert indicated during yesterday's guided tour that the room is 'available for the child or whatever'. If I expected to see silver stars on the ceiling, a pen full of children's toys, teddy bears and spidermen, hand paintings on the walls, a bunk bed where a friend could come to stay, I was disappointed. There is no trace of the world Sandra and I gave to our two boys when they were young, a time when our home was filled with love. Why is this so different?

Packing cases fill the room, some empty, some nailed shut. Small, ornate pieces of furniture with lacquered Buddhist designs stand amongst a mound of straw and other packaging materials. Prayer cushions in shrink wrap are piled up to the ceiling. This is a warehouse, a dispatch operation that condemns Francisco to sleep in the same room as his parents. It seems so callous, so unlike the image of care and concern I believed of Albert from the picture Madeleine painted. I desperately need to get to know him.

One last thought on the subject puzzles me. I would have expected a second wardrobe full of feminine attire and drawers full of a child's needs. There is nothing – just a suitcase open on the floor with a few clothes for Jasmin and a change of outfits for the boy.

The old Peugeot pulls up outside as I stand in the lounge, thumbing through the half dozen books on the shelf.

Francisco tugs at the belt on his car seat, anxious for his father to release him. He sees me and sprints into my arms.

'How's my favourite grandson today?'

Albert brushes his son's head with his free hand. For a few seconds, he stands motionless, his eyelids flickering as he looks past me. He exhales deeply as if recovering from the exertion of whatever thought has passed through his head. 'Your *only* grandchild.' He avoids my eyes and moves past us to release the plastic bag of shopping onto the kitchen table.

Whatever was on his mind has passed. 'It was non-stop gibberish from here to Porto airport and back, wasn't it? We stopped off in town to buy more croissants and a baguette. I'll make coffee?'

'Fine.' I'm confused. 'Have Sandra and Roger flown home? I thought when you talked of "we" yesterday that Sandra would have stayed on. There are things that still need to be said.'

'You must have misunderstood,' he says, either ignoring or dismissing the obvious disappointment in my voice. 'I managed to squeeze Tenzin in between Mum and Madeleine in the back of the Peugeot.'

'Tenzin?'

'He's the Buddhist monk you would have seen sitting next to us at the reception. We got to know him in Nepal. He's a good friend.' Something has amused him, but he keeps it to himself. 'Roger sat in the front, treating us to his strong and moody persona.'

I feel a real pang of disappointment to know Sandra won't be around but I'm not going to miss the chance to score a few brownie points. 'They certainly had a set-to at the end of the reception. Most of your in-laws seemed to find it highly amusing.'

'It's both comical and scary the way they let loose at each other, oblivious to the onlookers. No holds barred from Mum. She goes for the jugular.' There is the same sense of pride in his voice I recognise from my brief conversation with his brother.

'If history repeats itself, I bet when you picked her up this morning she was not only ready but looked a million dollars, and not a hint of the skinful she put down her throat yesterday?'

'Spot on. Although she did get a bit tetchy on the journey. She suggested to Tenzin that if he bothered to clean his teeth, his breath wouldn't stink of garlic.'

'Did he understand?'

'Not the words, but I think he got the tone. All the same, they parted as friends.'

Talking about his mother somehow softens the matter-of-fact way in which he normally speaks to me. He tells me, with a certain reverence, how close he feels to her, in a tone of voice that could have been uttered by a teenager describing his first infatuation. She has been through an awful lot, and he would do everything within his power to avoid her feelings being hurt again. Did I know she suffered from depression and had told him once that she had contemplated suicide? He will never let anybody hurt her again.

'That's as it should be,' I say. It's a weak response but I find to my surprise that I am embarrassed and somewhat overawed by the force of his sentiments.

There is a gruff voice from beyond the house calling Hugo's name, followed by the bark of a dog.

'Do you want to see who that is?' I suggest.

He turns his head towards the sound, then back to me. He shakes his head violently. 'No, it's nobody important. I'll make the coffee.'

I'm disappointed Sandra decided not to delay her departure, and fuck it being a definite no-no because Roger is the club president at a charity golf competition in Newport this afternoon. Some things are more important than Roger's social calendar. I crave a rite of passage back into the family, even if it means no more than a formal truce with Sandra and Vernon, the rancour gone and the occasional opportunities to see Francisco with his parents' blessing.

Albert calls me into the house. The baguette is crisp, the butter unsalted, and from somewhere a small flask of homemade strawberry confit appears. The coffee bubbles in a metal percolator on one of the gas rings above the oven. I take the mug he offers me. 'Jasmin not joining us?' I ask.

'She had to go to work. It's a busy practice.'

'No honeymoon?'

'There will be time for all that in the future.'

'Listen,' I say, 'apologies and expressions of regret count for nothing after all this time, I know, but I wanted to tell you all that I am sincerely sorry for all the hurt my selfish actions have caused. If I could turn the clock back, I really would. The one thing I've learned is, although moods change during marriage, however black you like to think things are, you should never give up hope you can put things right; not simply turn your back on them.'

He checks his watch and stands up. There is a puzzled expression on his face. 'Do you really feel that way?'

I nod.

'That's good to know,' he says, holding his hand out for me to shake. 'Even if it is too late.'

I panic at the remark. And the offer of a handshake? What for? We aren't concluding a business deal, two strangers saying goodbye. Too late for what?

Without another word, he calls Francisco and they wander off together around the corner of the house and out of sight.

What is happening to my son? Very little is making sense. His attitude to me is detached, distant, yet there are times when I feel he is concealing his emotions. Is he the same with everybody? Look at his relationship with Jasmin. There is no romance. They married just yesterday, young, seemingly full of energy for life, yet both totally devoid of the intensity that love brings. Sure, they are struggling financially, with a new house that needs a bundle of work doing to it, even basic stuff like finishing what has already been poorly started. Yes, they have to work, but is all this Buddhist paraphernalia a distraction rather than a job capable of producing a real income? I suspect it is.

And then there is the boy. Francisco is a child in a million, yet they seem to have minimal parental attachment to him, few hugs and kisses, warm embraces. All those sensitive and tender moments seem to emanate from the boy, not from his parents.

Albert has turned the corner of the house and is walking back towards me. He glances repeatedly over his shoulder. I can sense he is nervous.

'We've come to talk to you,' he says. 'It's about time you knew why you're here.'

CHAPTER SEVEN
Usk, South Wales – 1992

The last six months of 1992 passed as if I existed in some chimerical form, within an unreal bubble, witnessing events occurring but unable to influence the outcome or feel, let alone react, to the violent shocks exploding around me.

If I was feeling unkind, I could have said it was Sandra's fault in the first place. The physical side of our relationship had become predictable and ritualised, every move a well-rehearsed progression to a final spasm and mumbled satisfaction. It had been that way since the operation. They had tied her tubes. There could be no more pregnancies, not that we remotely wanted any. But it didn't stop her getting moany and irritable, just like she always used to around that time of the month when her excuse was a troubling menstrual cycle.

It was a Friday. I'd had a good morning with a flurry of orders from the sales team for new heating installations, a relatively peaceful wages payout session with few gripes about missing commissions and overtime, and a good lunchtime meeting in the pub with a new supplier offering attractive terms. I envisaged an afternoon away from the office, a bottle of expensive wine, those tender words and suggestive caresses; a prelude to the way lovemaking used to be in those halcyon days when we could not get enough of each other.

The rebuff is swift and clinical. Sandra is late for a bridge date with the girls, and where is the au pair? She is supposed to be here by now. Could I be a darling and wait in for her?

I'd thought it was the au pair's day off. That's why I came home to suggest an intimate afternoon together – just the two of us. But it was never just the two of us, was it? There was always the elephant in the room (her words, not mine), the tragedy we found so difficult to verbalise but that we had accepted and handled as best we could; mainly, as best as Sandra could.

Then, there were the boys. They would be home from school sometime before six. Be a good lad and hang around until Rosita shows up. A peck on the cheek, a squeeze on the arm, and she was gone.

There was just over half the bottle of Sancerre left and I was dozing in a lounger by the pool, when the patio doors clicked shut behind me. Rosita perched on the far edge of the lounger, sideways on, next to my feet.

Normally, when dressed in her workaday, loose-fitting housemaid's smock and covered with what my mother would have called a pinafore, her figure was well camouflaged. I had never really looked at her as anything other than the au pair. Sure, in the ten months or so she had been working for us, I had registered she was attractive, with those dark Latin features and a cascade of black hair customarily tied up in a bun, but no more than that.

She was older than the girls who had come before her, twenty-six when she arrived, and Spanish. It was a deliberate choice on Sandra's part, breaking away from the mould of Swiss and Austrians in their late teens; she swore the last little girl had a silent crush on me.

Up until today, Rosita had been an adjunct to my wife, just someone who did for us – one of my mother's many little sayings, God rest her soul.

The woman who now sat at my feet was clad in a skimpy bikini. The floral top barely contained her full breasts; a thin strap secured the lower square of material then, I guess, disappeared into the voluptuous curves of her backside. If the intention of the nylon beach cover-up was to preserve her modesty, it failed miserably.

'Did you go out dressed like that?'

She laughed. 'You sound like my father.' Her eyes made a pass across my body and hesitated, briefly, at my crotch. 'But you don't look like him, señor Hart.' She ran a hand through her hair.

'I'm serious,' I said, trying to sound friendly but paternal. 'You could end up in real trouble, wearing next to nothing.'

'Really? What sort of trouble?'

I was in serious denial. I had come home expecting at this very moment to be lying naked in bed with my wife, and I was aroused beyond belief. But I did try. Believe me, I tried.

'There are some very unsavoury characters about,' I said. 'This is not a beach on your Spanish Costas where everybody walks around covered by a handkerchief or two.'

'Don't be so *pesado*.'

I didn't understand, but I got the gist. Maybe I was trying to emphasise the age gap between us. The way the conversation was going, one of us needed to come to our senses.

'She don't let me sunbathe at home. Not appropriate for your sons. I have a place by the canal where I go to make my bronzing. Not often. You have shit weather.'

'A lot of people use the canal path. You are taking a risk.'

'Not where I stay. The only ones who spy on me are some boys from the school. They think I do not know they are there. So, I put on a little show; just a bit. They rush home to rub themselves.'

Were these words coming from that demure home help who barely acknowledged my presence in the house?

'Would you like to see?'

Confirmation was not required. I lay back in the lounger, my hands clasped behind my head.

She arranged a towel on the lawn alongside me and sat down, her back supported on the lounger. One hand began to gently feel inside her bikini top and massage her breast, slowly exposing the flesh above the material, until she had her nipple pinched between her thumb and index finger. In an exaggerated gesture, she extended her tongue to moisten the fingers on her other hand, which she then rubbed in a circular motion around the firm, dark nipple.

In a practised movement, the breast was back inside the bikini and the fingers of one hand, and then the other, played between her lips, inserted and retracted, matted with her saliva. She began to massage the inside of her thighs, along the bikini line, her middle finger sneaking under the material to play around the lips of her vagina. Her hips rotated and thrusted.

I have to say that I've seen a similar routine played out since, a hundred times or more, in seedy little Spanish backstreet nightclubs, without registering a second glance; but right then and there it was like I'd just scored on some powerful drug. My head was spinning, the pulse in my neck throbbing, my body hot and totally out of control.

I collapsed onto the towel alongside her, my mouth anxious for hers. Our tongues met, a frantic, needy thrust by me, a controlled, searching movement from her. The finger that had played with her labia was inside my mouth alongside her tongue, the scent, the movement, totally intoxicating. My hands pawed at her breasts, forcing them out of the bikini, my mouth dipping to kiss and caress the nipples she manoeuvred towards me. She was in total control and I was loving it.

At the time, I thought she was beginning to respond, those laboured sighs, erratic movements like mini electric shocks. In retrospect, I think she was a damned good actor, and I was about as effective as the guy pumping air into a punctured bicycle tyre: working hard but achieving nothing.

There and then, convinced my technique was stimulating her as much as it was me, I dropped my hand to the bikini bottom and pulled the thin band of material to one side. I played with my finger around the lips of her vagina, trying to enter her, but there was no way in. The material was forcing her lips to close tight and as I struggled, moving the band to the other side, with precisely the same result, I could feel she was laughing at me.

Holding me off with surprisingly strong arms, she put her hand behind her back, pulled at the material to release a press stud, watching me intently as the bikini bottom fell away at the same time as her hand began to snake inside my shorts to push them down.

I needed to back off, to distract my overriding and shameful desire to come into that probing hand. I didn't want the release; I needed to hold myself in check until the crescendo that would surely possess me when I could move into her.

I summoned my concentration. 'Are you sure everything is all right inside?' My words came out as a croak. I glued my eyes to the patio doors and centred on them. How long had it been since the glass had last been cleaned? One week, a couple of months? Never? What did we use? Glass cleaner? A condom? Did I need a condom?

My trousers and briefs were around my ankles, her moist hands gently massaging me.

'All right inside where?' she asked.

It was going to be so wonderful inside there, I thought. 'The house,' I stammered.

'Everything is just fine.' She pulled me closer and I went to mount her, but the movement of her body was adroit. She had turned me and, legs apart, was astride my body, her hand directing me slowly into her. I had never felt anything like that in my life. Her muscles were gripping me so tight, I could not move inside her. The pain was exquisite. Then, she was rising gently, leaving me almost outside her, hesitating so that the tip of my penis flicked around her clitoris, before feeding me, once more, into the unimaginable pleasure.

If I was being economical with the truth, I'd say I held out for two minutes before I spasmed and came inside her with no other desire than the pure animal urge to transfer every last drop of my being into her.

She jumped up, the tail of the bikini bottom trailing between her legs, and dived into the pool. She swam to the bottom and reappeared, maybe twenty seconds later, shaking her head, a spout of water propelled from her mouth.

'Got to wash them away. Don't want any of the little ones to survive, do we?' She arched her back and disappeared once more under the water. A responsible man would have paid heed to that comment, however biologically inaccurate it might have been, but I was already dreaming of the next time.

I'd never realised just how thoughtless and uncaring I could be when I really wanted something. For the next six weeks, I would skip hours, half days away from work, overnight absences from home to fictitious business meetings. I convinced Sandra to change the au pair's day off to a Wednesday, which was far more convenient for me than Friday, and persuaded her that a lively social life with her friends from the golf club was exactly what she needed to brighten her existence, with me so busy building the business. She even complimented me on how I had developed a really caring nature, all of a sudden.

At every conceivable opportunity, I would take Rosita to bed; sometimes in the house, afternoon hotel assignations, a Wednesday trip up to London to take in dinner, a show and a night in a five-star hotel.

Most of the time I used a condom. I hadn't really given the possibility of pregnancy a thought; more the means to prolong the lovemaking, to try to give her back just a little of the ecstasy that she gave me. I said that without thinking. Bullshit! At least I can be truthful now. That magnanimous nonsense about giving her back something; what I really meant was that I didn't want to feel a berk in bed whose speciality was premature ejaculation.

With a little willpower and self-control, I could hold off my climax for sometimes thirty minutes before my resolve evaporated. It was enough time for her to run through a series of gestures and touches that left me moaning with pleasure, my hands gripping tight to the mattress, my head buried deep into the pillow.

When time permitted and we would come together maybe two, or even three times, the passion was softer, less frantic, the actions slower and more controlled. It was on these occasions I sensed she might be enjoying the experience more, the little grunts, groans and gasps expressions of genuine satisfaction. At the end of the day, I guess I wasn't so very different from most men. My sexual gratification was what really counted, and any pleasure she derived, just an add-on to grease the pole for our next encounter.

In the four years we were together, I don't think I ever asked Rosita where she had learned all those lovemaking techniques. Maybe I was afraid what the answer might be. I brushed over the subject once, only to receive a reply that it was something that came naturally to Latin women. I had looked at her mother and immediately known it was a lie.

In my real world, almost imperceptibly, the walls were beginning to close in. Sandra had never been given cause to doubt my faithfulness or to question my attitude in relation to other women or, as time had worn on, to do anything other than take my moral compass for granted. She was, however, starting to ask questions about Rosita.

Whether the questions were really directed at me or were more rhetorical, with me as a sounding board, I wasn't sure, but could it be that the au pair had a boyfriend? Wasn't it strange: in the past she had always come back to her room to sleep following her day off, and now she didn't? Since her day off had been changed to Wednesday, she was staying out all night. Did I have any idea where she went? Had I noticed that Rosita's attitude around the house had changed? She used to be willing and receptive. Now, there was a hint of arrogance, cockiness almost, in her manner. What did I put it down to?

I parried all these probes with the stock answer that I was too busy to concern myself with the bloody au pair, who was entirely Sandra's province. If she had questions to ask, why not pose them directly to Rosita? I knew she wouldn't and I continued to feign total disinterest.

On the other hand, Vernon, now aged fifteen and sexually aware, was a different kettle of fish. I made a conscious effort to keep my distance from Rosita around the house, but on the odd occasion when our paths crossed and there was a brief exchange of conversation, it seemed that Vernon was always looking on. At family meals, I would catch him looking from me to Rosita and back again before making some leading comment which could easily be misconstrued. He would look towards Sandra, I guessed to detect any sign of concern or acknowledgement of a problem, and then back to me, as if warning me off. At least, my guilt made it feel that way. Suspicions he might have; proof, he did not.

Not so, Albert, thank God. Nearly two years younger than his brother, his private time was spent behind a closed bedroom door, family life a distraction from his real passion of reading aloud in a language that sounded like the chattering of an agitated monkey. He assured us this was Tibetan, and who were we to challenge the assertion? There was probably nobody within a five-hundred-mile radius who could contradict him.

For that brief interlude, I had it all under control: a loving if undemonstrative wife who trusted me; a stable family life; a circumspect mistress who was an utter whore in the bedroom; and, to fund an expensive lifestyle, a business that was on the up.

It was all too good to last. And it didn't.

In the bedroom, I had begun to shun Sandra. Although sex together had become little more than a bimonthly ritual, I had now completely rejected her. That ebony-coloured body which had for so long excited me now left me cold. As she positioned herself to take me into her, I felt myself go flaccid, disgusted at the sight of the pads of cellulite starting to develop around her thighs and buttocks.

The strains of love and passion had given way to an image of my stepdad sitting in the frayed armchair in the lounge of the semi-detached in Sidcup, a cigarette propped in the corner of his mouth, a bottle of brown ale warming between his thighs. He'd had them all, so he said. All colours and nationalities. A life in the services got you that, moving around the world, always in transit. Women liked men in uniform. Don't go overboard just because she's coloured, he used to say. Take it from me, boy, they're all pink inside.

Those were the days long before political correctness, when you'd see signs outside hotels saying no blacks or Irish or travellers and everybody's favourite jam had a golliwog as a trademark. You're taking a big step if you marry her, he would say. Your friends will start to avoid you and hers won't talk to her. Think twice. She looks a cracker now, doesn't she just? But in forty years' time she'll probably have a huge arse and a moustache on her top lip. That's just the way things are. We evolved differently and haven't all learned to live together. Probably never will.

But my high ideals had transcended his world of racism and bigotry, or so I believed. I was truly in love and there could be no constraints in the world that would knock off course my feelings for this woman. The old man's words had almost faded into oblivion. For twenty-seven years I had been true to the credo of 'until death us do part', but not any more. In the half-light of a late September evening in 1992, I kept repeating to myself that I did not love or want any more the woman I had married.

'Is it me?' she asked. 'Am I doing something wrong?'

Does a woman really believe her husband when he blames the stress of work, or the medication he is taking for the blood pressure problem, or just being out of sorts? I hoped so because they were the only excuses I could offer. Yet, there was even one occasion when I turned over to face her, my penis limp and aching from having climaxed twice into Rosita that very afternoon, when I was on the point of telling her my love had been transferred to someone else. Instead, I mumbled something about a big meeting with the bank the next day and sought the solace of a soft pillow in which to bury my head.

There was an outside chance that if circumstances had remained unchanged, I could have outlived the crisis. As soon as familiarity and predictability became an integral part of the relationship with Rosita and the novelty began to fade, I would look for other things outside of the physical response to sustain my interest. Up until now, our conversations had stayed at the superficial, the occasional family anecdote, our social likes and dislikes, always ending with some titillation that would preface what we, or should I say I, was there for. I really knew nothing about Rosita, but she knew all she wanted to about me.

One Thursday morning in early October, just as she was rushing to get dressed to arrive before ten at the house, she made the announcement. The situation was becoming untenable – my words, her English was far more unstructured – and she felt that it was time for her to leave.

I listened to that casual statement with the dread of a heroin addict who's been told he's had his last fix. What could I say? As she stood halfway out of the door to the hotel room, there was a parting comment. She could see the relationship was going nowhere; there was no way I would ever leave my wife and family and she needed to think about her future. She had a lot to offer the right man.

You could say that again. I had never met anyone in my life who could turn me on that easily and keep me on the verge of such anticipation for so long. It might be all to do with sex, but wasn't that one of the most fundamental bedrocks of any relationship? Didn't the rest just follow on from a loving, physical relationship?

I gave myself a week to think things over and I asked her to defer doing anything until we had spoken again at length.

Since the affair had begun, I might have toyed on a few occasions with the consequences of what her ultimatum implied, but the status quo was always easier to live with; a time bomb perhaps, but nobody at that stage had lit the fuse. Now, Rosita had.

If I had to describe the turmoil in which I spent that week, trying to appear as normal as possible yet frantic to resolve the struggle that consumed me, I would say I longed for an event, good or bad, a decision taken by someone else to relieve me of the burden of choice. As the week progressed, with sleepless nights and the oppression of normality, I was having difficulty rationalising, in deciding whether I was caught between reality or fantasy, courage or cowardice, conviction or resolution.

In more reflective moments, I would think about the personal repercussions of leaving; how Sandra would react, the impact on the boys – there were already patent signs of problems ahead with Vernon – the attitude of my mother, the in-laws and Sandra's extended family, the people who worked for me, close friends, neighbours. I had make-believe conversations in my head with so many people.

And what about our elephant in the room? To jump ship in these circumstances would be seen as particularly callous and unfeeling and place an unfair weight on a lot of other people's shoulders. I would be despised, hated, for shunning the burden that nature – God, if you believe in the creator – had placed on us equally.

I thought about the financial implications as well. The equity in the house was probably in line with what the business was worth. Sandra would obviously keep the house and contents plus a fair chunk of maintenance to cover the mortgage, bills and other family running costs. As all the share capital of the company was in my name, I would expect to keep the business and use the cash flow to meet my obligations to support the family. I guessed that the rest of our assets, a self-employed pension fund, some savings accounts and a few small shareholdings would be cashed in and split between us.

What nobody knew about was the slush fund. That is, except for possibly Karen in the office, who had asked a few searching questions over the years but had no specific knowledge. In earlier times, when the plumbing and heating operations had been less structured, I did a number of jobs for cash, no invoices, no VAT and no questions asked. A couple of big cash-only contracts on some dodgy residential construction sites had considerably upped the fund, which I hid in the name of a bogus offshore shell company with a bank account in Liechtenstein. At the last count there was sixty grand tucked away for a rainy day. I did not intend that anybody would get to know about this little nest egg. The consequences could be very damaging, as a client, Harry Black, had learned to his cost. As one of the partners in a construction operation, he was currently doing a six-year stretch in an open prison somewhere in Norfolk for claiming the VAT back on a string of bogus invoices.

The following Wednesday, Rosita's day off, I stayed around the house, ostensibly to do some paperwork but primarily to avoid any suspicion I might be with her. My mind was still far from made up.

Sandra was playing golf the next day in a ladies' four ball at the club in Newport, so I arranged a reservation in our secret little hotel in Bristol, false name, of course, and all bills settled in cash.

It's the God's honest truth I intended a conversation and no more, but when I arrived she was already in the room, wearing nothing but a black négligée and a warm smile. I had no defence against this sort of onslaught. Today we were going to do something just a little different, she advised, as if a schoolteacher talking to her class.

I was stripped with my hands and feet splayed apart and bound to the corners of the bed with bands of red velvet cloth. First would come the body massage with a blend of exotic-smelling oils. The moment the finger sponge touched my skin I was as hard as a rock, the mix of smells intoxicating my senses, my head fuzzy from lack of sleep and about to melt into a slumber for the first time in days. I must have dozed off.

***

Porto, Portugal – 2008

Shite! That hurt! Stop that!

The sponge is rough around my genitals. Water is splashing against my thigh, followed by the brusque rub of a hand towel. Someone is lifting my bottom up and pulling out material from underneath me. The smell is disgusting. More water and another fierce rub of the towel before I am again raised by the bottom and a new piece of material placed under me. I feel press studs close and my shirt pulled down.

It is time to think about opening my eyes. I have made my decision and I know it's not what she wants to hear, but I have to say it. 'Rosita,' I call, my eyes finally alive and present.

Two women in identical pink dresses with prim, white-coloured collars turn together to look at me, their expressions of surprise evaporating into practised smiles and their mouths framing words I cannot hear.

'Sorry,' I say automatically. 'I don't speak the language.' My breathing is becoming rapid. My body is damp with sweat. This can't be happening. Where am I? The vein in my leg begins to throb. For the first time, I wince at the tightness in my chest and stomach, punctuated by sharp, piercing stabs as if someone is throwing darts at me. I am dying.

One of the women draws near to me, bending low, saying something with a smile, a comforting hand on my forehead. As if in a dream, I watch in slow motion as her dress grazes the sheet under which I am lying. She speaks again, raising her eyebrows as if expecting an answer. Don't look at me like that. I'm not an idiot. Don't you understand?

'I mean I can't hear you.' I sense the words have been fumbled. Calm down. Think straight. I look directly into her eyes. 'Whatever language you are speaking, I cannot understand because I am not able to hear you. ¿*Lo entiendes*?' I try to enunciate slowly, emphasising every word.

Alongside the woman is an IV bag suspended on a stand. My gaze follows the drop of clear liquid down a tube into the plastic connector in the back of my hand.

'I'm in hospital?' I realise suddenly, out loud.

She nods and then holds one index finger horizontally over the other. I was to wait. It is a pointless gesture. As I look down, my right leg is in traction, suspended in a pulley system. I'm not going anywhere.

It's a private ward. I cannot see anything out of the window other than a blue sky dotted with puffy white clouds. Sitting as upright as my stricture allows, I can just make out the end of the building, some five storeys above the ground. The information posters on the far wall are in Portuguese.

Of course, I was at the wedding. The morning after. A cup of coffee. I recall looking around to see where Francisco was, but beyond that? I really try to focus. What happened? Why am I here? Concentrate. Why can't I remember? Why can't I hear?

Someone is tapping on my arm. I open my eyes. Did I fall asleep? The man is dressed in a blue tunic with a V-neck. It's the uniform that surgeons wear. Are they going to operate on me?

My pleading look is answered by a knowing smile. The thin moustache is twirled up at the ends over a mean mouth and pointed chin. He looks like the figure of a king on a set of playing cards. I can tell he is speaking slowly and try to read his lips, but it's useless. I shake my head.

'I've gone deaf,' I say.

He turns on the heels of his white rubber slip-ons and is gone, only to return a few minutes later with two other men dressed in similar tunics, but in a darkish red colour. One of them examines my ears with an otoscope, a protracted examination that requires the second man to follow suit, presumably to confirm the findings. There is general head nodding and assent.

The first doctor has acquired an A4 pad and a pencil. His writing is laboriously slow, eventually turning the page around for me to read.

'No, I don't know where I am and I don't know what happened,' I answer. I sense panic in my voice.

Again, he starts writing. I am in the Santo Antonio hospital in Porto, in a specialist unit that deals mainly with old people, as he puts it. I am suffering from a series of puncture wounds caused by flying glass in my legs and lower abdomen plus a broken femur. Their main concern is the possibility of head trauma which has caused the loss of hearing and apparent partial memory failure. Further tests would be carried out the following day.

'What day is it?'

Wednesday. The wedding was on the Sunday. I have been out cold for at least two days.

'I don't understand,' I say. 'What happened to cause these injuries?'

His brow furrows. Do I remember nothing?

'No!' I say, rather too violently. 'If I remembered, I wouldn't be asking.'

He didn't know all the details. Someone who has the information will come and speak with me as soon as possible.

'You must have some idea,' I plead.

He writes again, arduously, his tongue poking out between his lips in concentration, finally turning the sheet of paper towards me.

Suddenly, from nowhere, a childhood recollection fills my head: a holiday where there had been a forest fire; flames crackling above the pine trees; black clouds turning day into night; a thunderstorm soaking the parched soil and releasing the fetid smell of heat from the earth; Mum turning to my stepfather, saying it seemed like the world was coming to an end.

I read aloud the words. 'An accident. A gas explosion in a house.'

PART TWO – GILBERT – REALISATION

CHAPTER EIGHT
Porto – 2008

I drift in and out of sleep throughout the rest of that day. Prodded awake at around seven, I'm lifted into a sitting position and served with a tray of food, a homemade pâté as a starter, followed by a plate of what turned out to be a very tasty meal of diced chicken, lentils and puréed broccoli, with a rich chocolate mousse for dessert, all washed down with some chilled mineral water. The whole experience made me wonder what was for dinner at the Royal Gwent in Newport; perhaps rack of Welsh lamb with a redcurrant sauce? I somehow doubt it.

Somebody has kindly written 'sleeping pill' on a piece of paper the nurse hands me with the medication and a glass of water. I've always had a thing about taking medicine when you don't need it. She fusses, pulls and pushes at the sheets. I palm the pill and make a big show of swallowing a mouthful of water.

The painkillers and whatever else they put into me when I regained consciousness have made me fuzzy and my concentration patchy. My mind flits from one loose thought to another. I am grateful for a clear head now to take stock of the situation. The nurse dims the lights and closes the door behind her.

All I know is there has been an explosion somewhere that caused the deafness in my one good ear – a personal crisis I feel surprisingly unconcerned about – and a memory loss that spanned the period from when I was drinking coffee in Albert's garden until I regained consciousness. Was Albert's the house involved? There are other properties in the vicinity. Could it have been one of them?

My eyes are half shut but I notice the emergency light in the corridor become brighter and then dim again. The door to my room opens and closes, its shadow traced faintly on the wall. I feign sleep, my eyes pressed almost closed, leaving a slot through which I can barely see. A hand reaches for the IV bag, fumbling hurriedly to detach it from the stand. It is clumsily replaced with another bag taken from the pocket of a full-length white coat. The configuration is checked, the positioning adjusted. The sense of light and dark play on my eyelids, prompting me to open my eyes a little wider to watch the door close and the figure disappear from view.

For thirty seconds, I try to allay my fears. There is no reason why the replacement of the IV bag with the saline drip is anything other than standard night-time procedure in the hospital. But there is something about the incompetent way it was handled that grates on me. I sit up as high as my aching leg will allow to release the IV bag and seal the top with the flexible stopper attached to halt the flow into my body and hook the bag back onto the stand. There is no point in maintaining the feed into the vein on the back of my hand, so I remove the plaster and withdraw the needle. I'm prepared to take the flak from the nursing staff in the morning with a disarming smile and a mumbled apology.

This minimal exertion has tired me out.

I awake to the smell of freshly brewed coffee. My broken leg aches whenever I move, but the pains around my thigh and stomach have receded to little more than a tingling sensation.

The nurse who speaks English with some fluency reacts to my waving hand. She hands me a pad and pencil, reads the question, her forehead creasing as she does so, and then scribbles a reply. Yes, it is not uncommon for the night staff to check the IV bags on their rounds and change them when necessary. If they feel the patient might be disturbed, they will leave the clinical chart unaltered until their shift is about to finish and then make the annotation. For a moment, I think the shake of the head and finger-waving is to tell me off for removing the saline feed, but it's just to confirm the drip is no longer required. She dismantles the equipment and places it all in a white plastic tray at the foot of the bed.

Lino arrives late morning, smartly dressed in an impeccable double-breasted suit, trousers with razor-sharp creases and lacquered shoes with a mirrored finish; my first unkind thought is a double for a tailor's dummy.

My impression of him from the reception is of somebody who really doesn't like me very much, and his bearing today seems to reinforce the fact. He gives me a cursory nod as he perches on the edge of a chair next to the bed and, in a totally exaggerated fashion, unfastens the catches to a briefcase. He removes three large pieces of white board which he balances carefully against his legs. A surreal sight in the hands of a grown man follows: a magic erasure slate of the kind children use to draw and then erase the image by turning a brightly coloured plastic knob at the slate's base.

He takes the marker from its holder and, with the slate balanced on his lap, begins to write. He holds the message out for me to see. I stifle my amusement.

'Yes, good morning to you,' I respond, 'and thanks to the family for their good wishes, but what I need, Lino, is information. How did I come to be here, what happened, and how extensive are my injuries?'

The temptation for him to speak must be hard to suppress, but he simply smiles and fingers through the three white boards until he finds the one he wants.

All three must have been prepared outside after reference to the medical staff. They are written in a fairly intelligible hand, albeit small lettering, the words sloping downwards slightly from the horizontal at the end of each line, as if penned with difficulty by somebody in their declining years.

There was a gas leak from the installation in Albert and Jasmin's house which had caused an explosion. I was found unconscious, my injuries, primarily a fractured leg, caused by the kitchen door as it was blown off its hinges. Fragments of glass were embedded in my thighs and lower abdomen. There is no internal damage and I am expected to heal relatively rapidly.

He waits for me to read the words a second time, then pulls the next board into position.

Doctor Mattias will be speaking to me later today concerning the head trauma I suffered. Again, there is no apparent brain damage but I am scheduled for a further MRI scan. There is also no damage to my inner ear. The hope is my hearing will return but there are no guarantees. The memory loss I am suffering is not an uncommon reaction to a trauma. When it comes to recovery, my age works against me.

'Thanks,' I say. 'That's a cheerful summary to brighten up my day.'

He scribbles on the magic slate again.

'I know you didn't come to tell me fairy stories,' I reply. 'And I'm sorry it had to be you who drew the short straw when it came to deciding who would make this visit.'

'It is not like that,' he wrote.

'Why you, then?' It is the second time he glances down nervously at the third white board still propped up against his leg, the writing turned towards him.

The realisation hits me like an uppercut to the chin. I have been so preoccupied with my own sorry state the thought had never occurred to me. Hartless, Potless and now totally Thoughtless.

I can feel my body give an involuntary shudder.

'Turn it over, please,' I mumble.

I can almost feel the air escaping from his mouth as he reverses the board. The message is in larger letters, all written with careful precision. There isn't so much to say. There can be no misunderstanding.

'Tragically, Albert was killed by the explosion. There were no other casualties. We are all very sorry for your loss.'

He has bowed his head, purposefully studying the floor.

There is a flash of bright light before my eyes. I feel murderous and suicidal at the same time. I'm not going to show this unfeeling peacock of a man my grief and tears. How could this have happened?

'Jasmin and Francisco?' I ask.

He puts his thumbs up and then writes. 'They were out when the explosion occurred. Naturally, they are distraught and confused, heartbroken, as we all are,' he emphasises.

I can't imagine Lino heartbroken. Maybe if they were out of stock of his favourite cufflinks or he had lost his tailor's telephone number, but otherwise I would be surprised if he sheds too many tears over his fellow man.

His duty call is done. He stands up, brushing and straightening the crease in his trousers as he does so. He directs my attention to his mouth and for the first time since he arrived, he speaks. Every word is enunciated slowly with an exaggerated movement of those mean, thin lips.

I look closely. 'I must go now,' he says. 'Somebody will come to see you in a day or two. When you are feeling better, the police will need to talk with you.' I pick up most of it. The rest, I guess.

Nobody came, not even the police.

Three days pass. I survive in a kind of zombie-like existence, sometimes depressed, saddened and full of the guilt that my fragile attempt to rejoin the clan has precipitated this disaster; often angry, my temper boiling inside me, resentment of how fate has treated me with such contempt. Yet all these intense reactions, however desperately felt, are somehow absorbed into a swirling mist separating me from just where I am right now and the real world. I am not as angry or as sad or as bereaved as I should be if the fog of my failed memory and soundless world were to clear and restore me to the very moment I sipped a coffee and Albert said to me ... What had he said?

Lino left his magic erasure slate with me to assist other visitors. It proves a godsend for Dr Mattias who becomes very adroit at writing clipped sentences, abbreviated words and clearing the slate with a pretentious flick of the wrist as he turns the knob. Even the nursing staff take to using it when prompted to explain what they are saying. I am also starting to get a grasp of messages written in Portuguese, many of the words similar to my recollection of Spanish.

From a medical standpoint, there is no physical injury to my head, no apparent explanation for the loss of my faculties other than the ferocious noise of the explosion and the related stress and shock. It's fifty–fifty on recovering one or both of the senses and, for the time being, I should plan my life to adapt to the reality of my situation. My wounds and fractured leg are responding well to treatment and Dr Mattias hopes to see the back of me within the next week.

A delivery from Amazon Spain is a book on the art of lip-reading. There is no indication as to the sender's name but I have my money on Lino. I have not yet got past the title page, perhaps an admission I cannot yet let myself contemplate the prospect of a life of silence.

Apart from the ever more infrequent visits from Mattias, the days merge into a sterilised routine which I try to anticipate and exploit by turning it into a guessing game as to the number of minutes' difference between the time I calculate a scheduled event will occur and the exact time it does. I am getting quite good, with few variations greater than five minutes.

It's on Saturday when the routine really goes to the dogs. There seems to be an air of controlled panic around the corridor with people moving hurriedly, little short of breaking into a run. Lunch is almost an hour behind schedule and the regular pill-dispensing session in the late afternoon fails to materialise. A saucer with our daily dosage is placed on the dinner tray and we are left to our own devices.

The following day, the English-speaking nurse confides in me. A female patient came out of surgery after a routine operation for varicose veins and died suddenly two hours later. Such an occurrence is virtually unheard of and all sorts of investigations are in train. Care staff are under investigation by the management, quite unfairly in her opinion.

On Monday, the routine is back to normal, and I have visitors.

Loud voices in the corridor precede the arrival of the tall, black policeman I saw in Cavalla on the night I arrived. Today, he is dressed in a uniform of dark-blue bomber jacket distinguished with the official shield badge and black collar; he wears a white shirt with a black tie which reaches the belt of mid-blue jodhpurs firmly tucked into black riding boots polished to a perfection that would even make Lino jealous. He looks more impressive than I first remember and carries an air of authority to match his appearance. Trailing behind him are a bag-carrying junior officer and two civilians.

The first civilian is a thin man with a slight limp, well into his fifties. He proffers me his card. Pedro Borodin is an official representative of the Ministério Público. It means nothing to me. If someone had told me it was the Portuguese equivalent of the Crown Prosecution Service, I might have been distinctly more nervous about his presence.

The other civilian, a young woman, is an official court-appointed interpreter. The badge pinned to a summery blouse says 'Louisa Campos'. She hands me a typed sheet in English, explaining her role and pointing out today's meeting is not a formal interview but a fact-finding mission to assist with the investigation into the tragic death of Albert Hart.

Whilst I'm reading, I can sense Lannier's questioning stare. Of course, when I first saw him at the police station, Albert treated me as a passing tourist seeking directions, not as a long-lost relative. He has a right to be suspicious but makes no comment.

I manage to break the ice, forcing a smile from all the visitors as I offer the magic eraser slate as a means of communication. Louisa gives me a gracious shake of her head and indicates she will rely on a pencil and writing pad.

'That's your loss,' I say. 'It works very well.'

As I imagine, the meeting turns out to be long and laborious, complicated as it is by the language and my hearing difficulties.

The first part, a rundown of my movements since I arrived up until the moment my memory lapsed, is straightforward. I do all of the talking, stopping at regular intervals for Louisa to translate. At this stage, nobody interrupts or asks for clarification or questions my actions.

Phase two is the background to my personal and family life. Again, the progression is fairly quick as I do all of the talking and nobody tries to interrupt or follow-up.

My lunch arrives, forcing a break in the meeting. They will be back in an hour. I play with the tagliatelle and think about Albert. How short and ultimately lacking his life was in all those experiences we claim existence is about. It took him until thirty to find the woman he wanted to share his life with, and then death deprived him of the opportunity to watch his family grow. Maybe he left it later for a reason – to avoid making all those stupid mistakes his father had made.

A little hand pulls at the sheet, desperately feeling for me to react. Francisco is peering up at me, his head barely past the level of the mattress. He smiles as his eyes cast around for some new novelty with which to engage. Jasmin stands at the foot of the bed, a solitary figure with a demeanour bordering on the apologetic.

She goes to speak but I put my finger over my lips and reach for the trusty magic eraser. Francisco immediately turns his attention to the slate and its colourful plastic frame and knobs. She parries away his inquisitive fingers as she writes. Has she been crying for a whole week? She looks terrible. Her hair is unwashed, matted and unkempt; cheeks sallow and framed by red blotches; her eyes, tired and scared.

'You don't have to apologise for not coming before this, Jasmin.' I feel so sorry for her. 'You must have had so much to deal with. I understand totally.'

She holds the slate she has written on low enough for Francisco to see, puts her hand over his and twists the knob. As the letters disappear, he laughs and starts to jump up and down, demanding she give it to him.

'You have started something now,' I say. 'He won't let you write.'

For the first time, she gives a half-smile.

I wait for her to write again, fighting all the time as she does to keep his demanding hands at bay.

The judge's *procurador* – she didn't know the word in English – has informed her the burial permit was held up because of the post-mortem but can now be issued. There are still difficulties to resolve, on which she does not elaborate, but a provisional date has been set for the funeral and, hopefully, the burial.

'When?' I ask, involuntarily wiggling the toes of my bad leg as if to test my readiness.

Blind fury possesses me as I read her response. 'What do you mean, moved from Saturday to next Monday to accommodate Roger's diary commitments? Are you suggesting he's trying to find time to fit in the funeral of my son? And why do you keep saying hopefully? Is there some doubt that he is to be buried?' I can feel my temper surfacing.

She raises her eyebrows and writes.

'What does "In Portugal" mean, for God's sake?' I must have been shouting because Francisco looks scared and she has moved back a step. 'I'm sorry,' I correct. 'I can't hear my own voice. Please forgive me.' I smile longingly at the boy, but he turns his head into his mother's lap.

'When I come out of hospital, I shall need somewhere to stay for a day or two and I don't have a great deal of money.'

She comes over, clutches my hand and kisses me gently on the cheek. I am taken aback before I realise the gesture is to demonstrate to Francisco everything is all right. I hold my hand out to him and, much to my relief, he takes it. 'Sorry,' I repeat.

I should have realised she has already worked out all of the details.

Had I heard Albert talk about Adele? Yes, I did recall the name. She is a good friend who runs the local pharmacy, close to town. She is single and lives in a three-bedroom flat above the shop premises with her dog, an energetic Portuguese water breed named Pom-Pom. At the sound of the name, Francisco's eyes light up, and I watch his lips repeat 'Pom-Pom' as his hands pretend to stroke the animal.

My four visitors have made their way back into the room, standing, obviously impatient for Jasmin to leave. She feels the vibe and scribbles hurriedly on the slate. Her brother, Hugo, will be in contact with the hospital to collect me when I'm discharged. He will take me to meet Adele.

'Until next Monday,' I say.

'I'm counting on you,' she writes.

'It goes without saying.'

She waves a goodbye and grabs Francisco's hand, pulling him roughly towards the door. He is confused. There is a brief moment as she and Lannier look at each other. I am no expert but there is fear in her eyes and a cold indifference in his.

The meeting resumes but this time in a much more laborious and time-consuming fashion. Either Lannier or Borodin speak, Louisa writes down the question in English, shows it to me and I reply, giving her the time to translate my comments.

We start by talking about my motives for coming to Portugal after such a long absence from the family. What had I hoped to achieve? No, I did not feel any resentment or anger towards any members of the family. I was looking for reconciliation, not confrontation.

Had I not been involved in an argument with Albert in the garden of his house on the morning of the explosion? A person in the vicinity has testified to such an occurrence.

I cannot recall anything which happened past drinking coffee at breakfast, and there were never any angry words between us, no disagreements, nothing said to provoke an argument. No, there was nobody else present who could corroborate my statement.

'Hang on.' I begin to understand. 'What is all this? If you are trying to suggest that I have something to do with my son's death, you are out of your minds. This is getting ridiculous. I'm beginning to think I need a lawyer present.'

Certain allegations have been made. They must be investigated. Surely I can understand their position?

I take some time to mull over a reply. It could only be Sandra. 'If you are talking about the desperate comments of a bereaved mother who hates and despises her former husband, who sees his appearance and the death of her son as beyond coincidence, then of course you will hear her cry, but it is not a cry based on evidence or logic, it is—'

Louisa holds up her hand to stop me while she translates, indicating when she has done so for me to continue.

'It is the need to both come to terms with his death and to condemn the person guilty of deserting the family.'

They appear to receive the comment at face value and move on to the next topic. Did I inspect the house in some detail?

I wouldn't say some detail. I was given a quick guided tour by Albert and, yes, it did include looking at the plumbing and heating installation.

That was my profession, wasn't it?

Originally, but I haven't been in the business for more than twelve years.

What did I think of the installation in the house?

From memory, my impression was it would not conform to the safety standards required in the UK.

And to Portuguese standards?

I have no specific knowledge of Portuguese regulations, but I would imagine that EU rules standardise everything.

Why did I think the installation was faulty?

What was all this? 'I didn't say that. Don't put words into my mouth. There's a difference between not conforming to standards and being faulty. In Britain, we would have used more copper piping and compression fittings, not the push-fit solution for which Albert had opted. It would do the job, but it wasn't ideal.'

It obviously didn't do the job. Did I notice the electric wiring connected to the switch alongside the gas boiler?

No.

I did not see a bare wire?

I finally begin to see where we are going with this series of stilted exchanges. 'Are you saying that the explosion was caused by an electrical short-circuit and a gas leak?'

It is still under investigation.

Borodin is beginning to pack away his various papers into a battered briefcase and I take the meeting as coming to an end.

Lannier turns to the interpreter, speaking at length; not one specific question, but a number of observations.

I wait patiently and read the sheet she eventually hands me. I understand now why Jasmin looked so distraught. Sandra and her cronies must have given her hell with the pressure they applied.

Yes, I have already heard the news about the release of Albert's body. 'As for Sandra's attempts to have her son repatriated and buried in Wales, I had no idea. She has not contacted me. That she is tenacious and persistent, I can well believe. Until now, I was not aware she has hired one of the most foremost lawyers in Lisbon to counter Jasmin's decision to have Albert's remains buried locally, but I'm not surprised. She is angry and blames anybody and everybody.'

As they troop out of the door, Lannier turns to me, coursing the saliva around inside his closed mouth and shaking his head. It's the second time today I manage to read somebody's lips.

'*Boa sorte,*' he says. 'You will need all the luck you can get.'

I take it as a warning, not a prophesy, but, as usual, I'm wrong.

CHAPTER NINE
Cavalla – 2008

I have forgotten what time Hugo said he would arrive, but there's nothing to do but wait in the hospital reception area.

As my clothes were literally cut off of me the day I was admitted, it is hospital lost property I have to thank for a T-shirt with a Dutch beer brand logo, a pair of pyjama-like baggy trousers and some cheap rubber flip-flops. The wretched phoney Rolex has, regrettably, withstood the blast, and along with a wedding ring which I used to wear on a string around my neck, these are my only personal possessions, not counting the pair of aluminium crutches I have just acquired.

Whilst I might not be prepared to admit it, the exertion of trying to dress, coordinating movements with the crutches and a ten-minute session of cheek kissing, saying thank you and handshaking has tired me out. If I can just close my eyes.

***

Usk – 1992

Deciding to tell my wife I was leaving her when she had a boiling kettle in her hand could be construed as both poor timing and asking for trouble, but that's exactly the way it happened. My prepared speech, one of several I had rehearsed in my head over the previous weekend, came to nothing, and I blurted it out like a schoolboy admitting a classroom indiscretion.

And she reacted exactly as if I was an errant pupil. This is an aberration! The girl will get the sack. We will talk about it tomorrow. Don't be stupid. You're not going to give up all this, and me, she adds belatedly, just for some little tart who wiggles her bum at you.

I told her Rosita had already left and was waiting for me. We will talk about the way forward in a day or two, when she has got over the initial shock.

She stared wide-eyed at me, hands on hips, legs spread apart. Slowly, her head began to shake. Realisation? Condemnation? Confusion? Hard to tell;

perhaps all three. Her eyes were moist, her voice softened. Maybe we have both been working too hard and need to take a holiday together, talk things over, get to know each other again. After all, we have both been subject to a lot of stress, what with the boys doing what teenagers do and, of course, our other important family obligation – our shared obligation, she emphasises. I should rest and take time to think things over. Remember, it wasn't for her sake I must abandon the slut. Think of the boys and what it will do to them.

Her appealing words, soft and reconciling, momentarily knocked me out of kilter. This wasn't the fire and brimstone reaction I had expected. I was certain she wouldn't try and hold our relationship together. Was I missing something? Too late now; I had to go through with it. I forced myself to say I was sorry, but my mind was made up and there was no way I was prepared to turn back.

In the blink of an eyelid, her mood changed again, much more in line with what I had calculated and could handle. She told me to fuck off until I came to my senses. Mark her words, I would come crawling back. Close the door on your way out.

That was more like it. That was the way I had painted the scenario. My suitcase was already packed.

I had lied about Rosita waiting for me. She had gone to stay with a friend in Cardiff for two nights, a mutual decision to create a space whilst I started to sort things out. I had to tell my mum what was going on.

I was just five when Grace lost my father, a victim of simply being born at the wrong time. The heart disorder that slowly and painfully killed him, a procedure they now treat as an outpatient with a local anaesthetic, left a widowed mother of a five-year-old whose childhood was about to take on a multiple role. Of course, I was an infant, a boy growing up into a teenager, but to her, I was something else. An attractive single mother in those days was both an unfortunate victim and a target; kept at a distance by the female neighbours wary of their husbands' moral compasses, yet prey to the innuendos and sleights of men keen to test the water.

As the years passed, I became confidant, consultant and decision maker, roles that took me far beyond my developed capacity to handle them. When she married for a second time, her reliance upon me became even greater. Marrying solely for financial security in exchange for housekeeping services and, until the drunken old bastard couldn't demand it any more, sexual gratification were unhappy motives.

In the circumstances, it is hardly surprising she actively disliked and resented the few girlfriends I had, and possibly even less surprising that as I finished my extended apprenticeship with a local plumbing outfit, I suffered some kind of breakdown. Sandra had just arrived on the scene and Grace had the ideal bête noire upon whom to heap the blame. On top of that, like many of her generation, Mum was a cupboard racist, gracious and caring to Sandra's face, fiercely critical behind her back – sometimes not quite waiting until her back was turned.

At work, I was fast becoming a pariah. None of these beer-swigging, shagging, sporty types whom I had worked with for years now wanted to pair up with a nutjob. My nickname was PWAS (pronounced peewaz), an acronym for Plumber With A Shrink, and even the boss, a fair-minded man, was beginning to tire of my programmed weekly absences for therapy.

Although we were not conscious of it, these influences were driving Sandra and I into taking the only decision that made sense if we were to make our lives together. Her qualification as a bookkeeper would help to support us whilst I set up my own plumbing and heating operation and could get onto a stable financial footing. We were Londoners and the objective was to find a place to live and work, far enough away from the prejudices we were trying to deal with, yet within weekend visiting distance of friends and relatives.

Wales was never on our drawing board, but when the boss suggested I look at the operation of an old friend of his who was retiring, it was too good to ignore. It was a one-man business based in a town in the Valleys. He didn't want much for it and was willing for me to pay him in instalments to supplement his pension. My boss was both enthusiastic and supportive, though I knew his motives were anything but selfless.

A lot of water has gone under the bridge since then. In time, after Mum buried my stepfather and became frailer, she moved down to be closer to us and her grandchildren.

As I let myself into the bungalow, sat down beside her, kissed her on the cheek and used the remote to turn the sound down on the TV, I expected her reaction to be one of 'I never could stand that money-grabbing wife of yours anyway'. She thought all my friends and employees were only out to take advantage of me, and trusted no one.

Expecting at best an ally, and at worst, a neutral response, I was staggered at her reaction.

'You've become a fool, with your head in the clouds. Whatever you think you're looking for, it's right in front of your eyes. The frying pan is almost down to just about the right temperature and you choose this moment to jump into the fiercest of fires with that au pair of yours. Believe me, Gil, she's only after one thing.'

I tried to put my point of view, to reach that unspoken harmony we had always managed in the past, but she was unmoved.

'I don't know why I waste my breath,' she said. 'You'll do exactly what you want, anyway. You always do. It's just selfish and hurtful what you're doing to those two boys. And as for—' She stopped in mid-sentence and as if reading my mind. 'You know, Gil, sex isn't everything. In fact, in the scheme of things, it's not very much at all. Take my word for it. Do something for me, Gil, please.'

'What's that, Mum?' I asked with forced cheer.

I didn't even know she had the words in her vocabulary to be so crude and forthright. I guess she had lived the part so often of the victim in the scenario she now described.

'The next time you shoot your bolt inside her, look away and think to yourself, do I really know this woman? Do I love her? Be honest with yourself and live with the answer your heart and head give you now your cock is out of action.'

We never said another word on the subject and, until her dying day, as much as she was still Mum and I was her son, the dependence had finally ceased and she was her own woman, fiercely loyal to Sandra and the boys, never once speaking or responding to Rosita's attempts, or mine on her behalf, to make peace. There was even no reaction, other than a bland smile and nod of the head, when I told her years later that I was to be a father again. When the end came, we were many miles apart and she had died in the nursing home before I had time to fly back and hold her hand and tell her I loved her.

I did try what she had so crudely suggested the next time Rosita and I were together, but the result was all fuzzy in my head and I dismissed the experiment as flawed.

Three days passed before I decided sufficient time had elapsed for the raw emotion to have been dulled by the reality and for Sandra and me to discuss the practicalities. Rosita and I were close to a deal on renting a two-bedroomed apartment just outside Newport, and I had made my first return visit to a subdued and uncertain office environment. Conversations were restricted to the minutiae of our business world, avoiding any mention of my family or personal issues.

I must have phrased my request for a meeting in the wrong terms, because when I reached the house, there was an air of expectancy around Sandra that suggested I had finally come to my senses. As I started to talk about dividing our assets, she deflated like a balloon, the bottle of wine unopened on the table, her attention elsewhere and a sudden anxiety for me to leave.

I had intended to write a letter setting out my proposals when the rug was very definitely pulled out from under my feet.

The first sign control was being wrested out of my grasp was a registered letter from a firm of solicitors with a Bristol address, serving a statutory notice on me, stating that Sandra was suing for divorce on the grounds of my adultery with a person or persons unnamed. I was requested, in order to avoid any further anguish to my wife, to provide within seven days a complete list of all properties, bank or other accounts, assets and all goods and chattels in my, joint or nominee names, in the UK or outside, that would represent a complete and true statement of our financial position.

My solicitor, Paul Duggan, was a mutual friend from the golf club Sandra and I had joined shortly after arriving in Wales. The objective had been to build up a group of influential contacts who would help in the development of my fledgling business, and whilst my interest in flogging a golf ball to death quickly waned, Sandra became reasonably competent and had kept up her membership long after mine had lapsed.

In retrospect, I should have ditched Paul at stage one, but the naivety that everything would fall into line with my wishes, the passive nature of Sandra's reaction so far and my idea of what was just and fair blinded me to the reality. Paul, an avid fan of American cop films, was a competent local solicitor who specialised in residential conveyancing, minor litigation and matrimonial issues, mainly where legal aid was involved and neither party had a pot to piss in.

I thought when he first read the letter from Radnott, Pinner, he was about to genuflect and fall to his knees in silent prayer. 'These are heavy dudes,' he said. 'London based, totally beyond my pay grade. You need to tool up with someone who can interreact with these people.'

'How could she afford a firm like that?' I queried.

'They've probably looked at an estimate of your wealth, taken a fee hike and gone pro bono on the balance. They'll take a slice of whatever she gets.'

'Can they do that?'

'Who's going to stop them? The Law Society? I doubt it.'

Like a fool, I told him to get a grip and act for me. I was sure he could achieve a result. After all, I wasn't going to create any problems or make life difficult for Sandra.

The trouble was, she didn't feel that way.

Paul's reply to Radnott, Pinner was almost reverential. He acknowledged the service on my behalf, thanked them for leaving the co-respondent's name as not disclosed and confirmed that the petition would not be contested. He hoped that an amicable settlement could be reached between the parties and made an offer along the lines I had drafted.

The following Monday, my arrival at the office was delayed following a visit to the estate agents to sign off on the shorthold tenancy for the flat. We would be moving in on the Thursday and I was feeling elated. Rosita had fancied a waterbed, sulked when I said it was too expensive, but what the hell. Business was buoyant and I figured four grand was a small price to pay for the pleasure I would get out of it.

You could have cut the atmosphere with a knife. Sandra was sitting around the oval table in the boardroom, Karen standing at her side, talking earnestly, flicking through files of invoices, oblivious to my presence as I stood by the door.

'Having a good time, girls?'

Karen stood upright with a jerk, her hand releasing the file which spiralled down onto the table. Sandra glanced up briefly and returned to study the page she had separated for inspection.

'Fine, thanks. You?'

'Can I ask what you think you are doing here?'

'I'm sorry.'

'You heard me, Sandra. Don't play games.'

There was a nervous cough from Karen and a mumbled excuse that preceded a hasty exit from the room.

Sandra raised her eyes to hold my angry stare. 'As far as I remember, I am a director and shareholder in this company. Do I need a reason to be here?'

'Up until now, your interest in the business has been to appear once a fortnight to countersign cheques and distract the staff for an hour or so with your tales of how the other half live.' I was livid inside, but I thought some tongue-in-cheek humour might make me sound relaxed about the intrusion into what I considered as my world.

She had no time to reply. The door to the warehouse crashed open as a face I recognised from another environment staggered into the office laden with files that had been consigned to the archive years ago. He hadn't seen me, announcing to all and sundry in his booming voice there were eight gas boilers with the M740 pressure release valve left in stock. 'Does that tally?' he asked, equally loudly.

'Tally with what, may I ask?' I interrupted, again, before Sandra could react.

'Ahhh …' He dragged out the word for five seconds as if weighing me up. 'You've finally arrived, old man.' He balanced the files on the desk Sandra was occupying, turning and thrusting his hand out. 'Glad you could make it.' His approach made me feel as if I were the interloper.

Roger had been membership secretary at the golf club those many years before when we had first applied to join. He had made a big thing about the munificent gesture he would bestow by taking us under his wing and ensuring we got to know everybody who was anybody in the club. He would tap his index finger on the side of his nose. 'I've learned during my role in procurement with the Ministry of Defence, it's never what you know, it's who you know that can really make a difference. Look at me.'

And I had, for about the first four months, until I had lost interest and the pressure of business took over all those spare hours. I had thought about selling my set of clubs, but they were still tucked into a corner in the garage. It crossed my mind Roger might get his hairy mitts on them. What I could do right there and then with that driver lingered on my mind.

Although I had never given it a thought, I imagined Sandra would have seen him around the club on a regular basis and exchanged pleasantries. I never once conceived she knew him well enough to solicit his help to poke his nose into my – yes, that's what I said – my business.

'What are you doing here?' I snapped. 'And what concern is it of yours how many gas boilers I have in stock?'

Roger would have been about five years older than me, of a similar build but a good deal taller. With all that golf and the running I recalled he loved to do, he was in good shape, muscular and clothes conscious, as I guessed would befit his role as a middle-manager civil servant. He would probably be well up the greasy pole in the Ministry by now.

'Good Lord, old man, nothing personal.' There was a defensive smile on his face and he was watching my hands. 'Sandra's a brick amongst the girls at the club and she told me you'd both decided to sever the old ties that bind and all that.' He looked over at her. 'I told her I'd been through the process a couple of years ago when Constance sailed away into the blue yonder, and if you both needed any advice, well, she just had to ask. And she did.'

I could tell, even though the door was closed, his booming voice had reached the outer office, and Jimmy, one of my lead plumbers, was trying desperately not to laugh but failing. I went to speak, but Roger hadn't finished.

'I know the financials can be pretty scary for both parties, all that form filling and baring the old soul with the gruesome details. San' – I'd never called her that in my life – 'asked if I'd give her a hand in trying to work out what your' – his arm extended to include the two of us in the remark – 'little show here is worth. I told her it would be a pleasure and she could count on me.'

My fist was pumping and I was trying hard to control myself. 'Would you mind if I had a private word with my wife?' I said through clenched teeth.

'My word, no,' he said. 'Never too late for the old kiss and make up, is it?' His comforting smile at Sandra lingered just a fraction too long. He swept the files up into his arms. 'I've got plenty to be getting on with, looking over this little lot.'

Then, there was silence. She looked up questioningly at me with eyes as cold as a dead fish, but did not speak.

'What's going on, Sandra? Or should I call you San?' I mimicked. 'What on earth is the sodding laughing cavalier doing here? I thought we had a deal.'

'No. You had a deal and I listened.' Her voice was flat and as cold as her eyes. 'My solicitors tell me you are putting the cart before the horse. Until we have both made a full report of our assets and expenses, no deal is possible.' She hesitated, as if deciding whether to broach a new topic. 'They have written to Paul to set out the framework. By the way, I think it's really unfair on Paul that you have instructed him to act. Damn it, Gil, he's a mutual friend. It's the last job he wants.'

'He's spoken with you?'

'Of course. He phoned to apologise.'

'To apologise?' I was flabbergasted.

'No. Wrong word. More to explain. What he said was he had known you a long time and did not feel he could refuse to act when you insisted. He would do his very best for you and that might involve issues I might find hurtful. He didn't know what they might be, but experience had taught him spiteful allegations between divorcing couples are all too common. He asked me not to think any less of him when it was all over.'

I nodded. It wasn't the first time I thought I should probably change solicitors but, like the fool I was, and to my cost, I didn't take my own advice.

'How does that explain the presence of your tame gamekeeper here today?'

'Don't be cruel. It's not necessary. I have to put a value on my shareholding in the company and Roger is here to try to help me do that. He knows more about the ins and outs than I do, so I asked him. As he said, he's recently divorced, although his was on the grounds of incompatibility.'

'Your shareholding?' I could not keep the sarcasm out of my voice. 'You own one fucking share, for Christ's sake. And that was just to make up numbers. At the time, every company needed two shareholders. The rest are in my name.'

'There is no need to sound angry.' She was so calm. Solicitor's instructions, I calculated. Whatever you do, Mrs Hart, do not let him see you are losing your temper.

'I'm not angry. I'm incredulous.'

'The solicitors tell me we both have an equal interest in the company, in whatever names the shares are registered. That goes for everything. After all, we both started together with nothing.'

'And that is why I made the proposal I did.'

'It will probably work out that way, but we have to go through all the procedures.'

I waved my hand in the general direction of Roger. 'But is all this really necessary? Does knowing how many pieces of stock of a particular item are in hand tell you what the business is really worth?' I should have given that question a lot more thought than I did. If I had, I might have been able to forestall what was to come. Instead, I tried to play on her emotions. 'Is there no trust between us? I still respect you. Don't you have any feelings for me?'

She put down the piece of paper she was playing with and looked directly into my eyes. 'What do you want, Gil? Do you want me to say I love you when I know you cannot say the same in return? That would be self-destructive. Now, let me get on, please.'

For four weeks there was some semblance of normality, if you discounted filling in something called a Form E which ran over about twelve pages and asked about everything anybody could wish to know regarding your personal circumstances; that, and following the relentless progression of solicitors' letters and court notices which led to the decree nisi.

There was to be a meeting. We were now six weeks into our new apartment. Rosita had taken a temporary job as a peak-capped minion in the local branch of a burger franchise, although she made it plain she was angling for a role as my secretary once the divorce was finalised. Our relationship was still dominated by sex, which I craved like a drug that obsessed me and which she satisfied with a dedication that matched my intensity. The waterbed, which had taken a team to install and position, proved to be an amazing acquisition. It took a while to get used to, but once we had learned to manipulate our bodies, the sensation of coming together could be achieved in some truly unconventional poses.

The lingering memory of that morning's fantastic climax was uppermost in my mind as we sat around an enormous oval mahogany table in the well-appointed boardroom of Radnott, Pinner in the centre of Bristol. Paul seemed distant, distracted, a self-imposed defence to the knowledge he was out of his comfort zone. I didn't care. I was not going to be bullied by some jumped-up lawyer who thought he could dominate the proceedings.

Mr Suman introduced himself as a partner in the firm and offhandedly presented the two younger men sitting alongside as junior solicitors who specialised in family litigation. Sandra sat the other side of him, staring steadfastly in front of her. Paul and I faced them.

Suman was of Indian extraction, a small man with delicate features and a clipped accent. Even from the distance we sat apart, I could smell the stench of tobacco on his breath and marvel at the thought a man with such a healthy income should have such disgusting teeth. Several were missing and others were misshapen or broken. He must have sensed my reaction and apologised for his appearance. He was in the initial stages of a very long and complicated dental procedure. It was the only fleeting moment in a long and painful meeting that he humbled himself before me.

We had come together, he explained, to decide whether the divorce would proceed through the FDA process or be treated as an FDR matter. FDA was an appointment procedure where the parties had reached an agreed financial settlement, and FDR, where a dispute existed.

Everybody around the table hoped there would be no cause for disagreement, and Paul indicated a fair and equitable proposal had been made by me which, upon further considered reflection, he hoped was acceptable to Mrs Hart. He turned to smile at Sandra but her gaze was cast down at a point on the leather-bound blotter in front of her.

Suman tipped his head and gave a 'we are not amused' smile.

'Your proposal is rejected,' he said. 'We have a counterproposal.'

'Which is?'

He looked straight at me. 'The equity in the property in which you live, plus all the chattels therein, other than your personal clothing and effects. The savings accounts, bank accounts and market investments, and fifty per cent of the pension fund in the name of Mr Hart, which will be converted into cash.'

Apart from the pension fund, which had not crossed my mind and which I could not object to, the proposal was in line with my original offer.

'Agreed,' I said.

'I haven't finished.'

For a moment, I was confused. 'Oh, you mean maintenance payments?'

He ignored my question. 'Mrs Hart will also be entitled to the entire share capital in GH Plumbing & Heating Services Ltd, and any amounts loaned or owed to you by said company will be considered as discharged.'

I was too taken aback to say anything.

'In addition,' he went on, 'you will pay eight hundred pounds per month until the majority of your eldest son, reducing to six hundred pounds until the majority of your second son, and at the rate of three hundred pounds for a further five years.' He sat back in his chair. 'That is Mrs Hart's offer to you.'

'You are crazy,' I said, looking at Sandra who now returned my gaze. 'What am I supposed to live on?' I asked. 'And what could you possibly know about running a plumbing company?'

Suman leaned forward again. 'The answer to the second question is that it would be no concern of yours. The answer to your first is the bank account in the name of your offshore company, Brass Tacks SA, held in Liechtenstein.'

I tried not to show my panic as Paul looked at me quizzically. 'I have no idea what you are talking about.' I hoped I sounded both annoyed and confused at the allegation.

Suman indicated to the colleague on his far left, a younger man with a face of pitted skin and lank brown hair. 'Mr Hopkins, please,' he said.

Hopkins asked me if I denied being in possession of such an account and I replied emphatically that I did. He then went on to explain the penalties and attitude of the courts for failure to disclose assets in a matrimonial dispute. 'The judges take a very dim view of such devious behaviour.'

'I'm sure they do,' I said, sounding offended by the implication.

'Do you know a Mr Harry Black, formerly of Blackstone Constructions?' he asked.

'What's he got to do with anything?'

'You carried out a contract for Blackstone, did you not?'

I remembered the invoices. They were for peanuts. 'Bits and pieces. Nothing very significant.'

'Do you class complete plumbing and heating installations in sixty houses as "nothing very significant"?'

'Not if we had done the work, no.'

Hopkins pulled a document from a folder. 'As you may be aware, Mr Black is currently at Her Majesty's Pleasure for the next two years or so. I have a signed affidavit from Mr Black stating that he contracted the services of

Gilbert Hart to complete the installations I referred to during the course of 1986. Mr Hart did not render invoices and was paid in cash. Two things occurred. Mr Black raised phoney and exorbitant invoices from a bogus company he had formed himself to substantiate the plumbing and heating work, so as to enable him to pay Mr Hart and to keep a sizeable chunk plus the VAT for himself, an action which led to his incarceration.'

I laughed, but inside I knew I was doomed. 'You mean he used his own money to pay himself? Sounds rather ridiculous.'

'Don't be naïve, Mr Hart.' Hopkins sounded threatening. 'The bank was financing the construction and Mr Black had a partner whom he was effectively defrauding.' He went back to his paperwork. 'The second thing that occurred is you tried to deposit a large sum of cash in your secret account, but the bank would not accept it without understanding the provenance. You went back to Mr Black and exchanged a substantial part of the cash for cheques drawn on Mrs Black's personal account, made out to Brass Tacks SA.'

More pieces of paper appeared. 'This is an affidavit from Mrs Black plus copies of the cancelled cheques showing clearly they were deposited in your Liechtenstein account.'

'I daresay Black would say anything that might help to reduce his sentence.'

Hopkins shook his head. 'No coercion or inducement was used to encourage Mr or Mrs Black to swear the affidavits.'

This was the only thing he said that turned out not to be strictly true. I found out later Sandra and Roger had gone to see Black in prison once they were hot on my trail. To encourage the man to shop me, Roger had given his ebullient performance of a freemason's relationship with a fellow in chambers who was a hotshot at getting people out on appeal or sentences reduced. True or not, Black was probably sufficiently bitter at taking the rap for all the other subcontractors to have named and shamed.

'There is one other thing you should be aware of, Mr Hart.' Hopkins could already see that I had nowhere to go. 'The houses in the residential site were all fitted with something called a gas boiler with an M740 pressure release valve. Checks have shown that over the years your company purchased thirty more boilers than were sold. We will let the facts speak for themselves.'

He was right. I had tried to buy all sixty for cash, but the supplier had insisted on invoicing half of them.

I avoided everybody's eyes. Bang to rights.

Suman had returned to the fray. 'As your legal adviser will no doubt tell you, the option remains for you to reject Mrs Hart's counterproposal and pursue the matter via the courts. However, I must warn you we have strongly advised our client, should you pursue this course of action, that in order to preserve the integrity of her claim against you, it would be necessary to disclose to the relevant authorities all of the circumstances surrounding the transaction, the offshore company and the suspect bank account.'

Of course, I had lost, and Sandra had ended up with everything. The irony of it all was Roger not only knew somebody who did get Black's sentence reduced, he also knew somebody who knew somebody with a keen interest in acquiring plumbing and heating companies now the regulations were being tightened and prices were rising in tandem. Within six months of gaining control of the business, Sandra had sold out for three million and was financially set for life. Another year, and cunning old Roger was sharing the marital bed.

Talking about beds, I have to say that Rosita's reaction to the news was not what I expected. She more or less shrugged and suggested that we leave the UK and settle back in Spain. Her parents had a holiday home we could live in whilst I started up a new plumbing and heating operation on the Costas. Property in Spain was booming, she said, and everybody was crying out for tradesmen to keep up with the growth. It sounded like a really stimulating challenge and she never once doubted my prowess as a businessman.

The owner of the apartment in Newport took the news badly that I would have to break the shorthold tenancy. He was an excitable Italian whose family had built up an ice cream business after the Second World War and had surely not ended up owning a flat like the one we had rented by giving the taxman a lick of all the choc ices he had sold. I had no sympathy for him, especially after the company cheque I had issued to pay the last month's rent bounced and he called me a crook. Sandra had wasted no time in changing the authorised signatories at the bank and had caught me out.

I offered the waterbed to the landlord for a thousand pounds and the rent arrears. He told me to fuck off and the sooner I left the country, the better.

The taxi was waiting with Rosita and the luggage. Sorry, I had just forgotten something. I ran back into the flat, took the kitchen knife out of my pocket and made a savage cut in the mattress. Water began to flow from the wound. With any luck, we would be out of the country before the water had seeped through the floorboards and the downstairs bedroom ceiling collapsed.

CHAPTER TEN
Cavalla – 2008

The car has just run through a hollow filled with water that splashes up around the doors. Hugo taps me on the shoulder to attract my attention. He has looked at me quizzically on two occasions since meeting me at the hospital, as if he is having trouble grasping the man he spoke with normally a week ago could now no longer hear a word he is saying.

His gestures tell me the car needs petrol and he proposes stopping for a coffee. I hobble clumsily to a table where I hand him the indispensable magic eraser slate. Although his face punctures with a weak smile from time to time, I can tell from his tired, puffy eyes and unkempt appearance he has also been feeling the immense strain of Albert's death.

I mention how tired and distressed Jasmin looked when she visited me. Everybody close to my son has taken his tragic death badly, he tells me, but there are other personal and professional factors Jasmin has to deal with which put her under pressure.

I press him for details. He refers to the issue with Sandra, her insistence on repatriating the body and the demands of the lawyer she has hired. Then, there is the veterinary practice. It's very busy at the moment.

Couldn't she get someone to substitute her at this time, I ask.

It's not that easy. The practice has one important client, a safari park outside the town of Lamego, replete with various species of African animals, an area in which Jasmin is well versed having spent part of her practical training in Kenya and a two-year contract working full-time for a zoo in Strasbourg. During the past week, there has been an outbreak of a dietary infection amongst some of the animals at the park and management insist Jasmin be available to supervise the treatment. The park has been forced to close temporarily, and time is money.

'If I can do anything to help.' I point at my leg. 'Given the state I'm in, whatever I'm able. Perhaps some babysitting at night when the boy is in bed?'

He will pass on the message. For the time being, Jasmin and Francisco are staying with her mother, Inés. She is the headmistress of the local primary school. For the next two weeks, the schools are still on holidays and Inés has time to look after Francisco, but after that … He shrugs.

Hugo is a puzzling individual. He is tall with soft features, yet possesses an air of self-assurance and arrogance I recognise in his uncle Lino, if not the same brashness of approach. There is something deeper, more troubled or apprehensive underpinning his personality. Maybe I'm reading the signals wrongly, but I sense he is constantly plucking up courage to ask me something but never does.

I look at the question on the slate. 'No,' I say, 'I'm not afraid that I might not get my memory back. There's only a very short period missing and I seem to remember everything else. They say my age is against me. After all, it's at my time of life you start forgetting things as a matter of course.'

He smiles, seemingly relieved that he has broached a sensitive personal issue and I was not offended, though I feel the lengthy, comforting pat on the shoulder overplays the sympathy card.

'I'm much more concerned about recovering my hearing. The thought I might be confined to this arrangement for the rest of my life is terrifying.' I point towards the slate.

As he starts to write, I anticipate the next question. 'As it happens, someone sent me a book on lip-reading and I will get around to studying it. As far as sign language is concerned, I can't see me getting the hang of it.'

Hugo shows me into Adele's apartment, where we are set upon by a frenzied ball of black and white fur, desperate to lick us to death before its features disappear behind a long, furry fringe, his tail still wagging furiously. This, I guess, is Pom-Pom, the Portuguese water dog who is such a hit with Francisco. I can understand why. His energy is all positive and friendly, with a determination to achieve immediate bonding.

My temporary accommodation above the pharmacy in Cavalla turns out to be a pleasant surprise. Whilst the rest of the apartment is cluttered and untidy, my bedroom, with a window overlooking the road into the centre of town, feels like an oasis of calm. The room is large, simply furnished in bright colours with a bedspread displaying da Vinci's *Vitruvian Man*, neatly positioned so the head is symmetrically arranged between my two pillows.

Judging by the confusion in the adjoining rooms, someone has gone to a great deal of trouble to ensure my stay will be as comfortable as possible. The posters pinned around the walls showing folk having a good time at

Woodstock, Glastonbury and a handful of other places I had never heard of doubtless provide a clue as to the personality of my hostess.

Adele will be up to see me as soon as the pharmacy closes and Hugo will pick me up in three days' time, the following Monday, at ten, to take me to the funeral.

My stomach rumbling, I try the fridge. Sadly, as I'm not into hummus, lentils and soya milk, I will have to go hungry. Pom-Pom watches intently, following me at a polite distance as I hobble around, only responding to be pampered whenever I summon him.

At around nine, the front door crashes open and two pizza boxes herald the arrival of the last possible person I would have imagined responsible for running a pharmacy.

Still dressed in her working pink smock, this apparition from another age smiles and holds out her hand. Adele would have been born in the mid-seventies and could never have known the real age of Aquarius, flower power, free love and all that, but I would never have guessed it from looking at her. Her tousled blonde hair is pinned back with large clips in the shape of stars and shuffled into a short, ragged ponytail at the back which rather resembles Pom-Pom's tail.

Her face is heavily tanned, with the trace of crack lines in her skin that sun worshippers tend to develop mingled with a sprinkling of light-brown freckles. On the top of her left cheek, alongside her eye, are two small henna tattoos in white, one of a heart and the other of a star that matches the clips in her hair.

She is slightly smaller than average height, with what can only be described as a fulsome figure, but her most striking feature is the array of tattoos visible on her body. There is little free space. From the highly coloured butterfly on her neck to the solemn hippie woman on her arm (a self-portrait?) to the long floral display on her leg and, on the top of her foot, visible between the thong of her sandals, the anti-nuclear symbol intertwined with a white daisy, she is a walking advertisement for peace and harmony.

Her mouth is moving at such breakneck speed I cannot decipher a single word or even the language in which she is speaking. I put my hands up to my ears and then up in the air, hunching my shoulders in a gesture of incomprehension. It works, and without saying a word, I hand her the slate.

Her command of English is good, courtesy of a university degree where most of the reading matter originated in the US or UK, although talking or writing so rapidly she cannot avoid misspellings or the odd grammatical confusion.

She is a vegetarian, hence the two pizzas: mine with chicken and chorizo; hers, highly colourful, but unappealing to a steak and chips philistine like me. Tomorrow, she will shop for things I will like but would I mind if it's not red meat, which turns her stomach on sight? I offer a twenty euro note from my dwindling resources. Happily, she declines, getting up to clear away the empty boxes and glasses so as to avoid any attempt by me to force the cash onto her. She need not have worried. It was a duty offer and the money is soon back in my pocket.

I see little of her over the next three days and learn next to nothing of her background, other than she has never been married, attended university in Porto where she met Hugo, and, through him, came to be friends with Albert. Tears well in her eyes when she mentions his name and, although curious, I back off from pushing for more personal details until we get to know each other better.

After lunch on Saturday, and with the pharmacy closed for the weekend, she announces her intention of going on a trip with a friend and will be back on Sunday evening. Normally, she would take the dog, but as I am here, this is an ideal opportunity to enjoy that little extra freedom; so, would I mind? By this time, Pom-Pom and I have become firm friends and I will be glad of the company.

The fridge is now full of items I could not imagine Adele countenancing in a hundred years and which I am sure will all be ceremoniously dumped as soon as I have departed.

Left to my own devices, the solitude bears down on me, a painful concoction of dread, grief and culpability. I have never been particularly religious, but I find myself in a conversation with God. To be more exact, I curse him. Less than a fortnight earlier, I held a glass in my hand to toast the start of a fresh start, not just the beginning of a journey for Albert and his new wife and son, but, at last – at long last – an affirmation that I could begin to make amends. If my son's death is punishment for my wrongdoings, and, yes, there is a litany of sins for which I could be condemned, then, for both our sakes, God, take it out on me! Why steal the life of a man who has done nothing but good, just to torture the sinner and wreak misery and sadness on family and loved ones? Even Adele is in pain.

Yet, there is still something wrong with this argument. Something troubles me; the reality does not quite match the scenario I have painted, something I cannot yet identify.

I begin to see my struggle as personal, exclusive to God and me, a wrestling match with me as the aggressor and my opponent unable to do anything but parry my blows. I attribute malignance to his so-called benign divinity; the falsehood which claims one man's evil can be balanced by another's good; a demonstration that hell is really here on earth and, above all, an old man's inability to blame anybody else for his own guilt.

I cannot say this with any certainty but, when drowsy from the lack of sleep that did not come and with my mind in torment, I believe it was only the comforting presence of my faceless companion, Pom-Pom, that stopped me from swallowing all the painkillers I had been given. As my hand reaches out for the container, a pink tongue appears from between the mass of fur to lick my fingers, then a cold, damp snout buries into my palm until I begin to respond and gently stroke him until sleep comes.

By Sunday afternoon, and after a takeaway of chicken piri-piri washed down by a potent local white wine, the depression begins to lift. I must resist these waves of morbid fatalism. I can't handle the reality of Albert's death because I don't know all the facts. Take Adele, for instance. What was her relationship with my son? Do I need a reason to go looking or is it just an excuse to poke around in things that have nothing to do with me? It's becoming a habit.

Amongst all the bric-a-brac around the apartment there are no personal photographs on display, no evidence of family and friends. I find that curious. Her bedroom is slightly smaller than mine but untidy and uncared for, clothes strewn around the floor, magazines discarded amidst several mugs with traces of the camomile tea she favours. She sleeps on a king-sized futon but there is no evidence of a partner.

The wardrobe door opens onto a dozen or so outfits, mostly colourful summer clothes with a sprinkling of drabber and heavier winter wear. The top drawers of her chest of drawers contain nothing but underwear. The lower drawers are all slacks, blouses and jumpers. Except for the very bottom one. There are the missing photographs, a dozen or so, large postcard size, all in decorative metal frames, bound together with tape.

Every photo is of Adele, at various ages from about twenty onwards, in company with one person or another. I don't recognise most of the companions but in three of the most recent, I do. My guess is they must have been taken about four years earlier. Albert looked a very happy man, and the intimate poses and looks between the two suggest the relationship was far from platonic.

Adele must have returned late and risen early, because after I awake on the alarm and emerge, showered, shaved and dressed, the apartment is deserted. I hear a familiar bark from the outside enclosure to which Pom-Pom is confined whilst Adele is at work. Today, there will be no morning romp with my adorable ball of fur. Today will be filled with sadness and regret. Today, Sandra and I will suffer the worst experience any parent has to bear. We will bury our child. So, why do I no longer feel the pain of remorse?

I check my appearance. I have lost weight, and the suit recovered from the boot of the Astra hangs on my shoulders, limp and creased, whilst the trouser leg is stretched taut by the plaster cast on my thigh; overall, the reflection of a sad old man, a misfit who is about to gatecrash a virtual stranger's funeral.

Adele has left a note. She will close the pharmacy in time to attend the church service. Hugo is on his way.

I find myself back in the large room where we had celebrated the marriage, Hugo by my side, his head bowed, hands clasped tightly as he tries to hold himself in check.

In the centre of the room a group of four monks, clad in saffron-coloured robes, move their heads up and down in unison to the chant as they shuffle around the simple pine coffin. Hugo uses the slate to explain they are making a whining sound intended to chase away the evil spirits which orbit the body.

I hobble forward until I can look down on the peaceful face, so natural and unblemished, as if asleep and, at any moment, able to wake and smile at me. I raise two fingers to my lips in a kiss and place them against his mouth. I flinch at the chill of the touch and wait for the tears to come. But they don't. I look again at the remains of my son and my eyes cloud as his face becomes a blank canvas.

The only other people in the room, standing by the exit door, are Jasmin and Vernon, her eyes averted as she listens to him. He is standing uncomfortably close to her, eyes wide and fierce, his hands pumping, flecks of spittle at the corner of his mouth as he speaks. Francisco sits in his buggy, one hand dragging a plastic robot along the floor, the other gripping his mother's skirt. I look at him and smile, but he stares through me and I see that blank canvas again. We are all born innocent, an innocence that is corrupted and eventually extinguished, unintentionally or otherwise, by the people who are supposed to nurture and protect us. The canvas that is Francisco is today being painted with the savage, black strokes of hate and anger, not love and compassion.

On Sunday, I read and re-read three chapters of the book on lip-reading. It was difficult. The idea of separating words from the way they are spelled to the way they sound; recognising phonetic text, and the classification of the lip movements into various groupings. I couldn't say I had taken much in, but it taught me to start studying the lips of the people around me.

The word 'fuck' is easy to lip-read because it is written exactly as it sounds. If spoken vehemently, the nose crinkles upwards and the upper teeth are bared in rabbit fashion. When followed by 'you', the mouth adopts an open, pouting movement. Vernon is giving me plenty of practice in recognising that particular profanity.

Hugo starts to move towards them but I restrain him. Neither physically nor mentally is he a match for Vernon.

Instead, I call Jasmin's name and wait for Vernon to turn, distracted by the interruption. He recognises me, utters another profanity, this time in my direction, and strides away. As he does so, he glances over at Hugo. There is a barely imperceptible nod in return which I take as indicating both recognition and relief.

The plastic cover on my magic erasure slate is becoming creased and a little tear has appeared near one of the corners. I make a mental note to buy another, but for today, the one I hand to Jasmin will have to do.

'What was all that about?' I ask.

She has started to use text message abbreviations. Everybody is waiting at the evangelical church in Godim and Vernon insists we finish all this mumbo jumbo, as he puts it. His mother is anxious to get the funeral started. The mourners are getting impatient.

'I could tell those were not the words he was using.'

'He is a rude and uncouth man.'

Apparently, the terms of the compromise reached a week ago were that if Sandra was prepared to concede to the burial near to their home, Jasmin would agree to a Christian burial in a local church. Sandra made every effort to have the body repatriated to Wales and is both bitter and angry at Jasmin's persistent and stubborn resistance.

I point at the monks. 'Is this what he would have wanted?'

She nods and writes on the slate.

Like the Buddhists, Albert believed in samsara, a conviction his actions in life will lead to reincarnation. As far as the monks are concerned, he is simply going to a refuge, and when the last rite is chanted, The Three Jewels, his entry into Nirvana will be secure.

Before I can press for more details, the double doors open with a bang and Vernon enters with a group of men in sombre suits, pall-bearers, I guess, employed by the undertaker. Vernon roughly pushes away two of the monks, pointing frantically at one of the men to seal the coffin.

Jasmin rushes towards him. There is a fierce exchange of words. Vernon raises his hand to strike her across the face.

'Get away from her!' I shout.

His face is full of hate. He walks over to me, his hand still raised, his mouth framing words I cannot hear or understand, except for his repeated profanities and a word that looks like a smile but I take as 'kill', or 'k.ee.l' in its phonetic form.

My earlier brief encounter in the cloakroom with Vernon should have primed me as to what to expect, but the sense of his pent-up aggression is frightening. Close up, I feel intimidated by his aggressive bearing, the clenched fists and gritted teeth. He is struggling to hold himself in check. Even when he starts to back away from me, I feel a sense of raw fear in the pit of my stomach. It isn't his height or build. He is no taller than me but boasts a wiry frame, muscular and agile. Perhaps it's the colour of his skin that makes him appear more imposing. That's racist. I'm not racist. How could I be? After all, I chose to marry a beautiful black woman at a time when it was socially frowned upon, if not openly voiced. No, it wasn't anything to do with colour. I imagine a white man in his place and it would be equally intimidating. Vernon is out of control, a bitter, angry man. I could blame all his anti-social behaviour on the drugs, alcohol, maybe some other substance abuse, but the truth is I sired a son with an evil and destructive personality.

Once again, I force myself to acknowledge his troubled mind was evident in those early years and my response was to run away.

Vernon and his retinue take the coffin, leaving our little group and a band of very confused and unhappy monks. I propose to Hugo he suggest they follow on to the cemetery in Godim and complete their blessing when the Christian ceremony is complete.

We journey in silence. As I sit with Francisco, playing with his robot in the back of Hugo's car, I can sense the boy recognises today is not like any other. His concentration is directed solely on the toy, avoiding eye contact with any of the adults, as if doing what he is doing will make everything all right and looking at us will tell him it is not.

Arriving late, our little grouping stands alongside Lino and Inés who have been deliberately ostracised by Sandra and her clan. Lino hands me a brand-new magic erasure slate with a look that says it all: you may have pooh-poohed this originally but now you see how right I was. I thank him.

I interpret the weak, apologetic smile from Madeleine as saying she isn't brave enough to defy her best friend's will. My response is a half-smile and nod of the head to convey that I sort of understand and we need to talk. Nobody else bothers to acknowledge my presence. Throughout the entire proceedings my hand is entwined with a little hand with soft fingernails digging into my palm, relentlessly squeezing and releasing in an unspoken plea to not let go. And I won't. Not now. Not ever.

As the burial service comes to an end, the monks resume their chanting to Sandra's obvious disgust. An attractive woman breaks away from the group as she catches my eye. With a broad smile, she walks towards me. A sideways glance tells me she's already come onto Lino's radar.

To tell the truth, I would have passed her on the street did she not look so much like her mother.

Sandra comes from a large family. She is somewhere in the middle order, one of three girls and three boys. By the time I arrived on the scene, it was a source of family bemusement that the youngest of the sisters, Florence, had adopted Sandra as her soulmate and mentor, following her fashions, her likes and dislikes, and being easily swayed by her opinions.

I suppose it was hardly surprising within six months of our move to Wales and with Sandra regularly waxing lyrical about her new environment, Florence and new husband Humbert had also relocated. They were both NHS nursing assistants, and a transfer to the Royal Gwent in Newport was a matter of course.

The sisters lived in each other's pockets and as our family grew, so, eventually, did theirs, with the arrival of a daughter. Botany, four years Albert's junior. As a child, she hero-worshipped him. I last saw her as a nine-year-old but I could never mistake the beaming smile and infectious laugh inherited from her mother. She has grown into a real beauty. As she approaches, Lino intercepts her with a ridiculously exaggerated bow of the head, a kiss on the hand and what I read as a gasped '*Encantado*', as if he is about to be overcome with emotion.

'Excuse Jasmin's uncle Lino,' I say. 'He's just arrived out of a fifties movie. Lovely to see you, Botany, after all these years.'

Natural enough, perhaps, given the passage of time, but somehow strangely formal, we shake hands. She returns my smile and says nothing, obviously primed as to my condition. Gauging by the flush on his cheeks, whatever comment she exchanges with Lino evidently appeals to his less than understated ego. He is clearly keen to follow up but she purposefully turns her back on him to speak directly to me. I strip the wrapping from the new slate and hand it to her.

As we start to talk, I feel a little piqued that my fate has already been decided by Madeleine and Botany without considering it necessary to refer to me. A seat with extra legroom has been booked on a flight back to Cardiff the following day. Botany will accompany me and ensure I get back to Chepstow. Her car is at the airport.

'What about Madeleine's Astra?' I ask.

It suffered some minor damage in the explosion and would be repaired and parked up. When my wounds are healed, I can return to collect it and drive it back to the UK. Madeleine is in no rush. My few belongings were collected from the remains of the house and delivered to Adele. The police were unwilling for anything to be touched, but Hugo managed to get the necessary authority.

'Why are the police still involved?'

Haven't I been told? Botany is surprised. The house and garden have been sealed off. It's a crime scene and the forensic examination has still not been concluded.

'They don't think Albert's death was an accident?' I am incredulous.

She shrugs her shoulders.

Sandra walks over to Jasmin, casting a glance towards me and Francisco, who is still holding my hand. I get the words 'Happy families?' She is looking directly at me as she speaks but there is no compromise in her expression, just a cold stare through hurt and troubled eyes. She is clearly having difficulty holding herself in check, a lava of emotion hovering just below the thin veneer of civility. They speak briefly.

'What was all that about?' I ask, holding out my slate. Jasmin is shivering with the emotion, tears welled but not falling from her eyes.

Sandra's entourage is returning to the UK tomorrow. Jasmin has been summoned to the Crowne Plaza in Porto after breakfast to discuss Albert's belongings and his will. Sandra's lawyer is to be present.

'Did Albert have a will?' It doesn't seem consistent with my impression of the man.

Not to her knowledge, but she never got involved in his personal affairs.

'Personal affairs' is the term on my mind when I sit in an armchair later that evening, following a very palatable courgette and mushroom cannelloni which Adele prepared. She is sitting cross-legged on the floor in front of me, watching the news, whilst I bide my time by studying the tattoos on the back of her arms and the line drawing of Cupid with a bow on the nape of her neck. Our conversation at dinner meandered over nothing in particular at the snail's pace dictated by all the writing and reading now so much a part of my communication needs.

I was intrigued to learn more about my son. 'Did you know Albert well at one time?'

She turns, her brow creases.

'I mean ...' I am searching for the right words. 'Were you close? More than friends?'

She writes, 'WHO'S BEEN TALKING?'

'Nobody,' I say, hurriedly. 'It's just that you seemed very fond of him.'

'I expect it's Lino,' she writes. 'Was it him?' He's interested in everybody else's relationships.' She hesitates, then writes again. 'Except he can't arrange one for himself.'

I can believe it. Lino must have spent a good twenty minutes chatting up Botany, only to watch her slip out from under the arm that was pressed against the wall, wave goodbye and hurry to join Sandra. I managed to grab Madeleine's hand to hold her back and thank her for buying my plane ticket. I will give her the money as soon as I return home. 'We need to talk,' I said, as she tried to release herself from my grip. 'Especially after our last encounter.' I think her reply was, 'It's too late now.'

Adele is waiting patiently for confirmation. 'No. Just an old man's intuition,' I reassure her.

'I thought Albert was serious about me, at one time,' she prints in tiny letters. 'But he changed. And because he changed, I was forced to change.'

'Change how?'

'He had different options. They didn't include me.' With a flourish, she hands back the slate and turns back to the television. The conversation is over.

My immediate reaction is the incursion into her private life might have distanced her from me, but the next morning, as Hugo waits patiently to take me to the airport, she hugs me and, poking her finger into her mouth as if it were an inkwell, writes a symbolic message on my forehead.

'What does it say?' I ask.

She speaks by moving her lips in exaggerated fashion. 'That is for Albert to read,' she says and kisses me delicately on both cheeks.

Hugo is preoccupied and distant. Apart from enquiries about my hearing and memory, which I acknowledge with a 'no change' comment, the thirty-minute drive to Porto passes in silence.

I half expected and dreaded the prospect Sandra and family would be on the same flight back to Bristol, but, happily, as Botany tells me, they are on the later BA scheduled service.

The slate comes in for some heavy activity as we pass the time, with Botany bringing me up to date on all the family, her development and education. As she writes, she has the arm holding the slate linked through mine and I can relive the affection she felt for me as a little girl all those years ago. She does not hold back from letting herself get close to me. I am still Uncle Gil and it's a feeling that makes me glow inside.

'Does your mum still hate me?' I ask.

She nods.

The whole family, but Florence in particular, took the break-up very badly. At the time I felt it became more than a relationship issue. Discarding the black wife for the white mistress was easier for them to deal with rather than look on me as a fool who sacrificed his family for a romp in the hay.

'Why don't you?'

'Guess.'

I toy with the possibilities. 'We always got on when you were a kid and came around to visit Albert?'

She makes a maybe, maybe not gesture by holding her hand out and moving it up and down.

'Something else?'

She nods again.

I delve back into my memory, picturing a little girl with pigtails, in a floral dress, standing patiently by the kitchen door, with her mother and aunt deep in conversation and unaware of her presence.

'I'll take a wild guess,' I say, rather enjoying the game. 'But if I'm wrong, promise you won't get angry with me and not be my friend any more?' I say it as if I were a little boy and she laughs her agreement.

'This is just a stab in the dark. I'm no shrink, but I would say that the little Botany was jealous of the hold that Sandra had over her mum.' I always saw Florence as being under her sister's control and dominance, possibly seen through a child's eyes as a threat to the intimate relationship between mother and daughter. 'Maybe you didn't like Sandra at the time, and I was an okay uncle who didn't get in the way and made you laugh.'

She gives a thoughtful nod and writes on the slate. 'I still don't like her,' she puts. 'There have been plenty of relationships, but I don't let anybody get too close. Sandra did that for me.'

'I'm sorry,' I say. 'I'm afraid you are talking to the wrong person about meaningful relationships.'

She laughs. The ice has been well and truly broken between us. One thing she tells me, I did not know. For the past ten years, the two sisters have not spoken or maintained contact. Something serious happened to stall their relationship but Botany has no idea what it was. Her mother would not say, only hinting it was something to do with Vernon.

She deliberately changes the subject. Did I know the woman who had been standing next to Sandra at the funeral and who spent a lot of time talking to Vernon?

'Yes. Of course I do. It's Madeleine. She is Sandra's best friend. I've known her for years, since my schooldays. She moved to Wales long before Sandra and me. Her husband was in the steel industry. We met again by chance as members of the same golf club.'

I wait for her next question. 'No,' I say. 'Her name is not Smith. She's a widow now. If I'm not mistaken, her married name was Forbes. You've got me hooked. What's all this about?'

She insists I keep it a secret. Botany is employed in the back office reception at The Golden Swan Hotel in Usk. She recognised Madeleine immediately. In fact, she is famous amongst the front-of-house staff.

'Famous for what?' I ask.

Madeleine, or Mrs Smith, as per the registration card, is known as number six of an elite group the front office had christened the Bang Gang. She is one of the regulars who book in late morning for the afternoon. They have lunch with their partners, either in the restaurant or room service, and then spend a few pleasurable hours before going home, presumably to their spouses.

'Are you sure it's Madeleine? She has no ties to anybody, as far as I know.'

Botany writes. 'It's probably the man friend who has to be discreet.'

'Who is?' I ask, but I've already guessed.

He is careful. He always comes in after she has registered and goes directly upstairs; always leaving first, minutes before his companion comes down to pay the bill in cash. Botany put two and two together and, remembering the bearing of the man who always tried to shield his face from view but never quite managed, well … She had reached the bottom of the slate.

'Roger.' I savour the thought. 'You're saying she's having an affair with Roger.' An image comes into my mind of the two walking and talking intimately together in the church car park the previous day. 'Are you sure?'

She writes, covering the final comment with one hand. 'What do you take

me for, Uncle?'
 I laugh as she pretends to be offended.
 She takes her hand away.
 'A telltale?'

CHAPTER ELEVEN
Chepstow – 2008

The self-help book on lip-reading is beginning to look a little dog-eared around the corners, and there are some water stains where I balanced it too near the washbasin when practising lip shapes in the bathroom mirror, but it has been useful. I won't say I have assimilated a great deal, but with the odd half hour working on the various vowel and consonant lip groupings, spotting sliding vowels and sounds with lookalike lip shapings, the basics are gradually percolating through my ancient brain.

There is constant emphasis in the book on the need for someone to practice with, but a pocket mirror from the Pound Shop has to serve as my stand-in. I've even got to the point where I try to spell everyday words in the phonetic form they take when I speak. At first, it took time to gel as 'M.l.ee.s.m.uu.n' and 'V.l.ay.v.er.s' appeared on the page, but after six weeks of being back in Chepstow on my own, I am really getting the hang of it.

The problem is not so much identifying individual words. I can watch the supermarket checkout girl's lips and read any number of words, but even though I understand the context of what she is saying, when one lip shape runs rapidly into another I easily get lost, my brain panics and I shut down.

As soon as I am able, I pay Madeleine a visit, ostensibly to reimburse her for the airfare, but my primary motive is to find out why she was so scared of Vernon when she cornered me at the wedding reception. Had I taken her advice to return directly to the UK, perhaps the entire tragedy could have been avoided. It's a sobering thought.

She is all dressed up and smells like she's tried every sample bottle in the perfume shop. I wonder if she's on her way to the Golden Swan to assume her secret identity. How would she react if she understood she's known as number six of the Gang Bang? The thought crosses my mind to telephone Sandra's number later and check if good old Roger is at home. But I'm glad I don't. Even though I don't approve of her choice, good luck to her; and as for him, one day he'll slip up and blot his copy book. I'd love to be a fly on the wall in Sandra's lounge when that happens.

She avoids my gaze, her head raised to the side as if in serious contemplation. The tragedy has put everything into perspective. A terrible accident. Like Vernon, she drank too much that night and overreacted to his empty threats.

'It seemed more than that, as though he planned to harm me, and you were worried enough to warn me to leave.'

She shakes her head, snatching the slate from my hand. She speaks as she writes and I'm pleased with myself for picking up most of it. 'Nothing like that, Gil. I'm sorry to say that your son can be a nasty piece of work and manages to put the fear of God into people. He did me, but it's water under the bridge now. Since Albert's death, he's calmed down. It's got to us all. Things will never be the same for any of us.'

As I say my goodbyes, I am left with the uncomfortable feeling she knows more than she is prepared to divulge. Madeleine is still running scared.

Throughout the weeks that follow, I try to phone her on several occasions, always unsuccessfully. I can't count the messages I've left. There's even some good news I feel I want to share with her. My hearing has started to return. The car crash occurred in the road outside the block of flats. One of the vehicles tried desperately to brake and I heard the screech. I didn't hear the impact; maybe the pitch wasn't right, but I definitely heard the violent tyre squeal shortly before the collision. Funny how your senses can jog your memory.

***

Sanlazer, Costa de la Luz, Spain – 1992

I had been in Spain about two months before my first car accident. It wasn't a car, in fact. It was a hired van, and I turned left out of a driveway, holding the nearside lane and forcing a Land Cruiser to swerve into the gap I had just left. It was close, but thankfully nobody was hurt, and although the cars came into contact, neither vehicle was damaged. I must have seemed offhand to the other driver, as throughout my profuse apologies I was still thinking about the outspoken comments of the customer whose villa I had just left.

Our first weeks in Spain had been almost surreal. I hadn't placed any importance on Rosita's decision to relocate direct to the family's seaside apartment on the Costa de la Luz, just west of Huelva and close to the river border with Portugal's Algarve. Looking back, her option was the easy one; the alternative, having to deal with the reception we were likely to receive if we just turned up at the family's address in Madrid – the soon-to-be divorced Englishman, so much older than their vulnerable daughter or sister on whom he now depended to restore stability in his shattered life.

I had heard their names, not paying much attention to her descriptions and assuming they must be wealthy to live in the capital and have a holiday retreat by the sea. I understood nothing about the southern Mediterranean Latin attitude to family life. You didn't have to be well-off to own a second home. Amongst middle-class families it was almost the norm, and Rosita's father, a butcher with his own business in the suburbs, certainly fitted into that category.

Families lived together, many in the homes they had grown up in that now served for the three or four generations who cohabited and fended for each other. Their house or apartment or villa had been paid for long ago, and the capital they had accumulated during their working lives saved and invested for the future.

Financing the purchase of a property was something the Spanish banks were promoting to encourage home ownership amongst an emerging middle class of young professionals. Taken in isolation, this initiative was not enough to fuel demand for the supply of properties which were becoming available as the construction boom got underway. Attracting expatriates to invest in sun and sea housing projects helped, but the real tidal movement was appealing to the rump of the Spanish population to invest in a second home with wild, speculative promises of special deals and exaggerated simulations of self-funding holiday rentals that would easily cover the monthly mortgage repayments.

Rosita's family had been swept along in this property maelstrom, finally settling on a four-bedroom villa in a small complex that faced the beach and the ocean beyond. There were eight detached villas in all, four in a line parallel with the beach and two properties on either side to form the three sides of a rectangle. Each property had its own small garden and barbecue area with a gate leading to the communal swimming pool, spa tub and gardens. A wire fence separated the complex from the beach, with access via another gate controlled by a keypad with a six-digit code which the management company changed twice a year.

As I was to discover to my cost, the area west of Huelva was particularly popular with the Spanish and less so with the expatriate community, who either preferred the solitary wilds of Andalucia's interior or the more populated areas of the coastline between Malaga and Marbella where immigrant residents could gravitate to the appropriate enclave and talk about the weather, the appalling conditions back in their native country, their prowess on the golf course and the likely rise or fall of the euro. Their contact with the local community was relived in anecdotes about their tame electrician or gardener, or a timely reminder to José in the local supermarket that he was running out of baked beans, sauerkraut or pickled herrings, or some other dietary indispensable.

By the time Rosita and I arrived at the villa in Sanlazer, it was October and the resort seemed virtually deserted. The exodus of the July and August hordes back to their northern homes had long since come to pass. Even the September stragglers had now gone away. The resident population could be no more than a few thousand, made up of local trades people and the elderly long-term boarders who would spend the daylight hours feeling their way slowly along the mosaic pavements, tottering and cursing as they came across patches with missing stones and waving their walking sticks in anger at the odd car which failed to stop at barely discernible pedestrian crossings.

At night, amongst the blocks of deserted apartment buildings shrouded in darkness, there was a profound silence, often interrupted by the bark of a dog or cats screeching as they fought over scraps. It was as if the world had come to an end and we were the only survivors, locked in each other's arms, waiting for fate to decide what would happen to us.

Whilst I had been well and truly shafted financially by Sandra and her lawyers, I still had the Liechtenstein bank account, which had not yet suffered the impact of the monthly maintenance payments, and we were living rent-free with relatively few outgoings. Nevertheless, as I explained to Rosita, I had to look to the future by organising a few domestic clients who needed plumbing work done, learning all the local techniques and, eventually, setting up a company to tackle larger-scale jobs with bigger profit margins. And, to be truthful, with little else to talk about, I was getting bored just hanging around the house.

Most days I had the communal pool to myself, and I would try to swim in the morning and again as the sun was setting. An elderly gardener, Santos, came around once a week to check and clean the pool and fiddle around in the garden. He was sorry, but the owner's committee, who ran the condominium, had instructed him to cover the pool at the end of October and turn off the pumps. Through Rosita, I implored him to leave things as they were, at least for another month. Neither of them could understand why I still wanted to swim in such cold conditions, but when I explained to Santos that the current temperature was equivalent to a warm summer's day in Wales, he capitulated and gave me a one-week reprieve. November seventh and that was it!

With some tools and equipment I had salvaged from the firm, and a few new acquisitions, I placed an advertisement in the English-speaking newspaper covering the area from Malaga along the Costa del Sol, through to our coastline and as far as the eastern Algarve. I had never given much thought to the distances involved and was happily accepting enquiries from locations hundreds of kilometres apart, even though I had not studied a map or tried to structure the visits. I was just relieved to get the enquiries, all from expats who had contacted the mobile number under the business title I had styled: Pipe Dreams.

For fear of offending, I didn't talk about better or worse, but I had to admit that Spanish plumbing was quite a challenge when compared to what I was used to. I expected the pipework to be metric, but when it came to the glaring lack of compression fittings and the obsession with burying traps and plastic pipework unprotected in cement walls, where they would eventually rot, I began to realise the scale of the difficulties I faced.

As business did little more than hiccup along, my temper shortened, and insomnia became a problem as desperate feelings of anger and jealousy filled my head and refused to abandon me into sleep.

It all started with the website. With little else to do, I would spend hours combing the internet, finding sites of local interest where I could pretend to be Bob or Charlie and report on forums as to the wonderful plumbing service I had received from Gilbert Hart. Eventually, bored and disheartened, I would give up and find myself scrolling back to the Chepstow golf club site to read about the world I had left behind.

The festive mixed Stableford pairs competition was played by couples all wearing Father Christmas gear. The pictures were of happy couples waving golf clubs at the camera. I flicked down the cursor. A ton weight landed in my stomach. The competition had been won by the embracing couple of Sandra Hart and Roger Davenport, who held out their trophy as they stared into each other's eyes, their red and white hats askew on their heads. There were more photos, many more. The couple kissing; the couple amongst fellow competitors; the couple toasting each other; the couple … I threw the mouse across the table. The only thing the fucking couple weren't pictured doing was fucking! But that would come later. I banged my fist on the glass surface. The prize was a weekend in the Presidential Suite at the Celtic Manor Hotel, all expenses paid.

How could she? What had possessed her? We had always laughed together about Roger – what a buffoon he was, a flirt with no style, a harmless charmer. Now this. Perhaps my critique of the man had always been a little sterner than hers, more acerbic and less forgiving; but even so, how could she?

I lay awake at night, imagining them on a king-sized bed, her naked, the beads of sweat on her ebony skin, his hands probing around her body. Was he a good lover? Did he satisfy her more than I had? Did she crave the sex? The pillow was damp under my head. It's nothing, I told Rosita, just worried about the business.

And how would the boys handle Roger's involvement in their life? Albert would take it in his stride, no doubt. Buddhism was a shield for Albert, protecting him from having to deal with issues confronting him in the real world. His approach would be to chant an incoherent dirge and regurgitate some incomprehensible teaching on the subject of human relationships from a learned monk who had died five hundred years ago and had been reincarnated various times, most recently into the body of a portly Asian lad with a double chin who sat cross-legged on a mat, or so the photograph above Albert's shrine suggested.

Vernon's reaction would be far more complex. If he saw Roger as simply satisfying Sandra's social and physical needs, Vernon would probably stomach the man's presence around the house, probably treating him as Sandra's male concubine and offering him little respect. But Roger had better beware if he tried to act the father figure or exert his moral compass over Sandra. A father figure implied an adult relationship and, as far as Vernon was concerned, Sandra's only meaningful bond was with the son who looked after her. Roger was no weakling but Vernon's temper when tested produced the most violent physical response. I had seen his temper flare up from nothing over something quite trivial to a point where two people were necessary to restrain him.

I turned over my pillow and felt the damp chill against my cheek. Go on, Roger! Chance your luck and stand up to him.

In those early days in November, any profit I made was easily consumed in vehicle hire and diesel costs, travelling a hundred kilometres to fix a leaking tap or days spent chiselling and replastering brickwork once a problem had been identified and resolved. Most of the customers were Brits of pension age, few of whom seemed overenthusiastic about my work, especially when I presented the bill. My efforts produced none of the recommendations I had expected.

It was the retired bookmaker in the villa on the golf course in Estepona who really let go, no holds barred. I had spent the best part of a week working on a new installation he had asked for, in a refurbished annex for his newly divorced daughter who was coming to live with her parents after a messy break-up. I knew the old guy and his wife were cut up about the daughter's state of mind, but I didn't expect to be the brunt of his frustration.

'You know, Mr Hart,' he said, his glasses perched on the tip of his nose as he studied the bill, which I had costed at something marginally less than I would have charged in the UK. 'I'm not saying that you are a bad person or even an opportunist, but I'll lay you even money you are out of the plumbing game in six months. This isn't paradise or Pimlico where you can charge fancy prices and take twice as long to do a job as the average local wallah.'

'You think I'm overcharging you?' I was genuinely offended.

'I don't think, I know. Your idea of reasonable is my idea of extortion. You have to relate your prices to the local market and not imagine somehow that your work is worth more than the others because, plainly, it is not. The job looks, and is, second-rate, and you need a reality check.'

'You don't propose to pay?' I asked.

'No, I'll pay. I've never taken a bet – mind you, it was a bet contracting you – that I've ever refused to pay out on. I'm simply saying this: the expat community is large but small-minded and bad news travels like wildfire. You are bad news, and few will come looking for Pipe Dreams when they know they will end up instead with Expensive Nightmares. The Spanish will never hire you. They stick to their own. Besides, you don't even have a tax number and can't issue an invoice. Carry on as you are, and you are doomed.'

I left with a cheque, grave doubts, and nearly crashed the van.

As December came around, I could tell that Rosita was becoming more on edge. Sanlazer was beginning to wake up from its temporary hibernation, more people were about, and the prices had gone up on most things in the local supermarket. The council had adorned the major roads with sprays of festive symbols amongst strings of coloured lights, and nativity scenes had started to appear in garden displays and shop windows.

The entire Rodriguez family, minus Rosita's father, the grandly named Thiago Maximiliano, was due to arrive the day before Christmas Eve. The head of the family would remain at his premises with the staff and travel down the following day. I had never seen Rosita so active, cleaning, changing bed linen, harassing me not to make a mess and relocating all our belongings to the fourth bedroom with just a single bed and a plywood wardrobe. The mood of casual living was about to change.

There was a tension as the minivan drew up outside and the passengers disembarked.

Romina hugged her daughter passionately, clasping Rosita to her ample frame, holding her out at arm's length to study her face and then pulling her once more into an embrace. To me, it seemed excessive, like the parent who had just recovered the kidnap victim. Her glance in my direction suggested I was the misguided perpetrator.

Greetings with the other female family members were less intense, with brief hugs and summary kisses, hurried questions and replies as they stood awkwardly with embarrassed smiles, waiting to be introduced to the stranger in their midst.

The driver, a tall, good-looking man in his early thirties, ignored Rosita and walked over towards me, stone-faced, his hand extended. 'I'm Salvador, Rosita's brother.' His accent was heavy, mildly aggressive. 'You are Gilbert.'

I shook his hand, which he quickly withdrew.

'Help me with the luggage, please,' he said, turning to the rear of the vehicle. I followed him, smiling an acknowledgement as I did so at the people I was forced to shimmy past.

Once everybody was inside, Rosita introduced me in Spanish to her family. Her voice had a false confidence with an edge of apprehension, as if she expected disapproval but hoped otherwise. There was none. Everybody reacted well to my *'Encantado'* and faltering Spanish greeting. Naturally enough, Romina's reaction bordered on the inquisitive going on suspicious, but this rotund, homely woman with traces of a moustache of dark hairs along her top lip was friendly enough. Someone had once told me if you wanted to see what your wife would look like in old age, take a few hints from the mother. They both had jet black hair, but I couldn't see Rosita with a double chin and a tube of Veet in her handbag as we slipped into our dotage.

Salvador was going back and forth with suitcases and baby supplies. He dismissed my offer of further help with a curt shake of the head.

Grandmother Aurora was perched on the edge of the sofa, a small suitcase wedged between her legs. She looked anxious to be somewhere else. This small, frail woman seemed to burst into life like a flower in bloom as soon as there was a ring at the door. Rosita explained. Grandmother Aurora would not be staying in the villa this time as we were occupying her room. Her bosom friend had come to collect her. She would be celebrating Christmas with us, but staying in a nearby block of apartments. Bosom friend was right. The woman who came to collect her was of a similar age, with a chest built like a Sherman tank.

The little boy stepped forward and, obviously primed to do so by his mother, formally shook my hand before turning to rush back and stand between her legs.

'That was Miguel,' the mother said in perfect English. 'And I am Eliana.' She indicated Salvador as if to say 'I am with him', but the gesture was offhand and suggested that there had been some family discord on the six-hour drive from Madrid. She was tall and gangly with untidy auburn hair, her height accentuated by the severely cut trouser suit she wore.

Eliana was not conventionally beautiful, but her sharply defined features that appeared to stand out as if trying to flee her face gave an impression of both intrigue and disappointment. Her smile, however, was disarming. 'You are not what I had imagined,' she said.

'What did you imagine?' I asked, immediately regretting the rejoinder as a hostage to fortune.

'I expected you to look younger,' she said, and there was a sarcastic laugh from the teenage girl astride the arm of the couch that Rosita and I had made love on two nights earlier.

'Pity your English is too good to be misunderstood.'

'Sorry, but you did ask. My husband, the policeman, has taught me, you know, the truth, the whole truth and nothing but …'

The younger girl laughed again as if she knew a secret, and I turned towards her. She was the last family member present.

Rosita relaxed the challenging look she had fixed on her sister-in-law and turned towards the girl. 'This is my sister, Isabel. She is still at school.' She emphasised the last sentence, elongating the middle word.

'Good to know you,' I said.

I recognised the implied warning in Rosita's introduction. Years later, when I ran the bar, I'd seen the look Isabel gave me a hundred times; the leap into womanhood with the only weapon yet acquired, holding out sexuality like a badge to see whether it attracted or repelled. Neither response satisfied. A rejection dented that fragile self-confidence; a positive reaction, difficult, maybe dangerous to deal with, unless previous attempts had brought neither love nor satisfaction and the drug was now simply an addiction to increase the victim count.

I'll give Isabel one thing; she had quite a lot in her armoury. The flight from schoolgirl to femme fatale involved a frizzy Afro haircut and a lot of make-up, but, however hard she had tried, she could not disguise a natural, Moorish beauty. The T-shirt flopped over her shoulders and around her waist but stretched tight around her breasts, firm nipples outlined against the material, distorting the print of the face of an ugly, unshaven, staring male with the word 'Zucchero' under it. The material was tied in a knot, leaving a gap of tanned flesh and a pierced belly button implanted with a silver stud above a pair of tight shorts in white denim with a ragged hole cut out suggestively, just to the left of her crotch.

The look said it all. Sexual contempt. Come on, if you think you can, it said, and I'll show the world you are just a dirty old man.

I laughed and she turned away abruptly, saying something hurriedly in Spanish to Rosita, and then casually ambled to the kitchen.

For once, the house was full of noise as people moved about, unpacking, recovering items stored since the last visit and generally settling in. Rosita had prepared a large chicken and seafood paella which was well received and eaten hurriedly from plates on people's laps, rather than on the table she had laid.

By midnight, everybody was in bed and Rosita and I were trying to get comfortable in a single bed with a mattress that seemed to be full of straw. She asked me what I thought of her family, to which I made all the right noises. I posed the same question with the prompt I thought Salvador resented my presence.

'He's concerned, over-protective around his sister and suspicious of your long-term motives. He'll grow to like you.'

'Maybe he wishes his wife had the beauty, charm and personality of his sister.'

She kissed me, a long and lingering kiss. 'What are you after?' she teased.

'Nothing in this bed, believe me. We'd wake the whole house up.'

She turned her back on me and I snuggled into the contours of her body. 'It doesn't feel like nothing,' she said.

'Don't pay any attention, it's only arthritis.'

'Hope not. We don't want to confirm Isabel's parting comment.' There was humour in her voice, but none in my reply.

I straightened up. 'Which was?'

'You laughed at her. Young girls are sensitive.'

'You still haven't told me what she said.'

'It was intended to get at me, not you,' she whispered into my ear. 'She said that at some stage in their lives, every woman goes for the older man. I'll get over it.'

I didn't comment. Between Rosita and I, the age gap issue had only ever been mentioned once, by me, soon after we both realised the relationship was getting serious. Now, in the space of an evening, the topic had been the subject of negative reactions from three members of her family. As far as her brother and his wife were concerned, I could understand their reservations, but as for that little slut, I promised myself, one day I'd teach her a lesson.

I had trouble sleeping and was up early to find Salvador playing with Miguel in the garden. I had agreed to go over to Ayamonte and help out an Irish guy who had opened up his bar for the Christmas period, only to find that he had a problem with blocked drains. He was a regular who didn't pay much but plied me with drinks during and after whatever job he'd called me for. It was a lively bar and a good craic, as they say.

There was no point in setting off for another hour so I decided to make some toast and coffee, extending the offer to Salvador, who, to my surprise, accepted. We sat in the kitchen as Miguel careered across the tiled floor with a plastic dumper truck, transporting alphabet blocks from one side to another and pressing his father to assist whenever he felt his attention was waning.

Rosita's big brother was square-chinned with dark features and deep-set brown eyes, the atypical idea of a Spanish male had it not been for his height and stature, which were imposing and not the squat, ample-bellied figure so prevalent in the older generation who patrolled the streets of Sanlazer.

He obviously saw it as his role as protector of the family honour to appraise and vet me as suitable or otherwise, except his technique was crude, and his none too subtle warnings he didn't want to see his sister get hurt, given in the manner of a caution for excessive speeding to an errant motorist. In spite of all the hacking away at my past and adulterous behaviour, I began to feel a certain empathy for him. I could sense Eliana would have been much more direct and efficient at extracting the information than this fish out of water.

He was mildly less aggressive than on the previous evening, but even so, I recognised the abrupt attitude as nothing more than the professional stance he adopted on a working day. Underneath it all, he didn't really want to be talking about me; he wanted to talk about himself, to impress his personality upon me, to identify to another mature adult male that he was his own man. It made me curious to know the character I would meet later that day, the patriarch who had raised this man, not as Salvador but with the faceless identity as the son of Thiago Maximiliano.

I began to shift the conversation away from me. 'Do you speak English much on a day-to-day basis? Spotting the Brits driving on the wrong side of the road?'

'In the summer months, yes. In the other times, not so much. Each car, two men, has a monthly target. Fines we must collect. Every time we succeed, a star on our assessment. Every month we fail, a mark against.'

'A black mark.'

'Yes, a black mark. People say your work must be beautiful, but it is not. I have only stars, but my pay and conditions are no better than the man who empties the trash. We are fortunate my wife is still able to work.'

It had never occurred to me the traffic police might be enthusiastic about people breaking the law. Apparently, they all had stretches on the major roads where speed limits or overtaking restrictions demanded more patience than could be shown by the average Spanish driver – that, I could believe – and they would lay in wait, picking up maybe nine or ten transgressors in an hour.

'What if they don't have the cash to pay?' I asked.

He smiled at my naivety. 'Some of the vans have credit card machines. In other cases, we escort the driver to the nearest cash machine. Most people have cards.'

'And if they still don't have enough to pay?'

He shrugged and bent to propel the dumper truck across the kitchen floor. 'We are supposed to confiscate the vehicle, but that is much paperwork and takes a long time. Mostly, we take as much as he can give and tell him to send the rest. Sometimes they do; sometimes, no.'

Eliana had appeared at the kitchen door, a matronly looking dressing gown pulled tight around her waist. The blouse had covered the bump last night, but now I could see she was pregnant, probably four or five months gone. Her eyes followed mine down.

'A girl,' she said. 'Due the end of April.'

'Congratulations.'

'Is that right?' she said, smiling briefly at Salvador before turning her attention to the coffee percolator and the demands of her son. If anybody knew the definition of 'offhand', it was her.

CHAPTER TWELVE
Sanlazer – 1992

I would like to blame 'Mad Max' Madden for the state in which I arrived back at the villa eight hours later, but the truth is I hadn't wanted to return to deal with inquisitive faces and invasive questions, so accepting yet one last round before I left was a no-brainer.

It had taken less than thirty minutes to clear the blockage – a rat had been trapped in the pipework – and another twenty to clean up the mess and clear away the kit. By eleven, I was on my second pint, propped on a stool with the rolled-up sleeves of my shirt smelling mildly of raw sewage where I had not been quite quick enough to retreat from a backflow discharge as the blockage cleared.

By the time the three Belfast girls arrived, the bar was filling up and I was on my fourth pint, with the world looking a lot better than it had been a couple of hours earlier. Once they had traded some inoffensive sectarian banter with Max, the girls got talking to the guys on a couple of the tables who were happy to ply them with drinks. As far as I could see, all three of them were still under the influence from the night before. To be honest, I didn't really pay much attention. It was all smutty, sexual innuendo and false laughter at exaggerated shaggy dog stories about yesterday's exploits and what the girls would do if they got their hands on Father Christmas.

The quieter one of the three – and, to use racing parlance, that was only by a short head – was a redhead with excessively long false eyelashes and heavy make-up. She had a passable figure and must have been in her early thirties. She was explaining to the old guy with the sad-looking dog how she just could not stand one more Christmas at home with all the boring old relatives, roast turkey, crackers and those disgusting Brussel sprouts that smelt like old ladies' armpits. Despite the pejoratives, it made me feel a little homesick.

Months after, Mad Max had told me she looked over in my direction on several occasions and had asked the old guy if he knew who I was. He had seen me at work and must have told her I was the plumber who had unblocked the drains.

I looked up from my beer to see Mad Max trying to attract my attention.

There was somebody in the ladies' calling out that the toilet wouldn't flush. 'Go over and sort it out, would you?' he asked. 'I'm busy serving.'

Suffering from beer fatigue, I ambled over to tell whoever it was to use the other cubicle. Nobody reacted to my warning knock on the outer door and the hesitant 'excuse me, is somebody in there?'

There was no sign of anybody inside. As I walked towards the first cubicle, a hand reached out and grabbed at my arm, pulling me in and turning me around, forcing me to sit down on the toilet. The alcohol had slowed my reflexes and I found myself looking up at the woman, standing there barely clothed in a half bra and a pair of flimsy panties. She locked the door. Before I could react, she had leaned unsteadily over me, her hand scooping a handful of bleached white breast coursed with blue veins from within the bra and holding it up under her chin, the chestnut nipple hovering in front of my mouth. Beneath the make-up and painted lips, the muscles in her face were sagging through drink and I had this momentary vision of a Saint Bernard offering the brandy flask around its neck as succour to the needy.

'Do something then, you fucker!' she hissed at me. So, I did. I bit the nipple.

The effect was electric. She shivered and began to run her mouth down my shirt front, pinching at the skin beneath with her teeth as her hand felt feverishly inside my trousers, ripping at the belt and exposing my penis above the elastic of my pants. In one movement, she had kicked off her panties and had her legs astride my waist, easing me into her as she began to move up and down at a frantic pace to which I began to react with an involuntary desire to flay out at her. I could feel my hands tighten around her arms and a fierce contradiction inside me that knew I should push her away from me, yet wanted to yield to the naked animal desire her actions demanded I fulfil.

I could not recall an experience so sobering as the sudden realisation I was about to climax at entirely the wrong time and in the most inappropriate of circumstances. As I started to spasm, she was strong at first, resisting my attempts to force her away, but I had enough purchase on her arms to withdraw from her.

'Fuck me properly!' she whispered furiously between gritted teeth.

But I was already out, my penis pressed against her, ejaculating into the dark matt of pubic hair around her vulva.

The outer door had opened. 'Are you in there, Siobhan?' a drunken woman's voice called out.

She had sunk to the floor, her legs spread open around the base of the toilet, head down on her chest. 'Just a minute. Had to puke,' she stammered.

'Hurry up, will you? There's a couple of horny young ones out here desperate to buy us drinks.'

'Won't be long.' The door slammed.

I had pulled on my pants and trousers. Down the front of my shirt, there was lipstick, foundation smudges and a thin trail of blood where she must have snagged her lip on a button. I could not go home like that.

I helped her to her feet. 'You stink,' she said. I was unsure whether she meant my performance or my shirt.

'Comes with the job,' I said.

'You won't say anything about this to anyone, will yer? My mates are a gabby pair. It'd be all around Woodvale. You can't trust Angela. She'd be desperate to tell my old man. Can't wait to fuck him, can she?' She snorted. 'She'd have to join the fucking queue he's working his way through. Bastard!'

'My lips are sealed.' There was total conviction in my voice.

'I made up my mind. One way or another, I was going to have it away with a Spaniard before I got back onto that sodding plane.'

I didn't want to disillusion her about her trophy catch. I told her to wait two minutes until I had made it to the gents' toilet, and then go back to her friends. She nodded, pulling on her panties over the semen-sodden pubic hair and slipping the dress back over her head.

Fortunately, a small corridor separated the bar from the toilets and I was able to slip into the gents without anyone seeing me. I heard her leave and loud voices cheer as she returned to the bar.

I removed the plastic cover from one of the cisterns, wrapped my shirt into a ball and waited until two guys had come in to use the urinals. They looked around at the source of the noise as I pretended to mess with the cistern.

'Do me a favour,' I said. 'Can you ask the guvnor to pop in, please? There's been a small leak and my shirt has got soaked.'

Mad Max appeared, a confused look on his face. 'I thought that the problem was in the ladies,' he queried.

'She's pissed,' I said. 'Got confused with the doors. I put her right.

Anyway, I've fixed it as best I can. The problem is calcification. Next time around, I'll change the cistern and clean the joints.'

He nodded, seemingly satisfied with the explanation.

'Help me out, will you?'

Ten minutes later, I was walking out through the bar dressed in a Real Madrid football shirt that I had convinced Mad Max to take down from the large collection of football memorabilia he had pinned up on the walls around the bar. It was one size too small for me and smelt of a season's accumulated beer and fags, but it was a life saver. He had another one at home, he told me, so don't bother about bringing it back or charging him for the work I'd done there today. Call it quits.

I glanced across to see Siobhan and her friends in animated conversation with two bearded guys of North African origin. A hand was resting casually on her knee. She hadn't even noticed my leaving and I was both relieved and annoyed at myself for having been a willing participant in her aberration.

Tossing my compromised shirt into a waste bin, I headed back to Sanlazer. The idea for the replacement had been a touch of genius. Rosita had told me on numerous occasions how passionate her father was about football, and Real Madrid in particular. How he had a season ticket at the Santiago Bernabéu for every home match and, whenever he could, would travel with his drinking friends to the away games. With work always foremost in my mind, football had never stimulated me beyond watching some particularly important game on the television, but I had taken the trouble to swat up on a few facts, if only to establish my credentials with him.

The entire family was assembled in the lounge when I arrived. It was late afternoon and both Rosita and her mother sympathised with the ill fortune that had kept me at work for so many hours of the Nochebuena, the day before Christmas. Eliana was amusing her son whilst Isabel had a bare foot perched on the dining table as she varnished her toenails and studiously ignored me.

Salvador sat on the arm of the chair, bending to talk to his father. They both looked up as Rosita hustled me over. I don't know exactly what I had expected; I suppose Thiago Maximiliano sounded like a Roman general, but in stature and attitude, this man was far from imposing or overbearing. He was in his late fifties and looked ten years older, with veined red cheeks and a walrus moustache he constantly pressed with his thumb and index finger, following the growth from the centre of his top lip down to the edge of his chin. Small in stature, but with broad shoulders and muscular arms, he reminded me of a retired wrestler who, by the girth of his stomach, liked his glass of beer. The most striking features were his large, penetrating eyes, recessed behind a prominent forehead. The expression was not hostile, more the studied look of a man who did not rush to conclusions or take decisions lightly. He greeted me in Spanish whilst maintaining eye contact, as if assessing a customer to see whether he was worthy of credit for a side of pork.

His interest in the shirt was far more proactive. He said something to Salvador and beckoned with his hand for me to turn around.

'My father says the shirt is from two seasons ago.' The old man spoke again for his son to translate. 'Hagi left to join Brescia at the start of this season. It was a bad move. Brescia will be sent down to second level.'

'Who?' I had no idea what he was talking about.

'The player's name printed on the back of your shirt. Don't you know who it is?' He laughed, as did his father, at my ignorance. 'Where did you get it?' he asked.

I tried to steer as near to the truth as possible, telling him that my shirt had been soiled whilst at work and a friend had lent me this one.

'It is a good shirt,' the father said in faltering English. 'He is a good player. From Romania. Bad to sell him.'

'Is he on a par with Butragueño or Luis Enrique?' Time to impress, I felt.

The old man puckered his lips and nodded in admiration at the question, speaking and waiting with a smile as Salvador translated.

'He said these are good men. When you find a good man, you should keep him. No place in my father's team for bad players. When you cannot keep up, it is time to go.'

A celebration of Christmas on Christmas Eve was a novelty for me. The women decamped as one to the kitchen, where hectic chatter and laughter preceded a wonderful meal of fresh grilled prawns, large bream, oven-baked, expertly filleted by Rosita's father – or TM, as I began to call him – followed by leg of lamb served with small roast potatoes in their skins. Dessert was a selection of small cakes and *turrón*, a wonderful nougat made of sweet, roasted almonds. A chilled red wine followed by cava accompanied the feast, and although I drank sparingly, conscious that my system had already taken a beating through alcohol, it was great to see the relaxing effect it had on the adults, especially in relation to my presence amongst them.

Only Isabel remained distant and aloof, ignoring me whenever possible and passing dishes to me without looking round. Her ridiculous attitude began to amuse me. Apart from anything else, I was staggered that her parents – a patriarch like TM, and Romina, who came over as quite straight-laced – would allow their daughter to appear in public in the way she did. They seemed totally relaxed about her dress sense. Her outfit, or what there was of it, was so provocative that, with a paper hat on, she looked like the participant in a seasonal porn film. When Rosita told me later we were all going to midnight mass, I nearly choked on my nougat.

The one thing I didn't think stacked up about the Spanish Christmas was the present arrangements. All the adults exchanged gifts, amassing their spoils around them, packed in the gift wrapping arranged by the retailer. Even I ended up with a leather waistcoat, which I intended to donate to refugee relief as soon as circumstances allowed, and a bottle of aftershave, aptly named 'Diesel'. For Miguel, however, there was only a single present, a soft toy of a Sesame Street character.

Noticing my discomfort, Rosita laughed. 'My family are traditionalists. In Spain, it is the custom to give the children gifts on the day of The Three Kings. Instead of Santa, the children write to the Kings who visited baby Jesus, and they are supposed to arrive on their horses and leave the presents.'

'When's that?'

'January the sixth.'

'Unfair on the kids, making them wait that long.'

'It's what we grow up with.'

By the time the midnight mass was over, I was more than ready and expecting to go to bed, but the taxis lined up outside the church told me otherwise. Romina would take Miguel, who was already fast asleep, back to the villa. For everybody else, we were off to Lepe and a disco bar. I groaned inwardly, but Rosita was so excited I managed to feign mild enthusiasm.

We were in a side street, the flashing neon lights illuminating the pitch blackness. Throngs of people milled around the entrance which was patrolled by two impressive-looking bouncers. Relieved to think we would be summarily refused admittance and be obliged to return to the villa, I had not counted on TM's persuasive powers. Dressed in a lightweight bomber jacket over a black silk shirt, he had sidled up to the front of the queue, his arm draped around Isabel's shoulder. Somewhere en route she had discarded the black scarf and shawl that she had used to hide her modesty in the church and was back in full slapper gear. To be fair, in this environment, amongst the girls and boys around her own age, many of whom she appeared to know, she did not look at all out of place.

One of the bouncers smiled at something TM said and we were waved inside, Rosita tugging at me to keep up with our little group.

Inside was a raging inferno, a sea of people milling around, dancing anywhere there was a space, standing, trying to talk, or pushing and weaving to get to the bar. Salvador spoke to two lads in the corner who relinquished their table like greyhounds out of the trap. I asked him afterwards what he had said to encourage them. His tactic was the flash of a warrant card and the proposition they might not be of an age to be legally consuming alcohol. It always worked like a charm, he said.

Rosita prompted me to take the initiative and order a round of drinks before anybody else, with Eliana seconded to help me do the ordering and carry back the trays. With the noise level at deafening and the repetitive heavy bass accompaniment to the house music, any attempt at conversation would have been pointless, so I fished in my pocket for a fifty euro note whilst Eliana lent over the counter to shout in the barman's ear. It was a pretty straightforward order, two bottles of cava and six glasses in exchange for my note and no change. The barman winked at Eliana and mouthed '*Gracias*'. 'I told him to keep the change,' she shouted in my direction.

'That was big of you,' I replied.

A glass of chilled bubbly, a change of mood and I had shaken off the effects of a day of crazy, irresponsible behaviour and the hangover that had succeeded it. The music in the bar changed to retro with a disco beat. Alison Moyet began to sing 'All Cried Out' with a pulsating upbeat backing track and I was leading Rosita onto what passed for a dance floor.

Okay, I'll admit that my dancing style was a little overenthusiastic, born out of the era of John Travolta and Saturday Night Fever, exaggerated limb movements, stomach and bum thrusting, but, lost in the moment, I felt up there with the stars, Olivia Newton John's next leading man.

Not even Isabel, standing between two friends and obviously finding my antics worthy of her vitriolic tongue, could dissuade me. As far as I could see, the friends were far more interested in eyeing up the boys of their own age than passing judgement on any of the number of old men who were prancing around, reliving their youth. One of the girls said something in Isabel's ear which must have infuriated her. She glanced back briefly at me, turned and hurried back to sit next to her father.

'What's wrong with her?' I shouted into Rosita's ear.

Rosita made a disparaging gesture. 'Highly strung,' she replied.

I made it through Michael Jackson's 'Billie Jean' and 'Don't You Want Me' from The Human League before Salvador tapped me on the shoulder to say that we were leaving. Isabel and TM were already halfway towards the exit with Rosita chasing after them. Eliana came up next to me, hooking her arm through mine as we made our way to the door.

There was still a throng of people outside the entrance, milling around. It was 2 a.m. and it seemed that for many, the night was still young.

'You know how to enjoy yourself, don't you?' Eliana commented.

'That's what life's for, isn't it?' I looked over at her as she gave the slightest shake of the head and that shrug of the shoulders I had previously interpreted as disinterest in the answer. I didn't see that now. I had got it wrong. It was the attitude of somebody saying 'Why don't I feel like that? What am I missing?' I felt sorry for her.

I was about to say something else when I came face-to-face with one of the two friends who had been with Siobhan in Mad Max's that morning. I went to turn my head, but she had not recognised me. Her stare, empty of any emotion, looked straight through me. The other friend walked alongside her and they were sandwiched between two men in identical blue jackets with white open-necked shirts. I looked around as one of the men spoke briefly with the bouncer, who stood aside to let them enter the bar.

'A friend of yours?' Eliana asked.

I shook my head. 'No. Reminded me of somebody I knew at college.'

It wasn't until I opened the English language newspaper two days later that I saw the face of Siobhan staring back at me. The plain clothes division of the Guardia Civil were investigating the death of a tourist from Belfast who had fallen to her death on Christmas Eve from the fourth floor of an apartment complex in Isla Canela in Ayamonte. There was a picture of the building and another of the two friends accompanied by police officers, the men who had escorted them into the disco bar.

My hands were shaking as I came to the closing paragraphs. The police were holding a man in custody, a local vagrant and addict who was wearing a shirt with traces of the deceased's blood and who claimed to have recovered it from a trash can near the marina. Police were appealing for anybody who had met or knew the dead woman to contact them.

TM had planned for the family to lunch in a local beach restaurant. I told Rosita that I would join them as soon as I had quoted for a job in Huelva. Most of the shops were closed, but I remembered the gypsy market close to the beach car park. I found a shirt vaguely resembling the one I had ditched and paid cash. Back in Sanlazer, I took the shirt from its packaging, crushing it to give a worn look and passing my dirty hands across the front. To complete the task, I rubbed the sleeves in my urine and rolled them up. Satisfied with the result, I held it up as I walked to the toilet door, only to bump into Eliana who was standing outside with Miguel in her arms.

'You definitely can't wear that,' she said, letting Miguel to the floor and ushering him into the toilet.

'I was checking to see if it had been washed or not.'

'Missing your English maid, are you?' I wasn't sure whether it was a sarcastic remark or a reference to my relationship with Rosita.

I smiled. 'I'll just get another shirt,' I said.

'If you give me five minutes, we can go to the restaurant together. Junior has only just woken up.' She took it as read and disappeared into the toilet.

For the next few days, I tried to hide my edginess, but Rosita, always sensitive to me when around her family, finally quizzed me on my attitude. The first thing that came into my head was a lecture from Salvador on my business potential in Spain. He had told me to forget the plumbing and concentrate on the opportunities in home heating. Solar panels were all the rage, not price sensitive and financially attractive to the consumer. A friend of his was making a fortune in Madrid, mainly installations in new developments. As always, he finished off any conversation that revolved around money or career with his stock comment.

'But what do I know?' he would say, 'I'm just a policeman living on a shit salary and with no prospects. If only I could go back, I'd do things differently.'

'Why don't you?' I argued. 'You're only thirty. Hardly old, is it?'

'Ah! It's too late now,' he would say. 'I'm in now until I retire.'

'So?' Rosita asked me. 'What is troubling you?'

'Salvador is trying to convince me I should go into the solar panel business. It's preying on my mind,' I lied.

'Something to think about next week, not today. Aren't you going to say goodbye to them?'

I had forgotten. It was the thirtieth of December and Salvador and family had to be back in Madrid. He was on duty over the New Year. 'Big night for fines,' he had said. 'Excess of alcohol and it's between two and six hundred euros. All the force will be on duty tomorrow night.'

Eliana had just settled Miguel in the child's seat in the car. I went to give her the customary air kisses on the cheeks, but she turned her lips briefly into mine and they met. We both pulled away from each other.

I don't know what on earth possessed me to say it. Was I somehow tempting fate or seeing if she suspected something? A photograph of the shirt had been in the national papers and on the local television news service. 'By the way,' I said. 'Thanks for ironing my clothes. It wasn't necessary, but much appreciated.'

She was looking away, fiddling with the holdall of babies' necessities. 'I don't know how you can wear a shirt with the price tag still attached to it. Maybe it is a case of no sense, no feeling. Anyway, your secret is safe with me. I took the tag off and threw it away.'

CHAPTER THIRTEEN
Chepstow – 2008

As time passes, so my hearing continues to improve. Although a long way from where it was prior to the accident, I can now make out higher-pitched sounds distinctly and an unusual resonance when trying to read speech, almost like a hollow echo of the words in my brain as my lips move.

There was no epiphanic moment that made me decide to hide my improving hearing from the rest of the world; it was more an evolution, a gradual realisation people reacted better to me if they went on believing I was stone deaf. I have to admit the sample on which I based this conclusion was limited to the postman, the girls at the supermarket checkout and the frigid old cow who runs the post office and hands out my pension. Hardly representative, I would agree, but conclusive, if you accept it was the only time since arriving in Chepstow I have seen the old bag offer a sympathetic smile to anybody in the queue.

The other advantage of playing the deaf card is the thinking time it allows; if necessary, asking people to repeat slowly what they have said so I have the opportunity to work out a suitable answer. Of course, it demands I remain conscious of my supposed condition, not rushing to reply based on what I hear or failing to look at the person's lips as they are talking. There are pitfalls but I have both persisted with the self-help book and become proficient in my newly acquired art of deception. The last factor I cannot discount is the small increment the benefit office has given me as an award for my disability. It isn't much, but why give it up? It isn't hurting anybody. A carer has also been arranged to come in twice a week, wash and clean and make me a meal. All in all, being deaf has its compensations.

On the memory front, I am resigned to report no development, not a glimmer of any recollection of the period since breakfast on that fatal day until my awakening in hospital. It doesn't overly concern me, even when listening to my local doctor tell me I should come to terms with the real likelihood that neither my hearing nor memory will ever return, given my age and the deteriorating state of my faculties. He even compliments me on my prowess at learning lip-reading so rapidly.

This game I am playing takes my mind off of a lot of things, but from time to time I find myself slipping back into a mood of anger and self-pity, maudlin with bitter regrets at the tragic passing out of my life of Albert and Rosita and the child that was never born. It is on one of these mornings as I am moping around the apartment that the letter arrives.

Written with a fountain pen, I recall Jasmin's neat hand from the wedding invitation. The recollection does nothing to improve my mood, until I read the contents.

She opens by expressing her and her family's hopes that my physical recovery is complete and, although she understands my hearing and memory have not returned, she trusts I am able to cope.

I have almost forgotten the injury to my leg which is now in an elastic sock and gives me no problem other than a slight limp I am certain will pass with time.

There is a paragraph on the house, which will need to be demolished and is causing Hugo some concern as he cannot complete the insurance claim until the investigating judge has ruled on the cause of the explosion. The relevance of this remark is lost on me. I should have realised its significance, but at the time I was anxious to read on.

Until everything is sorted out, Jasmin has rented an old house close to the centre of town and the veterinary practice. She describes the property as big, with four bedrooms and a large garden in which Francisco enjoys playing.

Now, I come to the nub of the letter:

> Gilbert, I need to ask a big favour of you. My professional duties as the person responsible for the veterinary practice are many and leave me with little time to devote to a home life with Francisco. You may think I am not serious when I say that he misses you but it is true, and he needs the influence of a man in his life now that Albert is no longer with us. Francisco attends the crèche in Godim during the weekdays and, when I am too busy to attend, which is often, others must take and bring him home to stay until I return. Of course, my family would like to help, but nobody can guarantee to be available as my circumstances demand. You will ask why my mother, Inés, is not available, as she has

> more flexibility as headmistress of the school, but she is very committed to her community responsibilities and she never has time for Francisco.

I hesitate. Is it simply a case of a poor choice of words in her second language? She makes it sound as though Inés is callously indifferent to her grandson's needs. Maybe I'm just reading too much into a simple sentence.

> I have, naturally, been in contact with the social services to help me, but they must have a set timetable and cannot always send the same person. What I am trying to ask is for you to come to Cavalla for some months to take care of Francisco when I am not able. You are retired, so I guess that free time is not a problem, and as it is only for a few hours most days, you will have plenty of spare moments to rest and do things for yourself. You will have your own bedroom and the house and garden are big enough for us all. How do you feel about it? Please say yes and come as soon as you like. With the rent and everything, I cannot pay so much, but you will have all your food and some – how do you English say? – pocket money for the fine Douro wine and beer. Good, eh?
>
> Both Francisco and I send our love and look forward to seeing you.
>
> Jasmin Hart XX

I like the touch of putting our surname at the end of the letter; the implied family association is not lost on me.

My first reaction is to reply immediately by email. Yes! Yes! Yes! Since Rosita, there has been nobody who has really needed or wanted me. Sure, there have been a few women who claimed a special bond, but they disappeared like prairie grass on an ill wind. The invitation to the wedding had rekindled the faint hope I might not die a solitary old man, then dashed by the death of Albert; now, brought alive again by the prospect of a lasting relationship with my grandson.

After the euphoria come the doubts and fears. Am I really in a physical and mental state to tackle looking after a toddler? I am not able to hear or understand, even if I can make out some of the sounds. The responsibility is enormous. This is a task that should be entrusted to a younger person trained to do the job. Supposing something happened, there was an accident; could I ever forgive myself?

And the money? Jasmin is effectively saying I would be doing it for love. I am retired. Retired people, sensible people, have savings, a proper pension, a house with a bundle of equity in it. Grandparents don't need paying to look after their kith and kin. They can afford to upset the parents by lavishing treats on the grandchildren. Don't spoil them, the sons and daughters say – you're ruining their teeth, their diet, their routine, their psyche – but with a shake of the head, a smile and a 'What are you like, you grandparents?'

How can I be expected to give my grandson treats when I don't even have enough money to live on properly, barely survive? I am feeling extremely sorry for myself; fertile ground for what is to come, as it transpires.

I guess it's easy to follow my thought process. Firstly comes the resentment of having let Sandra and Roger take me to the cleaners over the divorce; then, the self-justification that what I have in mind is not for my sake; it won't hurt anybody and they can easily afford it. A drop in the ocean. Okay, call it despicable, because it is, but that's me. I am despicable. I have been for years. What the hell! There isn't any other option and it will be a small price for Roger to pay to have me out of his hair for good. I can take my pension, settle down in Portugal with a little nest egg, learn the language and watch my grandson grow into a man. It's the perfect fit.

I compose an email in reply to Jasmin's letter. I need a week or two to sort out my affairs, and, if all goes well, I would give her a positive reply within the next few days. I press the send icon. As the Beatles would say, I will definitely need a little help from my friends. Well, maybe 'friends' is stretching it just a little too far.

In all fairness, I did contemplate simply explaining the circumstances and asking Roger for a loan, but I soon discounted the idea, relying on the old maxim that, in financial dealings, it is best not to ask if a refusal might offend. I need an unequivocal 'yes'.

***

Two days after my visit to see Botany at The Golden Swan, she sends me the text I've been waiting for. Mrs Smith has booked a room for the following Friday.

The receptionist gives me a welcoming smile. I leave a message and make my way to the bar. The room is sprinkled with various couples and groups either lunching on bar meals or just drinking. I choose a seat out of earshot in an alcove formed by the bay window. I'm nervous about dealing with Madeleine. She doesn't deserve to become embroiled in my little plot, and the least I can do is offer an explanation and ask her not to judge me too harshly.

Plastic room key fob in hand and a puzzled look on her face, she catches sight of me.

'Good to see you, Madeleine.' I hand her the slate and say that I will try and lip-read as much as possible. In fact, I can hear and piece together about fifty per cent of what she says.

'This is a surprise,' she stammers, taking a deep breath. Her face is glowing.

'I notice you didn't say pleasant surprise,' I acknowledge with a smile. 'I somehow suspect it might not be. How did you know I'd be here, Gil?' I have no wish to get Botany involved. My tame explanation about having followed her never even surfaces before she begins to scribble hurriedly on the slate. 'It was you, was it? Rifling through my car? You found the note!' Another thought. 'You took the spare petrol money as well, from the glove box?'

I am totally flummoxed. 'I don't know what you are talking about, Madeleine. I haven't been anywhere near your car and I don't know anything about any money. I don't think I even know what car you drive.'

She must see the illogicality of her accusation and stills her anger. 'I thought it must have been Vernon from the start,' she says. 'He always seems to be watching me. Sandra can't seem to control him any more. He's into drugs and everything. I keep imagining I see him everywhere I go. There was somebody just here in the car park with a motorcycle and dressed in those black leathers. It looked just like Vernon, but why would he be here? He's become a fixation.' She's clearly agitated but striving to regain her composure.

'I can't stop long, Gil. You'll have to forgive me. I've arranged to meet someone.' She goes to stand up.

'I know exactly why you're here and who you've come to meet.' She slumps back into the chair. 'Whilst I might think you're a bloody fool, your private life is no concern of mine and it's not why I'm here.'

She ignores the comment, just stares into my eyes. When she speaks, it's almost a whisper, as if she's resigned to the consequences. 'So, now you know. Funny. Shit timing. I've been thinking for some time Roger and I needed to call it a day.'

For the sake of appearances, I ask her to repeat a couple of comments, but I've already got the gist.

'I came to see Roger before he joins you. We have a little business to discuss and I knew I'd find him here. I thought I owed you the heads-up before I spoke to him.'

'What business?' Her voiced is strained.

I tell her about my plan.

She breaths deeply, her lips pursed together, appearing to weigh up what I've said. 'Roger won't lend you any money, Gil. He can't stand the sight of you.'

'I'm sure he'll come round to my way of thinking.'

'And if he doesn't?'

'I haven't even considered the alternative.'

She stands up, a pinched smile on her lips. 'It's a low blow. Not much more I can say, is there, Gil? Other than I'm disappointed in you.'

What is an appropriate response? I ask her to repeat the last sentence.

Say what you feel, I tell myself. 'I'd say the same to you, Madeleine – for different reasons.'

She doesn't turn around or react, just straightens her back and walks away.

From the information Botany gave me, I can expect Roger to arrive in about twenty minutes. I don't feel the same trepidation in confronting Roger as I did in speaking to Madeleine. As much as it's of her own making, I know all about sliding into messy relationships, and she had probably succumbed to Roger's advances secure in the belief he ran a greater risk if Sandra ever discovered the truth. He would take steps to keep the affair well hidden from his wife. Loneliness, the need for a soul mate; these things must have played a big part in her decision and, I have to admit it, Roger is an attractive and sensuous man with a romantic appeal.

He shows no surprise at finding me waiting in the lobby. Perhaps she managed to contact him in advance. Nor does he react to the implied threat in my proposal. I pass the slate and give him the lip-reading spiel.

'Don't call it a loan, Gilbert. A loan implies that it's going to be paid back at some point. Hardly the case for somebody who hasn't got a cent to their name and isn't likely to have.' I see the sneer of contempt in his expression. 'Let's call it blackmail or extortion. Which of the two words do you prefer?'

'As the terminology isn't important, let's keep calling it a loan, because that is the way I want to treat it.'

'No due date? No interest?'

'No. A simple gentleman's agreement.'

His mouth forms a forced smile. 'A blackmailer and an adulterer; what a fine pair of gentlemen we make. The only difference is that you are scum, Gilbert, and, whatever my morals, I do have integrity. You make me sick.'

I refuse to be baited. I have one objective and a mounting desire to achieve it. 'Now you have got all that off your chest, what's it to be?'

'Five thousand, you say. By when?'

'The day after tomorrow. In cash. I need to book a flight.'

'That's a tall order.'

'I don't think so. Not for a man of your *integrity* and social status. Look at it this way. The quicker you organise the loan – draw up a document, by the way, I'll sign it – the quicker I am off your radar, possibly forever. Who knows?'

'And what stops you from asking for more when the five grand runs out?'

I smile. 'The answer's easy. I hope Madeleine understands why I'm doing this and will one day have it in her heart to forgive me. I care about what *she* thinks of me. If I came back for more …'

A final agreement is reached. He studiously reminds me Madeleine's Astra is still in Portugal and cautions I must get it back to her as quickly as possible. On second thoughts, he will send somebody to collect it as soon as it's repaired.

'Take my advice, Gil,' he says with that pompous look on his face that makes me want to punch him. 'Find a hole in Portugal, crawl into it and don't come back. There is no one or anything for you any more in Chepstow. Nobody will be interested in having any contact with you, and I'm sure the government will be happy to send the money you sponge off them to a Portuguese bank account.'

I watch as he saunters to the guest lift. I can only imagine the reaction between the couple when he gets to her room.

'I'll give it some serious thought,' I say to myself as the lift doors closes.

CHAPTER FOURTEEN
Cavalla – 2008

Settling down in Cavalla is a lot easier than I imagined. A passport and a smile get me most things around town, even if I do play on the sympathy vote with my hearing deficiency, and my new surrogate parent role when entertaining my grandson in front of the townsfolk. Although suspicious at first, the neighbours have now begun to recognise and accept me, either by waving their hands in greeting or by coming up to make a fuss of Francisco.

With Jasmin's assistance, opening a local bank account proved straightforward, and with my loan from Roger as a deposit, I can now boast a debit card and internet banking, everyday necessities for almost all of the population but a novelty as far as this reincarnation of my life is concerned. My pension and disability allowance have been redirected to my new account and, I have told myself, if everything works out, I will let the housing authorities in Chepstow know of my changed circumstances. For the time being, while they're still paying for my apartment, best not to mess with the status quo.

Before I left the UK, I had no option but to trust nosey neighbour with a door key together with a mobile number in case the place burned to the ground. I left the details of my absence as casual as possible. Nosey neighbour thinks I will be away for around six weeks to take care of my grandson. Although my stay will probably be for a lot longer, I fully intend to return briefly to check out everything and visit the local authority to raise some spurious and trivial enquiry just so they record my presence.

A month or so passes before I ask Jasmin to ring nosey neighbour on my behalf, more as a courtesy than anything else. During a three-minute call, Jasmin's contribution is limited to explaining who she is, the reason for the call plus versions of 'Can you please speak more slowly?' or 'Would you repeat that?' She holds the phone away from her ear and pulls faces at me.

As she says 'Thank you' and switches off the phone, her expression is one of confusion. 'She speaks so quickly with a strange accent and on many subjects. Maybe I understand wrong.' I explain what a gossip is in English. *'Fofoqueira,'* she says. 'We have lots of those in Cavalla.'

It seems nosey neighbour was angry, claiming I had left one of the kitchen windows on the latch. There had been a storm a few days earlier and the window had banged constantly throughout the night, keeping her awake. She had to wait until the next morning to go in and lock it, only to discover the pane of glass was broken. I was certain everything had been checked before I left. Maybe it was just her excuse for a nose around in my flat.

Francisco enjoys watching us communicate, enthralled as Jasmin sits in front of me and carefully mouths the words whilst I pretend I can't hear and mimic her lip movements as if trying to understand. 'The woman said your friend passed your way.' She hesitates. 'That means come to visit you?' she queries.

'You mean passed away?' She nods. 'No. It means someone died.'

She looks alarmed. 'She said the lady who comes to find you at the football match.'

For a moment, it doesn't register. 'Madeleine? She was talking about Madeleine?'

There is a look of horror on her face. Of course, I realise. She knows Madeleine from the wedding and, again, at Albert's funeral.

I can't believe it. There it is in black and white in the online edition of the local Chepstow paper. I scroll through the article. It happened the very day I left. A freak domestic accident, the report says. Her feet appear to have become entangled in the belt of a dressing gown at the top of the stairs and she tumbled down, breaking her neck as she landed. There is a picture, taken at a charity dinner a number of years earlier when her husband was alive. Finally, a comment from a close friend, Sandra Davenport, who explains how she is too devastated to comment on the loss of such a warm and sensitive companion whom she has known for nearly twenty-five years.

The search engine highlights a link to a later edition under the heading 'Gwent Woman's Tragic Death'. The coroner had opened and immediately suspended the inquest pending further reports from the competent authorities. What on earth are the implications of this statement? Is there a suggestion the death was other than accidental?

The blackness descends on me that night. Who am I? A bad omen; a man who bestows the kiss of death on those who have done nothing worse than show him kindness. Both Albert and Madeleine have been cursed by me.

I awake, afraid, the sensation of my body bathed in sweat, yet my skin is ice cold to the touch. In the pitch-black of night, the clustered branches of the holm oak scrape eerily against the windows of my bedroom as the southerly wind causes the branches to groan and strain in constant movement. There are sounds that can drive the breath from your body, and, as I lie there, I can hear them, low and mournful.

During the day, the detached house stands in a half-light, cloaked in the shadows of the trees that surround and enclose it on three sides. Built in the thirties, long before the world had heard of energy conservation or double glazing, the rooms are spacious with high ceilings, large bay windows and heavy, musty-scented curtains running full length to the varnished floorboards. An estate agent would say the house had character – a realtor's euphemism, in this case – to describe the intermittent change from dark to light as daylight penetrates in spikes across the rooms, only to be doused by the shadow of a leafy canopy in constant movement.

At night, there is a sinister, threatening air to the property. There are houses close by of a similar age, but none have the ivy cladding nor the sentinel of tall trees that sets this house apart from the others.

The one outstanding feature is a large garden beyond the trees, set to lawn, where Francisco and I, as non-participants in the working world that exists beyond the stone-clad wall, can laugh and play in our fantasy bubble. He is a delightful child to be around and I like to think that we both experience the very special relationship when grandparent and grandchild have the time for each other without the constraints parents are obliged to impose.

I have to acknowledge the violent mood swings which possessed me in those early weeks back in the Douro. Exhilaration could morph into depression at the drop of a hat; a laughing and committed participant transformed into a lone figure hunched in an armchair, gazing off into space. Yet what I could never fathom was the amazing sensitivity of a mere infant, capable of reacting to my change of mood as if he can read my mind. As keen as he is to play endlessly with me, when my mood darkens Francisco is prepared to sit quietly on my lap or at my feet, waiting for a reaction and demanding nothing. I begin to fear for this sensitive and seemingly unselfish child.

My bouts of depression are finally dispelled one balmy autumn evening when out walking with Francisco in his buggy on our once-a-week routine of meeting up with Adele and Pom-Pom and taking a long stroll together around town.

It's a comfortable arrangement. Francisco adores the dog and I suspect the feeling is mutual. As far as Adele and I are concerned, a third of the way into our prescribed route we regularly sit on a park bench whilst dog and child play, and I will earnestly study Adele's lips as I listen to her recounting the events of the week. From then on, we are content to move on without the need for communication to cement our growing friendship.

Our journey always takes us past the remains of the house in which Albert and Jasmin lived. It's a shrine we feel obliged to visit, somehow frozen in time, cloaked in tarpaulins and fenced with police barriers warning onlookers to keep their distance. We stop briefly, each with our private thoughts, before a nod from one or other breaks the spell.

On this occasion, Pom-Pom interrupts the silence with a warning bark as he lurches forward on the leash. How he manages to see through the fur which covers his eyes defeats me, but, sure enough, the object of his attention has now turned the corner and is straining to reach him. Despite its size, the little dog is sturdy and the old lady struggles to hold it back. She gasps for breath as the two animals begin their frenetic tail-wagging and sniffing appraisal.

Adele's welcoming smile quickly fades as the old woman, with one eye on the dogs, begins an earnest tirade, speaking so rapidly in the guttural local accent that I understand nothing. On occasions, she looks over and points at me as if to emphasise something but she sounds so hostile and accusing, I begin to feel guilty by association for whatever it is Adele is being berated for.

'What was all that about?' I ask as I watch the old lady stride off into the distance, the little dog trying to keep pace. 'She seemed so upset with us.'

Adele looks puzzled. The old lady was indeed distressed, but not with us. Senhora Garcia's problem is one of a public-spirited citizen who has spoken out, only to have her concerns dismissed by the authorities.

Apparently, whatever the weather, the old lady has a set routine. At a veterinary appointment when the pup was just weeks old, Jasmin had told her Boston terriers require lots of exercise; and so, every day at precisely ten in the morning, three in the afternoon and eight at night, she sets out with Massif for a two-point-six-kilometre walk. Massif is a misnomer, as this black and white, short-haired, stocky dog with the turned-down mouth and sad, pathetic eyes could easily fit into a shopping bag.

As they passed the house early on the morning of the explosion, Massif pricked up his ears, a sure sign that somebody else was in the vicinity. Senhora Garcia knew better than to doubt Massif's radar, so she stood still and waited.

Somewhere at the back of the house there were raised voices, men, angry with each other, but that was not what had attracted Massif's attention. The dog pulled her forward until she was to one side of the bushes that separated the road from the house. Waiting by the front gate were two men.

'Let's wait until he's alone,' said the slimmer of the two men as he made to move away.

'Hang on, Walid. Let's check with Yannik.' The other man cursed in some strange tongue that was not Portuguese as his phone slipped from his hand to fall onto the driveway. He retrieved it and made the call. He spoke briefly and listened to the reply.

'What did he say?' Walid prompted.

'Under no circumstances do we go back without what we came for. We must wait. It takes as long as it takes. Hugo and his English friend need to know they are in big trouble if—'

At that moment, Senhora Garcia tugged at the dog's lead, anxious to pull the animal back around the corner and out of sight of the men. But the dog resisted. Massif was crouched, back legs apart, defecating into his chosen spot and using his muscular body to avoid being interrupted part way through. In a gesture of defiance, he finished, looked up at the two men as they looked over, and clawed frantically at the grass and leaves with paddling back legs to try and cover his contribution to the hedgerow.

Before the two men had time to react, Senhora Garcia turned about and was urging the dog to retrace its steps. She was scared by the look on the men's faces but felt it was her civic duty to report the incident to the police as soon as news of the explosion became public knowledge.

'What did the police do?' I ask.

As far as Senhora Garcia was concerned, the answer was nothing. Sargento Lannier had politely thanked her, promising to make contact when a formal statement was required, but did not do so.

My first reaction is to fathom why Lannier dismissed the old lady's report. Adele is reticent to approach him on my behalf. Their paths have crossed before, she tells me, but is unwilling to explain further. A private matter, she insists, in no way connected with the accident. I take it at face value; my concern is trying to find something in Senhora Garcia's story that would trigger a recollection in my mind. But there is no shaft of light or sudden realisation. I am still in a dark place.

Without Adele's help, I cannot contemplate approaching Lannier, so we agree on a compromise. Senhora Garcia would be asked to press the police officer for a formal response. If the reply doesn't satisfy me, I will arrange a meeting with Lannier, explaining Adele's presence as simply that of my interpreter.

To my surprise, Senhora Garcia does not hesitate and, two days later, reports back. Following their investigation, the police ruled out the individuals concerned from their enquiry. Pressed by her for more information, Lannier said the two men were waiting to speak to Albert about a shipment for delivery and, on hearing there were visitors, decided to return later in the day. They left the scene long before the explosion occurred.

Lannier does not make appointments. The apologetic female police officer on counter duty explains that the public turn up and expect to wait as long as necessary. I could expect to hang around for two to three hours. She looks down at the little hand holding mine and must have realised the proposition was unrealistic. She runs her fingers through Francisco's curly hair before starting to write on the slate. Friday would be the best day to return. Sargento Lannier is normally in the building all day to attend to paperwork.

Adele arranges for a stand-in at the pharmacy while we are at the police station. Pedro is a retired doctor who likes to feel wanted and helps out from time to time. She can take as long as she likes. He will make up any prescriptions and wait for Adele to return to dispense them to the recipients.

As we sit in the waiting area, I can sense Adele is nervous. I ask her what she knows of Lannier's background but stop short of posing any probing questions. I have the distinct impression that, at some time, the two knew each other socially, possibly intimately. She knows quite a lot about him.

His origins are in Cape Verde, from an impoverished family who scraped a living from fishing. That's where he would have been today, he laughingly once told her, had the insinuations around the village that such a tall and muscular young man looked more like his uncle than his father proved to be a lie. He escaped a charge of attempted murder by no more than a few hours, working his passage on a freighter to Setubal and a new life that left behind his mother, shamed, and a man who would be in pain every time he pissed for the rest of his life. By lying his way into the police force, Lannier had climbed the greasy pole of the *Guardia Nacional Republicana* to achieve his appointment to the relative backwater of Cavalla, where he ruled with an iron hand.

'Is his history common knowledge?' I ask.

She laughs. It's established folklore in the town. Lannier is more than happy to perpetuate the story for his own ends.

Sitting before him in the cramped and uncomfortably hot office, watching him as he speaks slowly to Adele, I see in his hostile demeanour a man who prefers to rely on fear rather than respect to achieve control. Unlike our previous encounter, when he stared me out with those milky white eyes clouded with red, today he talks down at the table, deliberately avoiding eye contact, flecks of saliva caught in strands between his cracked lips. Unattractive grey stubble is dotted around his chin and thick top lip, which quivers slightly as he listens. I get the overall impression of a weary man short on patience, ready to explode.

His head jerks up and he looks at me intently as Adele translates the list of my requests. He screws his hands together until the bones make a sharp cracking sound, the preface to his brief reply. I hear the words, but I understand nothing. As usual, we go through the laborious process of translating onto the slate and Adele repeating my spoken reply back to Lannier in Portuguese. I'm fairly certain he understands most of the English, but he gives no hint as he waits for the translation.

The shake of the head continues as I read the words on the slate.

'This means you are not prepared to tell me anything about my son's death,' I object, 'unless and until it is done through a solicitor and approved by some judge in Porto?' I sound and feel exasperated. 'That's callous. I have a right to know. I was his father. Surely that counts for something amongst all this bureaucracy? What about these two men who were outside the house that morning? What do they have to say for themselves?'

He repeats exactly what he told the old lady. Again, looking pitifully up at me, he writes on a slip of paper and hands it to Adele as he stands up. The meeting is over.

'He's recommended a solicitor we can speak to,' she says as we collect Francisco from the waiting room where he has been playing happily with the female officer. I smile my thanks and push the buggy towards the door. 'It's only down the road,' she indicates as she reads the name on the slip of paper.

Ten minutes later, we are sitting in another waiting room, this time in a three-storey building just off the main square. A secretary-cum-receptionist occupies the centre space, close to the wall, protecting the walkway into the inner offices, busy typing with earphones she moves regally from her head whenever someone approaches to speak with her.

Five minutes pass before I hear the telephone ring on her desk. She looks directly at me as she recognises the caller's voice, as if to include me in the conversation she is about to have. She adjusts the mini microphone alongside her cheek, attached to the headset. Out of curiosity, I watch her lips as she answers. I get *'Bom Dia'*, but that's a pretty obvious piece of guesswork. The conversation ceases as she makes to transfer the call to the intended recipient. Again, I understand *'Doutor'*, then a name, followed by the movement of the underside of her tongue into the roof of her mouth. The *'L'* was followed by the open-mouthed *'A'*. The flicked tongue in between her teeth fooled me for a moment. I put it down as a *'T'*, but it suddenly came to me. The formation of *'D'*, *'N' and 'T'* are all basically similar. The split-mouthed *'AY'* at the end said it all. I had lip-read L.AN.EE.AY.

'Let's go,' I say to Adele. 'We are in the wrong place.'

She looks bemused, her raised eyebrows questioning my actions.

'Tell her we have to attend to the child. We'll make another appointment.'

There is a kiddies' play area in the hamburger restaurant on the other side of the square. We can watch on as Francisco plays whilst we talk.

'We were being directed to Lannier's lawyer friend. I guess he was about to be put on notice of our visit and react according to the policeman's prompting. We need somebody independent who can represent our interests.'

'I doubt you will find one in Cavalla.'

Francisco is the first one to notice the female police officer, as he jumps up and down in the ball pond, shouting to her one of the few words he knows, *'Brincar! Brincar!'* The officer has a bomber jacket over her uniform and is accompanied by a male colleague. She leaves him to order their food. Half playing with Francisco, she begins to talk with Adele, finishing the conversation by handing over a piece of paper on which she has scribbled a name and telephone number.

'What was all that about?' I ask.

Adele told her we needed a young, with-it solicitor who could stand up to Lannier, rather than somebody who was in his pocket. The woman gave a knowing smile and suggested we contact her fiancée, a recently qualified advocate who lives and practices law in Lamego, a regional centre some twenty-five kilometres from Cavalla. Twice a week, Domingos Cabral travels to Cavalla to spend the night with his fiancée. Their next date is the day after tomorrow. She will pass on the contact.

My misgivings that hiring any local lawyer with a lead into the Cavalla police force is like putting your head in the lion's mouth are soon dispelled. Domingos is an earnest young man with a permanently creased brow and thick, black-rimmed glasses that give him a Clark Kent look. His command of English is good, if not fluent. As a young boy, an aunt who had emigrated to live with her American husband in Boston before eventually returning to Portugal had insisted he speak only in English with her, but time has passed and most of his contacts in Lamego speak only Portuguese. He apologises for any shortcomings.

I happily play my deaf role with the expertise I have acquired over the past weeks. Any noise I hear, irrespective of from where it comes, I immediately repeat two words to myself: no reaction. The next task is the painfully slow and deliberately purposeful repositioning, so I'm in a direct line of sight of the speaker. This gives me thinking time. Sometimes, I speak too loudly or with a squeak in my voice. The whole charade becomes a challenge, a game I enjoy playing, the satisfaction of deceiving the other person and the reward of relishing the comment that of course they are so sorry for my affliction, but, my word, haven't I managed to pick up lip-reading rapidly.

In truth, I have reached a stage where I believe the hearing in my good ear is better than it was prior to the explosion, but I have become so competent at playing deaf, I am certain a gun could be fired behind me and I wouldn't react.

From the start, it is obvious Domingos actively dislikes the fact his fiancée works for Lannier. I had already guessed the policeman fancies himself as a ladies' man. The lawyer's gritted-teeth reaction tells me his girlfriend has also been the subject of Lannier's unwanted attentions.

Whatever Lannier's agenda, the facts surrounding Albert's death are under the control of the authorities in Porto. Any incidence of violent death ends up on the desk of someone in the Ministério Público, the Public Prosecutor, who will authorise issuing the post-mortem report, as had happened in this case. The aspect which puzzles Domingos is why the burial permit stipulated Albert's remains be buried in Portugal and could not be cremated. Such an order he has never come across. Using the authority I have given him, an application will be made to gain access to the police file. The authorities could dig their heels in, he warns, leaving me no course of action in Portugal. In that case, I would be forced to seek an inquest in the UK and leave it to the coroner via the British Consulate to request access to the file.

Two weeks pass before there is a response to his application. In that time, life settles into a predictable routine. Paradoxically, the more I get to know Jasmin, the less I really know about her. The initial expression of formal warmth and friendliness does not progress to the more relaxed and casual approach I would have expected from living in the same house. At first, I put it down to fatigue. She works long hours with little respite. I remembered Hugo telling me she has a contract with a wildlife park and there was an outbreak of a gastric infection amongst some of the animals.

As much as I can excuse her somewhat offhand relationship with me, I am beginning to feel it isn't entirely directed solely at me. Even with her brother, a regular visitor, and uncles Lino and Lourenco, who pop round occasionally on the off chance, she shows a certain reserve as her initial welcoming reaction tails into a series of bland exchanges lacking any emotion. Not so with her mother. There is a strong bond between them. Sometimes they remind me of two conspiratorial schoolgirls sharing secrets in whispered voices. Yet, it cannot have escaped Jasmin's notice that Francisco is wary around his grandmother. The boy clings to his mother's legs, hiding his face and moving around to avoid reacting to Inés's attempts to appeal to him. It strikes me as odd but conveniently fits in with my backstop for all childhood inconsistencies: growing pains.

On the other hand, the more time I spend together with Francisco, our relationship grows stronger and closer. We rely on each other. As obvious as his dependency is on me, I find myself talking to him as we play, as if he were an adult, recounting my stories and misgivings, trying to rationalise what life has really meant to me and what hope exists for the future. Stupidly, I frame make-believe questions he has asked me, contemplating the answers before replying. He seems impervious to my constant monologues, happy to play or snuggle into my lap to sleep. Perhaps my droning on has something to do with that. There are even times when I come into the lounge and he will leave Jasmin's lap to come and sit on mine. Had it been me, I would feel a twinge of jealousy, possibly resentment, but she seems happy, relieved almost, that he has shown me his favouritism.

***

Domingos had suggested we meet at his office in Lamego. It is on one of the few days I can count on Jasmin being around to take over from me. The change of scenery is just what I need.

I arrive early, prepped with a tourist guide that describes the town as nestled amongst the terraced slopes of the Douro valley wine-growing region, famous for its port wine, and overlooked by the ornate shrine of Our Ladies of Remedies. Unlike the rural style of Cavalla, my impression of Lamego is of a sophisticated elegance, inspired by the ornate Baroque architecture and the area's history as the birthplace of Portugal. I have an hour to spend just wandering through the streets and around the colourful market.

Domingos's office is on the first floor of a converted house, close to the Praca do Comercio, with an impressive view of the remains of the medieval castle and the bow in the river Balsemão. There is no secretary or waiting area, just a Sam Spade-style frosted glass-panelled door leading directly into one room. At least I won't be paying for expensive overheads.

He turns the official-looking papers to face me. I look blankly at them. I'm getting good at ordering various flavoured ice creams in Portuguese and telling people Francisco is just three years old and I am his grandfather, but present me with two pages of closely knit technical language and I'm lost.

'The process – we call it that; it means the investigation – into the death of your son has become more complicated than we imagined.' He stops to reject an incoming call on his mobile. 'I believe that you met a man called Borodin whilst you were in hospital?'

I vaguely remember Lannier's companion, a slight man in his fifties with a limp. I nod.

'He was charged by the prosecuting authority to examine the facts surrounding the accident. His role is to decide whether the process should be closed or taken a stage further.'

It is time to slow down, feign incomprehension, so I ask him to carefully repeat the last sentence. He does so, and I perform my charade.

'What does a stage further mean?'

'In essence, the Ministério Público believes that there is the possibility of a crime; how do you say ... foul play? A silly term, is it not? The process has been transferred to the Policia Judicial for further investigation. All the persons who entered and left the property around the time of the explosion will be considered suspects and again questioned by the police.'

'All the persons,' I repeat. 'As far as I can remember, only Albert and I were in the garden at the time. You are telling me there were other people. Who?'

I had started to sweat. I could tell my pulse was racing. There was a sensation of acid burning the inside of my nostrils. The wretched bile in the back of my mouth was as if I had just tasted my own death. I held my head in my hands, eyes shut tight, until the searing pain had passed and my parched mouth ached for water. In my brain, I could hear the distant echo of laughter and retreating footsteps.

'Are you feeling all right?' I can hear him say.

No, I feel like shouting, but I say nothing. Remember: no reaction.

He touches my shoulder, prompting me to open my eyes. He is holding out a glass of water. I gulp it down. It takes a minute or two, but I regain my composure.

The official document is back in his hands. Unusually, he takes his glasses off to read it. 'This is a *citação*, a court authority if you like, stating that your ability to assist the investigation, impaired as it is by the fact that you have no recollection of events at the crucial moments, may be aided if you are given access to certain of the details thus far accumulated.' He looks pleased with himself. 'This was the argument I presented to the judge in my submission, and which, happily, she has accepted.'

I decide on another mini 'didn't get what you were saying' interlude before we carry on.

'Does that mean we can see the police file?' I ask eventually.

Domingos shakes his head. 'Large elements of the file pertaining to the investigation will be excluded or comments redacted. Lannier will be appraised of what you can or cannot know. You will ask questions through me and, where appropriate, he will answer.'

'Sounds highly subjective to me.'

'It's the best we are going to get, so let's play ball, as you say.'

And we do. Another two weeks pass. It is late November and we are sitting in Lannier's office. His ebony features glisten under the flow of hot air from the air conditioning unit, hardly necessary on such a mild day.

It's the first time I become aware that he understands and speaks some English. Following my comment about how unnecessary the heating is, he turns to Domingos and asks how you said 'ritual' in English. Told that the word is the same, he says, 'It is a fucking ritual. We arrive at twenty November and heat, he goes on. We arrive at thirty-one March and heat, he goes off. We live by rules.'

There is an urgency about him, an impatience, I sense, that he will try to hurry us through the laborious question–answer–translation sequence of our first meeting in the hospital. Before we start, he asks Domingos if he has remembered to bring a mobile with a good-quality camera. It might be useful to photograph one or two pages to circumvent part of the question–answer session. Domingos takes the recently released Apple iPhone 3G from his pocket, taps the camera icon and takes a picture of the calendar on Lannier's desk. 'Good enough?' he queries proudly, showing us the image. He deletes the frame and places the phone on the desk. 'Shall we start?' he prompts.

Before we move on to our detailed list of questions, Lannier is keen to establish a timeline, the exact moment I can remember on that fateful day and the first thought I had as I awoke in hospital. He pulls a blue file from the desk drawer. It has the process number I recognise printed on it, but it is slimmer than I imagined it would be. He makes a point of keeping the contents hidden from us as he compares my answers to the information in the file.

At this juncture the internal telephone rings. Remember, no reaction. My gaze is drifting to the handset but I turn my head away. Lannier listens intently, saying little, before putting the phone down and suggesting to Domingos they have a word outside.

Both men apologise and close the door, leaving me alone, staring at the blue file and a mobile with an inbuilt camera. As the kids say, it was a no-brainer. I have the file open, taking photos page by page, not reading or understanding a word, my concentration bent on listening for any sound that tells me the two men are on the point of returning to the room. I reach the final page and put the mobile into standby long before anybody returns. Domingos enters on his own. Lannier has been called to attend a serious road traffic accident and regrets it is necessary to defer the meeting until another day.

He looks at the file, picks up his mobile and we make our way out. We are in his car and on the way back to Jasmin's house before I confess. He expresses surprise but doesn't give me the lecture on improper or illegal behaviour I anticipated. This being the night dedicated to some free time with his fiancée, he does not have time to review the paperwork until tomorrow. The best thing he can do is ensure the photos are transferred to the memory chip, remove the SIM card from his phone and put it in the spare mobile he carries. The iPhone will remain with me overnight and we will meet up the next day to discuss our findings.

'I should transfer the photos to your PC, if I were you,' he says. 'The touchscreen takes some getting used to and I wouldn't want you to accidentally erase them without realising.'

Jasmin is being extra considerate. She has to go out this evening and needs me to babysit outside of our agreed schedule. My quid pro quo is she configures the mobile to her printer and lets me use it while she is out. Anxious as she is, no explanation is sought. With practised expertise, she rapidly completes the synchronisation and produces a test sheet from the printer. As she hands it to me, I realise she's all dressed up. Who is she out to impress on a dinner date? I feel my face flush with anger. I'm about to say something when Hugo appears at the door. Under my breath, I apologise to Albert for thinking the worst of his widow. 'Have a nice night,' I say.

Francisco must somehow grasp that I am desperate to do something that does not involve him and chooses this evening to be particularly fractious and demanding. It is the first time I have felt irritated, angry almost, at the spate of continued interruptions and whining. He must have sensed for once we are not both on the same wavelength and resents it.

A voice inside my head says stop, step back. Was I like this with my two sons when they were growing up? Not once, but continuously, day after day, failing to balance their needs with the demands on my working life which, in retrospect, were nothing compared to my parental responsibilities?

I recall promising to turn up for the school operetta, *Huckleberry Finn*, adapted from Mark Twain's novel. They both had small parts but were enthusiastic. 'Promise you'll be there,' Albert said. I swore on the Bible. 'Don't hold your breath,' Vernon told him. 'The play hasn't got plumbing or heating in the title, so there's no chance he'll be there.' And he was right. A faulty boiler on a big job and I stayed late while it was fixed. Looking back, I didn't really have to stay. I wasn't Mr Indispensable. I just thought I was. It was so easy now to understand how Vernon's resentment had developed into the hate and contempt he now felt for me.

I shuffle the pages and place them on my bedside table. Plenty of time later when the little one is asleep in bed. With bones cracking, reminiscent of Lannier flexing his fingers, I sink slowly and painfully to my knees, voice wheezing from the back of my throat, signalling with my hands to mimic flames licking from my lips. 'The dragon is after you,' I grunt in Portuguese and begin to hustle across the floor on all fours. Little legs take off in front of me. There is a scream and then the persistent hysterical giggle I know so well. If I keep it up for long enough, he'll end up wetting himself. But who cares? If a game is worth playing, you go the whole hog.

CHAPTER FIFTEEN
Cavalla – 2008

I awake with a start, the pillow uncomfortably damp under my forehead, the pulse racing in my neck as it presses against the clenched fist gripping the sheet. I am petrified. Have I been dreaming? What has provoked such dread? I listen as the leafless branches of the oak scratch incessantly against the window. In the summer, when the leaves are on the trees, the sound is of rain beating on the glass. How often have I been deceived upon waking to imagine we are in the throes of some terrible storm, only to see the sun shining through a green canopy? Now, as winter begins to take hold, the image behind the curtains is of witches with pointed nails on long, bony fingers, scratching at the glass, pleading to come inside.

I turn onto my back and lie still, breathing in through my nose and out through my mouth, a deliberately controlled motion to calm my racing heart.

By the time I got to bed, I was worn out, with little energy to do much more than study the pages of photographs taken following the explosion. As I imagined, the worst of the damage occurred in the vicinity of the storage walk-in area next to the kitchen where the gas boiler was installed, the kitchen itself and the main lounge area and master bedroom, if you could call it that. The fire must have raged and abated quickly, because at ground level, whilst blackened with smoke and littered with debris, the second bedroom, or shrine room as it was, together with the garage, was relatively unscathed. At roof level, it was a different story. The timber joists were so badly scorched and deformed, I guessed the entire structure would have to be demolished and rebuilt.

All the photographs are dated and timed: early morning on the day following the accident. Something was preying on my mind last night and I fell asleep confused by my inability to understand what it was. Under the diffused glow from the bedside light, I pick up the four pages with the slideshow of photographs and look again. There is nothing. I reach the last page. In the garage-cum-workshop I had talked to Albert about his work, the prayer cushions piled up in the corner; ready to be dispatched, he had told me. I study the image closely. The cushions are not there any more. They had gone before the photograph was taken.

The sensation returns, slowly to start with and then with an intensity that scares me. My face creases in pain as the acid courses down my nostrils, rasping against the skin, that terrible taste in my mouth and the stench at the back of my throat. I gag. In the world between consciousness and sleep I watch, immobile, unable to move, as the cushions are carried out by indiscernible, shadowy figures. There is that laugh again, repeating and repeating, over and over again, until it comes to me. I suddenly realise whose laugh it is.

***

Sanlazer – 1993–1995

When Rosita laughed, it was one of her most endearing features. And she laughed a lot. In fact, we both laughed and loved a lot.

Those next few years were some of the happiest and carefree I can remember.

From the second of January, Sanlazer slipped back into a state of almost total hibernation. The remaining members of Rosita's family, along with the rest of the transient community who filled the bars and pavements on New Year's Eve, seemed to have vanished in a puff of smoke, back to their homes in the real world, leaving us to take a deep breath and get on with our lives where we had left off ten days earlier.

For a few days, Eliana's comment about the price tag on the shirt had rung alarm bells in my head, especially when Rosita had commented that her sister-in-law worked as a part-time counsellor in a special needs school for difficult children. I had never seen Eliana as anything other than a housewife and mother. Like everything else, time eventually dimmed and erased the memory of the unspoken implication of her remark and the concern it had caused me. Besides, Rosita and I were busy crafting our future together.

We had applied for and received my NIE – foreign identification number – residency card, social security and tax numbers. Our new business would be a partnership, a *sociedad civil*, Gilrosa – Clima y Solar, specialising in gas and solar heating, air conditioning and boiler installations. The letterhead and business cards gave me a new legitimacy and purpose, a reason to justify the dwindling balance in my Liechtenstein bank account, a worry that nagged at me constantly.

Business did not come rushing in, but with Rosita's undaunted enthusiasm as my right hand and interpreter, we began to quote for jobs and win a few orders. Most of the work came from expats who had responded to the ads in the English papers circulating throughout Andalucia, together with a sprinkling of small contracts from locals more infatuated with Rosita's compelling sales patter than any desire to invite an Englishman into their homes. For now, the big contracts eluded us, a nagging frustration as new housing complex after new housing complex began to dot the landscape. We were in a construction boom but barely surviving on the periphery, where the pickings were meagre and irregular.

Planning expansion was equally difficult. Expansion meant bank finance and that involved a track record, which we did not have. I cannot remember all the myriad ways a bank manager has of saying no. There must be a school that teaches them how to refuse without offending, although some of the arrogant arseholes I met must have forgotten this section of the curriculum.

During half of July and all of August, when Spain effectively shuts down, I was expecting the entire family to descend on us but was pleasantly surprised when it turned out to be only Rosita's parents and grandmother. TM had had what my mother would have described as 'a turn' just a month earlier. It hadn't been serious but the doctor had advised he stopped working so hard and gave some thought to retirement. On the face of it, he acted as if the advice would be comprehensively ignored but I got the feeling that for once in his life he felt vulnerable and was disappointed the rest of the family were not around to spend the summer with him.

Romina filled in the blanks. Rosita had every right to be upset that this was the first she knew of his heart problem, but her father had been adamant that nobody was to be told. After all, Rosita and her partner were busy building a new business together and they didn't need the worry.

As for Salvador, there was a chance of a course for promotion to captain with a move out of highway patrol into counternarcotics. He was working extra shifts and studying at night classes to improve his chances. Eliana barely merited a mention. Reading between the lines, Rosita told me there was some discord about the role of Eliana as mother to Miguel and their recently born daughter. TM stood four-square behind his son. Salvador was the breadwinner and needed to be given all possible encouragement to further his career. Eliana should accept her role as a full-time mother and cease to be so determined to follow her own career. Any wife had to understand that simple fact. I couldn't see Eliana kowtowing to such an outdated sexist attitude and she had probably spoken her mind, with the resultant temporary exile into purdah.

As for Isabel, well, I could just imagine the scenario. She was spending summer with a girlfriend on a cultural exchange in Southern Italy. Romina showed us a picture of the two standing in the Gabinetto Segreto in Pompeii, next to a statue of Pan with an enormous penis, about to have intercourse with a recumbent goat. Romina and Rosita seemed to find the whole thing quite amusing, though I doubt in the outfit Isabel was almost wearing she would be spending six weeks in Italy studying only stone genitalia. As far as I was concerned, her parents persisted with a strangely misplaced confidence in Isabel's moral compass.

I had some sympathy for Romina's mother and could now understand why, at Christmas, she had been so anxious to join her friend. Aurora's role appeared to be cook, cleaner and bottle washer. Romina had the technique of suggesting they tackle some chore together and then found some excuse to go off and do something else, normally involving a chair and a magazine. I felt sorry for the old dear but she seemed resigned to her lot, and her cooking skills were certainly a treat for the taste buds.

Apart from an evening meal together, we would see very little of our older generation during their stay. By this time, we had hired a small shop premises in an ageing apartment complex close by. With the three adjoining shops vacant and boarded-up, the rent we offered was peanuts and the space large enough to store our basic equipment stock and install a desk, telephone, computer and printer. With little work about in the area, we planned mail drops, designed leaflets and prepared simulated quotes for Rosita to use as an aid to her cold-calling telephone introduction. From time to time, I would check the telephone book for British-sounding names and follow her lead, but a rejection or adverse comment would tend to offend me and I would soon lose interest; call it my defence against dealing with rejection.

With all the apartments full during the high season, I came up with an annual boiler maintenance contract for owners. They would advise us when they were arriving, send or arrange keys for us, and I would service the boiler prior to their stay and be on call for the time they were in residence. I calculated a bargain basement price, but with sixty owners on our books, the income covered a fair chunk of our overheads and worked to everybody's satisfaction.

The next two years followed a roughly similar pattern. TM, Romina and her mother would turn up at Christmas and for six weeks in the summer, never with the rest of the family, their stays following a similar ritual to previous years. Rosita told me that TM had never fully recovered, although I have to say that the old man looked healthier and stronger than I had ever seen him. As far as I could tell, Salvador was still studying and working hard, Eliana was still persona non grata and Isabel was shagging her way around Europe. At least, that's the way it seemed.

Our partnership, Gilrosa, had begun to show signs of making some money; none too soon as far as I was concerned, with the Liechtenstein bank account now close to zero. At the end of summer 1995 we had taken on an assistant, Gonzalo, who had learned his skills with one of the big operators in Alicante and had come back to the area when his mother took ill. He came from a reasonably well-off family, tended to overestimate his capabilities, and resented criticism with the same haughtiness I had seen wearing a fancy suit and riding a ponced-up horse in a Spanish bullring. But he did his job, seemed to get on well with the customers and was happy to accept a deal for a lower wage with a bonus of ten per cent of the profits. 'It makes me a partner,' he would say. It didn't, but if it suited him to think that way, I wasn't going to object.

As we moved into 1996, I began to feel cautiously optimistic. The construction market was still strong, with plenty of EU money available, and Gilrosa was beginning to get a reputation in the sector. Just goes to show how wrong you can be. Little did I realise, as we toasted in the New Year, that the whole pack of cards was about to come crashing down.

CHAPTER SIXTEEN
Cavalla – 2008

Whatever the reasoning, I can't remember. I thought it might be better if I wore a suit. I only have the one, an off-the-peg pinstripe I found in the Red Cross shop. I needed it for the wedding, or so I thought. As it happened, there had been no dress code. I could have turned up in the chinos and a Ralph Lauren polo that were on the rail for a fiver. Anyway, I tidy the suit back into the wardrobe. What do you wear to confront a swarthy young North African as you ask him what he was really doing outside the house an hour or so before it burst into flames? I doubt he'll find me physically imposing whatever I'm wearing. It's my personality and bearing that will need to be intimidating, not my stature. I said it to myself but I had my fists clenched all the same.

Domingos has added little to my examination of the pages I photographed. The documents outlined the progress of the investigation, the preliminary post-mortem conclusions and the reasoning leading to the decision to release the body for burial. The intervention of Sandra's high-powered lawyer had clearly concentrated the magistrate's mind and circumvented the bureaucratic process.

The report from the prosecutor's office to determine the existence of possible criminal intent is supported by the need for further details regarding the movements and actions of the visitors to the house on the morning of the incident. The principal witness is believed to be suffering from temporary amnesia and apparent loss of hearing. Do they doubt the validity of my loss of memory? Do they believe I can hear, that I'm hiding something? My value as a witness is obviously dependent upon the recollection of events leading up to the explosion, but are the original statements made by Hugo and Vernon somehow open to question? I can't even remember either of them being there. I assumed Vernon had flown back to the UK with Sandra.

It's not just the papers stating he was present at some stage. If I can place any credence on my one recurring memory, it's the sound of laughter I keep hearing. That false, gruff bark, as if a cough and a laugh have got mixed up – that was a Vernon original. Whenever he was in trouble as a kid, I honed in on the sound as if it were a confession, as good as a guilty plea in court. How has it now taken me so long to recognise? In my subconscious, did I want to absolve him from being there?

What really captures my attention is the explanation Domingos provides for the last four pages, classified under the heading of *'Declarações de testemunhos'* – witness statements. Sure enough, there is the record of Senhora Garcia's report of her encounter with the two men, followed by extracts from the police records of Walid and Youssef Mahmoud. The two brothers are of Moroccan descent, first-generation Portuguese citizens with an address shown at an industrial complex on the outskirts of town. The sections on their police and criminal records have been heavily redacted in the thick black ink of a felt tip, but Domingos believes they are all to do with drug activity and the petty crime and threatening behaviour connected with the sale and distribution of narcotics.

'You seem fairly convinced,' I query.

Domingos flashes a beaming smile. 'Most of the hearings were at the Tribunal in Porto. I have contacts there. Cavalla is a closed provincial community run by the police chief and local magistrate. You learn what they want you to learn, and no more.'

'If so, why does the dossier mention these drug dealers?'

'We have already brought up the subject. Lannier knows he has to satisfy our curiosity or we are going to keep returning to press him on it. This way, he diffuses our concern.'

'He couldn't have known I would see the pages in the file.'

Domingos sits back in his chair, legs apart, and snorts a contemptuous laugh. 'I have been giving our visit some thought. Lannier was insistent I had a mobile with a camera available. He sent me a text message earlier suggesting I bring a spare with me. Then, there's the excuse of a private conversation with me. The explanation he gave was of a sensitive investigation in progress surrounding the activities of the Mahmoud brothers. He could not afford to have it prejudiced by us becoming involved. Nevertheless, he is convinced the two men have nothing to do with the explosion or your son's death. I thought that it was, how do you say, bullshit, at the time. Then his assistant appears, looking embarrassed, to advise him of some serious traffic accident but sounding very casual.'

'You think it was a put-up job?'

'I think he wanted to see if you were desperate enough and sufficiently emboldened to copy the file. Now, he has his answer. He also avoids a long and laborious session with us where we go through the question–answer–translation procedure to get to where we are now.'

'There was a surveillance camera in the room?'

'I believe so. Is it not the case I returned to the room shortly after you had finished taking photographs of the file?'

I nod. 'The cunning bastard. And I thought I was being clever, whilst all along I was doing exactly what he wanted.'

Domingos turns to the last photograph in the sequence. It's a copy of the page dealing with the witness statements. 'To say this report is cursory would be exaggerating its value. Both men say at Albert's request they paid a visit to the house to discuss a shipment of Buddhist artefacts. They run a delivery firm and handle a number of deliveries on behalf of the Dharma Meditation Centre, normally coordinated by Albert. They arrive at the house just after nine, hear a group of men talking in raised voices and decide to call back later. They recall seeing the lady with the dog but leave immediately after.' He puts down the photo. 'That's it.'

'He didn't question their alibis?'

'No. He appears to have accepted their explanation unconditionally. He asks whether they subsequently returned and is given the answer that other things cropped up and there was no time or opportunity that day.'

Although Domingos agrees more questions need to be asked, his refusal to accompany me and confront the two men is unequivocal. If there were ever formal proceedings, he could be accused of attempting to influence the witnesses and he is not prepared to take the risk. I thought about asking Adele, but she is bound to make excuses and I'm not prepared to tax our friendship by using emotional blackmail. She is afraid of Lannier and it will certainly put our fragile relationship at risk if she ends up in a confrontation with him. There may come a time when I need to depend on Adele's integrity.

Tomorrow, Jasmin has promised to be home by five and I will be free of my babysitting duties.

What I envisage is an unappetising prospect. With little Portuguese at my command and supposedly deaf to the rest of the world, I propose to ask detailed questions to two men who may or may not have had something to do with my son's death and will undoubtedly be hostile.

As for my hearing, I am aware that Domingos has his doubts. Our conversational toing and froing becomes so intense at times he must question my ability to speed lip-read with the proficiency I have seemingly achieved. From time to time, I remember to back off, question something he has said or ask for it to be repeated. He never challenges the charade but I sense he believes I am not as deaf as I make out. Maybe he doubts I ever lost my hearing – or my memory, come to that. Perhaps he suspects I'm living a complex lie and, in some way, I am complicit in Albert's death.

The slate lands on my lap whilst I'm lost in thought. We have just had breakfast and Jasmin is getting ready to leave for work as I play absent-mindedly with Francisco.

'Do you think he would do it?' I query.

'I'm sure he would, if you asked him nicely.'

Without going into detail, I mentioned to Jasmin the previous evening my having to speak to somebody in Portuguese. I doubted I would understand the replies even if I managed to ask the questions, which was highly unlikely. She suggests Hugo goes with me.

'Will you ask your brother for me? I don't really know him well enough.'

She laughs. 'You men! We live in a world of texts and social media and you still can't communicate with each other about things that matter. I take pity on you, Gilbert, because you cannot hear, but I suspect you would ask me to speak with him on your behalf even if your hearing was perfect.'

I pretend not to understand. With a dismissive shake of the head, she says unless I hear anything to the contrary, he will come around just after five.

He arrives five minutes early. I get into the car and we sit facing each other, one of those momentary awkward snapshots in time when you look into someone's eyes with something on your mind, yet you have no idea what that something is exactly; an irrelevance, perhaps, but the instance is engraved in your memory with a question mark.

He is first to react with a polite but brief smile. 'So, where are we off to?' he asks.

I had left the explanation with Jasmin sufficiently vague so as to avoid receiving a similar negative reaction to that I received from Domingos.

Meddling in affairs touching on Lannier's territory appears to put off most of the people around me.

Hugo's brow creases as the instant smile returns to his lips. 'Jasmin says that you can understand me if I speak slowly, more or less?'

'More or less,' I confirm. 'I may ask you to repeat stuff, but I can make out most of what you say.'

'I asked—'

'I understood. I need to speak with a couple of men at an address on the other side of town. It's on the road to Cambres.'

He turns, presses a button and the engine purrs into life with the gentle hum of a jet airliner in flight. Immediately, the seat moves around me, adjusting to the contours of my body. As he moves the automatic shift into forward, the picture on the navigation screen shows the present location.

Somehow, the car doesn't seem to match what I know about the driver. My knowledge of makes and models is very limited, but this long, luxurious coupe would be in one of those super German categories with a fancy price tag that could buy you a house or two in the Welsh valleys I once knew so well.

Up until now, I have never thought of Hugo outside of the box; that's to say, other than as Jasmin's brother or Albert's friend and best man, an adjunct to somebody else. The man himself, I know nothing about. Glancing across at the slender, muscular figure, his angular features, skin drawn tight over pronounced cheekbones, his eyes, a soft blue, clouded and humid, I can imagine ... what can I imagine? A high-powered salesman peddling cold cures and potions for athlete's foot, riding from call to call in some fancy expensive car? Hardly. All I know is the little I have overheard. He works at SantaCavalla, the pharmaceutical company that appears to employ half his family; or, at least, he did so shortly after university. But the car doesn't really jive with that profile. He must have moved on, an executive position with all the trappings. I am curious.

'Don't let me distract you from driving by trying to answer my questions,' I say. 'I can't see your lips from here. But when the opportunity arises, can you give me some background?'

He looks across, his glance a mixture of confusion and apprehension.

'I knew Albert as an adult for just two days. You were his friend, his brother-in-law, and you have known him since he was a teenager. Tell me about how you met, what you both got up to; what he was like as a person. Now he's gone, I need some connection with the man he was, as opposed to the boy I knew. I've been wrapped up with my own problems for too long. Maybe talking about him might help to restore my memory, recover those lost days that I need to bring back into focus. I suppose I need to grieve properly.'

There is another sideways glance, puzzled this time. 'Can you give me the exact address we are heading for?' he asks.

'Sorry. Yes.' I pull the offender's record sheet from my pocket and read off the address.

His back straightens as he reacts to the information, turning his head away from me to utter an expletive in English, followed by a string of Portuguese.

He did not mean for me to see his lips and I did not react. 'Do you know the place?' I ask innocently.

Hugo goes to say something but thinks better of it. He pulls the car over onto a grass verge and stops, turning to face me.

'These men have already been interrogated by the police. What do you expect to learn?'

I opt for a repeat request while I gather my thoughts. The man is scared.

'In the first place, from what I've seen, you could hardly call it an interrogation. I believe they may know more about the morning of the explosion than they're saying.' I watch him start to blink more rapidly. 'The reason for their being at the house sounds weak to me. Isn't discussing a shipment something you do over the phone? Would it need two men to talk about it?'

He dismisses my explanation. 'These men were Albert's contacts but I have met them. They are not people you mess around with.'

'They are just delivery men, aren't they? I only want to ask some questions about my son. What harm can there be in that?'

'As I say, I don't know them that well, but there are rumours they have been in trouble with the police on a number of occasions. They will be suspicious of a stranger.'

'All the more reason to talk to them with you along, to put their minds at rest. Shall we go?'

We come to a stop alongside a block of four small industrial units fronted by a communal parking area for staff and customers. The unit belonging to the transport company has no external signage. A white Transit with side doors and a rear hydraulic lift unit is parked outside the locked office door. A handwritten sign hanging inside the glass partition states the business is closed, reason enough for Hugo to propose we return on another day.

'Come on,' I say.

Outside the first of the units is a youth leaning against a wall, finishing a cigarette which he flicks into the air, following its flight as it lands in the drainage gutter. The waist-length smock he is wearing and the enormous panniers which dwarf the scooter on the stand alongside him carry fluorescent lettering publicising home deliveries for Pizza Wonderland.

'Ask him if he knows where we can find the guy from next door,' I say to Hugo.

The youth looks me up and down as if assessing whether I am worthy of an answer. 'What's in it for me?' he asks, slipping his hands casually into his trouser pockets.

I take a step towards him and he backs off. 'How about you just tell me where he is?'

He says something to Hugo.

'Who do you mean, Walid or Youssef?' Hugo is translating.

'Tell him either one.'

'You a customer?' is the comeback.

'Do you vet everyone who asks you a simple question?' I move closer to him just as a bell rings from inside the unit. He slips under my restraining arm and slouches towards the double doors. 'Try Café Palmeira.' He jerks his middle finger up. 'English,' he says as he spits on the ground.

We leave the car and walk across wasteland towards a row of shops set back on a lay-by in front of a large social housing estate of drab grey stone apartment buildings, all identical in design, all five storeys high. Café Palmeira is situated at the end of the block, with a space outside for the three plastic tables and chairs straddling the corner. To name a café after a palm tree, when there is not a single piece of greenery in sight other than tufts of grass poking up through the paving stones, defies the imagination, as does the prominent 'smoking is prohibited' notice, now heavily stained yellow from nicotine. Ashtrays sit on every table and the air is thick with the smell of tobacco.

About halfway down, in one of the inside booths, I pick out a group of three men, two of whom I remember from the police station on the night of my arrival and from the mugshots on the record sheets. The youngest, with the curly brown hair, and the other slim, gangly individual with a nasty scar on his cheek are laughing about something. The third man, sporting a dark, ragged beard and deep-set penetrating eyes, looks up unamused and aware long before his companions that their conversation is about to be interrupted.

Hugo hangs back, uncomfortable and apprehensive as I stand to the side of the table, effectively pinning two of the men into their seats. 'Walid *e* Youssef, *não é?*' I say, extending my hand. Nobody takes it.

All three are looking at Hugo with a mix of recognition and suspicion in their eyes. He acknowledges them and, without moving forward, gives a nervous and halting explanation as to why we are there.

The younger man turns, smiling, towards me. 'I am Walid. I study English since two years,' he says, as if we are about to start a conversational lesson. 'You may speak clearly to me.' He turns back to Hugo. 'We have already talk with Sargento Lannier. We know nothing more.'

'Would you just tell me why two of you went to Albert's house that morning?'

Walid glances furtively at his two companions. The third man with the beard is more muscular than I first realised. His hands are clenched tightly around a beer bottle. He gives an almost imperceptible nod of the head, raising his hand as if to bring the neck of the bottle to his mouth.

'Senhor Albert had a shipment for sending. I need to give a price.'

'And that needed two of you?'

'We needed payment.' Again, Walid looks around, waiting as Youssef nods gravely in support. I sense most of the other patrons have gone quiet as the atmosphere changes from casual to menacing.

I am making no pretence at feigning deafness, but Hugo doesn't seem to notice. He is looking steadfastly at the third man who, so far, has said nothing.

'You have to be paid before making a delivery?' I query.

He shakes his head. 'Pay for before consignments, not new one.'

'So, you were really there to collect debts. Is that right?' I lean down, closer to him, aware that the third man has tensed in his seat. His path to me is now unimpeded as Hugo has moved next to me, intent on saying something. I ignore him.

Walid shrugs with another nervous smile on his face. 'Same thing,' he says. 'Pay, collect, just business. Anyway, we sort it out.'

'How?'

'We speak with him.'

'Who? Albert?'

He nods.

'No more questions.' The third man is getting to his feet.

My face is so close to Walid I can smell the beer and stale cigarettes on his breath. 'Why did you tell the police that you heard voices from inside the house and walked on by? That was a lie, wasn't it. What did you say to Albert? When? Before or after you saw the lady with the dog?' Without realising, I grip the collar of his jacket.

The advancing years must have shaved a few seconds off my reaction time. Before I know it, the third man has reached the edge of the table, springing to his feet with a handful of my sweatshirt which he twists in a knot that tightens the material around my throat. Instinctively, my hands reach up to loosen his grip, giving him the opportunity to sweep my legs out from under me so that I am kneeling before him. The grip tightens as I gasp for breath. I feel a sharp twinge of pain from my recently injured leg.

'You call us liars when we have done nothing.' His English is accented but perfect. 'I will teach you a lesson.'

Walid is now on his feet. 'Let us all stay calm,' he says. 'My friend Yannik, he get very nervous when someone call us a liar. We tell the truth. I speak and then we go away. Albert, us, everybody happy. End of conversation.'

Hugo is rooted to the spot. I follow the point on which his eyes are focused; the glint of light on steel as the knife is drawn from its sheaf.

I strain to release my attacker's grip but he is strong. I can hardly breath. I wonder if I will pass out before or after he stabs me.

It all happens in a split second. I feel a rush of cold air on my back just as Yannik's grip on my sweatshirt relaxes slightly. He pulls me to my feet. His eyes are fixed on a point over my left shoulder. The knife has disappeared back into his pocket.

As I struggle for breath, I sense my one chance. The words the master at the school boxing club would repeat as we trained all those years ago are ringing in my head. Do not stop the uppercut when it strikes the opponent's chin but follow through as if your fist is destined to contact the ceiling. Yannik sees it coming and ducks out of the way, but, had it been intended, the punch was inch perfect. As I lurch forward with the impetus, I catch Walid a glancing blow under the chin, strafing his mouth and landing four-square on his nose. Time stands still, and then there is blood spattering everywhere.

Hands clamp around my arms, forcing them behind my back. Walid sinks back into the seat, his hands trying unsuccessfully to stem the flow of blood oozing between his fingers. I have broken his nose.

I register the sound of the café door as it swings shut behind me and the man appears at my side. I recognise the scent. Lannier moves his broad shoulders around inside a neatly ironed, blue short-sleeve shirt, folds a soft blue cap with white trim into the shoulder flap and adjusts the black holstered belt supporting matching dungaree-style trousers tucked at the ankles into a pair of highly polished black boots. He takes a pack of cigarettes from one of the many pockets in his trousers, accepts the Zippo lighter from an outstretched hand and blows a thin cloud of smoke into the air.

As the old cliché goes, you could hear a pin drop.

He nods towards the officer gripping my arms and I feel the cold steel of handcuffs around my wrists. Lannier's wrinkled black hand extends towards my shoulder but stops short of touching me, as if I have the plague.

He speaks briefly to Hugo, the café owner and, finally, Youssef, whose comment provokes him into leaning across to smell my breath. I nearly retch at the stench of a cocktail of cigarettes, garlic and red wine as I look up at him.

Nobody has said a word to me. A nod from Lannier and I'm led away to a waiting police car, unceremoniously dumped into the back seat and, after a series of photographs, blood test and mouth swab, left in a cell with a glass of water and, rather fetchingly, four decorated paper napkins to clean myself, compliments of the female police officer. She has written on one of them to tell me Domingos is on his way from Lamego.

To my surprise, what concerns me most are not the repercussions of my actions but the fact I am about to let down Jasmin and Francisco. She emphasised the weight of her commitments the following day and that I needed to be on hand from eight to give Francisco his breakfast. It's a breach of the faith she has in me and I can't understand why, in God's name, it's troubling me so much. Am I really developing a conscience this late in life?

Just before midnight, they release me. Domingos and Hugo are waiting in the outside office where I first saw the two men I now know as Walid and Youssef. I recall the image in my mind of Albert in a secretive huddle with the two of them. On that occasion, it also arose because of physical violence with a member of my family. Only this time, Albert is not around to deal with the consequences.

'Are you all right?' Domingos asks.

I nod.

Amongst all the legal jargon, precise articulation and laboured lip-reading, one thing is now clear. Hugo has convinced Walid and his cronies not to proceed with a complaint against me for assault. I thank him but he is in a strange mood and hardly reacts. He seems distant, lost in a world of his own. Maybe the adrenalin rush has left him drained, tired, and he needs his bed. I certainly need mine but Domingos insists on delaying my departure to lay down the law.

With Walid's waiver and the extenuating circumstances of the stress and grief I have suffered as a result of Albert's death coupled with my injuries, Lannier is prepared to take no further action. However, as the incident is now registered in a police report, the process will remain on file, confirming I was released with a caution; and should I be involved in any further incidents within the next two years, the matter will be taken into consideration.

'So, I now have a criminal record in Portugal. Is that so?' I ask.

'Afraid so,' Domingos replies. 'There is one other condition.'

'Which is?'

'We need to get together sometime tomorrow. Lannier wants a complete transcript of your conversation with the three men for the record.'

'Shouldn't take long,' I reply. 'We talked for about five minutes before coming to blows. Not much happened.'

It is whilst I am reliving the exchanges with Walid I realise something was said which is new to me. The revelations are of a conversation between Walid and Albert to discuss a debt, the reason offered for the two men turning up at the house. I have to know more. Somehow, I sense Walid is the key to unlocking something hidden away inside my head.

I tell Domingos everything I remember. What I cannot reveal is my intention to seek out Walid again and dig further into the events of that morning. I'm not in the mood for a censorious lecture. The next move needs to be planned carefully.

As unpredictable as the weather can be, one thing is a near certainty. With a bank holiday coming up next Tuesday, recognition of the Restoration of Independence on December the first, the climate has nosedived from pleasant autumn to bleak midwinter in the space of twenty-four hours and is likely to remain that way. Another certainty is that a large percentage of the working population will find an excuse to avoid the office on the intervening Monday.

Jasmin is taking Francisco to stay with her mother over the long weekend and I will be left to my own devices. I feel sorry for Francisco. Even at his tender young age, I can tell he doesn't want to go. If blending infant emotions with senile responses counts for anything, I know he will find four days in the company of his grandmother difficult to handle. I also know Jasmin would have refused an offer for me to look after him; perhaps she feels Francisco needs to confront this family reality at an early age. In any event, I need time on my own.

I spend most of Saturday watching at a distance the site from where Walid and partners operate. As the day wears on, the activity at the adjacent pizza delivery operation heightens. There are four or five young guys with motorbikes decked in publicity livery, and a steady stream of traffic for a takeaway service I did not realise existed on my first visit. But Walid's unit remains locked and deserted.

It's past four, dusk is falling and the drizzle has started. It's the drizzle you hardly notice which ends up soaking you in a matter of minutes. Although I'm wearing a light raincoat over my suit, my bones are chilled. I'm feeling dejected and on the point of giving up for the day, when a Citroën estate pulls up outside the unit. Three men in hoodies scurry about, taking a series of suitcase-size packages from the boot into the warehouse, where they remain.

My pulse rate increases. I try to find cover under the eaves of the last of the four units, seeking both protection from the rain and the opportunity to move around the corner and out of direct view, should they reappear. The cover is minimal. My suit, now damp and hanging loosely on me, gives off a stale and foreign odour I can only attribute to the previous wearer.

Another ten minutes pass before I back off at the sound of an opening door. I catch a glimpse of Yannik as he hurries to the driver's side of the Citroën. The engine starts and I wait as it halts at the junction and then disappears from view.

Five minutes pass before the man with the scarred face, Walid's brother Youssef, appears, fumbling for keys to unlock the Transit. Tyres squeal as he releases the clutch and guns the accelerator.

Walid must be on his own. This is my opportunity. Of the three, he is the only one who was prepared to talk and, as luck has it, the only one I feel capable of matching physically. If I'm able to corner him before he has the opportunity to alert the others, he will tell me.

I move to the door. As I expected, it's locked, but the door itself is set into a much larger sliding framework providing vehicle access to within the building. I inch it open. The noise seems deafening as the frame screeches against the runners but there is no reaction from within, no shout of 'who's there?' I make no attempt to close it. I am acutely aware this is my only exit route if things go wrong.

As my eyes accustom to the gloom, I begin to make out the interior of a medium-sized warehouse with little to suggest it is the base for a delivery operation. Apart from a few stacks of cardboard boxes, sacking and some empty wooden crates, the floor space is virtually empty. To the left, at the far end, is a steel staircase leading up to an office in total darkness. I make my way cautiously towards the rear of the building.

Time is of the essence. How long do I have before one of the others returns? At first, the place appears to be deserted. Moving forward beyond a makeshift plywood partition, I can just make out the glow of a single light bulb reflecting upwards onto the iron rafters and the discordant sound of wailing Arabic chanting coming from a radio. The sound is heavily distorted by the persistent crackle of interference from the steel structure of the building.

There is an open doorway at one end of the partition. I glance inside. Walid is standing at a large rectangular table, a table lamp the sole source of light close to him. His attention is directed to filling small plastic bags with what look like pills of some sort. As he works, his face screws up into an expression of what could be either ecstasy or agony as he wails along to the music.

'I need to talk to you.' It's hardly an appropriate introduction but I can't think of a suitable opening line. I step into view.

Things happen simultaneously. Startled by my presence, Walid staggers back, knocking the table lamp so that the light shines directly into his face. A monitor comes to life on a workstation behind him. The screen shows four images from cameras that must be installed about the premises and activated by motion sensors. One shows the main entrance and the gap I had left open. An image would have displayed my approach. He must have been too preoccupied to notice.

His violent cursing outstrips the noise from the radio as he lurches backwards, his forearms rapidly sweeping whatever was on the table into the partially opened drawer. He stabs his finger to turn off the radio. For a second, we stand facing each other in total silence, staring into the gloom as he fumbles with the table lamp.

'What you do here? This private property. Police put you in prison. Get out.'

I hold up my hands in supplication. 'I know the risk I'm taking. That's how desperate I am. Please, I must have your help.' I'm pleading. I sense the composure returning to his face as he makes out the words.

'You, crazy man coming here. Yannik very angry with you. He want to hurt you. He come back anytime.'

'Don't you understand, Walid? I don't care. I need to know everything that happened on the morning you went to the house.'

'I already tell you.' He looks around as the screen returns to sleep mode. A look of concern flashes across his face.

'Please tell me again. Every detail.' I still have my hands held in the air as if someone is pointing a gun at me. 'You went to the house to collect money. How much?'

He shakes his head and shrugs. The element of surprise has passed. 'I don't remember exact. *Dois mil*. Two thousand euros,' he corrects.

'A lot of money for deliveries.'

He shrugs again. 'A lot of deliveries.'

'Then what happened?' I press.

He is looking at the table and then turns his attention to the floor. 'We arrive at house and hear lot of shouting from garden at back.'

'Who was shouting? Albert? Me?'

'No. Man who get involved in fight. Police arrest him. You know. You there.'

'Are you talking about Vernon?'

He shrugs again. 'Don't know name. Know voice. Always angry man.'

'Then?' I make a circular motion with my hand as if to hurry him along. Bravado is one thing, but if one of the others returns, I am in big trouble.

'I phone Albert and he come to front of house. We talk. Then we leave.'

'What did you talk about?'

There is a moment's hesitation that tells me I'm not going to hear the truth, or, at least, the whole truth. 'We talk about money.'

'Is that all?'

I can see he's debating whether to say something else.

'Please. Tell me.'

The monitor springs into life again, but I can't make out anybody on the screen. The front entrance is still open.

'We needed' – he is searching for the word in English – '*almofadas*,' he says, finally. 'Our property.'

'Cushions?' I'm confused. On the floor behind him, there is indeed a small pile of cushions, the material and style of the prayer cushions Albert had made and that had been stored in the garage. 'What do you mean, your prop—'

A fist hits me from behind, slamming into my kidneys. As I sink to my knees, gasping for breath, the pain surges in nauseous waves. I turn my head to catch sight of his face. He is smiling. In that instant, I realise. Yannik must have his mobile linked through the internet to the security cameras in the unit. If a camera is activated, he'll be alerted. He has been aware of my presence from the second I pushed open the entrance door. How naïve of me.

'I just wanted to talk,' I manage to croak, but he pulls me upright by the hair and I realise what is coming; the sound of a harsh laugh and, then, darkness.

The concrete is cold against my cheek. My hand slides across the floor, fingers probing until I can reach what I see from the corner of my eye. I hold it tight in a clenched fist. The taste of blood is in my mouth. At least one tooth is loose. The pain in the small of my back is horrendous. There are raised voices. Now there are three of them. I try to focus, raising my head and gasping at the pain from the stabbing throbbing in my head. The man with the scar has my wallet in one hand, holding out something in the other. There is another flurry of excited conversation. If it's money they're after? Did I make that sound? Was it supposed to be a laugh?

I don't see the boot coming, just the stabbing shock of pain in my midriff before I pass out.

It isn't like regaining consciousness. My brain can't handle the agony, suspending me in the sort of hazy half-life you experience when the anaesthetic is beginning to wear off after an operation. There is the unique smell of a black plastic rubbish bag. It's over my head and shoulders. Panic. They are going to throw me into the river or bury me. Kill me first, for God's sake! My body shudders. I'm in a moving vehicle, careering over a bump in the road. Where are they taking me? I gasp for breath, sucking the plastic bag closer towards my mouth, yet I feel fresh air against my cheek. They have cut a slit into the plastic. Elation. They don't want me to suffocate. I feel like singing. I try to flex my legs. My feet are bound. I touch the side of the vehicle. I am in the boot of a car. Another bump, only this time my body seems to be suspended in mid-air. The pain is too much. Darkness. Blessed release.

CHAPTER SEVENTEEN
Porto, Portugal – 2008

If this is heaven, I think I might like it. I keep my eyes closed. The pillows under my head are full and soft, lightly scented with one of those cheap Spanish perfumes my mother used to swear by, Maja or 4711, or was that the name of a convenience store? I can't remember, yet the very association triggers memories of a widowed mother trying to bring up her child on a clerk's wage; as a young boy, waiting after primary school for her to come home and spending those long winter evenings sitting on the floor between her legs in front of a coal fire as I listened to her reading stories; Saturday morning pictures with a friend and, then, more waiting for her train to arrive from London and the weekend to start. I did so much waiting when I was a child. And with waiting, comes longing. And with longing, comes yearning. I yearned to see her again, if only to say sorry.

The mere scent of a Spanish perfume, and the memories come flooding back.

***

Sanlazer – 1996

The New Year celebrations that heralded in 1996 were amongst the happiest memories that I have of my time in Spain. As had become the custom, my parents-in-law had arrived with Aurora just before Christmas, and we slipped into the time-honoured ritual of TM holding court in his favourite chair while Romina complained about all the work she had to do and looked on as dear grandmother Aurora still managed at eighty-something to do most of it.

Romina had become fixated with health concerns, founded on several visits with TM to the hospital in Madrid. She had become superficially knowledgeable with an ever-expanding vocabulary of disease and illnesses, courtesy of Google, all designed to instil dread into anybody feeling slightly off colour. In her eyes, TM was clinging onto life by a thread, although I had honestly never seen him look so ruddy and fit. His changing moods and temper were entirely conditioned by how Real Madrid was performing.

Normally successful – the team had topped the league the previous season – it was struggling for results in the current round and TM was not approaching the New Year's Eve party he had arranged with his normal gusto and bonhomie.

When I said party, I meant a sedate get-together with a number of his old cronies from neighbouring properties. This year, he spent most of the evening sitting in a corner with Santos, the former gardener and pool cleaner, who had retired from the condominium as the season came to an end. He had been replaced by a swarthy young man with rugged good looks who always seemed as though he was about to burst out of his T-shirt. Everybody called him Robi, which was not his real name but an abbreviated corruption of some unpronounceable Eastern European surname. Apparently, Robi had been recommended for the job by his uncle, a man I had casually noticed as a visitor to the complex during the month of August. He was one of those people who look at you out of the corner of their eye and you sense they are about to say something, but they never do.

TM's monologue to an overly attentive Santos was an assurance that the pool had been much cleaner when the old man had been in charge, several reasons as to why Valdano should be sacked as the Real Manager, and his hope the rumours linking Arsenio to the club were accurate.

Despite the low-key nature of the celebrations, I was feeling elated. Gilrosa's business over the past few months had moved from the plain of local supplier to new heights of regional sub-contractor to a few national residential construction companies. The persistence of Rosita and the arrogant confidence of our second-in-command, Gonzalo, had started to produce dividends. We were involved in two big housing contracts: one in Almeria and the other in Torrevieja, east of Murcia. These were prestige developments, over two hundred units, where a good result would establish us as serious players, but tough negotiations had squeezed margins and we desperately needed to keep expenses down to come out in the black.

With over fifty operatives on short-term contracts working on sites hundreds of kilometres from our base, I had been spending a great deal of my time away from home, developing and supervising work rotas in an effort to control the mounting labour costs.

Back in Sanlazer, Rosita dealt with sourcing the complex inventory of equipment, chasing up suppliers, and becoming as expert at putting off requests for money with heart-rending excuses at the same time as ferociously chasing up the contractors for money owed to us. Gonzalo would split his time between helping me out on site and touting for new business amongst his burgeoning list of contacts.

As strange as it might sound, any language difficulties had ceased to become a serious problem. My Spanish was good enough to get me by on site, with a limited and specific vocabulary, and as far as my workforce was concerned, I was better off speaking English. The majority of the men came from Eastern Europe or one or other of the old Soviet bloc countries, knew little Spanish and had a few phrases in schoolboy English to get us over most hurdles. They were a resourceful bunch, hard workers who could turn their hands to most things. I admired the leaders amongst them, and when back in Sanlazer, I would often invite over pool man Robi for a beer to tell him how impressed I was with his fellow immigrant workers.

But business success was not the main reason for my elation. Although lovemaking with Rosita had slipped into a more predictable and established pattern, a lot less frequent since I had been travelling, we had seriously been trying for a child for the past two years. Neither of us wanted to leave it too late but every month came the same unhappy realisation. Earlier in the year we had even visited a clinic in Seville for tests, where I was given some revolutionary new and very expensive medicine to improve my sperm count. But still, nothing happened.

I had even started questioning our future together. I could never aspire to call myself an intellectual, but I began to despair that Rosita had absolutely no conversation or interest in anything beyond the business or the procession of television soap operas which crammed the airwaves. For the first time, I had really lost my temper with her one evening when, with a bored sigh and without asking, she had flicked the TV remote to change channels. The CNN documentary on White House shenanigans, in which I was engrossed, gave way to the image of a swarthy he-man pretending to play the ukulele in accompaniment to an overweight, middle-aged woman sporting too much make-up, as she mimed to some forgettable rural dirge. I accused Rosita of lacking culture, to which her reply was she needed something to take her mind off my sexual inadequacy.

I suppose in the end, rather than get uptight about it, I had come to terms with the situation, stopped stressing and relaxed into the reality that IVF would be the likely outcome. How many times has that happened and the woman gets pregnant shortly afterwards? Thousands, I bet.

For two days, I had been learning the Spanish translation parrot-fashion, but I was genuinely nervous. God knows why. Apart from the family, the room was full of strangers who couldn't have cared less about my news.

'If I could have your attention for a moment, I have an announcement,' I started.

TM gave me a dagger's look as my interruption had come midway through one of his long-winded, boring anecdotes.

'Rosita and I are pleased to tell you we are going to have a baby. He or she is due in August and we are both happy and excited with the news.' I hugged and kissed her as people gathered around to offer their congratulations and the cava began to flow.

I should have left it there, enjoyed the celebration and got on with my life. But I didn't, did I? I had to tell people. Trouble was, I didn't have any friends left to tell. Apart from Mad Max and a couple of the other bar owners, my social contacts had evaporated. My old address book was combed for possibles, but most of the names on the list either hated my guts or hadn't spoken to or heard from me in years. Stupidly, I settled on an email to Paul Duggan, the ineffectual solicitor who had helped cock up my divorce, and another, to Madeleine. I deleted the one to Madeleine before I sent it. She was too close to Sandra and I knew it wouldn't be well received in my family circle. As it happened, sending it to Paul had the same effect. The golf club was a tight-knit group of up-their-own-arseholes, and I should have realised once Paul had told him, Roger would happily broadcast any piece of news he thought would discredit me.

Looking back, I suppose I've known a few people whose experience of happiness could be measured in terms of oceans. Me? I guess, by comparison, I've had a leaky plastic cupful, a few precious memories of times when I felt some real stability in my life. The first three months of 1996 were that for me: the thought of parenthood, maybe a girl this time; watching Rosita bloom in those early months of pregnancy. Even the weather was on my side. A mini heatwave at the end of March. What more could I want?

'There's someone on the phone for you called Ramon Sikorsky,' Rosita called from the office. 'Says he knows you.'

I had recognised Robi's uncle when I saw him by chance at a motorway service station south of Alicante. He came up to me as I was sitting, drinking coffee, introduced himself and started spouting off in Spanish. I put my hand up and gave him my 'slow down, *no comprendo*' response, at which he pointed to the Seat van with Gilrosa's livery on its sides and I nodded. He was a diminutive man with a rotund figure, somewhere in his late forties with staring pinprick black eyes, a perpetual strained look on his face and a tuft of black hair at the front of a balding head. His frown had turned into a beaming smile when I asked why anybody would want to name their son after a helicopter. He said, 'Sikorsky man come first, helicopter second.'

The conversation in halting English in the car park had been brief. He was able to supply all sorts of things to the building industry. He could beat anybody's price, but there was one thing. All his deals were in cash with no paperwork. He had pocketed my business card as if it were a five hundred euro note.

I had forgotten the name and the chance meeting. 'Can I help you?' I said into the telephone, still blissfully ignorant.

'Señor Thart. You remember me. We talk in car park. I helicopter man.' The squeaky voice was unmistakeable.

A new Maxi Combi hot water boiler cost us around eight hundred euros. Sikorsky could lay his hands on around fifty, he told me, for three hundred and fifty euros a pop, brand new. They would come along ten at a time and I should feed them into my inventory chain, using one here, one there, if I knew what he meant? I did, and I'd let him know.

'Do not keep waiting long time, señor Thart. Lots of people know good deal.'

I discussed it with Rosita. She was as nervous as me, but the prospect of a twenty thousand euro cash flow windfall right at the time when we could really do with it was too good to resist. We would do a deal for ten boilers. If it worked out, we would think about it.

Seeing the units, I was in no doubt as to where they had come from. As buoyant as the construction industry was, plenty of developers had overstretched, relying on cheap credit that was suddenly not there any more.

Banks had foreclosed, large unfinished developments mothballed, and Sikorsky and his cronies had moved in.

These Maxis did not come in nice new boxes with a guarantee. Many with pipework still attached had been torn off the walls of homes in construction and I would need a good explanation to give my foremen as to their origin to avoid rumours starting to circulate. The story, sufficient to avoid arousing suspicion, was that the boilers had been over-specified on another site we were working on and had to be replaced with smaller units.

It all worked very smoothly, and by the time the summer came we had sourced over a hundred boilers, solar panels and various other items from Sikorsky. However tempting it was to make the most of our association with him, Rosita was becoming increasingly nervous. We had to take Gonzalo into our confidence; he had guessed anyway and could use it against me if our working relationship were to suffer a breach. Nevertheless, I was a risk-taker who was enjoying the luxury of something approaching a fifty thousand euro boost to my cash resources, enough to keep the creditors off our backs and give the business some breathing space. On top of which, Sikorsky appeared to have an endless supply of bent gear.

There was another problem, of course. The paperwork was light of all this equipment we were installing. The tax authorities were bound to spot the discrepancy. Again, it was Sikorsky who knew somebody who knew somebody who would issue some phoney invoices to us for ten per cent of face value.

The unholy trinity was now complete. With Sikorsky at one end, Rosita and I in the middle and Gonzalo capable of holding us to ransom, we carried on. As far as I was concerned, collapsing the pack of cards was like giving up smoking: choose a future date. In this instance, I had pledged to Rosita that we would stop as soon as the baby was born.

'Father has been on the phone,' Rosita announced. 'Everybody is coming down this year. It's their fortieth wedding anniversary in August. Hopefully, we can celebrate the birth of their grandson at the same time.' We were in mid-June. By the look of her, I doubted she would hang on that long.

'When are they descending on us?'

'Most of them, the third week in July.'

'Most of them?' I queried.

She looked a little shamefaced and I knew something was coming that I was not going to like. 'With their third child on the way, Salvador can't afford to take a holiday.'

My heart lifted. 'He's staying in Madrid?' I ventured, unable to control the gleeful tone. I knew that Salvador's promotion hopes had stalled for a second time, and on the odd occasion when I had joined in the group Skype call, the man looked ten years older than I remembered and had the air of somebody who had just been told they had a terminal illness and a week to live.

She breathed in deeply. 'No. On the contrary. With Madrid a ghost city in August, they transfer officers from the local force to supplement the squads in the holiday resorts. Sal has managed to get a posting to Huelva for the summer and Papá has insisted that he stay here.'

I could tell what was coming. I would shortly need to do a lot of travelling.

'It's good, really,' she said with that false bravado when on the defensive. 'We've drifted apart over the last few years. I think he gets a little pissed off we are doing so well—'

I couldn't help interrupting with a snorted laugh.

'Well, in his eyes,' she corrected. 'Remember, his life hasn't changed, other than more kids and money worries. For the first time in his life, I think he's a little jealous of me.'

'Little does he know of our struggles,' I said. 'When's he coming?'

'Ten days' time.' She looked nervous. 'You don't mind, do you?'

'If it's what you want. Who am I to object?' I may have said it grudgingly, but as far as Rosita was concerned, I meant it. The fact was I was over fifty, living in somebody else's house with no say as to who came and went, and still, as far as Rosita's family were concerned, existing on the periphery of their grace and favour. With the baby coming, it would all have to change. We needed a place of our own, away from all the ties. I would start putting out feelers in the morning. There were a couple of new developments about halfway between Seville and Cordoba. I knew the guys promoting the sites. The Spanish were always willing to talk a deal.

As it turned out, Salvador seemed quite upbeat and positive about life. Getting away from Madrid, a wife and two young kids, with another on the way, was an opportunity to escape the monotony of day-to-day life. Here, the working routines were different; he was making new friends and could recapture some of the spirit that was the old Salvador. Much to Rosita's chagrin, his bluster and bullying nature had started to reappear. Older brother knew what was right for younger sister and he wasn't afraid to say it, along with digs about some people who didn't deserve getting the breaks in life.

I kept low-key. Rosita needed to show her brother she was as good as, if not better, than him and deserved his respect. I knew she was whistling in the wind, but it would eventually help in persuading her a move away was the right course of action, so I let the drama play out, always too busy to pay more than token attention to the sullen moods into which she would get after a lecture from Salvador.

At the social level, I would go out for the occasional meal with him or, more likely, stand at some bar, listening to one story after another about the day's traffic infringements. Gonzalo would often be present. He was fascinated by Salvador's boring litanies, almost to the point of mild hero worship, which I found amusing in someone so amazingly arrogant in his attitude to most people. Fine, let them talk, become best buddies. I could feign listening whilst concentrating on the finer features of the barmaid.

We were into mid-July and the rest of the family would be on us within the next few days. Business in the construction industry was beginning to wind down for the August exodus and I could be grateful that the more time I could now spend at the villa coincided with the longer shift patterns that Salvador was now obliged to work. The closer it got to the arrival of Eliana and the two kids, the more morose his mood became. He would arrive from work as I left for the office; a passing hello and our worlds parted, which suited me just fine.

There was one more delivery due from Sikorsky before the summer break. I had taken to receiving his equipment in a small warehouse at the back of the shop unit in Sanlazer. There, I could sanitise it of any signs of having been previously installed before I allowed it to be shipped to one of the sites we were working on. Pipework was removed, joints cleaned and any scratches or surface marks polished out, work that I entrusted only to Rosita or Gonzalo if I was absent. Cartons and wrappings kept back from purchases from our normal suppliers were used to repackage the parts before they left the warehouse.

I had agreed a delivery time with Sikorsky of 10 p.m. Most of the neighbouring populace would be dining at this time, and we could have the delivery off his lorry and into the warehouse before anybody noticed; not that night-time loading or unloading was that unusual anyway.

Sikorsky was never late, but he didn't show; not a telephone call, a text message or even a carrier pigeon. In fact, I never saw or heard from him again. I waited until eleven before I called it a night. At the time I thought it strange, but I didn't put any store by it. Things happen.

* * *

Rosita was six weeks away from her due date and if I said she waddled into the lounge the following day with the news, nobody could have accused me of being inaccurate or unkind. TM had hired a minibus to bring everybody down; leaving at eleven, and with countless toilet breaks for young and old en route, we could expect them to arrive at around eight. Rosita would prepare dinner for half nine to give some leeway.

Salvador had just come off a double shift, ignoring my cheery greeting and avoiding eye contact as he made straight for his room, a shower and a change of clothes.

'Time for a drink at the bar?' It was more an order than an invitation and took me by surprise.

We were barely two hours away from the arrival of his wife and family. My memory of Salvador around Eliana was the portrayal of an abstemious protector, the face of virtue with the assumed gravitas of a Quaker on a mission. Things must have changed. He was on edge, strangely uncomfortable, yet his demeanour was somehow threatening.

'You smell like the Chelsea Flower Show,' I said. We were in a booth away from the other patrons, a group who had just come off the beach with the scent of sunscreen that collided brutally with Salvador's cologne.

'Sorry?' he replied, confused at the remark.

'Your perfume. Overdid it, did you?'

He shook his head. There was obviously going to be no small talk. He was looking over my left shoulder, the way policemen do when telling you they're going to fine you for speeding. 'We were on what you call a stop-and-search operation last night. I had a very interesting conversation with a man called

Sikorsky. Recognise the name?'

He had just pulled out the rug from under my feet, but I had learned in these instances to appear unconcerned and say nothing, just hold the gaze of the other man who was banking on the advantage of surprise. He was still looking over my shoulder.

'He knows you, very well. His truck was full of equipment reported stolen from a construction site in Jerez. Do I make sense?'

I still didn't say anything. It was irking him.

'Do you not propose to answer my questions?' He shook his head in apparent disdain.

'I don't think I can offer anything to this conversation. You're the one doing the talking.' I had no idea where we were going. Was I about to be arrested? Was he warning me to get out of town before the sheriff arrived?

'Señor Sikorsky was very cooperative. He talked a great deal. What he had to say could land you in prison for a very long time.'

'Could or will?'

For the first time, he looked at me. Confidence, and that smug policeman superiority hidden under a veil of pseudo-politeness, had started to reappear. 'I was on my own when I stopped the vehicle. I have yet to prepare and file my report. Sikorsky tried to convince me I should not do so.'

Jesus! This was a shakedown. My own would-be brother-in-law was on the take and I was the intended victim. 'Did he succeed?' I asked.

There was a wry smile. 'That depends on you.'

'How come?'

'Don't be naïve, Gilbert. Not only do I have Sikorsky for theft, but attempting to bribe a police officer. He needs you in as part of the deal to make our commitment to silence complete.'

'And how much is my contribution to this pact of silence?'

'The same as his.'

'And if I say no?'

He shrugged. 'I complete my report, charge you both and hand over the fifteen thousand with which Sikorsky tried to bribe me. Rosita and the baby can come and visit you in the Centro Penitenciario in Huelva.'

So that was it. Fifteen thousand. I knew Salvador had serious money problems and this was his way out. I had three times what he wanted stashed away in cash to avoid the taxman. It would hurt, but it was doable. It would make finding the deposit on a new house more difficult, but that was tomorrow's problem.

'One thing,' I said as we got up to leave. 'Rosita must never know of this. Agreed?'

'Naturally,' he said. 'It will always only be between the three of us. Eliana would divorce me.' That didn't sound to me as if it would be the end of the world. He sat down again, indicating I should follow suit. 'Whatever you think of me, you are where you are today because you are a criminal. I'm doing you a big favour.'

'Don't moralise about something called extortion. It doesn't suit you, police officer Salvador.' I hope that hurt. His failure to achieve promotion must have really soured him. No harm in rubbing salt in the wound.

Brushing a symbolic piece of dirt from his shoulder was meant to tell me his reaction to that comment. 'Look upon it as a joining fee,' he said with a sardonic smile.

'Joining fee?'

'To the family.'

'What the fuck are you talking about?'

'Rosita always does what I tell her. She has done so all her life. Sometimes it takes a little time and a few tears, but I'm her big brother who always knows what's best for her.'

'Svengali, are you?'

'Again?' His brow creased.

'It doesn't matter. You were saying?'

'When he heard that you were her latest lover, TM asked me to persuade her to get rid of you.'

I was thinking about bringing my fist into contact with his smarmy face. A bar filling up with locals; a Spanish policeman, a nodding acquaintance to many of the people who had come in … it wasn't worth it. 'Didn't it work?' I chided instead.

'On the contrary, had I done so, we would not be sitting here talking now.'

'You sound convinced.'

'I am. Since a young age, Rosita has been highly sexed.' He smiled as if he had intimate knowledge. 'Before you, I've had to get rid of quite a few undesirables who thought heaven lay between her legs.'

'So, what stopped you, in my case?' It was dripping in sarcasm and I was on the point of getting up and leaving. It would have been the smart tactic, but I wanted to hear the rest.

'When we met, I felt sorry for you. You were old. I knew it wouldn't last. The time would come when you would have a hard job getting it up, as they say in the movies. Rosita would find her creature comforts somewhere else. I could enjoy myself watching it play out. Sooner or later …'

'Seems as though I've defied the odds.'

This time he did get up to leave. 'We'll see,' he said. 'We'll see.' He eased me out in front of him. 'We now have a deal that binds us close together.' He was talking softly into my ear. 'Like when you are young and both take blood from your fingers.'

'Blood brothers?'

'That's it,' he sounded enthusiastic. 'Blood brothers.'

'I'd like that,' I said. And I would have, but not in the way he imagined.

CHAPTER EIGHTEEN
Porto – 2008

'You have lost quite a lot of blood.' The words are spoken in a soft female voice with the hint of a smile.

I keep my eyes closed. It somehow makes the pain more tolerable. I recognise the voice but I can't recall from where. It would mean opening my eyes, leaving behind those fluffy pillows and the scent of a childhood I thought I had long since forgotten. Those memories are so vivid, so real, so present. 'Let me sleep. I need to go back.'

'Afraid not,' comes the reply. 'Servicing the dreams of old men has definitely been crossed off my must-do list.'

My eyes blink open and I focus on the woman standing alongside the bed. My ribs hurt like hell, my chin feels twice its normal size and there is a dark, deep throbbing in my crotch. Despite my sorry state, I am feeling surprisingly well-disposed. If I had to open my eyes to focus on anybody, she would have been in the top five.

'So, it's true,' I say.

'What is?'

'You do have comfy slippers and a fleecy housecoat.'

'If I remember correctly, winceyette pyjamas were mentioned last time we met. Gonna have to disappoint you there.'

'I'll take one out of two. How did I get here, Brigitte?'

'All in good time. A doctor friend of mine checked you out. Serious bruising, a broken nose and a cracked rib. Nothing that careful convalescence and a quiet life won't cure. He confirmed that your hearing has returned; at least, in one ear.'

'Did he do some tests?'

'No. He asked you to lift your arm whilst you were semi-conscious and you told him to fuck off. No more proof was needed.'

I tried to smile back.

'When I last spoke with him, Hugo told me you were still deaf but learning to lip-read.'

Some semblance of reality is coming back to me, my reactions slowly returning to reasoned rather than instinctive. I take in my surroundings. The wallpaper is an aggressive floral pattern in dark reds and dirty North Sea blue, the blooms reaching upward as if struggling for air; the carpet, a thick shagpile in mottled greys. Only the ceiling is white, but overly decorated with a stuccoed series of pretentious cornices and a centrepiece that looks like a wreath, circling the most hideous ceiling light I have ever seen. It's the sort of bedroom in which you could imagine being kept prisoner. Stupidly, I involuntarily check to see if my hands or legs are bound.

'Interesting decor,' I say.

'Ghastly, isn't it?' She pulls the housecoat tight around her waist and sits on the edge of the bed. 'It was like this when we bought the place.'

I don't ask with which husband. It doesn't seem appropriate.

'At first, I thought I must change the decor immediately, but then I realised it was to be the guest bedroom, and as I didn't want guests staying and feeling comfortable enough to carry on staying – all that polite chatter, making meals, serving drinks, washing up; all that sort of domestic crap – the decoration began to grow on me. Now I love it because it's so awful.' She turns to look at me. 'We were talking about your hearing?'

'I only began to start making out sounds a few weeks ago. Something inside my head told me that some people tend, unreasonably, to relate physical disability to a degree of mental incompetence. I suppose if you have to shout at somebody to make yourself understood, you simplify the sentences, triggering something in your brain that questions their intelligence. Anyway, I decided as my hearing returned, I would carry on playing at being deaf until my memory of what happened came back to me. People talk, sometimes carelessly, if they think nobody is listening. I might learn something.'

'And have you?'

'I know that Walid and his violent friends know a lot more than they are prepared to admit. Which brings me back to what am I doing here? What is your connection to them? They were about to kill me.'

'I don't think so. They may be many things, but not murderers. You were probably in for a ride into the countryside, to be dropped off frightened, fearing for your life, with a warning to stay away from them.'

'How do you know all this?'

She reaches over and pulls my hand into hers. It isn't sexual; more what a mother might do to comfort a child. 'You were lucky. Youssef is the sensible one. He found my card as he was going through your wallet. I've got it, by the way.'

I remember. She had given her business card to me at the wedding.

'Rather sweet, really; keeping it, I mean. Did you actually consider taking advantage of my offer to visit?'

I feel embarrassed, a stupid and out-of-place reaction. All I end up doing is sounding pathetic. 'I don't get given many cards these days.'

She releases my hand. 'Youssef telephoned me. I sent Claudio to fetch you and bring you to Porto. You were in pain, almost unconscious. They gave you something' – she hesitates – 'shall we say, to challenge your senses. And here you are.'

'Why would they ring you? Are you something to do with them?'

She stalls again. 'Let's say they are clients of mine. They would not want to do anything that might offend me. Seeing my card in your wallet, I guess they thought it best to check it out with me.'

I try to sit up but the sharp pain in my chest forces me back onto the pillow and that scent again. Whatever they had given to knock me out, I needed some more. 'You mean you bankroll them? You finance drug dealers?'

She stands up, a forced expression of alarm on her face, her hands outstretched, telling me to stop. 'Whoa, boy! You are going way too fast. I lend money to people who can't get finance from regular sources. My concern is their ability to pay me back, not what they do with the money. I may suspect what my clients are up to, but I make it my business not to know too much. Youssef and his partners borrow from me big time, and they always repay on the dot. End of story.'

I remember Walid sweeping everything from the table into a drawer and, as I lay on the floor, my hand closing around the pill that must have fallen. I study my hand. The pill isn't there any more.

She is preparing to leave. 'Talking about repayments, it's Sunday, my busiest day of the week. I have to get going. Plenty to do.'

'You work on Sundays?'

There is the flicker of a smile. 'Most of my more reticent clients find reasons during the week not to see me, excuses to avoid my attentions. Sunday is a home day when family demands are too great to be gallivanting around.

It's the one day in the week when they feel obliged to talk to me.'

I nod. I had been on the receiving end of a few Sunday visits when running the bar in Spain. I had always paid up, but never to anybody who looked like Brigitte. 'What do you do, use your charm?'

'It seems to work. Claudio and two friends keep the door open whilst I do the talking. My clients find it an irresistible combination.' She laughs.

Twenty minutes later and I can understand exactly what she means. There is a deep male laugh in the hallway as a Sonny Liston lookalike puts his head around the door and leers at me. He must be over two metres tall with a hand as large as both of mine. 'I'm Claudio,' he says. 'We met last night.'

'I don't remember,' I say.

He says something in Portuguese as Brigitte eases into the bedroom, now dressed and sporting a black and white tweed coat with a fur collar.

'He said you probably don't remember trying to sing Roxanne either, but he does. That's why you spent two thirds of the journey in the trunk.'

'Remembering things seems to be my biggest problem at the moment.'

Brigitte's parting remarks play into just how I feel. I should take the opportunity to get some rest. As and when I fancy getting up, there are towels and shaving gear in the second bathroom and plenty of male outfits of all sizes in the wardrobe. I should be able to find something to wear to replace my suit which she has thrown away. There is food in the kitchen. Please feel free to help myself, but she will aim to be back by five with a Chinese takeaway for us. The run of the apartment is mine and I should make myself at home.

For a second, I panic. I need to be back in Cavalla to look after Francisco. Relax. Of course, it's the long holiday weekend. I'm not due back on duty until Tuesday evening.

Claudio is calling for her. They will be waiting in the car.

'You know, I think you have got two things mixed up,' she says, stroking the ends of the hairstyle that almost joins under her chin. 'You desperately want to remember what happened on the day Albert died. I understand that. But as far as both of your sons are concerned, there is a sixteen-year vacuum. It's as though you lost your memory of them during the entire period. Now you need to know how their lives evolved.'

There it is again, that sensation in my nose and throat, the stench of burning flesh, the searing pain and the vision of Vernon shouting at me, mouthing words I cannot hear because I'm deaf.

She has gone. The bedroom door closes slowly to the sound of a squeaky hinge.

* * *

I must have gone into a deep sleep because it's early afternoon before I awake. I'm sore everywhere, but the acute stabs of pain that racked my chest have eased. Staggering into the bathroom is an effort, but I relish a ten-minute shower of piercing, almost unbearably hot water and drying off with the feel of soft, Egyptian cotton towels wrapped around me. With the taste of Brigitte in my mouth as I use her toothbrush, I begin to feel well enough to realise whatever damage has been done, it has not affected my sexual drive. A shave from an ageing electric shaver with failing batteries, a splatter of what I hope is a flask of cologne and not air freshener, and I'm ready for the perfect quid pro quo for a serious beating: the prospect of spending an evening alone with Brigitte.

Dressed in a pair of beige chinos two sizes too small that compress at the waist as I force the button home, and the sort of short-sleeved floral shirt worn by drunkards on holiday on the Costas, I make scrambled eggs, strong coffee and three slices of heavily buttered toast, all arranged in front of me at an island breakfast unit in one of the most palatial kitchen-diners I have ever seen. The area of the kitchen comfortably exceeds my entire flat in Chepstow and is strictly in keeping with the remainder of the apartment.

Everything about the decor says money and a taste for modern styling, precise and functional, yet comfortable, all in muted colours. The expansive lounge boasts two seating areas; one, a set of three large sofas, arranged to form a square against a contemporary shelving unit housing a fitted television with surround sound and a home entertainment system. The smoked glass-topped coffee table, if you can call it that, is large enough to be accessible from any one of the sofas. Littered with magazines, books and a large iPad, a battered cardboard box has been placed in the centre, topped by a sheet of white A4 paper with large, scrawled writing in felt tip: 'You may find these enlightening'.

The second seating area is a study and library corner with two made-to-measure bookshelves, a small partner's desk with a laptop and hard-backed chair, all set off by three armchairs of different design and upholstery. One of the shelves is devoted to five black-framed photographs, all of Brigitte at varying ages, all with different men, standing stiffly alongside each other and posed outside official-looking buildings – except for one. In this black and white image, a much younger Brigitte is laughing as she tries to avoid the splashes from a fountain while the man in the shot points a camera towards her. A third person must be taking the picture. It looks so natural and spontaneous. Every photo has a small white label in the corner with a number from one to five on it and a date. This one says '1' and '1988'.

The lounge is brought to life by a set of curtains in a vivid Mexican design that frame the sliding glass doors leading onto the external balcony and a commanding view over the city. Today, the scene is shrouded in dark, fast-moving clouds that almost seem in touching distance of the penthouse apartment.

What particularly intrigues me are the paintings Brigitte has chosen, originals in violent colours of cartoon girls and women who all have one thing in common. They show surprise or distress, even one in resignation, at the moment of some unnatural discharge from their bodies: one, a series of smiling oranges, emerging from the open mouth of a girl with plaits; another, a monkey, breaking free from the shoulder of a deformed woman with smeared lipstick. As vivid as the colours are, the themes resonate a dark and sombre personality.

From the lounge there is a corridor which leads off to a dining room with a neglected feel about it. A left turn and I'm back in the bedroom area. Her room is large and sparsely furnished, dominated by two large curtainless picture windows with an exit to a small balcony and another view over the city, this time towards the university. I take some pointless satisfaction in noting that only one side of her double bed has been slept in, but a glance into the en suite bathroom leaves me literally with a bad taste in my mouth. The recently used toothbrush I employed with such relish could not have been hers. Brigitte's germs I would have enjoyed, but not those, I jealously countenance, of some male companion.

I nearly don't bother to open the door to the third bedroom, but my curiosity being what it is ... I'm taken totally by surprise. This is the private enclave of a young man, a teenager perhaps, with posters of landmark foreign films on the walls and the clutter of youth: trophies, memorabilia, textbooks on maths and chemistry and a wardrobe full of casual clothing. I vaguely recall she talked of not having children. Was this a family secret or would there be some harmless explanation?

I'm back in the lounge, rifling through the carton Brigitte left for me. There are two large photo albums and a series of packets, labelled and stuffed full of prints. I glance through the album pages in random fashion before pulling out one or two of the loose photos. As I go to follow suit with the fourth and last packet, the side of the envelope comes apart in my hands, the tightly packed prints now spread in ones and twos around the table.

I almost missed them. Most of the prints in the other packets are of Hugo as a teenager and as a college student, mainly on his own or with one or two male school friends, some with Brigitte and a number of end-of-term poses with his mother, Inés, and a man whom I assume to be his father. This last grouping shows Hugo in his late teens with Albert alongside, taken on different occasions but with various backdrops I recognise or assume to be in Brighton and the surrounding Sussex countryside. In two of the prints, hazy because of a shaking hand holding the camera and falling rain, they are huddling under an umbrella at an air show. I nearly fail to recognise the third person standing next to them. I never imagined Vernon knew Hugo at that time in their lives. Thinking about it, there is every reason why they should have met. After all, he was Albert's brother and Hugo was obviously a close friend. I suppose it was the offhand attitude and coldness between them at Albert's funeral that makes this revelation such a surprise.

Brigitte's parting words that morning are ringing in my ears. For the preservation of my sanity, I had created a sixteen-year vacuum as far as the boys were concerned. Their development as young men has never been permitted to cross my mind, never preyed on my conscience or sub-conscience. I have shut them away in a coffin marked 'gone forever', buried somewhere deep beyond my reach. But now, I contemplate their resurrection. I care desperately to know how they coped with my discarding them as vulnerable, impressionable teenagers and how their defence mechanism coped with being cast aside.

In their own way, the reactions were as radical as mine. Would Albert have become so committed as a Buddhist fanatic had I been there for them? Would Vernon's burning hatred, his aggressive and negative passions, have been as pronounced as they are today if I had tried to present a balanced view? I can't answer these questions. The photographs show three young men, seemingly happy and relaxed, just as they should be at that age. The smiles seem open and genuine, yet I find myself looking at them as if they are some kind of altricial species, cast off by their parents to fend for themselves. My life has become meaningless with no value in the eyes of others. Surely, there has to be a purpose.

With a heavy heart and time to spare, I set about closing my mind to all these negative thoughts and examining the entire collection of photographs in a more concise and ordered fashion. The call takes me by surprise. Had an hour passed? Brigitte will be back in five minutes and I am to switch on the oven.

By now, I have sifted through every single photo, separating a further four postcard-size prints of the three boys, this time on holiday, the first showing them in brief Speedo swimming trunks, toasting the photographer with cocktails as they stand framed by the beach and sea behind them; the remaining three with a date stamp some days later than the first, taken by each of them in turn and featuring the other two standing in front of a rustic beach bar with palm trees in the background. There is a distinct change in their reaction to the camera. In the two featuring Vernon, he looks decidedly upbeat, whereas his two friends have the downcast looks of serious hangovers. I put the selection featuring the boys to one side with a list of questions in my mind that I need to ask Brigitte.

The Citroën draws up outside the main entrance to the building as I'm standing on the balcony, easing the palms of my hands back and forth around my chest to dull the ache which is slowly returning. Dusk is almost turning to darkness as Claudio emerges from the car and opens the rear door. Two extremely well-built, olive-skinned gents exit from the front, deferentially bowing their heads as Brigitte steps from the rear door. Claudio merits a brief hug and receives a word in her ear as she glances up at the penthouse. I must have been spotted. I see her laugh as she moves out of sight, swinging the carrier bag playfully alongside her.

She likes her Chinese takeaway piping hot, so five minutes at 180°C gives just enough time to set the table and open a chilled red Pinot Noir. The food is transferred from plastic cartons into pre-heated fine china bowls, the dipping sauces into miniature ramekins.

'You like to pretend to eat well,' I say, expecting a caustic reply.

'Life's all pretence,' she says. 'Today we collected more than we managed throughout the whole week, by pretending.'

She's right. Beef in black bean sauce does taste different, piping hot, out of a fancy porcelain bowl. 'Pretending what?' My mouth is full.

'Pretending we might use force.'

'With two bodyguards and Claudio, you must have looked fairly dangerous. Scary, I'd say.'

'The question is, without them, would I have looked too harmless?'

'I take your point.'

'It's all a question of perception. Present the possibilities and let the imagination do the rest.' She lifts the wine glass to her mouth and toasts me.

'Is that what you did when you left me that box of photographs?' A shake of the head says time for all that later.

We are sitting facing each other on the sofas. She has kicked off her shoes, head resting on a cushion, knees bent, feet nestling under her velvet skirt. We are both nursing goblets of Remy VSOP between our hands.

'Somebody is coming to see you in the morning,' she says.

Right at that moment, I could not have cared a damn. It could be the Pope or the Devil's advocate. I am only interested in the here and now.

'Who?' It seemed the right thing to say.

'Somebody who might be able to help you make sense of all this.'

'Hugo?'

She shakes her head. 'Good Lord, no. Wait and see. In the meantime, you have some questions for me. Get the albums.'

I fetch the two volumes together with the loose photos I have sorted from the pile. She beckons me to keep them to hand.

'How are you feeling?' It's the first time she has mentioned my injuries since the morning.

'Believe me, my physical ailments have been eclipsed by the prospect of learning something new about my son.'

She looks over at me, waiting for a reaction to what she is about to say.

'My brother, Lino, thinks you are a pathetic idiot who has lost touch with reality.'

I frame an image of the arrogant bastard saying this. 'I could think of a few comments he might choose to savour in return.' I hesitate. It's not what she wants to hear. 'More important to me is, what do you think?'

'My view is that after all these years, you finally discover you have a conscience. How long is it again since you turned your back on your family?'

'Sixteen years.'

'Your remorse is not just for the loss of a single day when you were badly injured and your son died. The driving force which provoked you into that stupid attempt to mess with the Moroccans stems from the pain of neglect and the need to overcome the ignorance of not knowing what happened to the individuals you discarded throughout those missing years.'

I twist in my seat. There is something strangely arousing about her when her mood changes from flippant to serious. 'It doesn't sound like you talking.'

'It isn't,' she retorts. 'But we'll come to that tomorrow morning. It's important for you to know the truth, isn't it?' She doesn't wait for my acknowledgement. 'Let me try and fill in a few of the blanks for you.'

'That's why you left the photos out for me?'

She nods. 'What did they tell you?'

'Beyond the fact that my sons were friends with Hugo in their teens and holidayed together?'

She waits and I shrug. 'Nothing,' I add.

She clamps her arms around her legs and pulls them even closer, as if seeking protection. 'Let's start with Hugo,' she says.

Brigitte had been nearly thirty when she had met and married husband number one. He wasn't her first choice. An operation in her mid-twenties to remove a cyst had revealed she could not have children, and one or two intended partners had baulked at the news with lame and insincere excuses. And then Jacques came along. A society photographer with all the airs and graces, he genuinely did not care about the lack of an offspring, revelling in not only the charm and wit that Brigitte brought into his life, but the depth of love she had developed for him. They purchased the apartment she now lives in, spending those early years, the happiest of her life, enjoying the fruits of both his freelance work and her career as a highly-rated loan assessment officer in a national bank.

'Is that the reason for all the photographs around that time?' I ask.

She smiles at the memory. 'He was insatiable,' she says. 'He never stopped taking pictures, always with the latest model of camera available. He must have had twenty of the damn things.'

And then Hugo came to live with them. There had been a desperate argument with his parents.

'What about?' I ask.

She ignores the question, insisting that I turn to page six in one of the albums. 'Do you recognise the people?' she presses.

The photograph was of a christening outside a church. Everybody looked stiff and posed. Inés, holding the baby; Hugo in his mid-teens, standing to attention; and Jasmin, pale and distracted, sitting in a wheelchair, covered in a blanket. She was recovering from an appendectomy and had developed complications.

'You won't recognise the two men standing alongside Inés,' she says. 'My sister's husband and his twin brother, both dead. The stone-faced one looking straight ahead is Estevão, Inés's husband. Next to him is Vicente. Their parents are still alive. They were at Jasmin's wedding. I saw your *ex-wife* talking to them.' She waits for my reaction.

I ignore the invitation. 'Twins. Close, were they?'

'I was much younger, but from what I remember, as boys they were inseparable. As they reached manhood, Estevão ruled and Vicente followed.'

'The baby?'

She exhales. 'A boy. Martin. The birth went wrong. The cord was trapped around his neck. Lack of oxygen to the brain. He lived for three months. Better if he had died at birth. Inés took it badly. So did ...' She appears to be weighing her words. 'The pregnancy took us all by surprise, so many years after Jasmin. I'm sure it was the last thing she expected, or planned. But, in the end, she must have really wanted the baby. She had an amniocentesis at six months and decided to go and stay with relatives in Spain until the birth. Jasmin went with her.

'I appreciate the background information.' I'm impatient to get on and talk about Albert.

'It's not background. It's all relevant if you ever get to understand anything about the family to which your son became attached.' She holds out her brandy glass. 'Get me another, will you?'

'Don't think I'm prying, please, but my impression from the wedding was that you're not very close to your sister?' I pour a measure large enough to keep her talking.

She nods and settles back onto the sofa, the refilled glass nestling in the space between her legs.

'As soon as Inés went to Spain. Hugo came to live with me. He didn't get on with his father and refused to go back.'

Hugo's decision had been divisive, setting sister against sister, a rift which had never really healed, yet provided Brigitte and her husband with the one thing they would never otherwise have enjoyed: the presence of a child, albeit a demanding teenager, in their home.

In the weeks following his arrival, Inés would be on the phone from Spain every day, sometimes two or three times, either pleading with the boy or screaming at her sister, demanding his return home. Brigitte did everything possible to shield Hugo from the emotional turmoil, but even she could not temper the news, coming shortly after the christening, that his father, Estevão, had committed suicide. It was a particularly messy death that was reported all over the local and national press. The man had taken a strong sedative at the family's smallholding before slitting his wrists with the survival blade he used to slice the chickens' necks from their bodies.

From one day to the next, the gregarious and outward-going schoolboy had turned into a quiet, pensive and morose introvert. In the wake of the tragedy, the bond between aunt and nephew grew stronger, satisfying a mutual need that had remained, she claimed, to this day.

'And your husband's relationship with Hugo?'

'Jacques,' she says reflectively. 'Jacques. Yes. Open the other album, will you, pages ten to twelve?'

The three pages are covered with photos of the three of them on holiday in the countryside. If ever there were examples of a happy and complete family at play, these images are it.

'I loved Jacques,' she says, 'not only for the way he loved me, but for the care and concern he took over his relationship with Hugo. We were both prone to spoil the boy, but, from Jacques' side, there was discipline as well, but always with a reasoned explanation and never in anger. Hugo worshipped the ground he walked on and I felt very much that way too.'

I'm waiting for the punchline. After all, the marriage had ended.

'Those photos were taken in Normandy the year after Hugo came to live with us. The holiday lasted four days. We were booked for seven.' Further explanation needs to be preceded by a heavy draught of brandy. Her dimple cheeks have reddened but I doubt it's the alcohol.

'I used to try and keep myself fit in those days, a morning run, an hour or two in the gym. I left Jacques breakfasting in the country hotel at which we were staying. Hugo was at the age where getting up before eleven in the morning constituted sleep deprivaty. I found a fifteen-kilometre route that would take me the best part of two hours. A quick shower, and then we would all meet up for lunch to plan the afternoon.

'On this particular morning, I had not even run five kilometres before I twisted my ankle quite badly in a newly ploughed field. I staggered back to the hotel. I knew Jacques would be out walking, so I went straight to Hugo's room for help in removing the trainer from my swollen foot. They were in bed together, Jacques on the point of climaxing as I entered the room.'

'Jesus,' I exclaim. 'I wasn't expecting that.'

'It turns out I had married a paedophile. The worst thing about it was that most of his close friends knew except me. Apparently, he had started grooming Hugo not long after his arrival and the sex had been going on for five months. It was an acrimonious divorce. I reported him to the police, but the cunning bastard had waited until Hugo's sixteenth birthday before the sexual activity started. There was no question of rape. Hugo was a more than willing participant.'

'How did Hugo react to all of this?'

Brigitte was pleasantly surprised and relieved the boy appeared to take everything in his stride. From the day Jacques exited their lives, his name was never mentioned by either of them. Hugo's schooling had graduated from *Ensino básico* to *Secundária*, the intention being he would specialise in maths and chemistry until he was eighteen, when he could begin a degree course at university.

It's getting late and the aches and pains have worsened as tiredness begins to take hold of me, but I'm too intrigued at just where her story is going to call a halt. 'His experience with Jacques left no lasting scars?'

Her brow creases as she cocks her head sideways, as if deciding whether to continue. She takes a decision. 'I don't know whether Hugo had homosexual tendencies before Jacques got to him, but since he started to cultivate relationships, they have always been with males. As he got older, he would go to gay clubs and bring home friends for the night. I lost him just before his seventeenth birthday, but I am sure his sexual preferences have never changed.'

'What do you mean "lost him"?'

I should have guessed Lino would have something to do with it. The would-be patriarch of the family decided it was time for the breach between Hugo and his mother to be repaired. Rather than start a degree course, Hugo's uncle convinced him to join the commercial arm of SantaCavalla with a bursary to cover the cost of a four-year pharmacology degree course in Brighton. They literally packed him off shortly after he returned to Cavalla. The third of the four years was a placement year which Hugo would spend with the company in Cavalla. Brigitte reacted angrily, but in her heart of hearts she knew it was the right decision. Inés had the moral right of any mother to strive for a relationship with her own son and her gain was Brigitte's loss. But that was little consolation to the woman who came to love him as her own flesh and blood, especially in the light of all that happened.

'By all that happened, are you referring to Jacques?'

She shakes her head and yawns. She has said enough but I press on. 'A final nightcap?' I urge.

Another shake of the head. I can tell she is not used to drinking as much as we have. She is straining to keep her eyes open. 'I think I told you once about the dangers of the family pack instinct and their intimate secrets. There are things I know, other things I suspect that will go to the grave with me: promises I have made to Hugo that I will never break. I think it's time ...'

Time to change the subject, I think, otherwise the night is over. 'It was in Brighton that Hugo met up with Albert and Vernon?'

'I don't know anything about Vernon, other than they all went on a beach holiday one summer. I only met him once when they all stayed here just before they left, and I can't say I really took to him. He was nothing like the other two.'

I pick up the photographs I put aside earlier just as the penny drops. It's so obvious from the Brighton set, I'm surprised I hadn't noticed. 'Albert was gay?' I must have made it sound as though he came from Mars.

'You didn't know?'

'I had no idea; the wedding and all that.'

'I got to know Albert quite well. Hugo never went back to finish the degree course after the year in Cavalla. Again, Lino's doing. Eventually, Albert followed Hugo back here, and from time to time they would come to Porto for the weekend and stay with me. I've always kept Hugo's room for him. They were very close.'

'But the wedding?'

'These are questions for Jasmin, not for me. The only thing I will say is I believe Albert had a real struggle with his sexuality. Once, when Hugo and he had a lovers' tiff and split up, I heard Albert was seeing a local girl, someone called Adele.'

'I'm more confused than ever.'

'Help me up,' she says. 'It's time for our beds.'

The plural context isn't lost on me. She doesn't have to worry. If anybody touched me, I would scream in pain.

She gestures for me to help her stand. 'I don't want to offend your ex-wife, Gil, but having met and talked with her, I would have to say Albert's confusion was down to the fierce hostility she has towards homosexuality and lesbianism. He said his mother considers any non-heterosexual relationship as a mortal sin, borne of her family's strict Evangelical Christian roots in the Caribbean of which she is so proud. I think she would have been devastated to learn and unable to accept her son was gay, and, in his turn, Albert fought against his natural impulses to try and be the heterosexual son she took as given.'

I pull her to her feet and we walk hand in hand towards the bedrooms. At her door, she stops, planting the softest of kisses on my lips. 'Goodnight, Gil. I have to tell you that tonight has been a very cathartic experience for me. Thank you for your understanding.'

Sleep does not come, even after two painkillers and a litre of mineral water. Maybe I have more answers, but now there are a whole lot of new questions to go with them.

CHAPTER NINETEEN
Porto – 2008

The man looks up as I walk into the kitchen the next morning, following the aroma of freshly ground coffee, the liquid gurgling in the percolator as it completes the cycle. I expect to see Brigitte in that functional housecoat she likes to wear and bemoan our mutual hangovers, but she is nowhere to be seen. I take the mug of steaming liquid from the outstretched hand and watch his calculating gaze as he follows my movements.

'Brigitte thought you might need this,' he says in heavily accented English. 'Personally, I prefer a large glass of fizzy lemon and lime and a healthy portion of Eggs Benedict. Sees me right every time, although the Puerto Ricans suggest the foolproof remedy is to rub a slice of lemon under your drinking arm.'

'Sounds painful,' I say, easing myself into the high-backed stool across the tiled breakfast bar to face him.

As far as the ordeal with the Moroccans was concerned, I am moving a hundred times better than the previous day, but my head feels as if it's splitting in two. Before last night, I could honestly say I was the next best thing to a teetotaller, but the cognac I haven't touched in years, coupled with a lack of sleep as so many issues toss around in my mind, has left me in bits.

The Pedro Borodin who accompanied Lannier to question me at the hospital gave an impression of somebody limp and uncomfortable in his surroundings, like a cat soaked in a thunderstorm. He said very little on that occasion, appearing to rely on the female translator for an understanding of my replies, and obviously intended to mislead me. The man who faces me now is a far more confident and self-possessed individual.

I'm not going to let it pass without a comment. 'Your English has obviously come on a treat in the last few months,' I say, the sarcasm unmissable.

'Just like your hearing,' he retorts, picking at the crocodile emblem on his polo. In that expensive shirt and check sports jacket he could have been one of Roger's cronies from the golf club, except for the matted, unwashed hair and the uneven stubble around his weak-looking jaw, a lack of attention with a dull razor that gives him a slightly vagrant appearance – a tramp who has found somebody else's clothes.

'That was no pretence.'

'I know,' he assures me. 'However, Brigitte tells me you decided to perpetuate the condition?'

'I thought it might help, suggest frailty where there isn't any.'

'Not a bad idea. Has it worked?'

'No. I got a beating and a night in Brigitte's guest bedroom without anybody showing pity for my condition.'

He laughs. His teeth are stained from nicotine.

'Who the hell are you and what do you want with me?' I intended the ferocity of the question would unsettle him, but he seems to find it amusing.

'You know who I am. The name is Pedro Borodin, born and bred in Mozambique, and I am attached to the Portuguese Ministério Público service in a consultative capacity. By profession, I am a forensic psychologist. You have heard of that?'

'Only in the movies. You profile serial killers?'

'Nothing so glamorous, I regret. Most of my work is spent within the police force, dealing with behavioural problems that influence serving officers when handling serious crime.'

'What was, or is, your interest in me?'

'At the time, we were concerned that your memory and hearing loss might be faked in order to hide some degree of culpability in what happened to your son.'

'So, you gave me the all clear?'

'As far as your impairments are concerned, they were genuine enough. With regard to your involvement in the tragic incident, how do you say, the jury is still out.'

'Is that why this meeting has been set up?'

He shook his head. 'Not directly. Senhora Cousteau is well known to us. We have a number of mutual interests in certain sections of her clientele. She told us you were staying here and the circumstances of your arrival. We felt it useful if I came and had an informal conversation with you.'

I laugh. 'And that is what this is?' I hold out my empty mug. 'Do me a favour, will you?' He reaches for the percolator. It stretches to half a cup. 'Is

Brigitte around?'

He puts the percolator to one side. 'She apologises, but she had to go out on business. She promises to return and arrange for a car to take you back to Cavalla this afternoon. It is a holiday to recall Portugal's independence. People will go Christmas shopping to celebrate.' He shakes his head in apparent dismay.

'You don't like shopping?'

'Today is for pageant and reflection, not an excuse.'

'For what?'

'Shopping. Go down to ViaCatarina and see for yourself.'

'And the point of this conversation?'

He takes a few seconds before replying. 'Yes, this afternoon. Lots of traffic on the road. Leave yourself plenty of time.'

He has started to amuse me. 'I've had the history morality lesson and the traffic update. What's next?'

'Have you ever heard of a Senhora Fernanda Santos?'

I shake my head.

'She died instead of you. You should honour her memory.'

'What are you talking about?'

'Do you know what this is?' He holds out in the palm of his hand a small triangular white pill.

I flinch involuntarily, recalling the stab of pain in my chest. I had grasped that pill in my hand as I lay on the floor of the warehouse.

'I'm guessing it's not aspirin.'

'No,' he says. 'It's what you call in English a recreational drug, primarily an amphetamine, but it has one very unusual and frightening component. Have you heard of carfentanil or W18?'

Again, I shake my head. He is taking me into an area I know absolutely nothing about. A few spliffs at parties over the years, but drugs have never been my scene. If I had wanted a release from the daily grind, I would look no further than alcohol. He was continuing to speak – a synthetic opiate ten thousand times more potent than heroin had reappeared on the market around two years earlier and was already responsible for thousands of deaths.

'I'm no expert,' he says, 'but apparently it is a more potent form of fentanyl, the painkiller on which the artist Prince overdosed. There are minute traces in this pill you picked up. The problem is the opioid is tasteless and colourless and very difficult to detect, simply because there are no established tests to target the drug.'

'There's your answer, then. Pick up Walid and his mates and you'll solve your problem. He was messing with thousands of the things.'

'Narcotics have had the three men under surveillance for some time. That's how we know they had no direct involvement in the gas explosion at your son's house. We need to know where the supply is coming from. When we find out, they will be arrested.'

'Why not interrogate them? Make them tell you.'

His smile offends me, suggesting I am being naïve. 'We would achieve nothing other than to alert the source to our presence. They are more afraid of whoever is their contact than they are of the police, and would never talk. As it is, the supply has temporarily dried up.' He looks as though he's weighing something up in his mind. 'I am taking a risk even telling you.'

'Then why are you?'

'Shall we have some more coffee?' He seems to know his way around the kitchen which I find annoying. Did she have a thing for him? I can't see it. This one is no catch. In five minutes, both our mugs have been refilled.

Apparently, my foolish bravado in getting mixed up with the Moroccans was unhelpful in pursuing their investigation. The cursory interrogation of the men in Lannier's case file was also explained, as he had to be warned off as well.

'Your problem is the reason for me being here this morning.'

'My problem?' I query.

'It looks as though somebody wants you dead.' He must sense my confusion. 'Let me give you a possible scenario of what I consider is worth following up. I have to say in advance that my superiors are highly sceptical of my theory and are more inclined to believe you are somehow implicated in the explosion; that you simply did not manage to escape in time.'

'Until I heard about Walid and company being around the house, I never assumed it was anything other than a terrible accident.'

'Wrong. The forensics report clearly reveals that the gas fittings around the boiler had recently been tampered with. Just hear me out.' He checks his watch. It's either a genuine Rolex or the Somalian who sold me the phoney must have really put himself about.

'Let's assume you were supposed to die in that explosion.'

'That's preposterous.'

'Hear me out!'

'Calm down. I'm sorry.'

'Somehow, you survived and Albert died in your place. You are in hospital in an induced coma with whoever wanted you dead uncertain as to whether you would recover and, if you did, what state you would be in. Their best course of action is to try and ensure that you never wake up, so they manage to get into the hospital and leave your next saline drip available, expecting when it is changed you will die from the dose of carfentanil that has been mixed with the solution, enough to put an elephant to sleep; certainly, ten times that which would be needed to kill a human.'

I hold my hand up, like a schoolboy in class. 'Sorry to interrupt, but one of the things I do have a hazy recollection of is someone trying to change the drip in the middle of the night and, for some reason, I must have thought it was odd and taken it off.'

'Supports my theory, doesn't it?'

'And the lethal drip bag?' I know what is coming.

'You recover consciousness, are taken off the saline and the contaminated bag is replaced into stock. A day or so later, Senhora Fernanda Santos arrives for a routine varicose vein operation, needs rehydration and dies within seconds of receiving the drip. Until last week, nobody had even made the connection between the saline bag and her death, which was attributed to heart failure following surgical complications. As I talk to you, there are a dozen technicians checking stocks and manufacturing procedures at the supplier in Aachen and another team going through the hospital's personnel records to find somebody with a grudge, but my guess is it all centres around you.'

I am visibly sweating, rivulets running down my forehead. I can taste the salt in my mouth.

'Are you okay?'

'At the house, I remember a laugh. I think it was my son's.'

'Albert?'

'No. Vernon.'

He takes the mobile out of his inside pocket and begins to tap laboriously with one finger on the keyboard. 'I promised myself this morning I would avoid giving you an appraisal into the workings of the memory. My insights tend to turn into lectures and, however enthralling I might find the topic, some of my students have been known to yawn. I have made a note to send you a few links to websites you might find helpful. Please study them. We really do need you to start remembering what happened. Try to concentrate on the laugh and see what follows.'

My mouth must have fallen open at the sheer insensitivity of interrupting such a chilling analysis with this off-the-cuff distraction.

'Somebody is trying to kill me and you want me to start doing some fact finding on the internet?'

'It's a theory, no more. Don't become obsessed. And remember, you have lost your memory. You may well have met and spoken to the individual or individuals who would have you dead and shown absolutely no trace of recognition or realisation. For the time being, you are no threat.'

'For the time being? It's like a time bomb.' My mind is racing.

His smile is probably meant to reassure me.

'I'm really coming to the crux of why I am here this morning. To be blunt, we need your cooperation.'

He had put me on my guard. 'To do what?'

'We still have doubts as to whether you are an accomplice somebody wants out of the way or a genuine victim. Surely you want to help eliminate our concerns?'

'Not if the price is to end up dead.'

'They have missed their golden opportunity. The contaminated drip was the perfect crime. Nobody would have questioned the circumstances had you succumbed to your injuries. Whatever happens, they have to make it look like an accident. That is not easy.'

'Thanks for those comforting words. So, what are you proposing?'

There is that smile again. 'We think it is a good idea if you go on pretending to be deaf. I understand you have developed some lip-reading skills, and the apparent weakness will give your aggressors confidence. What you now need to do is start letting people know you are having flashbacks, isolated images of events on the day of the explosion.'

'Are you stark raving mad? I don't remember, but I have to pretend that I do so that somebody can try and kill me? No way.'

'You will have people, specially trained, from the force here in Porto, to watch your back 24/7. We will not let you come to any harm.'

I give him one of my sneered laughs. 'Very good. Sorry I won't be around to hear their apology for having fucked up the assignment.'

'The risk is minimal.'

'For you, maybe.'

'Your son is dead. Don't you want to help to bring those responsible to justice? Don't you owe him that much?'

'Quite frankly, I don't know what I owe him. I am learning that my son was living a lie, prepared to suppress his sexuality simply to keep his mother happy, if Brigitte's viewpoint is correct.' I need to think everything through.

Borodin is at the door, his contact details tucked safely into my wallet. 'Don't take too long. Somebody may be impatient and sense an opportunity. That would be most unfortunate.'

'Perhaps you are wrong about the whole thing. It could still be just a tragic accident.'

He raises his eyebrows. 'Not even you think like that any more, Mr Hart.'

It's as though the whole visit has been stage-managed. He was not out of the door more than two minutes before Brigitte walks in. She is in a woollen trouser suit, the jacket tailored tight to her waist partially covering a frilly white blouse with a black bolo tie and clasp. She flings her crocodile skin handbag onto the counter and kicks one of her black suede shoes with the ridiculously high heels across the floor. Everything about her looks vital, not a trace of last night's excesses in her eyes. 'Thank God for that. Meetings with new clients; always have to dress to impress. How did you get on?'

'Didn't he tell you?' I must have sounded sullen. I am jealous. They are conspirators.

'I saw his car drive off. Just as well, I find him very difficult to talk to. Everything okay?'

I nod. I was sworn to silence. 'I agree. He likes the sound of his own voice.'

She is upbeat. There was time before Claudio came to drive me back to Cavalla for a snack meal and a glass of something bubbly. Doesn't that sound inviting?

I can't help myself. I couldn't care less about the food. I'm intoxicated, not with the wine but with the woman who is pouring it into the two flutes.

Did I have any more thoughts about our conversation? Did I? A hundred questions had filled my mind last night. Today's conversation has dampened my curiosity, a starker perspective has changed my mood, but I still need answers.

Even if I went along with Albert's motives for marrying, what on earth were Jasmin's? Did she think she could influence his sexuality? What did Hugo think of this apparent change of heart? Was Albert really Francisco's father? How did Adele fit into his life?

Brigitte insists I stop. These are things she cannot tell me. The answers are in Cavalla, with people from whom she is disconnected. I must look there.

She puts the photos of the boys into a starched white envelope along with Martin's christening photograph showing Jasmin's parents and uncle Vicente.

'I'm guessing that you will need to borrow these,' she says. 'Please make sure that I get them back.'

We stand by the front door. Claudio is waiting for me outside. There is an uneasy silence whilst neither of us seem to know what the right thing is to say. I sense that last night's experience has somehow breached the defences she normally finds so easy to erect. Borodin said something to me about memory being a question of opening closed doors and reacting to the new light. As much as I have to deal with new facts, she has revealed details of her life that were a closed book. Does she feel vulnerable now I know?

She plants a kiss on my lips I desperately want to return a hundredfold, but I know it would be to misinterpret her intentions. It's the sort of kiss you give somebody close to you when you are saying goodbye.

'Do you remember at the wedding I likened my family to a pack of hyenas?' Her hands are pressed gently around my shoulders, holding me out at arm's length.

I nod, feeling the warmth on my shoulder blades.

'I read an article about a backpacker in Australia who was circled and attacked by a pack of hyenas. He was badly injured but had one striking memory of his ordeal. For a time the pack circled him, watching him and waiting, assessing his potential as an enemy. After a while two broke loose and began to move closer, each approaching him from a different direction. He said that just before they attacked, they seemed to be smiling at him, and he could not get the image out of his mind.'

'What saved him?'

'Divine intervention. There was an electric storm at the time. Lightning struck the tree next to him and they ran off. He managed to save himself.'

'And the moral of the story?'

She ushers me towards the front door. 'I don't think I need say any more.'

CHAPTER TWENTY
Sanlazer – 1996

'Tell me another story,' Miguel whined, tugging at his grandfather's shorts.

'Leave your grandfather alone,' Eliana said with that docile smile of hers. 'He's tired.'

Miguel and his younger sister apart, everybody in the house had that spent look I used to get after watching a marathon on the television, exhausted for no good reason. Nobody had done anything, but there was a lethargy about the place which emanated from TM and felt infectious.

According to Rosita, this was the first summer TM had failed to pre-order the new Real Madrid strip ready for the season, so disenchanted was he with the team. After finishing a lowly sixth in the league, their worst finish for nineteen years, and, as he constantly reiterated, not only sixth, but sixth behind arch-rival title holders, Atletico Madrid; plus the sacking of their coach, Arsenio, a month earlier, a consequence of having been unceremoniously dumped out of Europe in the quarter finals by Italy's Juventus. To add insult to injury, just look whom they had appointed as the new manager. A bloody Italian, some guy called Fabio Capello.

TM was inconsolable and his mood percolated throughout the household. Romina's conversation was obsessed with infections in hospitals and she would complain tirelessly at her domestic workload now her mother was too ill to travel with them, though it seemed to me she had again mastered the art of looking constantly busy but actually leaving all the chores to the other women in the house. That excluded Isabel, who spent most of every day alone by the pool, ignoring everybody, or locked in her bedroom.

Isabel was an enigma whom I just could not fathom. Now nearly twenty, she had lost that sexually-aware-but-not-quite-sure-how-to-handle-it schoolgirl look. Her taste in clothes had become conventional, drab almost, matching her rather downbeat approach to life. As far as men were concerned, apart from her father and Salvador, who merited the occasional forced smile, she was at best curt, or otherwise just plain rude. As far as her reaction to me was concerned, nothing had changed, but muscular young Robi, the gardener and pool man, who fancied himself as a lady's man and was obviously possessed by the voluptuous figure in the bikini, found her constant put-downs deeply offensive to his fragile ego.

I had the feeling Gonzalo might also have tried it on once and received a similar brush-off. He was supposed to have already left on holiday to visit his family, but when challenged, he pompously announced he had some vital administrative tasks to complete with Rosita before he could leave. I was fast reaching the conclusion Gonzalo had served his purpose and was increasingly doing less and less. I intended to tell him his idea of a partnership had just been dissolved and he should not bother coming back. I had met a number of guys on my travels whom I rated as being able to do a better job. It was time for a change. His initial willingness to follow my lead had been replaced by the annoying habit of challenging my decisions as a matter of course, whether he really agreed or not. When rebuffed, he would sulk around the office, making excuses as to why he had to remain in Sanlazer rather than get out on the road to visit prospective clients.

On this particular evening, I had just returned from one of the sites we were working on in Cadiz. As I walked into the villa, the only sounds were of Miguel teasing his sister, who was now in tears, followed by Eliana's weary pleas for him to stop. She looked up and gave me that 'it's all right for you; just look at what I have to put up with' face. She was pregnant again, only just, a slight bump which she would playfully exaggerate for the children's amusement by drawing comparisons with Rosita's distended stomach. Her sharp features had tended to blancmange with the weight gain she complained about but her mood was mainly laidback, apparently unconcerned, unless it came to dealing with the kids and, strangely, I thought, with Isabel. I noticed they would spend long periods in her bedroom, talking in whispered voices. I had also taken to discreetly studying Eliana to establish if she was complicit in her husband's extortion ploy, but if she did know what was going on, she was clever enough to hide it from me. I was keeping an open mind.

I dodged around the warring children, made some small talk with my downbeat housemates and entered the kitchen, only to be promptly shushed away with a hastily blown kiss by a harassed-looking Rosita. I decided to retreat to a bar for a beer before dinner and the opportunity to listen to the sound of some genuinely happy holidaymakers.

Our local on the corner I discounted. There was no air conditioning and the regulars were no more enticing company than the folk at home. I opted for the bar in the Tropisol, two blocks behind the front-line five-star luxury hotels which charged prices in line with London and Paris. The Tropisol knew its place, an all-inclusive three star that was always full and where I knew the barmaid well enough to guarantee happy hour prices whatever the time of day.

The large bar had been designed to front the restaurant and the place was crowded with a mix of pre-dinner drinkers and a melee of anxious guests playing nervously with the plastic identification strips around their wrists as they waited for the doors to open, so they could pretend not to be rushing to their seats for first pick at the evening's buffet. The cacophony of so many different languages in such a confined space meant the Georgian barmaid had to lean over the bar, adjusting a breast with one hand as she did so. She knew exactly what she was doing and I appreciated the compliment. I gave her my order. Should she get the waiter to take it over to where my brother was sitting? I looked over to where she was pointing and shook my head. I was just fine.

The two of them were side-on to me, facing the pool exit. The conversation was animated, Gonzalo gesticulating, pointing his finger angrily in the air as he leaned towards Salvador who grabbed his hand and forced it down onto the table. Salvador leaned forward to whisper in his ear in what seemed an attempt to calm the atmosphere. He moved back, releasing his grip as he did so. Gonzalo appeared to have reacted positively to what he had said.

It was then that my hackles rose. Salvador glanced behind to check that nobody close by was paying attention, before reaching into the bum bag he carried around his waist. He took out the brown padded envelope with the logo of our solar panel supplier. It was the envelope I had used to pack the fifteen thousand euros I had grudgingly handed over. A lot thinner than when he had counted it out in front of me, the envelope and its contents were now in Gonzalo's pocket. I had no time to study the result but I hoped the image on my mobile had captured the moment.

The whole sorry business began to fall into place. Salvador had not stumbled by accident into Sikorsky and his cargo of bent gear. How had he come to be on patrol on his own? The traffic police always worked in twos or threes. Gonzalo had tipped him off. He knew exactly at what time Sikorsky was supposed to arrive and the route he would take. Salvador was simply waiting for the bait to take the hook.

I watched as they finished up their conversation, each leaving by a separate exit.

My first reaction was to follow Gonzalo to confront him, to give the traitorous bastard a good hiding. Common sense prevailed. Whatever Salvador did with the money was up to him now and I was getting rid of Gonzalo anyway. Sacking him would be the highlight of my week.

I was lying in bed, unable to sleep, listening to Rosita snoring gently. There was something still troubling me. Why had Gonzalo done it? What was his share of the money; maybe five thousand, tops? Gonzalo's family were moderately wealthy. Surely he didn't need the money, and anyway, the bonus due out of Gilrosa's profits for the year was likely to be double what Salvador had handed over. He knew he could always ask Rosita for an advance if he had money worries. She would see him right even if I did protest after the event.

It was their conversation in the bar that concerned me as well. The only reason I could conceive to explain Gonzalo's anger was he expected more money than Salvador had given him. Surely they had to have agreed on the amount of the shakedown and the respective shares in advance of the event? What other explanation could there be?

One thing I had learned over the years was to avoid knee-jerk reactions, not to let emotions prompt me into hasty decisions I would later regret; take what people said or did on the chin, metaphorically count to ten and make a calculated response. Gonzalo would have to go, but as Rosita had once warned me, he knew too much about the operation and his spiteful retaliation could finish us. One way or the other, I would have to broach the matter with Rosita in as subtle a way as possible. I needed her guidance. She probably knew Gonzalo better than anyone.

I turned to look at her sleeping figure. She didn't need to have a care in the world. Fortunately for me, she never went to check on our cash fund I had used to pay off Salvador. She had the capacity to put anything shady or illegal we had done out of her mind, as if it had never happened, and to rely on me to provide whatever support was necessary when the time came.

Just to be on the safe side, I had covered my backside as far as the missing cash was concerned by an oblique reference to a holding deposit I had paid to one of the developers we knew, who was building a residential condominium near Cordoba. I said he had a nice plot and we had nothing to lose. If we backed out, we would get our money back. I knew she didn't want to live that far away and had been asking estate agents in Huelva about properties in the area, but the white lie would serve until I could somehow replace the money.

The following day, we had just finished the one ritual that TM always insisted upon, sitting down to the nightly family dinner which you missed at your peril, when Eliana made her announcement.

Next week would be the last week of July and the Fiesta da Velá de Santa Ana – the Festival of Santa Ana – in the Triana district of Seville. This local celebration was the religious highlight of the month, four days of people taking to the streets to visit the stalls and fairground activities, watching the processions and the famous *cucaña* or greasy pole competition. Hotel rooms had been booked for the night so we could all watch the young men on a river barge as they tried to walk the greasy pole and retrieve the flag tied to the end. Most would fall into the river, a spectacle which she was certain we and the children would enjoy. Salvador would drive us to Seville earlier in the day and rejoin us when his shift had finished.

Eliana saw me look hesitantly at Rosita, who shook her head. 'Rosita is, of course, too far gone to venture to Seville,' Eliana announced. 'Isabel and I will be staying behind with Rosita just in case the baby comes earlier than expected. I'll be honest, it's a chance to get you all out of the house and spend a couple of girlie days together and a little peace and quiet. You don't mind helping out with the kids, do you, Gilbert? After all, it will give you a little practice for the future.'

What could I say? It had been discussed, decided, done and dusted long before I had time to protest my heavy workload. I gave in with good grace but not without a look of amused reprimand in Rosita's direction for her apparent participation in the conspiracy.

The villa was in darkness as I sat in the lounge nursing a chilled can of San Miguel between my thighs. Salvador was working nights and the rest of the family had long since gone to bed. Apart from the constant hum of the air conditioning units from TM's bedroom and the family room where Eliana was with the kids, the air was still, heavy with the honey-vanilla scent from the weaver's broom growing around the perimeter of the common areas. Without the customary sea breeze, the heat was oppressive, way into the thirties, and I was stripped down to nothing but a pair of boxer-style swimming trunks.

'Get me a glass of wine, will you?' Eliana had suddenly appeared at the bottom of the stairs. 'She would not go to sleep tonight, restless and whimpering, I thought she would wake up Miguel.'

Coming from Eliana, the request for alcohol was surprising. She rarely drank, sipping from a small glass which usually remained partially full at the end of the meal. Tonight, following her announcement, she had managed two large glasses of a second rate Zalema and was now asking for more.

I handed her the glass and retook my seat. She was dressed in a creamy, synthetic silk dressing gown, belted tight around her waist. 'God, I hate kids,' she said, sitting on the floor, her back resting against the leg of my armchair. 'I don't mean that.' She took a large draught from the glass. 'What I really hate is their ceaseless energy-sapping demands that leave you screaming for release at the end of the day.'

'I have all that to come.' The way she was sitting had loosened the gap around the neck of the dressing gown. She had nothing on underneath, revealing the bikini strap lines traced in her lightly tanned skin.

'Rosita's young, full of vitality. You will be able to sit back and watch.'

'That was a very generous gesture you made tonight. Have you won El Gordo or something?'

She cocked her arm up to rest across my knee, half looking towards me. 'I won't pretend that the last few years have been anything but really difficult. I had to give up my job – it was well paid – after the kids came. Sal didn't get the promotion he expected. We had to keep asking TM for loans just to meet our expenses.'

'So, what changed?'

She swilled the wine around in her glass in a poor imitation of a sommelier. 'Sal sprang it on me a few days ago. They have been trying to claim back overtime for the last ten years. Apparently, the powers that be have finally given in and agreed. It's a big sum, coming in tranches. We've had the first one and paid TM back almost everything we borrowed.'

'That's good news,' I said, wondering what the hell 'coming in tranches' meant. Was he going to try and hit me again for more?

She twisted back to face away from me and held the empty glass out behind her. 'Any chance of a refill?'

I edged out from behind her back, took the glass and returned with it close to full. Either by accident or intent, the dressing gown had opened further to reveal a provocative view of two very full breasts.

'Rosita used to talk a lot about you,' she said.

'Used to?' I queried.

'I expect she still does, only we haven't really spoken for the last few years. I'm talking about when you first arrived.'

I was trying to look anywhere but down the front of her dressing gown.

'Rosita always loved to be the queen, to preach to her subjects about the world she knew their closed little lives had never experienced. Most of it was exaggerated, funny stories that would make me smile and indulge her, but then she started to speak of your relationship with her, intimate details.'

'Really?'

She was now sitting on the floor, her back between my legs, her shoulder blades barely touching my stomach. One side of the dressing gown had now slipped below her tanned breast, the large dark nipple distended. For a woman who had been pulled and pummelled by two kids, she was in pretty good nick.

'I think she felt it necessary to justify her actions. She had arrived here with a man so much older than she. There was a need to explain why she was in such a relationship.' Eliana took a deep breath, as if the memory was an exertion. 'She would explain just how gentle and considerate you were, attentive and loving. I could handle that. New relationships are full of such qualities that fade when the real person comes to the surface. It was her description of the lovemaking that captivated us.'

'Us?' Did Rosita have an invited audience as well?

'Isabel and I.'

'You're joking.' I sat up, involuntarily pushing her slightly forward. 'Isabel? She was a kid. She still is.'

She turned her head to briefly look at me. 'Isabel has been sexually aware for years. I doubt she was a virgin, even then. She loved to listen to Rosita and could not believe what she was hearing. Sex to her was frantic fumbling in a field somewhere with a sixteen-year-old, desperate physicality and furtive explanations.'

'But Isabel hates me, has done from the start. She could hardly stand to suffer my presence.'

'For an experienced man, you do not see the obvious in front of you. Isabel was totally infatuated with you. There was a need in her for a cross between the father figure that TM could never be and the prince who would rescue her from the ivory tower. At the start, she was too nervous to display her vulnerability to you, but when she finally tried, you put her down.'

'I did?' I had no recollection of offending Isabel. She had always seemed offhand.

'You belittled her by making her recognise her age and immaturity.'

'And now she hates me.'

There was a terse shake of the head. 'The opposite of love is not hate, it's indifference. As she has grown up, she has become indifferent to you.'

'She still seems upset whenever I venture a word in her direction.'

'Isabel has other problems, issues that don't concern you. Look, can we stop talking about Isabel? It's you and me I want to talk about.' She turned back to face the front, pressing her head into my lap as she slid slightly forward on the tiled floor.

'You were a new experience for Rosita. Most of her men friends up until then liked it rough, some more than others. You were totally different, soft and tender; someone who wanted to make it nice for the woman you were with.

'When Rosita talked of an hour of gentle petting and teasing, how you would play with her body, gradually increasing the intensity, how she would react to you, encouraging you, enticing and seducing so that when you joined together she was moist, expectant; you, rock hard, anxious.'

The monologue was beginning to turn me on. I prayed I wouldn't get an erection that would press into her back. My hands were on her shoulders, ready to push her away. Why didn't one of the kids start crying, for God's sake?

'Then, she said, you would stop in midstream, gently pulling out of her until the head of your penis nestled just outside her, gently caressing her clitoris until she began to tremble and urge you to come back inside her and climax together. Do you know how wonderful that sounds?'

It was a matter-of-fact question spoken with anger in her voice. She didn't give me time to answer, not that I had anything to say. My mouth was parched.

'Do you know what is my husband's idea of romance? It's saying "I love you" as he comes, thirty seconds after he's rolled on top of me and forced himself in against the dry walls of my vagina. He comes with a yelp, like a dog who's had its bollocks bitten, rolls off and wipes himself against my nightdress. Turning you on, is it?' She could feel me pressing against her.

'What's this all about, Eliana?' I tried to turn her head to look at me, but she resisted. I had never realised just how strong she was.

'I want to make a deal. I want you to fuck me, just once and never again. I want you to make love as if I were Rosita. Pretend, but do exactly what you do to her. Make me feel desired, loved, sexually irresistible.'

'And?' I was waiting for the sucker punch, something about Sikorsky. 'I promise that I will never mention to anybody my suspicions about a girl who fell off a balcony, a bloodstained shirt worn by a tramp and a new shirt, supposedly already worn, with the price tag still attached.'

I feigned confused ignorance but I was frightened at this bolt from the past. 'If I said that I don't know what you are talking about, but I fancied making love to you anyway?'

'Then I would tell Rosita what had happened. The last thing that I want is any emotional involvement with *you*. Do we have a deal?'

The memories of a stupid few hours in Mad Max's bar came back to me, but I had done nothing criminal. Why be afraid? I could look at it in a different light; the slimy, calculating way that Salvador had demanded money. This was my fifteen-grand shag, expensive but worth it just get to get back at Salvador. I would make sure I wiped my dick on her dressing gown when we had finished.

I licked the fingers of both hands and slid my hands over her breasts, playing with her nipples. 'I guess you've got yourself a deal,' I said.

There was a loud moan as she turned towards me, her hands wrestling frantically at the belt of my trousers, tearing at my zip.

'Take it easy,' I said, continuing to course my hands gently around her breasts. 'This is a marathon, not a sprint.'

'We'll make too much noise,' she said. 'Outside. Let's go.'

She had it all planned. TM had built a canvas lean-to for the kids alongside the barbecue, with some cushions and a blanket inside. We managed to squeeze inside, our legs dangling out of the end onto the concrete hardstand, stifling laughter as we manoeuvred into position.

The whole thing was taking too long. It was unnatural for her and we were both trying too hard. For me, neither of the sexual drivers was present. I felt no lust, and without the emotional warmth between us, the physicality was not about wanting to possess someone I loved. Her 'no kissing' demand left out an essential ingredient I relished as a precursor to penetration, the hunger and passion that joined you both.

'Now,' she said. 'Do it now!' Her voice had risen an octave. I moved her into a kneeling position, her head bowed forward, legs splayed out.

From the villa there came the sound of a window opening and an urgent voice calling in Spanish, 'Eliana, is that you?'

For a split second she froze, then scrambled to exit the lean-to and retrieve her dressing gown. It was pitch-dark save for the shadows cast by the solar lights around the perimeter of the communal swimming pool.

'Isabel? Are you all right?'

'What are you doing, Eliana?' The light in the bedroom came on, casting a glow down onto the patio and Eliana's robed outline.

'It's so hot, Isabel. I was trying to find a breeze.'

'Can you come up? I was having a bad dream and I'm scared.'

I had never heard Isabel talk like that. This was no headstrong, strong-willed teenager. This was the voice of a young woman with genuine fear in her voice.

'I'll be right there. Close the window or you will lose all the benefit of the air conditioning.'

The window slammed shut just as Eliana's head appeared at the entrance to the lean-to. Her voice was a penetrating whisper. 'There's no deal until we finish this. Do you understand?'

I nodded lamely and she was gone.

Never have I been so grateful to get into bed. My limp penis was sore and chapped from all the frenetic activity but I cherished the hand that sleepily reached out to couch it as Rosita snuggled her stomach, as best she could, into my back, our unborn child symbolically sandwiched between us. 'Thanks, Isabel,' I mouthed silently, as my head dug into the pillow.

Salvador was back for the weekend, fussing around, entertaining the kids whilst Eliana rested up. She had been overdoing it lately, he explained, too much boring routine. I knew exactly what he meant. Tomorrow, they would take the kids out for the day if the weather held up. I could not see it changing. The temperature was soaring in a clear blue sky and Sanlazer was packed with tourists.

It was difficult to choose the right time. The pool area was never that crowded, with most of the condominium residents preferring the adjacent beach. Rosita and I found a quiet corner with two plastic recliners. She was well past the bikini stage, choosing a loose one-piece and a white see-through cotton slipover. The effect was electric, whatever she wore, and it wasn't only me who thought so. Ostensibly attending to a strimmer, Robi had chosen a vantage point where he thought he could glance over at her without me noticing. At the time, I thought it was benign, the sort of thing a frustrated schoolboy might do; wanting what you cannot have, harmless voyeurism.

He was the least of my concerns. 'I need to talk to you about Gonzalo,' I said to Rosita.

To my surprise, the idea we should send our assistant packing did not provoke the reaction I had expected. Instead of the spirited defence of Gonzalo she had always shown whenever I had criticised his attitude in the past, she listened to my reasoning in silence. It was like me being the president of the USA; I had a nuclear weapon to destroy Gonzalo in her eyes, but I could not use it. The collateral damage would be too great. My conventional weaponry was pretty good, but there was no guarantee I could deliver the coup de grâce.

In most instances, you could count on a spontaneous, impetuous reaction from Rosita, in line with her Latin temperament. Today, she was pensive, saying nothing.

'Well?'

'Let me do it,' she said, finally. 'I know what will happen if you tell him. He will say something, you will lose your temper, and we will find him digging his heels in and demanding a big payout.'

'And you will tackle it how?'

'Persuade him, in the circumstances, that it is the best for all of us. I know him better than you.'

'Not too well, I hope.'

She laughed. 'Well enough to push the right buttons.'

It made sense. Gonzalo planned to finish up in the office on Tuesday and leave to join his family on Wednesday.

'We don't want him hanging around making trouble after you have told him,' I said. 'Pay him off and see him off the premises.'

It was agreed. She would speak with him whilst I was away on my enforced babysitting duties in Seville with her parents and Salvador.

Over the weekend, the weather changed. The storm clouds were gathering.

CHAPTER TWENTY-ONE
Cavalla – 2008

I hear the noise from the garden as Claudio pulls up outside the house. He helps me out of the car – the journey back has reawakened some uncomfortable aches from two days earlier – gives me one more of his 'poor sucker' smiles and drives off at speed.

The afternoon has a glorious autumnal feel, pleasantly warm in the sunshine yet chilly in the shadows of the trees. The side door is the best option of making it into the house without anybody seeing me and provides the opportunity to establish just what is going on before I make my presence known.

From behind the drab velvet curtains in the lounge I watch Lino attend expertly to a portable barbecue on the patio by the back door. His cashmere jumper, sleeves rolled up, is protected by a comical plastic pinafore-style apron with the print of large breasts and an obscene belly button. Together with the pair of tongs and the spatula he's wielding like a bandmaster with a baton, I reckon the whole ensemble rather suits him.

Just outside the conservatory, in the only area of the patio bathed in sunshine, Jasmin sits astride a pouffe alongside her mother, deep in conversation. I wait, expecting to catch sight of Francisco running around, but there's no sign of him.

They are obviously expecting me. The two magic slates I use to communicate in deaf mode have been placed on a spare chair, symbols of my invitation to join the party.

I am about to go to my room, change and freshen up before joining the family when I notice a movement close to the trunk of one of the large holm oaks. Francisco is hiding behind the tree and must have spotted the lounge curtain moving as I changed position. He springs from his hiding place, screaming '*Avô, Avô,*' in his shrill little voice and sprints across the ground, racing headlong past his family to find me. He leaps into my arms with the agility of a cat, clinging tightly to me, his body shaking as if he's in the midst of an earthquake.

'*O que é?*' I say. What's wrong? He's crying.

'I don't like it,' is all I understand.

'What don't you like?' I ask.

Jasmin bursts into the room, her expression a mix of anger and concern. She goes to take her son from me. As she moves towards him, his grip around me tightens. She mutters something under her breath.

'Look at me when you speak,' I bark.

The ferocity of my comment forces her take a step back. Her eyes stare at me as if I am about to harm her. She swallows hard.

'What's going on?' I ask. Francisco is whimpering into my good ear.

'Nothing,' she says, avoiding my eyes. 'We were waiting for you. Brigitte said you were on your way. We are going to have a barbecue.' She is regaining her composure.

'I mean with the boy. What is he scared of?'

Inés is standing in the doorway, a cigarette dangling from the side of her mouth with an inch of ash defying gravity on its end. 'It's nothing to do with you,' she says.

I shake my head, pretending not to understand.

Jasmin takes the lead. 'My mother says it is nothing to concern you,' she mouths.

'I asked you why Francisco is scared? I don't want to see my grandson like this.'

Jasmin strokes her son's back but the attempt to calm him makes him grip me even tighter, if that's possible.

'Let's go back outside,' Inés says to her daughter. 'Lino has the food ready for us.'

I get a first-hand appreciation of the situation as we join Lino in the ageing conservatory. Francisco turns his head dramatically, making it plain he is not prepared to look in the direction of Inés, just as I recognise the warm, damp sensation on my chest.

Inés is glaring at us. She turns, facing away from me to catch Lino's attention. I hear the words *'perigoso'* – dangerous – and *'eliminar'* – no translation necessary.

Lino gives me a beaming smile. 'Welcome,' he says, brushing past his sister, his hand outstretched. 'We decided on a family get-together today with some organic pork chops from a local farmer and some equally delicious red wine from a friend with a vineyard. I trust you are hungry?'

I am, and, to be fair to the cook, the meal is delicious. By the time we finish, I'm tiring of the effort of deception, interchanging between dealing with questions or comments written on the slates and pretending or, actually managing, to lip-read. If it was down to me, I would be relieved to announce my hearing has started to return, but I'm conscious different pressures on me are now in play.

The sub-plot of this family gathering is plainly to trash Brigitte in my eyes. She is the black sheep of the family, Lino explains, a devious and spiteful woman who has turned against the rest of her relatives, something he deeply regrets.

'How did you come to end up at her apartment?' he asks.

'She happened to invite me at the wedding, gave me her card,' I explain. 'But it was through some mutual contacts that I came to be in Porto.'

He nods, apparently accepting my explanation. 'She is a difficult individual with many personal problems. Her business is unconventional, some might say illegal, and she has had countless run-ins with the authorities.'

I recognise his hatchet job for what it is, but Inés's reaction is far more personal and vitriolic, accusing her sister of stealing her son from her with malicious lies and bribery.

'Lies?' I ask. 'What kind of lies?'

'About me, about the family. She ...'

Lino interrupts. Obviously, there is no way he is prepared to lose control of the conversation. 'If Hugo was to stay with her, she had to try and make him hate his mother. She made up all kinds of fancy stories that would convince his susceptible young mind.'

'And the bribery?'

'Money!' Inés spits out the word. 'Anything he wanted was his. Did you not notice? The bitch only ever married for money. Fucked anything and everything behind the backs of a string of husbands before she divorced or killed them off. She changed Hugo into what he is today.'

She makes her son sound like a demon. 'And what is he?' I ask.

Once again, Lino steps in before she can answer. 'Inés means that Brigitte poisoned his mind against us. Fortunately, I managed to save the boy from her. No harm was done and he is now a committed member of our family.'

If he allowed Inés to rant on, I might have learned something, but every time there is the likelihood of an emotional outburst, Lino changes the mood. His self-appointed brief is obviously to cast Brigitte as the outcast without divulging family confidences to a stranger, and I have to admire his competence.

Lino follows Jasmin out of the conservatory as she announces bedtime for Francisco. For one dread-filled moment, I think she is going to make her son kiss everyone, but she has the good sense to tell him to simply wave goodnight before ushering him smartly in front of her towards the stairs.

Inés and I are alone. She fusses in her handbag, mumbling to herself.

'I was sorry to learn about your loss,' I said. 'It must have been difficult for you.'

She looks up at me, an expression somewhere between bewilderment and apprehension. 'What do you mean?' Her voice is on edge.

'Your son. To die at birth is one thing; to survive for three months? It must have been terribly distressing for you. And, then, what with your husband ...'

Her shoulders relax. She chooses her words, speaking slowly. 'I knew from the start he would not survive. The doctors thought it was cerebral palsy at first but they changed their diagnosis when the symptoms worsened. Krabbe disease. It was a blessing when the end came. Poor little thing.' She looks up at the ceiling, remembering, perhaps thinking what she wanted to say next.

'I can sympathise,' I say. 'I have some knowledge of cerebral palsy.'

She ignores my attempt to find common ground. 'As for Estevão, my husband,' she explains, 'I believe he saw Hugo's leaving as ...' She searches for the word in English but fails. '*Traição*,' she says.

'Treachery,' Lino says from behind me. I wheel around. He has their coats draped over his arm. 'Estevão took his own life because he could not accept his son was prepared to turn his back on flesh and blood.' He motions to Inés not to interrupt. 'Tell me, how did you come to learn about our family history? Did Jasmin tell you?'

'I saw a picture of Martin's christening. Brigitte has a copy in her album. There were two men in the photograph. She told me who they were.'

Inés stands up, her stance rigid as she goes to take a step towards me. I edge backwards. I can't tell whether it's anger or alarm that has sharpened the look on her face. 'Why would Brigitte have a photograph of my family? She as good as disowned us when a rich meal ticket came along.'

'Maybe underneath the veneer she still clinged to her roots?'

Lino places his hand on my arm to lead me to one side. He suggests Inés puts on her coat and waits in the car. He hangs fire until she has left. 'Do you want me to write on the slate or speak?'

'Speak slowly.'

'You do not know any better, but there are some taboo subjects we do not talk about with my sister. They are personal, sensitive matters. As you can see, she hates Brigitte for what she did to Hugo. For you to raise the subject of her husband and his brother ...' He shakes his head. 'Just too painful. You do understand?' He gives me a patronising smile and follows his sister out of the door.

I expect Jasmin to make some excuse and seek the privacy of her own room as she tends to do. I now recognise her avoiding me socially is an escape from my prying questions. Looking back, I must have casually asked about her background and private life on a dozen occasions, but they were all fobbed off with generalities or oblique responses. I excused the reaction as that of a very private person, but now I begin to wonder if there is something more complex behind her unwillingness to engage with me.

Tonight she appears prepared to talk, making herself comfortable on the sofa, her feet tucked under a bunch of cushions at one end.

'So, what else did Aunt Brigitte have to say for herself?' she asks.

I mention the collection of family photographs and, specifically, the one that had so riled her mother.

'It's difficult for Inés,' she says. 'Estevão and his twin brother were very close, as you might expect. Both of them died tragically.'

'How?'

'Suicide. Both of them. My father when I was just a teenager; Vicente, just three years ago. Inés blames herself.'

'Why would she blame herself?'

'My father and uncle were both dreamers, fantasists with wild imaginations and short, violent tempers. My mother, if nothing else, is a realist with her feet on the ground. I think she feels that sometimes she was too hard on them, forcing them to see the world as it is; a dirty, evil place, controlled by people – men – who think they have the right to do exactly what they want.'

I have never heard her talk like this before. I intend to be provocative whilst she is in the mood. There may not be another occasion. 'Brigitte suggested that your brother, Hugo, had a homosexual relationship with Albert. Was Albert bisexual?'

Her eyes flicker with some sort of recognition and she clutches at a cushion, pulling it towards her chest and holding it tight. 'Brigitte is being ridiculous,' she says, 'making trouble, as she always does. Hugo and Albert were close, like brothers, but there was nothing sexual between them. Just think about it, Gilbert. Before Albert and I decided to get together, he was seeing Adele. You know, you stayed with her, at the apartment above the pharmacy.'

She laughs as if the notion is ridiculous and I have to admit to feeling a sense of relief. I have never seen myself as being in any way homophobic – live and let live has always been my credo – but I suppose I would somehow see Albert's homosexuality as a sort of manifestation of the failings in me, as his father, throughout his upbringing. We must have had conversations about sex. True, I can't remember any.

I have misjudged Jasmin. She is far more calculating than I imagined. There was a purpose behind her decision to remain in the lounge and engage me in conversation tonight and I just did not see it coming.

'I am really pleased to tell you that my workload at the practice has now been sorted out. I am going to have a lot more time to spend with Francisco, look after him, see him to and from infant school.'

'That's good,' I say, still not expecting the sucker punch.

'It has been very kind of you to stay all this time, but now we can let you get back to your good life in England. You can be home in time to spend Christmas with your friends.'

Those words, spoken so casually, are like a stake through my heart. Just the thought of that desolate apartment in Chepstow, living in solitude as I watch everyone around me enjoy the build-up to Christmas, only to spend those festive days alone, staring blankly at a television screen. The prospect fills me with a terrible dread.

'What about Francisco?' I blurt out. 'He needs constant stimulation, new things to challenge him. Look at the way he has started to draw since I've been here. I can help with that. I don't need to go back yet. I have no commitments.'

I can tell my reaction has taken her by surprise. She wasn't expecting me to protest and is unprepared to deal with it.

'Lino thinks that Francisco needs younger people around him. However much you enjoy being with him and he with you, Lino says he is too dependent upon you and that is not good for the boy.'

'Lino! Lino! Lino! All I hear is Lino! What the fuck does Lino know? He has no wife, no family. What gives him the right to preach about your son's best interests? You are the only person who knows instinctively what is best for Francisco, and right now, after what I witnessed this afternoon, I believe that I am best for him.' I'm scrambling for words. 'Can't you see, Jasmin, Lino dislikes and despises me? He does not want me around because I am not like him. He does not love, because he does not know how to love. He rules, the head of the family to whom everybody must listen, but I won't. The one thing I do know is how to love, and I love and care for my grandson.'

'I know you do,' she says, 'and you can come and see him as often as you like. Don't make it difficult for me, Gilbert. I have agreed with Lino and my mother on this course of action. I need you to accept our decision.'

I am fuming, the anger rising inside me like lava from a volcano. And with it, the frustration that comes with impotence when you have no grounds to challenge a decision you do not like.

An image of Borodin as he made his pitch comes into my head. *Your son is dead. Don't you want to help to bring those responsible to justice?* Now, I'm being sent away. Can the person who tried to kill me risk letting me leave? Is he or she prepared to take a chance my memory will never return? Being around Francisco has given me a purpose in life. I'm not heading back to Britain until the truth has surfaced.

'As I say, Jasmin, I am sorry and I will miss Francisco terribly. Still, there is one piece of encouraging news you will be pleased to hear.'

'There is?' I can sense the relief in her voice now I have backed down.

'I am starting to get flashbacks of images from the morning of the explosion, together with Albert, Hugo and – would you believe it – Vernon? I just hope that it is a prelude to a full recovery, don't you?'

CHAPTER TWENTY-TWO
Sanlazer – 1996

Unusually for July, the dark clouds rumbled across the sky, threatening rain that never came. The wind from the south-west was hot and humid with temperatures hovering in the early thirties.

These were the days I loved to go to the beach, with no need to shelter from the direct sunlight or spend ages religiously applying sun cream all over my body like a coat of armour, ready to confront the elements. I am certain the purists would tell me the conditions were just as harmful as if the sun were shining, but it never seemed that way or harmed my sensitive freckled skin.

Even so, I was clearly out of step with the rest of the holiday population, who appeared to equate sea and beach exclusively with blue sky and sun. For them, a cloudy day was an excuse to wander around the town, window-shop, pace themselves between each coffee or sit propped up in the corner of the esplanade of a bar with their happy hour two for one, aimlessly watching the screen of a television without the sound.

I could just imagine the crowds teeming around the commercial centre just outside Ayamonte, and it made me shiver with horror.

The Sanlazer post office was at the far end of the main street, known as The Strip, on a corner site just beyond the rows of bars, restaurants and souvenir shops. I threaded my way slowly amongst the crowds jamming the walkway as they stood watching pavement artists, sand sculptors and the African hawkers with their sacks of carved wooden animals, LED sunglasses for the kids and leather belts and wallets for dad. Brash touts blocked the path of oncoming families, enticing them into restaurants and bars with special offers. Worst of all, the parasites I really hated, were the timeshare OPCs who would latch onto their gullible victims like leeches, enticing them with false promises of free excursions to special attractions if they just accepted an invitation to visit an apartment complex that was out of this world.

In the early days, Rosita had been persuaded to work at one of these aparthotels as a so-called senior independent property consultant, selling these exaggeratedly described luxury apartments by the week at crazy prices plus exorbitant management fees. I went to pick her up on her second day.

She was in tears. Her instructions were not to let any punter walk away. If she felt she could not hold them, the brief was to call over one of the 'closers', the walnut-wizened bunch of old pros who let nobody escape without leaving a deposit on their 'new summer home'. Rosita described the operation as like the Venus flytrap with people instead of insects, unable to escape, families with children screaming to leave, yet ignored until a signature was on the dotted line. Two days was all she managed. With a salacious wink, the smarmy manager with the convertible BMW had told her she would be welcome back any time she fancied a change. He had looked directly at me as he finished the sentence.

It was mid-morning when Rosita took the call. To be honest, I had long since forgotten about the mailbox we had rented at the post office soon after we arrived. In those early days, we were not known at the villa address and neighbours had suggested we use the postbox facility to ensure we received our correspondence. Over time, we had become names familiar to the local postmen and I had stopped using the PO box number for return mail, switching to the home address. I had forgotten about it, and as the annual fee was debited direct from the business bank account, the call from the supervisor to advise the box was full and needed to be emptied came out of the blue.

Somebody had noticed leaflets were sticking out of the flap, she told me as I thanked her for making the call, my arms full of mostly junk mail which had accumulated over the last year. I decided to try and find a seat at the café-cum-ice cream parlour directly opposite the post office. The place was packed but as I walked over, three lads vacated a window seat which I hurriedly occupied before the other walk-ins got to it.

I had discarded ninety per cent of the rubbish mail before I came across the letters. There were two, both in identical lemon-coloured envelopes, both in Sandra's handwriting. They had been sent seven months earlier within two weeks of each other.

The first was brief and to the point.

Celine was our firstborn child, a difficult and horrendous birth that took over seven hours and left Sandra close to death. It was seven months before cerebral palsy was diagnosed and Celine was almost three before we knew the true severity of her condition. By the age of four, with complications and the presence of an inoperable tumour on her brain, she was in a totally vegetative state, well beyond our capacity to care for her.

Her very existence had, by this time, already damaged my relationship with Sandra to the point of us talking seriously about divorce, but the news of her pregnancy with Vernon, coupled with the relief we felt with the opportunity to move Celine from our home into residential care, reduced the strain on our relationship as well as providing some optimism for the future.

From the day Celine left, Sandra could never stand to refer to her by name. Tears would follow. Physically, she was no longer present, but going into the living room where Celine had spent her days, a prisoner in a tiny wheelchair gazing aimlessly out of the window, the conversation would always gravitate to her and she became known affectionately to us as the elephant in the room.

At the start, we visited the care home once a week, but it seemed to me so terribly pointless. An hour would pass with Sandra holding her daughter's hand and talking softly about the events of the previous week, but there was never a glimmer of recognition or a reaction. As the months passed, with business pressures to the forefront, my visits became less and less frequent. By the time Albert came along, Sandra had been obliged to reduce her visits to once a month and, I guess, I was joining her maybe three or four times a year.

You begin by expecting a telephone call to tell you the worst at any time, but it never comes and the years pass. There had even been some small signs of base responses but these had not amounted to much. Celine had survived until two days before her twenty-third birthday, but now she was dead.

The letter was matter of fact. The funeral would take place in ten days' time and Sandra expected me to be at the crematorium in Newport. That was over six months ago and I had known nothing about it.

The second letter was full of hurt and anger.

> Gilbert,
> True to form, as usual.
> What is it with you, The Queen is dead. Long live the Queen? I laid my darling Celine to rest on a dark day, with only strangers present.
> In those first three years of her life, before we knew the tragedy that lay before her, the only people she could have

ever recognised were me and, yes, you, her father. Yet, her father was not there to see her finally laid to rest. How callous can one man be?

Have you forgotten everything about the past? Have you sacrificed your conscience for the sake of that whore and your unborn child? I expect that you don't even acknowledge the existence of your sons any more.

The right thing to say would be I hope you never have to experience the pain and suffering I have endured all these years. But I don't feel like that. I hope that you, the whore and your new child all rot in hell, and the sooner the better.

By the way, if there were any of our friends who sympathised with you at the time of the divorce, forget them. There was not one person at the funeral who didn't think you were anything other than a total worthless bastard.

Sandra

PS. Your sons asked to be included as signatories to this letter.

And they had. There was Albert's scrawl, together with the small, tight-knit lettering in capitals I remembered. Vernon must have pressed so hard on the paper it had torn under his hand.

My first reaction was to reach for my mobile to explain. The callous side of my nature said the weight I felt in my stomach was not for the child who had died but for me having to suffer the unjust criticism of appearing to deliberately deny her existence. In the event, common sense and Rosita's counsel prevailed. I had long since missed the funeral. Another two or three days to calmly translate thoughts into words on paper, explain, regret and apologise, was the better option. The pressure of time was only mine.

I opted to drive my own car to Seville. The unpalatable thought of being in Salvador's family wagon with my in-laws and two excited kids in the mood I was in would not work. I explained I might need to rush back if Rosita went into labour and I preferred to keep my options open.

Whether she knew or not of our strained relationship, Eliana had booked Salvador and me into a twin-bedded room at the hotel. Fortunately, he had gone straight off to start his shift and I had both the room to myself and the afternoon to compose my thoughts whilst the kids and their grandparents went off to investigate the fiesta in Triana.

I decided on two copies of my letter of regret, explanation and contrition, just in case Sandra consigned hers to the waste bin before reading it. A second version, also handwritten, was addressed to Madeleine with a request that she show it to my boys. I was reasonably confident she might also mention its contents to a few old acquaintances, in the hope that they would not think too badly of me.

As I waited in the hotel bar for the folks to return, I began to feel I had finally been accepted as a member of this family. It appeared I had been totally discarded by the old one. Roots were important. With the birth of our daughter – we didn't know the sex but I was convinced – Rosita and I would have a new status in the family, the reality of a place of our own and, with Gonzalo gone, a seamless partnership in a fledgling business with prospects.

Things could be a lot worse.

Famous last words.

CHAPTER TWENTY-THREE
Cavalla – 2008

Nearly three weeks have passed since I telephoned Borodin to agree to his plan. To my surprise, he reacted to my decision with weary resignation and not the 'that's the spirit: let's get 'em' enthusiasm I anticipated. He will let me know when to start dropping hints my memory is showing signs of recovery, and I am to create a few vague but plausible scenarios in my head. I don't tell him I've already started.

In a line worthy of an American B-movie, he comes back to me a few days later to confirm 'we are in a go situation' and somebody will be watching out for me from now on. The instruction is for me to leave a message on a voicemail number every morning, setting out my intended movements for the day. Any significant changes to the schedule are to be separately advised by text message.

The tension of trying to act normally while imagining my life was on a knife-edge has left me exhausted. Yet, as the days pass, the whole experience turns out to be a total anticlimax. The various people to whom I pass on my good news simply treat it with a mild congratulatory disinterest, and I can only assume the team watching my back must be made up of highly experienced pros because I have never seen a single person on my tail. All in all, I have adopted an ambivalent attitude to the threat of somebody bent on seeing me dead.

The one thing for which I do have to thank Borodin is a vast array of website links to sites dealing with memory issues. Sifting through the various articles, I believe a simple understanding of implicit and explicit memory goes to the crux of my condition.

I have no problem with implicit memory, the things we do as a matter of course, without thinking, because we simply know, like getting onto a bicycle for the first time after many years and starting to ride. When it comes to explicit memory, again, my semantic retention of names, facts and general knowledge is as good as the norm for my age. My problem centres around episodic memory, the millions of doors in our brains constantly opening and closing, lighting up or darkening all the specific events throughout our lives we seek to recall and then return to storage. Apparently, I have a small batch of doors that do not let in the light.

Looking for cause and effect, I eventually find my answer in the story of an ex-combat soldier who loses his short-term memory as the result of a roadside explosion. He suffers from traumatic brain injury, known as closed-head TBI, even though there is no external physical evidence. An explosion creates a shock wave of high pressure, quickly followed by a reverse blast of low pressure. This rapid change in pressure leads to brain swelling and, as in my case, memory loss.

The closed doors of that soldier's memory lock away the shocking audio-visual images of the carnage taking place around him. I'm left with the disturbing impression of being unable to come to terms with something that occurred in Albert's house which was so distressing and so unacceptable to me.

Borodin's closing remarks hark back to the laugh I remember, Vernon's laugh. Concentrate on opening that one door, he wrote, and it may trigger others to spring open.

Jasmin has not mentioned the date of my leaving. There are oblique remarks about an aunt and some cousins coming from Granada in Spain to stay for Christmas. All the rooms in the house will be occupied by the twenty-second. She has not seen these relatives since staying with them some years ago and is naturally excited at the prospect of meeting up again. She holds out the letter from them as if she needs to justify herself to me. Jasmin might keep secrets, but I've never suspected her of lying.

With only a few weeks to go, I try to spend as much time as possible with Francisco. Whatever Lino might say, I believe my influence has helped the boy's development and his self-confidence. We bond naturally and I want to ensure I have done everything possible to help him overcome the fear that troubles him.

His new passion started when I drew a stickman hanging from a rope; the figure you construct as you fail to choose the correct letters during a game of hangman or guess the word. Something inside him must have sparked because the kitchen fridge, notice board and my bedroom wall are now plastered with page after page of stickpeople in varying poses. My stickman has no ears, Jasmin always has a plate in her hand and Inés, cigarette in mouth, has a big hand holding a kitchen knife. It strikes me, for Francisco's age, his powers of observation and attention to detail are quite exceptional, but again, like most grandparents, I see my grandchild as a very special little person.

One morning, he drew a stickwoman – I taught him to differentiate; stickwomen wear skirts, however outdated and sexist the concept is – with a dog. To save a few trees, I weaned him off one stick drawing per sheet of paper onto using my collection of slates, of which I now have six.

'Is it Pom-Pom?' I ask, recalling Adele's water dog we haven't seen for some time.

He nods his head vigorously.

'Shall we go and see him today?'

The reaction is as if I am offering him the moon and the stars.

From memory, Adele closes the pharmacy from one to two and, weather permitting, walks the dog on the riverbank, stopping at the picnic area to eat the sandwich lunch she shares with Pom-Pom. It's there we find her on this crisp December day, snuggled inside a grey Angora wool coat with the collar turned up, lobbing a stick for the dog to retrieve.

We sit together as Francisco takes over the stick-throwing role. His energetic attempts reach no more than two or three metres, upon which he desperately urges Pom-Pom to 'fetch' whilst the dog stays firmly on its haunches, its head tilted in a way which says, 'Is that your best shot?' Francisco wags his index finger in the dog's snout and runs off to retrieve the stick and repeat the process.

After a round of normal catch-up conversation in between bites of half a small baguette filled with some delicious soft cheese, which Adele insists I share, the opportunity arises to change the subject. I have a slate ready for some answers, which I'll combine with some earnest-looking, creased-brow lip-reading. As good as her English is, I now paraphrase some of the conversation to avoid stuttering pauses and grammatical hiccups.

'The affair?' she says. 'It's no secret. It lasted about nine months.'

'How long ago?'

'Let me see.' She pretends to be calculating dates. 'Four years, three months and nine days.'

'It wasn't you who broke it off, I take it?'

She slowly shakes her head. A flash of annoyance crosses her face. She takes the scribe and presses unnecessarily hard on the slate. 'I thought the final invitation was to ask me to marry him, not finish with me.'

'Why did he break it off?'

She shrugs her shoulders and looks away.

'I've been told Albert was a homosexual.'

It was the cue for her to open up. She didn't want to be the one to tell me. It wasn't her place. She has known Hugo for most of her adult life. It was at college in Porto she realised he was gay.

She stayed on at university to complete her pharmacist degree course and was introduced to Albert and his brother when they stayed with Hugo at his aunt's shortly before leaving on holiday. Albert was in his late teens at the time.

'Hugo has always been what they call in movies 'a tart'. He likes to sleep around with a variety of partners. I could tell Albert was involved with him but there was something more to your son. He looked at me the way I was used to being looked at by straight men, and he was very attractive.'

She did not see Albert again until a few years later, by which time he was living with Hugo in a small apartment in the centre of Cavalla. There was no more than a nod or a wave until around five years ago when she delivered a prescription to the nurse at the Dharma centre. He was there, decked in robes, teaching a class.

'I think it was one of the reasons he and Hugo had the argument and split up. Albert was really into Buddhism, spending periods away on retreat, putting his physical relationship to one side. I think it annoyed Hugo. He tended to be very jealous.'

'Of Buddhism?'

'Easily. Hugo is possessive, a real temperamental bitch sometimes, nasty and spiteful, especially if he doesn't get his own way.'

Albert found a soulmate in Adele. They were both sensitive, feeling people who enjoyed each other's company. Within a week, their friendship changed up a gear and Albert moved into her apartment. She admitted his bisexuality was sometimes a problem for them both, but they managed to overcome the depression that would cloud his mood whenever the physical side of their relationship faltered.

'Those bouts of depression he claimed he inherited from his mother, who suffered terribly as he grew up.' She is about to go on but checks, pauses and tightens the belt of her coat. 'I always felt there was a struggle going on inside Albert, the need to suppress certain urges countered by the desire to enhance others; a constant tug-of-war as he tried to reach a conclusion destined never to totally satisfy him.'

'Why did it end?'

'Why do you think? Hugo got his claws back into him. It was more than seduction. I think he would have stayed with me.'

'If?'

'Hugo had a hold over him, not just physical or emotional. Albert was scared when he broke it off with me; scared Hugo might say or do something that would cause trouble for him. It was as if he was going back against his will.'

It was said with a tinge of hubris, suggesting she was not only heartbroken but affronted when he ended the affair. 'But you stayed friends?'

She stifles a laugh. 'Of course. It was impossible to stay hurt and angry with Albert. Our paths were bound to cross. I hoped ...' She holds the slate up for me to read what I had already guessed.

'Weren't you upset when he started going out with Jasmin? They even had a child together.'

There is a real laugh, this time full of scorn and anger. 'Haven't you noticed anything since you've been here, Gilbert? The whole family is dysfunctional.' She points over towards Francisco who is persevering with the stick. 'I ask you. He's a lovely boy but does he look anything like Albert?'

It had never occurred to me. I took it as read. Francisco has a swarthy, olive-coloured skin, all right, I admit, with definite Caucasian features. But then, his strain is seventy-five per cent white. Why should he not look exactly as he does?

'Are you saying what I think you are?'

'I don't know what I'm saying, Gilbert. I feel like you are boxing me into a corner with all these questions. I loved Albert and I thought and hoped he might come back to me, but there were too many dark secrets that bound him to Hugo and Jasmin's family.' She has a downcast expression on her face as she calls for Pom-Pom to join her. She is bringing our conversation to an end.

'I came to see you for some answers, Adele.' I shake my head. 'After all you've said, I've got more questions than ever.'

'Sorry,' she says as she clips the lead onto the dog's collar. 'Albert never talked about Jasmin's family, except on two occasions. We were having a picnic. It was a lovely day, early spring. I brought sandwiches and a bottle of wine. Albert rarely drank but he did this day, almost the whole bottle. We were sitting in silence on the banks of the river, looking across at sheep in a field, both lost in our thoughts. One of the lambs – it can only have been a day or two old – it was lame with one leg withered. It struggled to stand up. Albert said in the animal world the mother will nudge at it with her snout, try to make it react. If she cannot, her attention turns to nurturing the fit lambs. In their own way, humans do the same thing, he said. The trouble is, humans have a conscience, some more than others. You can get rid of the problem, but the elephant stays in the room. I did not understand him.'

'I do,' I said. I wasn't prepared to explain. 'And the second occasion?'

Her brow creases. She points again at Francisco. 'When he was a tiny baby, Jasmin's mother brought him to the pharmacy. As you know, there is little space inside, so she left him in a pram next to the road. He was uncovered and it started to rain. I said to bring him in. She said no, he could get wet. He wouldn't feel a thing.'

The incident disturbed Adele, and when she next ran into Albert, she told him. She had never seen him angry before. It made her regret bringing up the subject, so she tried to paper over the issue by suggesting that perhaps Inés was jealous of Francisco because of the tragic death of her own child. Albert said she didn't understand. Inés was burdened with her sins. In every family, it seemed, there was always an elephant in the room.

'What did he mean?'

'I don't know, but soon after, he announced his engagement to Jasmin.' A single tear runs down her cheek.

She pulls on the lead, kisses Francisco on the forehead and starts to walk away.

'Just one more thing, Adele.' She stops in her tracks. 'Do you ever come across the drug carfentanil in your work?'

For a moment she looks as if she is going to carry on her way without answering, but she turns around, eyes and mouth wide open. 'Why do you ask?'

'Just curiosity. I was reading an article.'

'It's a very dangerous and highly controlled substance. I am not allowed to hold it, even in my secure storage.'

I pretend not to understand. She walks back towards me and repeats the sentence. I can sense she is nervous.

'Who does hold it?'

'It's rarely used legally.'

Slow down, I caution myself. I am supposed to be deaf. 'It's frustrating for me,' I apologise. 'I have started to hear a word every now and again and I become impatient. My memory is coming back in flashes as well. Apologies, I was asking who would hold it?'

'SantaCavalla are the registered importers. They keep a very small stock.'

'What for?'

She shakes her head. 'Why are you so interested?'

'Just bear with me. Who uses it?

'Vets are the only people who need it around here. Jasmin requisitions it whenever they have to anaesthetise a large animal, elephant or rhino, at the safari park. I have to countersign the requisition. What is all this about?' Apprehension turns to anger.

'It just came up in conversation. I hear even a small quantity can be fatal.'

'In the wrong hands,' she says with what sounds like suspicion in her voice.

'In the wrong hands.'

CHAPTER TWENTY-FOUR
Seville, Spain – 1996

I had to admit my role of chaperone to the elderly grandparents who were attending to their charges so responsibly was much more rewarding than I had imagined. Other than look on as the kids excitedly planned the day with TM at the breakfast table, I was pretty much left to my own devices.

Salvador had not returned to the room the previous evening, reappearing only at around eleven the following morning to shower and change. He would not be on call again until the early shift on Thursday, giving him plenty of time, as he earnestly explained, to bond with his kids.

It was early evening as we strolled through the gathering crowds in the streets of Triana. I followed behind the group as they moved between the stalls, stopping whenever the kids spotted something of interest or a fairground ride, on which Salvador would join them.

It was all very relaxing, a scene of families out to enjoy themselves, weaving their way happily past the street vendors and their myriad collections of artefacts, many with a religious context. Groups hovered around stalls selling tapas of all descriptions, wine in plastic flutes, *cañas* of beer, or *churros*, the deep-fried dough pastry coated in sugar which left a sweet, pungent scent mixed with the smell of cinnamon and boiling oil lingering on the hot summer air.

On the Guadalquivir river, which separates the Triana district from the centre of Seville, tired, muscular young men were concluding the rowing contests, the build-up in preparation for the next day's highlight, the *cucaña*, when streams of virile youths would try to retrieve the flag placed at the top of the greasy pole stretching out over the river.

I resented the sudden intrusion into my reverie. The mobile vibrated persistently in my trouser pocket. A no-name caller. I thought of the irrelevance of dealing with any minor business problem on a day like today and decided to ignore it. The caller rang off.

I was nearing the group as Salvador reached for his mobile, sheltering it around his ear as he tried to hear what the caller was saying. He stopped in his tracks, his face twisted in anger as he replied. Or was distress the expression? Had I missed a call about Rosita and the baby? Was it about to be born?

He finished speaking, pocketing the phone and looking around, anxiety etched on his face. He caught sight of me as my mobile vibrated again.

'Hello.'

There was a mix of anger and fear in Rosita's voice. 'Why don't you answer your phone?' she screamed.

'Calm down. Where's yours? Whose phone are you on?' I tried to sound sympathetic but my heart was racing. 'What's happened?'

The words came rushing out. 'I spoke with Gonzalo. He's crazy. You know that, don't you? He was shouting at me. I'm afraid of what he might do. Why aren't you here?'

'What do you mean, "what he might do"? What has he threatened?'

'To get us all. I've just spoken with Salvador. Come back with him as quickly as you can. I'm scared Gonzalo will return.' She started to sob into the phone.

My mind was racing. 'Find Eliana and Isabel and stay with them until I get there.'

'I'm on my own. They've gone to the clinic. I don't know what time they will be back.'

'Find Robi and tell him to stop Gonzalo from entering the villa. Lock all the doors and windows. I'll be back in about an hour.'

I was about to end the call when she spoke again. Her voice was calmer, composed. 'I know everything,' she said. 'I checked the money. I understand why you did it, but you should have told me.'

I didn't know what to say.

'I've told Salvador what I said to Eliana. I don't care what happens to us, but I will confirm to the authorities what Gonzalo told me he intends to tell them. Salvador is no longer my brother. He is a despicable man who would blackmail his own sister. He must pay.'

'We'll talk about all this when I get back. Just keep safe. I'm sure we can work it all out. Your immediate concern is Gonzalo, nothing else.'

Salvador was standing in front of me as I cleared the call.

'Whose car shall we take?' I asked.

'I've had time to think,' he replied. 'You know where Gonzalo lives, right?'

I nodded.

'Go and head him off. I'll take my car and go straight to the villa. I'll call Eliana and tell her to get home as quickly as possible. I can be there long before you. I'm a traffic cop, remember?'

'She knows all about our deal,' I said. 'Gonzalo told her.'

'I understand my sister better than anyone. I can talk her round. I am sure of that. Our problem is not Rosita. That's why you must go and find Gonzalo. Do whatever you have to and convince him to keep his mouth shut. Why did you want to fire the guy? Didn't she realise how he would react when she ended it?'

I was confused at his choice of words, but there was no time to ask questions.

'All right,' I said. 'It makes sense.'

It was nearly ten thirty before I was past Huelva and heading for La Antilla and the cabin in the woods where Gonzalo lived.

The screen on the mobile flashed on and off, illuminating the caller's name.

'Gonzalo!' I said. 'Where are you?'

'What do you think you are going to do by coming for me, Gil? Beat me up? It's all too late. You thought you were so fucking clever, such a real man who knows how to treat women. Well, let me tell you something.'

There was the sound of breaking glass.

'You won't get away with this, Gil. You can't do anything to hurt me.'

The line went dead.

CHAPTER TWENTY-FIVE
Cavalla – 2008

If proof were ever needed that physical appeal is sooner or later eclipsed by the power of personality, I need look no further than Jasmin. The woman whom I found so attractive when I first arrived in Cavalla is beginning to irritate me to the point where my frustration at her indifference makes me want to scream. I feel the urge to shake her and demand answers to the questions that constantly occupy my thoughts.

Whenever we come into contact, which is becoming increasingly infrequent, her conversation is limited to pressing me for a departure date, asking me to do something or avoiding any questions I try to slant about her personal history.

In the hope of softening her attitude, I give her a date. I will be out of her hair on the nineteenth, two weeks from today. It makes no difference. Jasmin has come to resent my presence for delving into personal issues she is unwilling or afraid to discuss.

Ostensibly, we are formally polite to each other, if only for the sake of Francisco who is blissfully unaware of the mounting tension. Whatever his parentage, he is my grandson and I will never see him in any other way.

We are in the town centre, passing time, when I literally bump into Domingos. Just the man I want to see. I haven't spoken to the lawyer since the aftermath of our meeting with Lannier. I suggest a coffee. It's a darn sight cheaper than paying for an hour of his time.

I make no pretence; my hearing has recovered.

'And your memory?' he asks politely.

'Slowly. I have flashbacks. Nothing definite yet,' I lie.

He smiles. 'And your reason for buying me this delightful hot chocolate? To enquire after my health?' He tilts his head to one side.

I point to Francisco who is trying to escape my grasp and reach a rather sad-looking dog lying beside its owner.

'I want to get hold of a copy of his birth certificate.'

'It's easy. He was born here, I take it? Go to the *Conservatória do Registo Civil* and request a copy of the *certidão de nascimento*. Pay the fee and it's yours.'

'A little delicate for me to be seen making enquiries. Is it something you could handle for me?'

'Cost you more than a cup of coffee.'

Domingos phones the next day. There is no record on file. Francisco could not have been born in Cavalla. Give him some more information to work on.

Coming straight out and asking Jasmin is out of the question. However, a chance lead arises that evening when Hugo comes over for dinner. He is being very solicitous about my health, keen to know all about the flashbacks I have experienced and rounding off a nervous monologue with an extremely enthusiastic yet wholly unconvincing performance of how sorry Francisco and the whole family are that I am leaving.

'I don't have to leave.' I'll make him suffer for his insincerity. 'Jasmin needs the space. I could stay at your place until the New Year.'

He huffs and puffs for a minute or so, talking about his commitments and how I should be back with my friends and relatives at this time of the year. I rather enjoy watching him squirm. He could just say, 'Nobody wants you around any more. Subject closed.'

I wait until Jasmin leaves the room to open the conversation with some crap I'd thought up about where we were born influencing us as adults.

'I'm Cavalla born and bred,' he replied as Jasmin returns. He looks up at her. 'Teresa's coming for Christmas with her relatives.' It was half question, half statement, a conversation filler. 'Granada to here is a good seven- to eight-hour drive. Will they do it all in one day?'

Jasmin nods absent-mindedly, concentrating on the cafetière and its stupid spout that always sends a trickle of coffee onto the table as you pour.

'They won't have seen Francisco since he was a baby,' he goes on. 'By the way, I was thinking. Is the safari park reopening for the holiday period?'

Jasmin moves a filled cup in front of me and looks up. 'Yes. We are giving some of the animals a health check this week to make sure everything is ready.'

'Let's make an afternoon of it before Gilbert leaves so that he and Francisco can spend a memorable few hours together. You would like that, wouldn't you, Gilbert?'

I react instinctively with a nod. My mind is elsewhere.

The following morning, I wait anxiously for the post to arrive. I ordered the kit just after I last spoke to Adele. Francisco saw it as a game. First, the cotton swab inside his mouth, and next, the second, in mine. Slip them both into the containers, the padded envelope, and the game is over. I paid the supplement for the express service. The results would be emailed to me within seven days of receipt.

Domingos sounds tired over the phone. 'Where?' he queries.

'Granada. In Spain,' I add, unnecessarily.

'You think he might have been born there?'

'It's a guess,' I say. 'Something I overheard.'

He has ties with a firm of lawyers in Seville and will make enquiries.

The next day, I have my answer. 'They are very quick,' Domingos says, 'but expensive. After all, time is money.'

'And the result?'

'The boy is indeed the child of Jasmin Guedes (Father: Estevão Guedes (*fallecido*) – Mother: Inés Reyes Guedes) and born on the day you indicated. I have asked them to send me a copy of the extract from the civil registry in Granada.'

'And the father?'

'He is recorded as *desconocido,* "not known".'

'What about registration with the Portuguese authorities?'

'As far as I can tell, it was never done.'

Friday comes with another opportunity to find Adele and Pom-Pom. The filled baguette in the plastic bag clutched in her hand appears untouched, but she is quickly on her feet as she catches sight of us. The pharmacy is very busy. She needs to get back.

Francisco lunges towards the dog who backs off out of reach with a practised leap. We watch as the boy tries in vain to encircle the dog by holding his arms out, a tactic which Pom-Pom has no difficulty in evading.

'Looks like you are stuck here for a few more minutes, Adele. Just enough time for you to tell me everything you know. I am not playing games, and we both know that there is no panic at the pharmacy.'

She goes to protest but I put up my hand.

'Somebody warned you off from talking to me, did they? It wouldn't surprise me. I'm beginning to get the distinct impression that the Reyes family has quite a few things it doesn't want the rest of the world to know. And me, in particular.'

She studies the ground in front of her, saying nothing.

'Which one was it: Jasmin, Hugo, Lino? I'll settle for Lino, the patriarch – protector of the Reyes family name.'

Her gaze remains steadfastly on the ground, but as my tone softens, so her eyes lift to meet mine.

'I need some information which I think you have, Adele.' I am trying to find the right way to phrase what I feel. 'But it's not one-sided. I'll tell you what I know, guess the rest and you can fill in the blanks for me. How about that?' I wait but there is no acknowledgement. 'Look at that little boy playing with your dog, that curly dark hair, those round, watery brown eyes that stare at everything in amazement and innocence. That is Francisco and he is my grandson and, whatever comes to pass, he will always be my grandson. Do you understand that? What exists between us goes beyond genes and blood. Do you understand that too?'

She nods, aware that I know.

I point towards Francisco. 'I had our DNA compared. The results came back yesterday. Of course, you know he is not Albert's child.'

Another acknowledgement.

'What you may not know is this.' I pull three sheets of paper from my pocket. The two sentences are shadowed in yellow marker. 'There is evidence of homogeneity, or a lack of variation, at key points in his chromosomes,' I read. 'These readings accounted for about a quarter of the genome – a finding most consistent with having been conceived by first-degree relatives.'

I wait, but there is no trace of surprise on her face.

'You know what that means?' I persist.

Her shoulders slump in resignation. 'Our relationship had finished.' It is little more than a whisper but her lips carefully frame the words. 'Albert would ask me to come over and help him with a large order of prayer cushions. He would cut and I would sew along three sides before they were filled. I loved the excuse to be near him again.' Her eyes begin to fill. The memory must be really painful.

'We used to talk about lots of things and he knew I still cared. I think it was to avoid the hurt that he told me. It was on one Sunday afternoon. Hugo and he had made a pact. Albert would claim parentage of Francisco and marry Jasmin. This would avoid problems for all three of them. Jasmin would no longer be quizzed about the boy's father; Albert could alleviate the pressure from his mother about producing a grandson for her; and Hugo and Albert could continue their ill-fated little tryst in private.'

'Why do you say 'ill-fated"?'

Her eyes come alive. 'It was doomed to fail. Hugo liked to play the field whilst Albert was strictly faithful. Albert knew about Hugo's little adventures, his one-night stands, but there was something else which bound them together, not to do with their personal relationship.'

'What?'

'I really don't know. Whatever it was, it was sinister; enough to make Albert become depressed.'

'And Francisco's natural father?'

She shakes her head. 'There was talk, but nothing more than wild gossip.'

'First-degree relatives,' I say. 'It's a fairly exclusive group of people.' I pull the christening photograph from my pocket. 'Sometimes putting two and two together can give you six and lead you off on the wrong tack. Sometimes, it can give you four. You'll recognise Jasmin's father, Estevão, and his twin brother, Vicente. Both committed suicide. Of course, it could be Lino, younger brother Lourenco, or, biologically possible, but unlikely, even Hugo. But I've seen Jasmin mixing socially with all these people and she acts perfectly naturally around them, so my money is on the twin who survived until one week after Francisco was born. What do you know about Vicente?'

There is not a flicker of surprise in her face, just the knowing look of somebody who came to the same conclusion a long time ago. 'Like I said, there were rumours, but they are a close and dangerous family. Inés warned me not to talk to you any more.'

'Warned or threatened?'

'She questioned my loyalty and the fact that, through SantaCavalla, Lino held a great deal of sway with the local pharmacy licencing authority.'

I nod. 'So, tell me what you know about Vicente and I will ask you no more compromising questions.'

We are strolling together back to the entrance to the pharmacy and her apartment. Francisco is instructing Pom-Pom to walk alongside him, but the dog has other ideas. Dark clouds are building overhead.

Whether it was always the case, she cannot say, but Vicente was a recluse who appeared rarely in public and, when he did, said very little. He lived in a small, tied cottage on the farm owned by his parents - did I remember? – the elderly couple who were at the sham wedding. 'That's about all I can tell you.'

'Does anybody live in the cottage now?'

'Not as far as I know,' she replies. 'It's not been lived in since he died. His mother treats it as some sort of shrine. They are simple people.'

'What about Vicente's father?'

'She dominates and he obeys. His only concern seems to be getting away with using the red diesel he buys for the tractor in his car. It's a joke around the town. I think even the police know. His is the only tractor that hasn't worked for years but uses ten litres of diesel per week.' She has lightened the mood but I can't leave it at that.

'How did Vicente kill himself?' I ask.

Her brow furrows. 'It was in the local newspaper. Drunk, with a shotgun wedged under his chin.'

By the time Friday arrives, I recognise the technique Jasmin and family are employing to stop my prying. The plan must be to keep me as busy as possible, looking after Francisco full-time because of a bout of infection at the crèche, running a series of unnecessary errands in the car and organising chores around the house which I have never been asked to perform before.

Next Tuesday is the planned trip to the safari park and I will leave the day after. Keeping me busy and my nose out of their affairs is most decidedly the Reyes family objective.

Saturday, supposedly my free day, will be the last opportunity to make myself a nuisance but I suspect someone will try to sabotage whatever plan I concoct. As luck would have it, a trip to the dry cleaners on the Friday gives me the opportunity for which I am looking.

It's a spur of the moment decision. As I adjust the strapping on Francisco's child seat, I see the old couple heading into town in an old Renault belching black smoke from the exhaust. Of course, today is market day, a special Christmas market in the centre of town. Jasmin asked me to take Francisco along later to look at the stalls and to meet Father Christmas.

It takes twenty minutes to get to the lay-by on the road running parallel to the old couple's farm. Beyond the copse bordering the inner edge of the field stands the cottage where Vicente lived. Francisco is hurriedly equipped with a spare magic slate and scribe. I ask him to draw me a picture. I promise to be back very soon.

Nobody locks doors in this trusting land and, as I anticipate, the back door is on the latch. The cottage is built of grey stone, with a tiled roof and a large lean-to filled with drums of diesel oil and bales of straw.

The back door leads into a kitchen and a small living room, paved in flagstones and sparsely decorated, with a narrow flight of bare concrete stairs in one corner. There is a sweet smell I can't identify.

The upper floor consists of two bedrooms and a narrow bathroom. Each bedroom has a single bed, one stripped to the mattress, the other unmade with sheets and a pillow. It could well be somebody has been sleeping there.

On the face of it, no effort has been made to remove the previous occupant's possessions or clean up other than a half-hearted attempt to remove the bloodstain on the kitchen floor next to the wooden table. As the stone is porous, I guess evidence of the tragedy will remain until the flagstone is replaced.

All I'm after is a sample of Vicente's DNA I can send-off to the laboratory; a hairbrush or a hat. Anything that holds a trace.

I am upstairs in the bathroom when I hear the sound of a door opening. Somebody is deliberately treading carefully. I pocket a dirt-laden comb with hairs wedged between the teeth from the bottom of a disused bathroom cabinet and move stealthily into the larger of the two bedrooms, praying the floor does not make a sound as I tiptoe across. The window is too small and the drop too severe for a man of my age in my condition. I open it to look out. I am bound to fall badly and break something if I try to force myself through and jump. I turn back. There is just the wardrobe, built in between two plastered brick walls. Steadying the hangers with my left hand, I pull the door shut. It fails to close properly. Where I am forced to crouch, my knee protrudes just beyond the door frame. I hold the door tight to my body.

Somebody is slowly climbing the stairs, the movement heavy and deliberate.

There is an inset wooden beam at the top of the wardrobe which I grip tight with both hands, giving me the impetus to push back against the wall and bring my knee slightly round at an angle. The wardrobe door clicks shut. The pain is excruciating, muscles and limbs wedged at unnatural angles. Seconds are all I have before I will be forced to give myself away.

The shuffling footsteps are in the room, moving towards the window. Whoever it is has stopped. They must be listening and looking. A fist thumps on the door of the wardrobe. Squares of what in the dark appear to be plastic slip from the top of the beam, falling onto the garments around me.

I wait for the wardrobe door to open but nothing happens. The sound of the steps recedes from the room. I hear someone muttering to themselves. There is a laugh I recognise. The front door is slammed with force. Silence.

Another ten seconds is all I can manage before I literally fall out of the wardrobe, unable to move and with the debilitating sensation of pins and needles as the blood returns to my limbs.

In my hurry to leave, I brush the plastic squares from my coat, but static electricity attaches two of what I now recognise as ageing Polaroid photographs to the material. I carefully pick them off and study the images. I collect the other six from the wardrobe, feeling along the beam for any more. There are none.

I pocket them and make for the car. There is no one in the field. I can't see Francisco's head above the rear window, but it's not concern for the boy that is making my heart pound.

CHAPTER TWENTY-SIX
Sanlazer – 1996

I must have banged on the front door a dozen times as I screamed his name. Apart from a solitary light bulb dangling from a cable in the porch, the cabin was in darkness. The kitchen door was unlocked. I needed to still the rage that was consuming me, to calm down and think straight. Drawers half-open, the cracked glass of a picture resting against the wall, a broken table lamp on the floor – all told me of a crazed man desperate to exact revenge.

Gonzalo had gone, along with the Transit van he used on business. Our tracks must have crossed. He had to be on his way back to the villa. I raced for the car.

Rosita! My God! My fingers trembled as I fumbled for the mobile. The call went straight to her message service. I got through to Salvador at the second attempt.

'Is everything all right? Is Rosita safe?'

'I'm not back yet. I had to stop off somewhere. I'll be there in a few minutes.'

I lost control. 'You said you would go straight there.' I was shouting. 'Gonzalo is not here. I heard glass breaking when I spoke to him. He must be trying to get into the villa. Rosita isn't answering her phone.' I swerved to avoid an antiquated motorcycle with no back light. 'I'm about ten minutes away. Meet me there.'

Most of the houses in the block were in darkness. Music and laughter were coming from the large villa on the end which belonged to the local councillor of a suburb in Madrid. TM had insisted the man must be on the take to have the best property on the block. I looked up and down the road. There was no sign of the Transit.

The entrance to the villa was in darkness. The front door was locked and bolted, just as I had instructed Rosita. As I moved around to the back of the house, I called out her name into the darkness of the communal gardens and swimming pool. The underwater pool lights should have been on, along with the concealed lamps under the bushes which partially shielded the pool surround from view. Robi's responsibility was to set the timer in the pool house. The lights were supposed to come on automatically at ten thirty this time of the year. It was almost midnight.

I ran towards the villa. It didn't really register with me until I had checked inside. The French windows were propped open. Nobody reacted to my frantic calls. The standard lamp was on alongside the chair in which Rosita would sit. It was the most comfortable for her, she said. It kept her back upright. The book she had been reading was open on the floor.

I hurled my jacket into the empty bedroom and banged on Isabel's door. No reply. She never went out. Why did she have to choose today not to be in?

I retraced my steps into the backyard. Two of Romina's yucca plants were lying on their sides, the earth spilling onto the concrete stand.

Somewhere in the darkness there was torchlight fanning the grass around the swimming pool.

'Rosita!' I called.

The light played up to meet me as I ran towards it.

'Rosita!' I felt a huge release of panic as I neared.

An arm barred my way, almost knocking me off my feet.

'Don't go there,' Salvador insisted. 'Call an ambulance and I will speak to the police. We daren't move her.'

I wrenched the torch from his hand and ran to the pool.

She was lying face down on the pool surround, the blue floral skirt of her dress around her waist. Her frilly briefs were wound about her knees. She was unconscious, her hands rigid, gripping the edge of the pool. Her legs were covered in dirt, matted with the pool of dark red blood oozing slowly from her insides.

I checked her neck for a pulse. She was alive. I searched in vain for my phone. Shit. It was in my jacket in our bedroom.

'Hold on, my darling,' I whispered into her ear. 'I'll be right back. Everything will be all right.'

The words evaporated into the night air as I began to run. 'Gonzalo!' I screamed, over and over again. 'I am going to kill you!'

CHAPTER TWENTY-SEVEN
Cavalla – 2008

My head is numb. For a split second, I'm back in the hospital. It's all been a dream – no, a nightmare. Nothing really happened. But it did. This is my room in Jasmin's house. People are talking in raised voices downstairs. Lino's voice is loudest. Something about *o velho sacana* – the old bastard. He's talking too fast for me to understand. Hang on! I do know what *pedófilo* means. Is it me he's calling a paedophile?

There is a push at my bedroom door. Nobody bothers to knock. Why should they? I'm deaf, aren't I?

It's all coming back to me. I look over. My heart is pounding. Somebody has put my jacket on a hanger. The photographs are in the button-down inside pocket. Or they were.

Jasmin strides over to the window and pulls back the curtains. There is condensation on the glass but I can tell it's one of those crisp winter days outside, when to walk in the sun is pleasant, not aggressive, yet once in the shadows, the chill bites.

'Are you feeling better?'

I study her face. Is my stare giving the game away? There is nothing in her demeanour to suggest she is aware I know the truth. I feel nothing but compassion. I yearn to say something meaningful but I must act normally. You poor girl. Why do these things happen? What makes people commit such terrible acts?

'The doctor said it was just a heart murmur.' She fluffs up the pillow. 'Too much adrenalin for your body to cope with. I got the medicine he prescribed from the pharmacy this morning. Rest up for the day.' She hesitates, as though choosing her words carefully. 'Adele says that you met her yesterday to chat about Albert?'

My fingers play around the frame of the magic slate. Somehow, it's comforting.

I just smile.

'We are going out for the day. Lino has suggested that as it is the last Saturday before Christmas, we should make a day of it. There is a fair in

Lamego. Inés is coming. Francisco will love it.'

No, he won't, I think. He will hate it. 'I thought he had somehow got out of the car,' I say. 'Did he sleep all right?'

I had run back to the car. There was a sharp pain in my chest and a single spasm in my left arm. I sank to my knees as I reached the rear door. I was fighting for breath, as if a metal spring was closing around my chest. It wasn't the fear of not finding Francisco in the car that brought on the attack, although I told everybody that was the reason. It was the first thing I thought of. It was looking at those photographs in daylight that did for me.

'Grandpapa?' I heard the little voice.

I struggled to look up and over the rear window. He had buried his head under the level of the driver's seat headrest. Tears were streaming from his eyes and he was trembling. His little tracksuit bottom was drenched in urine.

I had let him down. My promise not to be long had been broken; his trust in me, somehow betrayed. I began to feel the muscles in my chest relax. My arms enveloped him. 'I am so sorry,' I said. 'I am so sorry.'

He had smiled through the tears and handed me the magic slate with the outline of a house and a man on a bicycle. As I looked at him, he started to draw a bubble full of dots around the man's mouth.

I managed to drive us home but I must have blacked out as soon as we arrived.

Jasmin's voice eclipses my train of thought. 'One or two nightmares, I think,' she replies, 'but he'll be fine.' She looks at me quizzically. 'Why did you leave him on his own, anyway?'

Jasmin had helped me into the house. I remember that much. She is a lot stronger than she looks. As we waited for the doctor to arrive, I needed an excuse. I mumbled something about the shock of not seeing Francisco in the car. The doctor appeared and gave me something. I don't remember any more until I woke up just now.

'You know what it's like when you get older? When you have to go, you have to go. I stopped for a "*xixi*". I thought I saw a baby rabbit in the long grass and I would catch it to show Francisco. I followed it into the field and must have spent five minutes looking for it, without success.' I shrug my shoulders. 'He must have thought I had left him.'

It was the first time I have seen her laugh in days. 'Sometimes, I don't know which one of you is the child.'

'If he's not up to going with you, he is welcome to stay with me.'

'He will be okay.'

'He has a problem with his grandmother. Please, don't force him.'

She smiles again. 'I know. Inés is taking her own car, so we don't have to travel together.' She stands up. 'It's good you care. I'll not let him forget that.'

I wait until the purr of Lino's car fades into the distance, replaced by a comforting silence save for the customary brushing of the naked tree branches against the window frame and the far-off hum of traffic noise.

All the desperate sounds in my head are imagined, transposed from the group of photographs that are laid out on the bed before me. Screams. Laughter. The sounds of lust and violation.

Jasmin was young, a year or two younger than the family photograph taken when she was in the wheelchair at the christening. She is on a shabby-looking single bed, naked, spread out legs astride, her wrists and ankles bound and tied to the metal bed frame. The man adopts various stances around her, some posed for the camera, others with macho gestures as he prepares to penetrate her or smiling as he holds his penis close to her mouth. In every image, she has her eyes closed tight.

I recognise the man as Estevão, her father. I assume it must be Vicente who is taking the photographs. Eight images show incest, abuse and depravity in all its horror. I have no idea what I should do next. Both of the perpetrators are dead at their own hands. The only person who will be prejudiced if these images were ever to see the light of day would be the victim, Jasmin.

I gather the photographs, shuffling them behind the prints that Brigitte lent me. I study the prints of Albert. Did he know anything about Jasmin's past? Did she confide in him?

I find myself concentrating on the images of the three boys – young men, as they were – on holiday in the sunshine, clad in flimsy trunks with the beach bar in the background. With what I now know, I can look in a new light at Albert and Hugo with their arms around each other's shoulders as they stand, half directed towards each other, half turned to the camera, portraying a much deeper relationship than simple male bonding.

The photo of the two brothers together provides a different insight. Albert's arm is hovering above Vernon's shoulder, their bodies a distance apart. As arrogantly relaxed as Vernon appears, there is a tight expression on Albert's face. They are worlds apart, brothers in name only. Vernon has obviously been in some sort of struggle if the scratches under his eye and the welts on his arm are anything to go by. There is something strangely familiar about the second photograph I find puzzling. It has been taken from a slightly different angle to the first, with more of the background in the frame.

There is somebody at the front door.

I sweep up the pack of photos, hiding them under the bedcover, and pull on a dressing gown. Through the side window, I can make out the figure of Walid stamping his feet up and down, his posture agitated. There is nobody else in my field of vision. I check the chain lock on the door as he moves closer.

'What do you want?' I try not to sound as hostile as I feel. 'We're done.' I look searchingly over his shoulder.

'I am here alone. I no want any trouble with Madame Brigitte. She told me to come.'

'What does that mean?'

He holds out a gold link necklace with a pendant on it. 'Your son needed things from us. He said this was worth a lot of money.' He spits to one side. 'It not solid, just plated. Worth nothing. Take it.' He pushes it through the gap in the door into my hand. 'Tell him not to come again. We want nothing more with you Harts. You make trouble for us with police. You shit English!'

He turns to walk away. I'm confused. 'Just a minute. My son, you say. When was this?'

There is a moment's hesitation as he stops and turns around. 'When you think? When we first see him and you.'

I should have the presence of mind to press for more information but I'm just relieved to shut the door. Through the window, I follow his movement back out of the drive. I shove the necklace into the pocket of the dressing gown which I hang on the bedroom door before climbing back into bed.

The stress of seeing one of my aggressors again has left me confused. What prompted him to come round now after all this time? Is it possible Vernon has returned to Cavalla? My mind is all over the place.

My fingers touch the magic slate under the bed clothes. It is the picture Francisco sketched whilst I was in Vicente's cottage. What did he mean by it?

Had whoever was in the cottage cycled past the car and caused Francisco to become so distressed he hid in his chair as he wet himself? If so, what did the bubble and the dots mean?

The sensation was back. The smell of dead flesh. The acid burning inside my nostrils that made my face rack with pain. Only this time, it was more powerful and overwhelming than ever. There was that laugh – but not just the laugh; a voice as well. It kept saying one thing over and over again.

'You know, it wasn't an accident.'

CHAPTER TWENTY-EIGHT
Sanlazer – 1996

I could have sworn I heard a sniffling sound coming from Isabel's bedroom.

'Help!' I cried out as I careered into our bedroom and fumbled for my mobile. I sobbed out a disjointed stream of information and shouted demands at the emergency operator, who seemed to dissect my words with practised precision.

'Stay with the lady, please,' the measured voice said. 'We will be there very shortly.'

I could make out the sound of Salvador's voice on the road at the front of the villa. He was talking into his phone.

My knee juddered against the metal upright at the bottom of the stairs. Calm down. I hesitated, stroking at the jarring pain, hobbling forward into the darkness of the backyard and the communal gardens.

Where was she? I looked at the spot where she had been laying. There was nothing but the bloodstain over the concrete surround next to the pool. I was on my hands and knees, trying to peer into the darkness. 'Rosita! Rosita!'

The pool lights suddenly came on. Bulbs flickered into life from under the bushes. I looked up to see Salvador and a uniformed police officer running towards me. The palms of my hands were covered in blood. They were looking past me at something else.

I turned my head. Rosita was lying face down, hands outstretched, a foot or so under the surface of the water. Salvador yanked me out of the way as I tried to rise. He was in the pool and lifting her bodily out of the water. Her face looked so ashen white, no sign of her perpetual tan. I tried to stagger on my knees towards her, but two firm hands held me back.

The next few hours were a blur. Somebody had wrapped me in a blanket. A medic wearing a luminous yellow waistcoat looked at me anxiously as he gave me an injection. I watched people moving around me as if in slow motion. Fierce beams from arc lights illuminated the whole scene. Beyond the police cordon, a small group of people looked on. People covered from head to toe in white plastic suits began to move around. Eliana appeared alongside me to ask how I was.

'Come on,' the medic said with a forced half-smile. 'We take you to the hospital.'

I imagined that I could feel Rosita's firm body next to mine.

'Let's go to sleep now,' I heard myself say.

CHAPTER TWENTY-NINE
Cavalla – 2008

'You never talk about yourself much, Jasmin. What you were like as a girl. What it was like growing up in Cavalla. I really know very little about you.'

We have just put Francisco to bed together. Jasmin assures me his day was a series of wonderful sights and sounds. I'm sure, in the main, it's true, but the intensity with which he hugs me, the constant glances over his shoulder to see if anybody is behind him, I have my doubts. The trouble is, Jasmin possesses a special skill, the capacity to lock away the unpleasant and uncomfortable, to believe everything will be all right. Having seen the photographs, I can understand why, but if she continues to avoid the truth, she will reach a tipping point with desperate consequences. I have thought long and hard over whether and how to approach the topic. I don't want to put her through it, but I have to know.

We are sitting in the lounge. The atmosphere is far from relaxed. My prying has again set the tone. Does she know if Vernon is in town? It was as if I uncorked a demon from the bottle. She knows nothing and, in any event, there is no way she or any of her relatives want anything to do with my family, especially my vindictive ex-wife and deranged son. Thanks to Lino, I suspect, it's obvious the context of 'my family' now includes me.

Her fiery response turns into a sulk. She has a magazine balanced on her knees and I can sense an excuse is on the way to free her from answering.

I press home my point before she has the opportunity. 'Tell me something about you. For instance, how did you get on with your parents as you were growing up?'

She wriggles uncomfortably in her seat. 'Nothing much to tell. It was a very normal childhood. Nothing exciting ever really happens in Cavalla.' There she goes, trying to broaden the question into some banal generality.

'Did your father love you?'

She looks like a rabbit caught in the headlights. 'I don't know what you mean by that.' She looks away at the floor and I ask her to look at me and repeat what she said. 'Of course he did.'

'Did you ever tell anyone just how your father loved you?' I ask, expecting her to jump up and say goodnight. But, just like the rabbit, she stays frozen to the spot, seemingly unable to move. Her eyes stray to the photograph of Inés on the mantelpiece.

'Did your mother know before or did you tell her?'

She begins to shake her head violently. Tears well in her eyes.

I have to take a chance or the moment will pass. 'Answer me!' I say sternly. 'Can't you see the benefit of talking to somebody who has nothing to do with your past and, after next week, will have nothing to do with your future? I believe I know what happened.' I sound a damn sight more certain than I really am. I am drawing conclusions out of thin air.

'About what? About me? How could you?' she stammers.

'Because I do. Let's leave it at that.' I am about to walk on some really thin ice. 'Severe physical and mental deformity in the newborn can often be the result of inbreeding. It must have been a difficult birth for a young, frail girl to handle. It's no wonder you were in a wheelchair at the christening.'

Her head stops shaking. Her eyes are pleading. She is looking at me in absolute amazement.

I am right. I have to follow-up. 'I expect if I research Martin's birth certificate, I'll find it says that Inés was the mother and Estevão was the father. But you and I know that's not true. DNA can prove it.' I smile at her. 'I don't want to persecute you, Jasmin. For God's sake, you have gone through enough. Just tell me what I need to know and I won't ask any more questions. I have seen Francisco's birth certificate. Just who is Francisco's father? I have a right to know.'

She is about to say something, but instead she blinks several times. It's just as if curtains have been drawn. Her fists are clenched as she gets to her feet. For a second, I think she is about to strike me. 'Just who are you?' The words are hissed. 'What are you doing here? You have no place in our lives.' She moves towards the door.

'Whether I do or not is exactly what I'm trying to find out,' I say calmly.

The door nearly comes off its hinges as she slams it shut behind her.

CHAPTER THIRTY
Sanlazer – 1996

It did not take long for expressions of concern and sympathy to turn into innuendo and suspicion. It was perfectly natural, Salvador had assured me as he waited at the hospital for the emergency room doctor to prescribe the medication I should take to deal with the crisis. Ninety per cent of all domestic violence was perpetrated or arranged by the spouse and, until it was shown to the contrary, preconceptions within the local community and the press would indirectly point a finger at me.

The nursing staff had looked after me, treated my knee and washed Rosita's blood from my hands, but it was still caked under my fingernails. I tried to pick them clean but my hands were shaking. They were still shaking as we made our way through the silent crowd of blank faces in the road outside the villa. Thankfully, TM and Romina were still in Seville with the children. Eliana and Isabel had driven to break the news, but they intended to wait until the morning when medical support for the elderly parents would be at hand.

The cocktail of drugs they had given me had started to take effect. I could hardly stand or keep my eyes open. Salvador would stay close by throughout the night. He had given the police a rundown of events sufficient to raise a nationwide alert to apprehend Gonzalo. They had found the details of the Transit and his family address. The police would be round to collect me in the morning for a briefing. We'll get the bastard, Salvador had assured me.

For the first thirty seconds when I awoke, everything was gloriously as it had been days earlier. Rosita was having the baby, life was good and everything would be just fine. The enormity of the tragedy came in a sudden surge, as if a plastic bag had been thrust over my head and was being gripped tight around my neck. I struggled for breath, the tears filling my eyes, the realisation of just how much I had loved her; and now, with her gone, I was all alone.

The crowd was still outside when the police car arrived, damning in their silence as their gaze followed every move. It felt as though the officers were bundling, not helping me into the car. Salvador was not with me any more.

La Comisaría in Huelva was an unimposing, single-storey building a few blocks back from the Odiel river. As we climbed the steps to the entrance, a policeman supporting or perhaps securing my arm led me up the few stairs past a gaggle of photographers and reporters waiting for anything to provide a story. They kept me in a waiting room, sitting on a bench seat alongside my appointed minder, staring at a pair of highly varnished light-pine doors, above which was a clock that was actually ticking. I felt numb from head to toe.

It was nearly one in the afternoon, with the smell of cooking oil coming from somewhere in the building, when I was led into the interview room. There were two men and a woman waiting for me.

'I am Inspector Jefe Hernando Sanchez.' He smiled briefly, avoiding my outstretched hand. 'This is Inspector Almeida.' He pointed to the thin, angular man with designer stubble and a goatee beard. 'And there is Marianne. Under our rules, we are obliged to have a translator present when conducting an inter—' I sensed he went to say 'interrogation' but corrected himself in time. 'An interview,' he said. 'But I speak English fairly well and I am sure you understand some Spanish.'

Condescending bastard, I thought to myself, but just nodded.

'Unfortunately, Marianne was on court duty until some moments ago – the reason, you understand, why we have to keep you waiting.'

His English was clipped and guttural. Listening to him speak in Castilian to his colleagues with that grating monotone, I guessed he originated in the Basque country. He had a pronounced high forehead made more prominent by a receding hairline and short-cropped hair. There was a cleft above a rather effeminate-looking bowed top lip and a mean, stretched bottom lip that was hardly visible. I put him in his early forties.

I listened to what I believed were heartfelt sentiments about my terrible loss and the circumstances surrounding this heinous crime. Rosita's parents were on their way back from Seville and he would be speaking to them as soon as we had finished.

I must have been looking at the floor, lost in my memories of the previous night, but his words had registered.

'Are you feeling all right?' he asked. 'We can leave it until later, but it would help to understand what you know. If you like, we can ask someone to sit with you, a lawyer perhaps.'

I looked up into those deep-set brown eyes shielded by bushy, unkempt eyebrows and shook my head violently. 'No, I'm fine. I don't need anybody, certainly not a lawyer. I haven't done anything. If you want to know, I feel desperately sad and desolate. How would you expect me to feel? Go ahead and ask your questions. Just catch the sick fuck who did this.'

He coughed and raised a sheet of paper from which he started reading. 'Let me bring you up to date with the investigation. Firstly, your wife was assaulted and left for dead. Apparently, according to the pathologist's initial report and the chain of events as we understand them, although both were badly injured, neither she nor your unborn child died from this attack. Somehow, she crawled to the edge of the pool and slid into the water. She perished from drowning and, as a consequence, could no longer pass oxygenated blood via the umbilical cord to the child. Had a shorter time elapsed before medical aid could be administered, perhaps the baby …'

'Are you saying—'

'I am saying nothing. There will be a full autopsy today. We would expect to release the bodies for burial within two days. The wounds suffered resulted in substantial blood loss.'

There was still the blood caked underneath my fingernails. I didn't want to get rid of it any more.

'Have you found Gonzalo? Was she …?' I could not bring myself to ask the question.

It was as though he had been waiting for this moment. He must have given a great deal of thought to the words he chose. 'These are early moments in the investigation and there is much work still to do. I can tell you that from a preliminary examination it does not appear the señora was violated. There is, however, some evidence of recent sexual activity. Can you comment on that?'

Bewildered, I shook my head. 'What does that mean?'

He ignored the question. 'As to the whereabouts of señor Ramirez, I will come to that.' There was a watery smile on his lips. 'Firstly, to piece together a timeline, we need to know exactly what you were doing. Please start with your visit to Seville.'

With a great deal of effort, I stumbled into a recital of my movements over the last forty-eight hours, gradually gaining pace and fluency as the vivid memories of the last hours came sharply into focus.

He stopped me only once. 'You heard the sound of breaking glass?'

'Yes. I guessed Gonzalo was trying to get into the villa to attack Rosita.'

'Did you see any broken glass at the villa?'

I hadn't been looking, but I didn't recall seeing any.

'Tell me a little bit about the relationship you had with your wife. I call her your wife, but you were not married, were you?' He sounded censorious.

'What's there to tell? We were happy and we loved each other. I am sure we would have got married when the baby was born.' I stopped to compose myself as the sadness descended on me again.

'You would have disagreements from time to time?'

'What's that supposed to mean?'

'What I say. Did you have arguments?'

'Like any couple, we would have spats from time to time. Nothing serious.'

'I am sorry. "Spats"?'

The translator spoke for the first time.

He looked into my eyes without blinking. And did these' – he hesitated, for effect, I guessed – 'spats develop into a violent argument some days earlier on the subject of Gonzalo?'

'No, they did not. I mean, there was no argument about Gonzalo. Who told you that?'

'Isn't it true that you thought your wife was getting too close to Gonzalo? Perhaps too intimate?'

'Rubbish. What is this? Are you trying to suggest I had something to do with Rosita's death? If you are, you're crazy.'

'Maybe you were jealous of your employee. You wanted to fire him, is it not?'

'We both thought it was time he should leave. He was not doing his job properly.'

'Why did you argue with your wife about it if you both agreed?'

I was beginning to lose my temper. 'I've told you once. I'll tell you again. We did not argue. Rather than me sack him, Rosita said it would sound better coming from her and I accepted the argument. I didn't want to lose my temper with him.' As the words left my mouth, I realised I'd overstepped the mark.

'You get violent when you lose your temper, do you?' He looked down at a piece of paper couched in his hand beneath the level of the table. 'Did you get angry when you found out she was having an affair with Gonzalo Ramirez?'

'Who's feeding you this rubbish? There was no affair with Gonzalo. He just worked for us.'

There was a sharp rap on the door and a uniformed officer beckoned for Sanchez to join him. We waited in uncomfortable silence. Marianne fidgeted in her chair, her cheeks puffed in apparent exasperation. The other policeman casually pulled at the end of his goatee beard as he leaned back and stared at the ceiling.

'Can I have a glass of water?'

They must have been looking and listening in another room. Sanchez returned with a chilled plastic bottle in his hand and gave it to me.

'Do you know the whereabouts of Rinat Kryvorobycho?' He stumbled over the pronunciation, carefully emphasising each syllable.

'Who? Never heard of him.' My patience was being sorely tested. 'Are we finished? In case you've forgotten, I've lost my wife and baby and I need to be on my own.'

'I think you may know him as Robi. He works as a gardener for the condominium.'

'Of course I know Robi and I have no idea where he is. Why?'

'He did not report for work this morning.'

I went to stand up. Goatee nearly slipped back in his chair, only just managing to regain his balance.

'This is ridiculous,' I said. 'I come here to help and you treat me as somehow implicated in my wife's death. I want to go.'

Sanchez gestured for me to sit down. His voice was placatory. 'Just one more thing. You have a Furgon, a Transit van which you use for your business?'

'Yes. Gonzalo uses it. It's normally kept at his place.'

'Was it there last night?'

'No. That's how I knew he was not at home.'

'Did you check around his house?'

'What for? I've told you. The van was not parked up. I assumed he had gone back to our villa and went after him.'

'You did not go to the back entrance?'

'The kitchen door was open, so I went in to establish whether he was there.'

'The glass in the kitchen door to his house had been broken. You know nothing about that, I suppose?'

My fist thumped on the table, knocking the plastic bottle onto its side. 'I can't say I noticed. It was getting dark and I hadn't gone there to give his place a security check. Where is all this leading?'

He ignored the outburst, treating the question as rhetorical. 'You may be interested to know that we located the vehicle early this morning. It was on a piece of waste ground near the Santa Justa railway station in Seville. You know the area? It's the main station. He could have taken a train to anywhere.'

I gritted my teeth and shook my head. I had never met such an infuriating man.

'The strange thing is that when our forensic team went to check it out, there was not a fingerprint in the van. Now, I ask myself, why would Gonzalo, who normally drives the van, bother to wipe all trace of his presence from its interior? It doesn't make sense, does it?'

Beyond a shrug of the shoulders, it was my turn to treat a question as rhetorical.

Rosita's parents were sitting in the waiting room, Eliana in attendance. She gave me a weak smile as I passed and looked away. Romina looked up at me as if in the expectation that I had somehow managed to bring Rosita back to life. TM turned sideways, his demeanour intent on ignoring me. At this stage, there seemed little I could say, so I mumbled a brief 'Good afternoon' and followed the policeman who would take me back to Sanlazer.

By the time I got back to the villa, I could see that Robi was back at work, shuffling aimlessly around the pool, a barrier around the area of the bloodstain which had been treated with some chemical in an attempt to lift the stark reminder from the paving stones. The collection of plastic furniture arranged in a protective circle was hardly necessary. Nobody was coming to sunbathe or swim, nor, I doubted, would they do so for some time to come.

Robi looked shattered. He had spoken to the police, he told me. He was devastated. He should have been around. I assured him that the fact he had left earlier the previous day for what turned out to be an all-night drinking session with some friends was irrelevant. As it was, Gonzalo might well have shown up for the meeting with Rosita whilst Robi was still there, but the crime had been committed many hours later. He should not blame himself, but I could see that he did. He was giving a week's notice, he announced. There was no way he could carry on after what had happened. I could understand that. I felt much the same.

There was not much noise in the villa beyond the perpetual drone of the television news channel in the lounge, which TM insisted remain on during the day. A full-scale manhunt was in progress for Gonzalo with repetitive images of his face on the screen, a twenty-second filler showing his parents avoiding the press, a still of Rosita taken from her passport photo and confirmation that police forces throughout Europe had been alerted. TM would religiously watch every repeat, muttering that death would be too kind a sentence for what he had done. Gonzalo had been tried, convicted and sentenced by the media as far as TM was concerned, and, by association, I was equally guilty for having wreaked this disaster upon the family.

I kept to my room as much as possible, avoiding contact with anybody. Initially, I had left the villa to walk on my own, but I had gathered local celebrity status, with people pointing at me with uncertain glances as if I had some rare infectious disease. So I tended to stay in the villa.

None of the family would talk much. Even Salvador, who was the most resilient of us, kept his conversation to a minimum. He did tell me as Rosita and I had not married, the responsibility for the funeral arrangements rested with the family, and TM had insisted that I play no part in Saturday's proceedings beyond my attendance. There was no point in arguing. There had to be a flesh and blood scapegoat to channel the grief and, as unfair as it was on me, I could understand the need. The converse was also becoming a reality. I had started to actively dislike and resent all of them for their attitude towards me. It took my mind off Rosita, and the sense of hostility channelled my grief into a reaction with which I could deal.

The funeral was a turgid affair, full of dour, lengthy prayers and eulogies in Spanish I did not understand. I was treated as if a casual bystander, purposefully excluded from the family group and left to my own devices. I saw Sanchez and two other plain clothes policemen circulating around the perimeter of the large crowd of mourners together with a photographer who was trying discreetly, but unsuccessfully so, to take pictures of various individuals. A pointless operation, I thought.

I hardly recognised the muscular Robi dressed in an ill-fitting suit with a skew-whiff tie around his shirt collar, looking both extremely uncomfortable and distressed by the occasion. He was the only person who came up to me and shook my hand.

Rosita and our unborn daughter were laid to rest together. I picked up a handful of earth to drop onto the coffin and said a quiet, tearful goodbye to the woman I loved.

Reality descended upon me hard and fast. I had wondered why Isabel had not attended the funeral, and now I knew. The villa was empty. They had all gone off somewhere without telling me. On the doorstep were two suitcases and a note from Salvador. Isabel had packed all of my belongings she could find. If there was anything else, I should advise a forwarding address and Salvador would send it on to me. I was no longer welcome in the house, nor did any of the family ever wish to speak to me again. Please respect their wishes.

I slept in a sleeping bag on the floor of our rented office-cum-storeroom for the next few days. I tried desperately to keep our business intact, but it was as if the whole Spanish-speaking community had as one turned against me. Nobody appeared to understand English any more, existing contracts were curtailed with banal excuses and the new work we had been ready to undertake was cancelled without explanation. I got angry at first, resentful, ready to fight the world, and then suddenly a calm descended upon me.

I spent a week collecting outstanding debts from clients. I won't pretend it was easy. My technique was to sit in reception, sometimes for hours at a time, until they were so desperate to get rid of me they paid up. Apart from one hard-nosed ex-boxer turned construction entrepreneur, who threatened to do what the rest of Spain would like to do to me, or so he said, I had an almost perfect result. At least I had enough to survive for a year or so. Perhaps I'd look for a business opportunity in a new field. I was as disenchanted with the Spanish as they were with me. There was nothing like some English-speaking companionship, so I drifted to the Costa del Sol, a world of foreign tourists, expat residents and, sadly, a new life amongst a transient and predictable population.

The rest, as they say, is history, and a fake Rolex watch.
Or so I thought.

CHAPTER THIRTY-ONE
Cavalla – 2008

I make my daily call to Borodin's voice mail number. For once I can say my movements will involve something a little more interesting than the crèche, the pharmacy or the coffee shop in the centre of town. Between 2 and 5 p.m. I will be visiting the safari park near Lamego at Tamboreira, just off the A24 motorway, the cross-country link that straddles Northern Portugal and extends to the Spanish border. It's a good forty-minute car journey and we will be travelling in convoy.

I pass by the pharmacy to tell Adele I won't be seeing her again as I'm leaving for the UK the next day. She looks and sounds relieved. I guess at last things in Cavalla will be back to their three-monkey status of see no evil, hear no evil, speak no evil. I wish her a Merry Christmas and get a half-hearted blown kiss in reply. At least Pom-Pom reacts with his customary enthusiasm at seeing me.

Since our truncated conversation, Jasmin has purposely avoided me. Hugo made an appearance yesterday afternoon to tell me the arrangements for the trip to the safari park. He was aching to leave, but I felt like provoking a reaction and we were way past tact.

'I expect you would know. Is Vernon back in town?'

He looks to one side. 'News to me if he is,' he says. 'I knew he was due back to collect some of Albert's bits and pieces, possibly the car, but I haven't seen him.'

I ask him to look at me and repeat what he said. He does.

'Brigitte told me you weren't a very good liar.'

'Sorry?' My remark has caught him off guard.

'Not to worry. Can't you see I'm just an old man wanting to understand what made his son get involved with your dysfunctional family?' I don't give him time to react. 'How long had your affair with my son been going on?'

He stares at me with a mixture of alarm and hostility. 'Since Brighton,' he replies. 'Off and on.'

'Did you love each other?'

He presses his lips together and looks upward as if thinking time is somehow necessary to give a spontaneous answer. 'I think so. Like any couple, we had good and bad moments.'

'I'll put it on his tombstone, shall I? Albert – who was maybe loved, off and on.'

'More by me than his own father.'

'You can only take that at face value, Hugo. You really don't know anything about me and the way I have always felt about Albert.' Again, I don't wait for a rejoinder. 'Did he know Jasmin gave birth to a child when she was still a child herself? Did he know who the father of the child he introduced to me as his own is?' I was beginning to get angry.

'Listen. Jasmin told me all about your wild and slanderous theories. They are all bullshit. The best thing you can do is keep them to yourself.'

'I probably will, Hugo. I probably will, if only not to cause any more hurt to the suffering which your poor sister has gone through at the hands of her father. But if you force me to, well … DNA is infallible, I understand.'

'What do you want?'

'I need to know who Francisco's father is. Somebody has to tell me, or my slanderous theories, as you call them, will rule the day.'

I watch him turn and leave without saying another word.

Francisco careers into the lounge and jumps onto my lap. His rucksack, adorned with cartoon characters, rests against my chest. 'Safawi,' he keeps repeating excitedly.

I check the Rolex. We are due to leave.

'Where is Mummy?' I ask.

'I'm here.' She taps me on the shoulder from behind.

I don't look round. 'You have been avoiding me.'

'I had nothing to say to you.' As I cannot see her, she must have assumed I did not hear.

'I have told you. I don't want to cause you distress. I feel pity …' The word is out before I realise I've said it. However true, it's a poor choice. 'Sympathy' would have been a better option.

She's in front of me in an instant, her face flushed with anger. The rucksack is pressed hard into my chest. 'I don't need your pity,' she hisses. 'I don't need a man's pity. I don't need anybody's pity. You're all pathetic individuals without depth or substance. You just take what you can get.'

I apologise for my choice of words. 'I can understand why you feel like that.'

'You have no idea what I feel. I know, because Albert used to tell me. You lived in a world of adult male dominance where your wife and children were your subjects and what you said was what happened. You wanted to rule, just like all the men I have ever known, Albert excepted. But I guess he had a lot of non-male aspects to his character.'

'I didn't know Albert felt like that about me. I don't recognise myself in your description.'

There is a ring at the doorbell. She pulls Francisco off my lap. 'You should study yourself in the mirror,' she says.

If it were not for Francisco's incessant monologue in the car, I doubt more than half a dozen words were exchanged between the three of us. Hugo concentrated on driving whilst Jasmin, in the front passenger seat, looked steadfastly out of the window. I pretended to be paying attention to the little chatterbox, but I was a million miles away.

Aventura Selvagem is just south of the town, signposted from the motorway and set in rolling, tree-lined countryside on a large swathe of land at the perimeter of parkland. The impressive entrance to the safari park is through an archway built in the form of a lion's roaring mouth, alongside which are a dozen or so deserted ticket booths, fronted by a large sign which announces the park will reopen to the public for the end-of-year holiday season as from tomorrow.

We park alongside Lino's car where he and Inés are waiting. As he catches sight of his grandmother, Francisco stiffens. I wait for his soft fingernails to dig into the back of my hand, pulling me towards him. I try to comfort him as we all exchange cursory greetings.

When closed, the two sets of tall metal entrance gates, complete with speakers broadcasting jungle noises, give the impression wild animals are close at hand. I recognise the marketing technique. Build tension. The idea is for the public to assemble apprehensively in groups as they wait for the first door to swing open and close, leaving them confined, facing an inner gate, much like a boat confined in a canal lock. They are trapped. Nervous anticipation grows as the volume of jungle sounds increases. When the inner gate swings open, the expectation is to come face-to-face with some fearsome jungle scene. The sense of relief is palpable.

Directly beyond the gate stand two employees, one dressed head to foot as a lion, the other as a tiger, intent on welcoming their guests and, as they do so, intentionally barring the passageway through to the entrance into a large courtyard with a variety of point-of-sale stalls. Today, the stalls are empty. Tomorrow, they will be decked out with all sorts of souvenirs, confectionery and snacks for the visitors to buy before starting their adventure. As each visitor enters, he or she is hugged by the lion man or his tiger friend while the official photographer takes a photo, available, of course, to purchase on the way out. Beyond the courtyard is a martialling area for the clients to assemble into escorted groups, where a dozen open-sided passenger vehicles are parked, ready for a guided tour around the park.

We are introduced to Emilio, a serious-looking, balding man in his forties with rosy, veined cheeks, dressed in a park security uniform, who explains that for reasons of safety we will be using a closed vehicle to travel through the various enclosures. Today, as there is only a skeleton staff on site with no sector watchers, he will remain with us. By his relaxed but deferential attitude to Jasmin, I can tell she is not only a familiar face but a respected professional team member.

Lino instructs Francisco to sit next to his mother by the window on the two seats across the central walkway from me. The big diesel engine roars into life.

Emilio points his remote control at the first set of enclosure gates. They open and close behind us with a loud hydraulic hiss, and the adventure begins.

My memory comes alive. Day trips to Longleat and Windsor Safari Park with Sandra when the boys were nine or ten. I have never been one for looking at animals, either in this semi-wild state or in zoos. It seems like such a pointless occupation, staring at them as they stare back or, more likely, totally ignore you. Watching grown men stand in front of a cage mimicking a primate in the hope they can provoke a reaction seems to me to give the evolutionary advantage to the animal. It's rather like mewing at a cat or barking at a dog. The animal knows it's not real.

In those far-off days, the wonder of the safari park was not the herds of Watusi or wildebeest roaming around; the elephants, in a line, trunk to tail, in the background; the zebras and giraffes reacting to the sound of the vehicle;

and herbivores of all shapes and sizes, surviving together in their complex ecosystem. The wonder was the look of excitement and amazement on the faces of my boys.

Today, it is Francisco who captivates my attention. He is mesmerised by the scenes before him, jumping up and down in his seat, face pressed close to the window, breath clouding the glass and babbling in his own little language as he addresses the animals. I feel a tremendous sense of loss. Tears well in my eyes.

We move on through the monkey enclosure. I watch the expression on his little face change from anticipation to amusement as the various breeds of primates recognise the vehicle and rush towards it, clambering up and across, studying the inmates with unblinking eyes as they climb adroitly past the windows.

Finally, we are in the lion enclosure. Prides of these majestic animals rest under trees or amble along together. One large male stands in the road, blocking the way forward. Francisco roars at him, his hands raised in claws, fear in his face as the lion appears to hear him, tossing his head from side to side, his lips parted and teeth bared as the sound reaches us. Emilio gives several beeps on his horn and the animal turns, unconcerned, and moves slowly out of our path.

As the last gate shuts behind us, the vehicle comes to a halt with Emilio indicating for us to follow him. This is the African Trail, he explains. First comes the trek along a narrow path with savannah grass on either side. Just beyond the strip of grassland is an enormous aviary with birds of all descriptions, a cacophony of noise as they settle amongst the leaves and branches. Next, the Kenyan Homestead, a farm-like environment with pens of domestic and petting animals, including a family of meerkats standing on their hind legs with exaggerated head movements as they are attracted to the sound of Francisco as he points and laughs at them. Lastly, we arrive at the zoo with the caged or penned animals who are not allowed to roam within the enclosures, a reptile house and Mundo dos Mares, a world of sea creatures.

The large African-styled, thatched-roof cafeteria and the even bigger gift shop appear to be the high point of our visit, at least as far as Francisco is now concerned.

You haven't quite seen everything, Emilio tells us. Pointing upward, he indicates a canopied wooden construction some thirty metres above us. He turns to face the group.

'The grazing animals that we saw in the first quadrant have a replica of a watering hole made for them at the extreme of the area. From the observation platform up there you can view the animals in and around the water. You might also catch sight of the hippopotamus and white rhinoceros which spend most of the day in this area.'

I am on the point of saying I have already seen enough when Lino appears at my side.

'What a great idea,' he says. 'I don't know if you made out what he was saying, Gil, but it's something we've just got to see.' He tugs at my arm. The friendly approach baffles me. Is he just trying to improve the atmosphere between us before I leave? Hardly a Lino trait.

'There are two ways up,' Emilio says. 'The scenic route is to follow the trail up to the gorge bridge and cross. It was constructed to resemble a rickety rope bridge like you see on the films, but it's perfectly safe. Go up that way and come down via the elevator. That's the route we insist the public take. The elevator brings you down into the middle of the gift shop.'

'We'll stay here with Inés and Francisco,' Jasmin says. 'I need to speak with Emilio about something.'

Francisco looks confused at the turn of events. 'I can take the boy up with me, if you like,' I press, anxious to ease his anxiety.

'He's staying with me,' Jasmin snaps back. 'Can't you see he's tired out?'

It's not my place to take issue with her.

'Let's take a look before the light fades,' Lino insists jovially. 'Lead the way, Captain Hart.'

The trail leads up a winding single-file track until we are level with the bridge. I go to stop to take a breath but a hand urges me on. The bridge sways as we cross, our hands grasping upwards, feeling for purchase on the hemp guidelines, the securing ropes creaking as the weight of our bodies forces down on the wooden struts. It feels dangerous but in the gaps between the wood I can see the metal superstructure surrounding the bridge on three sides. There is no way anybody could fall to the ground from this carefully planned construction.

As we step off the bridge, there is a large observation terrace overlooking a muddy lake which Emilio evocatively described as the watering hole. A chest-high metal barrier runs around the perimeter with three coin-operated telescopes installed at intervals along it. At the far end, there is an entrance way and an arrow indicating access to the elevator. A plastic canopy has been erected in front of the metal doors, presumably to protect them from the worst of any bad weather.

A figure moves in the shadows.

What's going on—' I swing around to find Hugo following me. 'Where's Lino?' I ask.

'Telephone call,' he replies abruptly and turns away from me to walk hurriedly over in the direction of the elevator.

I move forward but I can barely make out their silhouettes in the half-light and the shadow of the canopy. There is nobody else on the terrace.

'No need to mention Spain,' Hugo says to the figure.

There's that laugh. 'You just did,' Vernon says.

'He can't hear us. He's deaf. Remember?'

'Poor sod! Deaf and vertigo. What a combination.'

'Just get it over with. Don't make a meal of it, like last time.'

'Keep your hair on. Does he remember anything?'

'I don't know. Jasmin said he keeps getting flashbacks.'

Vernon pushes Hugo to one side. 'Leave it to me.'

He ambles across to where I am standing, alongside one of the fixed telescopes. He is wearing a black leather bomber jacket with an imitation fur collar. Many years ago, I used to have one just like it. Very warm, as I recall. Maybe it explains why, in spite of the chill wind blowing across the exposed terrace, there are beads of sweat glistening on his brow. His bloodshot eyes fix me in a steadfast gaze.

'You're deaf, but you can lip-read. Is that right?'

'I understand every word you say. Now, what is this, Vernon?'

'Not even a hello or how are you, Vernon? Just "what is this"?' He tried to imitate my voice. 'Do you remember anything about the day Albert died?'

I choose to ignore the question. 'Why this complicated set-up to get me on my own up here?'

'Hugo's idea. We needed a quiet place to talk. As far as the rest of the world is concerned, I'm not here.'

'So talk, son. Whatever you've got to say, get it off your chest and we can all go home.'

He took a step closer towards me. 'Don't ever call me son! My father died sixteen years ago and he's the only one who had the right to call me that. Not you.' He spat out the last two words.

'As much as I understand it, I'm sorry you feel that way.'

'Sorry? Sorry? You have no idea what the word means. You've never been sorry about anything in your life. Do you really think Albert invited you over for some sort of kiss and make up session? Let's bring back dear father into the fold?'

'That was my hope.'

'You pathetic old bastard! He asked you to come as part of the plan.'

'What plan?'

'You were meant to pay for all the suffering you caused your family, especially Mum. You don't even realise you caused her breakdown.' I could feel the warmth of his breath, the stench of stale alcohol and something else I recognised but couldn't quite bring to mind. 'A new wife and then all the talk of a new baby to replace us; ignoring Mum's pleas for you to come when Celine died. You never cared about us. We were your past and could be thrown away, like rubbish in the bin.'

'I never felt like that. I explained about Celine to her.'

'Sandra took pills, tried to kill herself.' He blinks rapidly, his breathing noisy and aggressive, his fists pumping. 'So, I decided something needed to be done about it. I wanted a solution to get you out of the way forever.'

I begin to understand. Until that moment, I had felt in control of the situation. He was my son, the boy who had always backed off with a stern word or a slap to bring him to his senses. Now, there is something sinister, calculating, but at the same time I know he is out of control, under the influence of some substance or other, and it frightens me.

Hugo is at his side. 'Get on with it,' he urges, anxiety written over his face.

Vernon glances around and smiles. 'My brother and his bum buddy here were involved in a little illegal activity that meant the house and its contents needed to be destroyed and the insurance collected. A fire was too risky. If the finger was pointed at Hugo, the insurance company wouldn't pay out.'

I'm confused. 'This is Albert and Jasmin's house you are talking about?'

He snorts a laugh. 'Do me a favour. They were never going to live in that house. Jasmin can't stand men. She tolerated Albert, who was no threat as he was shacked up with this one in an apartment in town. The marriage charade was arranged to keep Mum happy, explain Jasmin's child to the rest of the world and, at the same time, provide the obligatory grandchild. The house belonged to Hugo. Nobody really lived there. He was doing it up to sell and, for the time being, Albert was using it to make his poncey cushions.'

He backs away, still holding me in his watery gaze. For a moment, I sense the threat has receded. The same question keeps going over and over in my head. I turn to face Hugo. 'So, will you tell me, who is Francisco's father? Surely, it doesn't matter now.'

He studies the ground. He isn't going to tell me.

'My guess is your Uncle Vicente.'

I can tell from the look on his face I am right.

'We haven't time for all this,' he says to Vernon. 'Hurry up.'

Vernon rushes at me, pushing my back hard against the railing with one hand. He is surprisingly strong. 'So, there you are, dear father. I needed, yearned, for you to pay for what you did to your loving wife and your discarded offspring, and Hugo had to set fire to a house. What better solution than to invite a qualified heating engineer to his son's wedding.' His grip around my coat tightens. He begins to twist the material tighter. It's like a tourniquet around my chest, making it difficult for me to breath.

He laughs, moving even closer so that our foreheads touch. Of course, I now recognise the smell, acetone on his breath, his intense body warmth, the glazed look in his eyes. I used cocaine a couple of times in my youth at some wild parties. That laugh, and now, the smell. Those closed doors in my mind begin to open. It's what happened on that fateful morning.

They arrived together as I was finishing coffee. Hugo was nervous. Vernon was high. He talked and talked; at first calm and measured, the words a blur to me still. But he couldn't control himself. He began to shout. His hands were on me, forcing me to the ground, his knee in my chest holding me down, our faces nearly touching.

I remember the bell ringing at the front gate. Albert went to answer. Out of sight there were raised voices, shouting, the metal gate crashing on its hinges.

All the time, Vernon had his knee pinning me down. He ordered me to keep quiet. Had Hugo brought the Benzo-whatever it was? There was a syringe with some clear-coloured liquid in it. Hugo wanted to know how much he should give me. How the hell should Vernon know? Hugo was supposed to be the expert on drugs. After all ... 'Give him the whole fucking lot,' was the instruction.

My head was spinning as I came round. How much time had passed, I don't know. I was on my knees, wedged into the cupboard alongside the gas boiler. The isolation valve had been loosened and the low hiss was gas escaping. Hands were under my armpits, gripping at me, pulling desperately, Albert's voice urging me to get to my feet. I was standing aimlessly, disorientated, just outside the back door. He ordered me to wait, went back inside the house, shutting the door behind him. There was a blinding flash, followed instantaneously by the explosion.

'Is it all coming back to you now?' The sound of an elephant trumpeting by the waterhole breaks the memory. Vernon starts to lift my feet from the ground, both hands now gripping my coat. 'Lost his bottle, Albert, didn't he? Just like the last time. Couldn't go through with it. Gave his bloody life trying to save somebody as worthless as you. Well, it won't happen this time. You can check out the animals as they're having their nightcap. I've heard the rhinos can be quite friendly. Give me a hand here, Hugo.'

His head turns away from me to focus on Hugo who is fumbling in a trouser pocket to answer his mobile. 'The police are waiting downstairs,' he says, his voice an octave higher than normal.

The hold on my coat relaxes slightly. I have one chance. With one hand, I start to release his grip. My other hand closes around the eyepiece of the telescope and I swing it around as hard as I can. The impact sounds like a golf club striking a ball. The metal optical tube hits the side of Vernon's head, knocking him off balance. He collapses unconscious onto the ground. I pray it's no worse than concussion.

Hugo is backing off. Someone has called the elevator. It starts its descent. I grab Hugo by the collar. He may be younger and fitter than me, but there is no fight left in him. He looks petrified. I slap him hard around the face. He winces.

'I was right about Francisco, wasn't I?'

He nods.

'The first child. The one that died. That was Jasmin's as well?'

There is no reaction, so I slap him again, even harder. He begins to sob.

'Answer me or I'll hit you. And this time, it will really hurt.'

'Yes.'

There's a movement behind me, the rustle of clothes. I turn to defend myself but Vernon has picked himself up and is moving quickly to the bridge and his escape. Blood is running from his ear, oozing through the fingers pressed against the side of his head.

Two large black hands push the elevator doors apart. Lannier is striding forward, two uniformed officers at his side.

'You took your time,' I say. 'I thought you were supposed to be watching my back.'

He looks at me with raised eyebrows, turning to take in the scene and give Hugo a cursory nod before concentrating on me. Hugo sidles past into the elevator, saying something to Lannier as he does so. Lannier nods again. The doors of the elevator close and we are left standing in the eerie light of a hazy moon.

Lannier has still said nothing to me. He is looking around to see if anybody else is present.

'Are you letting him go?' I ask. 'Borodin will want to talk to him. He's complicit in all of this.'

His forehead creases. 'I do not understand what you are talking about, Mr Hart. I was advised by Mr Reyes' office that there was a family meeting here today. You will accompany us to Cavalla, where you will be held in custody in connection with a European Arrest Warrant. The charges supporting this warrant will be read to you when you are formally charged. In the meantime, hold out your hands, please.' He brandishes a pair of handcuffs in my direction.

My mind is racing. 'This is some terrible mistake,' I say. 'Speak to Borodin. He will explain everything.'

He ignores me, reaching for my arms as he turns to speak with his colleagues.

'No,' I plead. 'Please. Please. Put the handcuffs on outside if you must, but give me five minutes to speak with the people down there. It's important that

I say something for the sake of the child. I'm an old man. Hardly likely to try to escape, am I? I'm sure I can explain everything back at Cavalla, but please, just let me have some dignity until we leave this place.'

He hesitates for a moment before returning the cuffs to his belt. He shakes his head. 'I will let you have five minutes, no more.' He nods towards his men. 'We could do with a coffee.'

Anxious faces look at us as the elevator doors open. They are lined up with Lino at one end, Jasmin and Francisco next to him. Inés and Hugo are nowhere in sight. Emilio walks over to the three policemen for a whispered conversation.

I look at Jasmin. 'You have all got your reasons for hoping there would be a tragic accident here today when I would fall to my death from the observation deck. It did not happen and I have to go on, knowing that my son would have killed me and will go on wanting me dead.'

She holds the palms of her hands out towards me. 'You don't know what you are saying. They just wanted to talk to you on their own, to convince you to give up trying to blame Albert's death on anybody else but yourself.'

Lino is walking across just as a tiny hand begins to tug at my trouser leg, at first gently, and then, more urgently.

'You have started to meddle in the private concerns of the Reyes family,' Lino says with that supercilious tone I find so offensive. 'You have been asked to leave and can have no ties with this family any more.'

I sweep Francisco up into my arms. 'Is that so?' I make a funny face at him that provokes a giggle and a hug. 'It doesn't feel that way to me.'

'Anyway,' he says, waving his hand in the direction of the police. 'It appears that your disagreeable past has caught up with you at last.'

I can tell Lannier is becoming impatient. I ignore Lino and turn back to Jasmin. 'Telling anybody what I know or believe about you and your family will only make your suffering greater. I cannot control what may happen in the future, but you have my word I will not volunteer the information I have to anybody else. For this little one's sake, speak to someone who can help you. It is a terrible burden to carry alone for the rest of your life. You deserve support.'

We are outside, walking to the police car, before I chance a smile at Lannier. 'That was a clever deception, the warrant and all that. Was it

Borodin's idea? Perhaps you can take the handcuffs off now.'

He wrinkles his nose. 'You are talking about the consultant psychologist who came with me to interview you at the hospital? Why do you keep mentioning his name?'

'It was his idea. The examining magistrate's office.'

'I have no idea what you are talking about. Doutor Borodin is not connected to the magistrate's office. He has a medical practice. We only use him when we require a psychological evaluation. You are confused.'

I go to protest but hold back. A phone call to Borodin later will resolve the confusion.

He says something in Portuguese to the driver and they both laugh. I am wedged between two well-built policemen in the rear seat. 'Was that about me?' I say.

He grins so wide the gold fillings in his back teeth are visible. 'You will not need a psychologist, but a damn good lawyer. You are wanted for questioning in connection with three suspected homicides, and that is not forgetting our investigation into the death of your son.'

CHAPTER THIRTY-TWO
Cavalla – 2008

There is indeed a twelve-page arrest warrant in Spanish on the table in front of the local magistrate, along with an English translation for me and one in Portuguese which Domingos is thumbing through as we wait for the proceedings to get underway.

In spite of the gravity of the occasion, I find myself paying little attention to the bustle around me in the compact courthouse in Cavalla. The impact of the conspiracy to get me onto the observation deck at the safari park has left me with a sense not only of profound weariness and resignation, but the realisation I might as well be dead than burdened with the weight of all the animosity directed towards me. I will never be able to rid myself of the look of naked hatred in Vernon's eyes, the urge to see me lying lifeless on the ground, as insignificant as stamping on an insect before it can seek cover. I feel I have no energy left to resist.

'Your Doutor Borodin is not available to take calls at the present.' Domingos interrupts my train of thought. I tell him I don't care.

I have been primed to expect the worst. Domingos will make every effort to convince the magistrate I am not a flight risk and could be freed to await the outcome of the hearing to enforce the warrant, but he is doubtful his plea will be successful. The charges are extremely serious.

The man from the prosecutor's office in Porto is a slender, nondescript individual with an annoyingly squeaky voice reminiscent of a cartoon character. As he speaks, the young girl standing next to me, my court-appointed translator, begins in a strident but nervously loud whisper to explain what he is saying.

When the man sits down, Domingos rises to make his case on my behalf. Following the tragic death of my son, I stayed in Cavalla to assist in whatever way I could with the investigation, even though my hearing and memory were seriously impaired. I have worked diligently and honestly as a babysitter for the last four months, and had it not been for the lack of space in the employer's home over the festive period, I would not have been forced to consider returning to the UK. He makes me sound like a whiter than white Mary

Poppins who is as capable of flight as a bird with its wings clipped, but I doubt his sterling efforts are impressing the magistrate, an elderly man, who looks to me as if he is hiding behind a pair of thick-rimmed tortoiseshell glasses.

The magistrate asks both advocates to join him for a private meeting. Sitting alone in that tiny courtroom, I cast my eyes around. The public seating is packed, mainly with cameramen and journalists interspersed with a few curious onlookers, none of whom I recognise. I feel as if the expressionless stares are already sealing my fate.

Domingos returns, looking glum. He will brief me in a minute. The room falls silent as the magistrate takes his seat. My interpreter readies herself.

'The warrant for the arrest and extradition of Gilbert Keith Hart is requested by the judge of the second district of the Huelva provincial court in connection with the charge of procuring the murder of Gonzalo Filipe Ramirez in or around July 1996. I have considered the comments of the parties and I am satisfied that the warrant satisfies the criteria of the EAW Framework Decision of 2005, and that no grounds exist for releasing the accused prior to the implementation of the warrant.'

He pauses, I guess more for effect than to recover his breath. 'However, as the accused is currently assisting the local authorities with their investigation into another matter, there will be a stay on the implementation of the warrant until these enquiries have been completed, and he will remain in the custody of the Cavalla police department. In the meantime, interrogation rights will be extended to our Spanish counterparts.'

The walls in the holding room for remand prisoners are dotted with graffiti in biro, most with the word '*inocente*' somewhere in the text. I know how they felt. Domingos is pretending to read them but all the time watching me out of the corner of his eye. He is becoming wary of me, just like the interpreter – am I about to become violent, somehow deranged? Doubt has crept into our relationship.

'Come on, man!' I prompt. 'Spit it out.'

'This is getting out of my league,' he says, apologetically. 'You need to be represented by somebody with more criminal experience. I don't think that I can represent you any longer.'

'Why's that? What went on in that room?'

'There was no way you were going to walk out of here today. The Spanish want to interview you in connection with another suspicious death in which you have been implicated.'

'Whose? It can only be my former partner, the woman who was attacked and died. I thought that was dealt with years ago.'

He shook his head. 'I don't know. Nor does the magistrate. It's not only that. They found the photographs.'

'What photographs, for God's sake?'

'The police searched the house you are living in. They took away various items including some indecent photographs taped under the lid of the sanitaryware in the bathroom.'

I react angrily, banging my fist into the wall, grazing my knuckles in the process. 'Don't they need a search warrant to do that? What's the fucking accusation now? That I'm some sort of pervert?'

'Young men, barely dressed, apparently.'

'They're my sons when they were kids, taken when they were on a beach holiday twenty years ago, for Christ's sake.'

'And the girl tied to the bed with the old man doing things to her?' His face is bright red, patently embarrassed by the situation in which he finds himself.

I stop blaspheming in midstream. How can I explain without breaking my promise to Jasmin? 'I found those photographs in a cottage whilst I was following up on Albert's past. They must have been taken many years ago, and certainly not by me.'

There will be a formal interview with the police the next day and, of course, Domingos will be there. I am urged to seriously consider his advice. He will give me a list of names and telephone numbers of colleagues better qualified to assist.

In the event, the meeting with Lannier, accompanied by the two stern-faced policemen who were with him at the safari park, lasts little more than ten minutes. He readily accepts my explanation regarding the photographs Brigitte gave me and, as I might have expected, concentrates his attention on the grainy images of Jasmin and her father.

The questions are predictable and, with time overnight to think, I have worked out what I think are plausible answers. Somebody suggested to me they thought Albert might have stayed at Vicente's cottage whilst he was doing up the house, and I came across the photographs as I was checking the wardrobe. I have no idea who the people are in the images. I intended to hand them over to Lino for him to deal with.

'Why Monsieur Reyes?' he asked.

'I found them in Vicente's cottage. It seemed the right thing to do.'

'And hiding them under the lid of the water closet? Why did you do that?'

'The opportunity to talk with Lino alone did not arise. In the meantime, as both Francisco and his mother have access to my room, I did not want them to come across the photos by chance.'

'Do you know who these people are?' he asks, pointing at the image with Jasmin spreadeagled on the bed.

'How would I? They were taken way before my time. Do you?'

He looks away from the photograph, fixing his eyes on mine and allowing a pensive half-smile to flicker on his lips. 'I know as much as you, I suspect.'

My responses are evasive, I know, but Lannier appears disinterested in probing further and we are done.

***

Time passes and my mood grows darker. Christmas Day leaves me feeling maudlin and depressed. From where I sit, in a windowless cell, there are no carols, no presents, no turkey dinner or lazy afternoons in front of the TV. My routine is the same as all the other days in this place, a world of grunted monosyllables from the guards that punctuate hour upon hour of solitude and silence. It isn't missing all the rituals of Christmas that make me feel so sorry for myself; it is the lack of a union, an anchor to fasten me to other people. Until I die I will be bereft of anybody who will call me father or husband or, above all, family. Francisco was my one last chance but now even that bond has been severed. Whatever justice is about to cast my way, guilty or not, I deserve to be locked up and the key thrown away.

Three days pass before there are any developments, not that I am in the mood to care one way or the other. Pending further evidence, the police have decided to shelve any further investigation into the explosion and have reached an understanding with the Spanish authorities. I will be handed over within the week and transported to the Centro Penitenciario in Huelva. It is not over, Lannier tells me. If new evidence comes to light, I will be brought back.

On my last day in Cavalla, Jasmin brings Francisco to see me. His face beams with delight as we catch sight of each other and I hug him tightly as he whispers in my ear, 'When are you coming home?' Fighting back the tears, I urge him to draw some stick policemen on the magic slate he now claims as his own and turn my attention to Jasmin. She seems genuinely distressed I am being shipped off to Spain, pressing for details of the background to the charges I face. I gloss over the history, conscious we are wasting time and that she needs to know about the photographs. I tell her how I came across the prints and emphasise that I have kept my promise and said nothing to the police about the identity of the individuals.

There is a look of resignation on her face as she shrugs her shoulders and tilts her head to one side. 'Perhaps it will be for the best,' she says, eventually. 'My father and his brother were evil men. I was six when he started to touch me in that way. You grow up thinking it is natural, the way things are meant to be. They tell you that, but you know, deep down, that it is wrong. These thoughts collide inside your head. Either they drive you wild or you become cold, unfeeling. Nobody can enter your world. I chose this path.'

'Forgive me. I have no right to talk about these things, but I cannot understand.'

'What?'

'You were a young girl, unable to stand up for yourself when you became pregnant by your father. That, I can appreciate. But why let yourself, when a mature woman, succumb to your uncle and …?' I look across at Francisco, absorbed with his drawing.

The guard stands up, the bunch of keys jangling against his leg. He points at his watch but makes no move towards the exit door.

She begins to shuffle in her chair and I suspect my question will remain unanswered. Her head drops, eyes fixed at a point on the table when she finally speaks. 'I have had a lot of time to think over the last few days. He missed you on Christmas Day, kept asking me where you were and had Father Christmas given you a present. It made me realise you are the only man who has ever really cared for him. The men in my family look upon him as an embarrassment. Albert was never really into children, though for the sake of appearances, he tried.

'Francisco really loves you and now you have to go away. If you ever have the chance, please come back to see him.' She raises her hand, checking behind her that the guard remains out of earshot. 'That is why I will answer your question, because I know you too love Francisco and will always want to be his grandfather. Because of this, you will never repeat what I am about to say.'

My throat is dry. I long to take her into my arms and say it doesn't matter, forget it, but she must have made her mind up long before coming to see me.

'Vicente was always the one holding the camera.' She gives a derisory laugh. 'He could do it with one hand whilst he masturbated with the other as he watched my father abuse me. While Estevão was alive, he never had the real thing, just photos that he could look at and fantasise. He was sick.'

The guard shuffles his feet impatiently, muttering something.

'The next time we meet,' she says. 'I promise to tell you.'

I study the guard as he checks his watch. My pleading look is acknowledged with a shake of the head.

'Just tell me this. Was Inés involved in your father's death?'

She stands up, motioning for Francisco to gather his things. 'I have never known whether Inés knew what was going on or not all those years ago. I've always been too afraid to ask her. She would probably say no whatever, and I would be none the wiser. What I do know is that when she discovered that I was pregnant with Estevão's child, she told me it would never happen again.'

'And Vicente's death?'

She shrugged. 'Who knows.'

She stands back as Francisco clings to me, whispers in my ear. When am I coming to see him? I say as soon as I can.

She kisses me on both cheeks. 'I take to heart your concern about him being scared of Inés. She has never been able to accept him. To her, he is the face of the suffering she has endured at the hands of her husband and his brother, the pain she must endure forever. She needs our help and support, not our condemnation.'

The guard slams the door shut behind them.

No longer the self-pity I have been dragging around like a ball and chain. Somehow, now, I need to make everything right.

CHAPTER THIRTY-THREE
Huelva, Spain – 2009

Inspector Jefe Hernando Sanchez has acquired the signs of good living since I last saw him over thirteen years ago. He still has the inquisitive, restless eyes of a bird of prey, small black pupils with a mesmerising effect, but they are now recessed behind chubby cheeks full of broken red veins. There are age marks all over his nearly bald head, accentuating a prominent forehead and the scholarly look I remember. Were it not for an overfed and out of condition body, I'd say he has weathered the storm of a lifetime in the police force reasonably successfully.

As the meeting gets underway, I realise they must have brought him out of retirement to handle the interview. A shirt collar so tight as to push up rolls of fat around his neck and a jacket, creased as it strains against the buttons, suggest to me items of clothing he rarely wears these days.

His colleague, Inspector Mahon, a self-assured, broad-chested man in his mid twenties with legs splayed apart either side of his chair, persistently refers to the older man as 'Inspector Jefe' in such an offhanded way it soon becomes obvious the title is now a courtesy rather than a concession to rank. I assume it's also intended to convey to me that Mahon is really the man in charge.

The tape recorder is switched on, with Mahon stating the process number and naming the persons present. Apparently, I have waved my right to an interpreter as both officials speak English and agree to answer questions whilst we are awaiting the arrival of the tribunal-appointed lawyer to represent me. In the meantime, he blithely states I acknowledge I am waving my statutory rights and understand sufficient Spanish to answer some personal information questions.

Up until this moment, I have not uttered a word.

He then reads me my Miranda rights in Spanish followed by a series of questions, all of which I am prompted to answer with '*Si*'.

I think about objecting, but the end result would be to send me back to my cell to wait, a prospect right now I find untenable. For three weeks I have spent every day in solitary confinement, patiently waiting for the guard with the permanently blocked nose to grunt '*abluciones*', heralding a twenty-minute bathroom break followed by an hour on my own in the exercise area.

The moron in the next cell has got hold of an MP3 player from somewhere with only one album on it and a track called 'Older' by George Michael which he plays at least once every half hour. That mournful voice and the soulful trumpet accompaniment is depressing enough for anybody in my position, but the constant repetition ... I used to like George Michael, but not any more.

'Did I hear you say "*Sí*", Mr Hart?' Mahon is leaning over the table.

'Sorry. *Sí.*'

Sanchez clears his throat. 'Can I take you back to the days shortly preceding the tragic death of Rosita Rodriguez?'

'If you must.'

'Do you recall the last time you saw Gonzalo Ramirez?'

'Two days before Rosita died. The day before I left for Seville with the family. It was just a hello and a brief chat about one of our clients.'

'Did you argue?'

'Far from it. The conversation was amicable.'

'But you wanted to get rid of him?'

'That's a very provocative way of putting it. I wanted to fire him.'

'Why?'

'Why do you fire anybody? He wasn't doing his job properly any more.'

'Is that the only reason?'

'Yes. What are you getting at?'

'It was nothing to do with the fact that he was in a relationship with your wife ... your partner?' he corrects himself.

I take a deep breath. 'We had all this out the last time we met. There was no affair. Where do you get all this nonsense from?'

Sanchez removes a large, bulging A4 folder from his briefcase. Gonzalo's name is on a label fixed to the front cover. He continues rummaging in the bottom of the case.

There are about a dozen letters and cards, bound in an elastic band. I recognise Gonzalo's writing. Sanchez flicks the envelopes as if they are a pack of cards.

'It appears that señor Ramirez was a born romantic. He was very graphic and explicit in detailing his feelings towards señora Rosita. Before you ask, her father found these when he was clearing out her personal effects. There can be little doubt. You are not telling me you have never seen them?'

'I am, yes.'

He starts upright in his chair. 'You have seen them, then?'

'No, I am telling you that, yes, I have never seen them.' I want to tear the letters out of his hand – my head is starting to swim – but I manage to hold myself together.

He sags back, his chair creaking, obviously dismayed the breakthrough he was hoping for is no more than a grammatical misunderstanding. 'You must be aware that the child the señora lost when she drowned was not yours?'

'So you're telling me.' I feel drained. What is the point of it all? 'No wonder Gonzalo kicked up a fuss about leaving. He must have been so angry with her.'

'It was not señor Ramirez who attacked your partner. That is certain.'

What the hell! He had to be wrong. 'You are crazy! Who else could it have been? He threatened her. She told me on the phone. I asked her to find the gardener to protect her from him.'

He reaches for the file and thumbs open one of the bookmarked pages. 'Do you recall somebody named Rinat Kryvorobycho?'

His stumble over the name brings back the memory. 'You asked me this once before. I knew him as Robi, the pool man.'

'And Roman Sikorsky?'

'Of course. Was that his name, Roman? He called himself Ramon. He used to sell me equipment when I was in the heating business.'

'What about Denys Hordiyenko or Yegor Dudik?'

'Sound like strikers for Dynamo Kiev. Never heard of them.'

'They have heard of you.'

The door slams back on its hinges and in strides an obese woman in her sixties with thinning, wispy dyed-blonde hair, blackening at the roots, and a mean, thin-lipped face with traces of stubble on her top lip. Had she worn a suit instead of a plain, knee-length pleated skirt, she could have passed for a man. The three files and leather briefcase balanced in her arms fall heavily onto the desk, dislodging the recording machine. In heavily accented English, she introduces herself as Bella Bastos, my tribunal-appointed attorney, passes a comment in Spanish which simultaneously makes Mahon smile and Sanchez look daggers, and collapses heavily into the seat alongside me, exhaling as she dabs at the perspiration on her forehead.

She motions for Mahon to halt the recording and points at Sanchez. 'I thought he was dead. Señor' – she checks the sheet of paper in front of her – 'Hart must be one of his processes still open.' Her head moves forward in a pronounced gesture to study me. 'Are you guilty or innocent?' she asks, with a smile that reveals nicotine-stained teeth.

'What?' I ask.

'You heard.'

If she wants to play games, I'll go along. 'I am guilty of many things, but not what is on the charge sheet. I did not seek to kill Gonzalo, or anybody else, for that matter.'

'There you are,' she says to Sanchez. 'You have your answer. Carry that simple fact in your head when you ask my client your questions.' The chair protests as she leans back in it. 'My clients are always innocent. Continue.'

The whole atmosphere in the room has changed. As if she waved a wand, the police officers are constrained by her presence, less hostile as they put their questions to me. Her technique must be to give the accused more confidence, although Mahon did initially try to reassert himself.

'That's why so many of your clients are found guilty, is it?' he smirks.

It's like water off a duck's back. 'Sometimes people lie to me,' she says. 'But you just have to look at this man to see he tells the truth.'

Sanchez chooses to ignore her as he presses the record button. 'Three months ago, the police were given information leading to the discovery of the body of Gonzalo Ramirez buried in marshlands in the Donana national park. As you might imagine, after all these years there only remained skeletal fragments, which allowed us to compare dental records and confirm his identity. Forensics were able to establish the victim was killed with a single bullet to the back of the skull, execution style. The informant named those responsible and the person who had ordered the assassination. He named you, señor Hart.'

She tugs at my sleeve. 'Doubtless a fine, upstanding member of the community,' she pronounces in a loud whisper, feigning confidentiality. 'Impeccable credentials and immediately believable.' She smiles sweetly at Sanchez. 'May we know the name of this socially-minded citizen?'

Mahon butts in. 'No. He has joined a special programme, *protección de testigos*, until the judgement. His name will be disclosed when the process is released to you.'

Bella Bastos sniffs the sniff of contempt as she moves her giant frame around in the chair to get comfortable. 'Probably a gang member who has revealed the name of his colleagues. They will be anxious to guarantee his silence.' She looks at Mahon, her gaze moving slowly downwards as if he has just vomited over her shoes. 'Is that all you have got? If so, I will be seeking a hearing for this man's release.'

Sanchez grits his teeth. 'Is it not the case that you asked your partner's brother, Salvador Rodriguez, to give five thousand euros to Gonzalo if he would finish the affair with her and go away permanently?'

'Absolutely not.'

'Is it not the case he took the money but came back to señor Rodriguez and asked for more? At this point, you decided to have Gonzalo killed. That is right, is it not?'

'This is all nonsense. No such thing happened.'

'Then tell us what did.'

I went through the story in detail, from the time I had first decided to fire Gonzalo, my conversation with Rosita and the events of the fatal day when she had managed to so incense him.

'When did you last contact Ramon Sikorsky?'

'I hadn't seen him for some weeks. He was supposed to have delivered heating equipment, but he was stopped by the police and did not make our meeting. From memory, I spoke to him on the phone a couple of days before I travelled to Seville.'

'To propose paying him ten thousand euros if he killed Gonzalo for you?'

It's on the tip of my tongue, but something inside my head tells me to hold off, keep my powder dry. Revealing Salvador's blackmail scheme can wait for another day.

'Do you have to think about your answer?' Sanchez presses.

'No. We talked about an incident he was involved in with the police and the likely outcome.'

'Señor Sikorsky says you begged him to kill Gonzalo for you, but he refused.'

'I don't believe you.'

Bella puts her arms on the seat of the chair to hoist herself up. The effort causes her to break wind, but she seems impervious to the stunned reaction. Mahon is having difficulty stopping himself from laughing, resulting in a grimace which makes him look as if he has serious toothache.

'That's enough for today,' Bella says. 'I need to talk to my client before he tells you anything else. Turn the recording off and give me a new time and date. I have to see justice served for another innocent client this afternoon.'

'Very well,' Mahon says, managing to compose himself, 'but there is also another matter we wish to speak to your client about.'

'Concerning what?' Neither policeman tries to assist her as she gathers the files and the briefcase into her arms.

'Señor Hart's involvement in the circumstances surrounding the suspicious death of a tourist some years earlier.'

'Are you charging him with anything?'

'Not yet,' Mahon replies.

She winks at me as she turns to leave. 'Probably a case of mistaken identity,' she announces to no one in particular. 'Bound to be.'

We eventually resume two days later, with the sound of George Michael still ringing in my ears as we enter the interview room. Nearly three hours were spent with Bella the previous afternoon, with me providing a detailed history of all the events leading up to Rosita's death, including the plot hatched by Gonzalo and Salvador to blackmail both Sikorsky and me.

This was another side of Bella Bastos. She was quiet and restrained, her questions timed and pertinent. She missed nothing. Pressed on Gonzalo's financial circumstances, I have to admit this aspect did not cross my mind. He was never paid that well but always seemed to have plenty of money and rarely asked for cash or advances when asked to incur charges on behalf of the business. Could I say if five thousand euros would have made a big difference to him? I could only say that it would to most employees.

'Did you know Gonzalo's family have a sunflower oil extraction plant in Cordoba?' Bella reads from a notebook. 'They are wealthy. Six months before he disappeared, his only surviving grandparent died, leaving Gonzalo a large sum of money and a twenty per cent interest in the company. His aunt told me he was about to return to help run the family business. He planned to leave you anyway.'

'I had no idea.'

'No? His father had told him to spend a couple of years working for somebody else to gain experience. They had asked him to go back two months earlier, but he said he couldn't let down his partner.'

'You have been busy. It's all news to me.'

'Criminal law in Andalucia is like a gossip-ridden village where everybody knows somebody who knows something. You just have to know who to call.' She takes my water bottle from the table and gulps down two large slugs. 'If it was just for the money, he wouldn't have waited around.'

'Meaning what?'

'I gained access to the file for the process today. Whatever we or the prosecution seek to use as evidence has to be included in the process. Mahon has tried to restrict its circulation with his witness protection bullshit, but I have a contact.' She is pleased with herself. 'The prosecutor's case will be built around the testimonies of Salvador Rodriguez and Roman Sikorsky. The secret witness is a sideshow, a career Ukrainian criminal who describes himself as an unwilling member of the gang Robi used to kidnap Gonzalo from his home and murder him.

'Robi? He killed Gonzalo?'

She nods, placing another sheet of paper carefully onto the table.

It is Salvador's testimony that damns me. According to him, Gonzalo had been having an affair with Rosita for over a year, believing the baby to be his and desperate for her to leave me and move to Cordoba. He was totally infatuated with her. I had found out about the affair and, in my determination not to lose my young 'wife', I had approached Salvador and asked him to bribe Gonzalo to get out of our lives. Gonzalo had initially agreed and taken the money but had then said he was staying around unless he was paid a great deal more.

I have to give Salvador credit. Apart from sounding totally credible, it explained why I would have given him cash and his hotel meeting with Gonzalo. He could deny the blackmail as an aberration on my part. What I could not fathom was how he had got Sikorsky onside.

Sikorsky's testimony is all pure fabrication, I tell Bella. He alleges that I offered him ten thousand euros to get rid of Gonzalo 'once and for all'. He turned me down, point-blank. He casually mentioned my approach to Robi and a couple of his friends, not realising at the time his nephew was 'knocking off' Rosita and was both angry and jealous that Gonzalo was also getting a piece of the action. As the story went on, Robi had offered to do my dirty work for the ten thousand but said he would need help. On the day agreed for the kill, when I was safely in Seville with an alibi, he asked for another six thousand euros to pay his two colleagues and I arranged for Rosita to draw the cash from the bank to pay him. There was indeed such a cash withdrawal which Eliana had collected from the bank on Rosita's authorisation.

And how did Sikorsky know all this, and where is Robi now, so that he can be questioned? Sanchez provides the answers when we are back in the interrogation room with the hum of the recording machine in the background. Mahon looks particularly sartorial in a maroon and beige check jacket like men wear to the golf course. Bella looks down her nose at him and says they must be paying the police too much if he can afford to waste money on trying to look like a Batman villain.

He launches into the attack. 'Three days after the day on which we believe Gonzalo Ramirez was murdered, Robi phoned his uncle to explain what had taken place and that he was back in Kiev until things 'cooled down'. Unfortunately, a week later when Sikorsky tried to contact his nephew, he was told that the man had died two days earlier in a road traffic accident. Are you denying that you agreed to pay this Robi a total of sixteen thousand euros to kill señor Ramirez?' Sanchez looks over his glasses at me.

'I most certainly am,' I replied.

'We have DNA confirmation that the unborn child señora Reyes was expecting had been fathered by the man you knew as Robi. You were aware of his involvement with your partner, were you not?'

I slump back in my chair. Some things are easy to accept because the suspicions exist at the back of your mind, in your subconscious maybe, awakened when the truth is revealed. Call me naïve, a man in his fifties preoccupied with his business career whilst his young wife craves attention and physical fulfilment, but it never once crossed my mind that Rosita was being unfaithful. Maybe I pleaded tiredness and shunned sex on too many occasions sufficient to see it coming down the track, but she was always caring and considerate. I should have realised I was trying to live in a relationship forged on the memory of our past sexual unity.

I try to summon anger, but I can't. Rosita possessed a voracious sexual appetite and I started to pay mere lip-service to her needs. She looked elsewhere.

'I had no idea,' I manage to say.

'At this time, we just have one other aspect to clarify.'

Bella looks up. She is doodling on a pad, drawing triangles and rectangles as if absent-mindedly trying to prove Pythagoras's theorem. It's tantamount to telling those around her that she doesn't need to make notes because she already has all the answers. I'm finding it disconcerting, and by the look on Mahon's face, he can't make it out either.

'I need to take you back to the night on which señora Rosita died,' Sanchez says in a monotone. 'Your testimony was that when you found her, she was unconscious, lying in a pool of blood on the paved surround of the pool. You ran into the villa to summon help, and when you returned, she was face down in the swimming pool. How do you account for the change in her position in what – the five- to ten-minute period it took for you to find the phone, make a call and return?'

'How can I know? I was not there. I have always assumed she regained consciousness and, in her confused state, moved to the edge of the pool without really being aware of her surroundings. Do you have a better theory?'

Bella tuts at the question.

'I do,' Mahon interrupts. 'We believe you were so annoyed at your partner's infidelity you dragged her to the edge of the pool and held her head under the water. Is that not the case?'

Mahon's eyes move across to look at Bella, who is scratching at her chest just underneath her two enormous breasts which bounce up and down as her hand moves. 'You should take up writing fiction,' she says. 'It would suit your fertile imagination. My client has already answered your question by telling you what the most plausible explanation is. What do you expect him to do, break down and say, yes, you are right, it was me all along? Really, Mahon.' She sounds exasperated.

Sanchez reaches across the table to pull over another file which he places on top of the one he has been reading from.

'Do you remember a young lady named Siobhan Mulcraine?'

I cannot recollect any such name.

'According to our information, you met her in a bar in Ayamonte in December of 1992. Correct?'

'What are we talking about now?' Bella seems both bored and weary as she puffs out her cheeks.

'A possible homicide. Do you remember now?'

I have already primed Bella as to what the other matter mentioned at the first interview was likely to be about. Her advice is to treat any questions as taxing my memory. I know she has press cuttings of the incident in her handbag.

'Vaguely. No exact recollection.'

'I'm surprised,' Mahon says, obviously not, 'as there were large amounts of your DNA, shall we say, all around the lower parts of her body. We had no match until recently, when the Portuguese posted your profile on the Europol biometrics system.'

'I sort of remember. It's an occurrence I would rather forget. It was out of character. Caught me at a bad time.'

'What do you remember?'

'It was Christmas. I'd done a small plumbing job for the bar owner when he asked me to look at the flush in the ladies' toilet. Somebody had complained. As I walked in, this young lady moved on me and I was too roused to refuse. We had sex and I left the bar. She stayed, talking to some friends. That was all there was to it. I went home.'

'The bar owner at the time said otherwise. He had not called anybody to do work for him and only noticed you because you followed a girl into the toilet. You came out with her and you left the bar together.'

'I don't believe it. I have known Max since I arrived in Spain. He would not say that. It's not true.'

'We have a sworn statement.'

'Then it's a lie.'

'The hotel receptionist also confirms that he remembers you entering the hotel with the girl. He never saw you leave. Two hours later, the girl falls to her death from the fourth floor.'

'This is getting ridiculous.' I feel the blood coursing through the vessels in my head. 'Where do you get these liars from? I know nothing about where this woman was staying. I knew her for ten minutes. I didn't even know her name until I read it in the newspaper.'

CHAPTER THIRTY-FOUR
Huelva – 2009

I once read a book in which the author imagined that for prisoners incarcerated behind four walls, the seasons all blend into one. Don't believe it. The passage from winter to spring sits heavy upon anybody who has served time. Those cold and humid days when the sun remains alive for so few hours; the soundless skies; the memory of people scurrying to and from somewhere, never relaxed and at peace. There is a sense of finality about the winter, a spell that is broken when the birds begin to sing and the sun is warm once more upon your back. Renewal comes with the spring, but not for those incarcerated, those merely existing in the shadows, waiting in anxious silence as they count how many more springs before their time will come again. Frustrations emerge, petty issues become major ones, violence stirs and grows, and the sense of imminent danger hangs permanently in the air.

As I move towards the end of my third month of remand, the acute bouts of depression return. Whatever happens, I can never expect to be a free man again. Perhaps it's for the best. In one way or another, I have brought nothing but pain and suffering to those who were once close to me. I can even accept that Vernon and Albert wanted to see me dead. Maybe I should think seriously about ending it all. At least it would save a great deal of the time and effort of a trial. Have I got the willpower to go through with it?

'You look like shit.'

It's the first time Bella has come to see me in a month. I thought she must have given me up as a lost cause. As pragmatically offhand and unsympathetic as she is, I am grateful to see her.

'The judgement is in three days,' she says. 'It has been moved to Seville. You are a high-profile defendant and the judge of the second division of Huelva province wants to make sure the cameras catch her right-side profile on a bigger stage.' She smiles, for once. 'I am only making fun. Where the outcome could be a sentence of five years or more, it is for the examining judge to decide if the case deserves to be heard in the appeal court. That means Seville.'

I put down her perpetual fidgeting as nerves before a big case, although outwardly she seems as nonplussed as ever. 'Do I have to worry about the issue of the tourist who fell to her death? Can they bring it up?'

'They will try, primarily as a means of staining your character rather than the imputation of criminal guilt. I have read the statements of both the former bar owner and the aparthotel receptionist. Both are flawed and would never stand cross-examination in court, and, on top of that, one of them is seriously ill and either unwilling or unable to testify.'

She watches me visibly relax before metaphorically aiming for my solar plexus. 'Your posture is one of the victim, the dedicated husband unaware of his wife's infidelity. If you testify, the prosecution will certainly ask you about the incident with the tourist to demonstrate you are as, or even more, sexually promiscuous than your wife. It is my advice, therefore, that you say nothing.'

'Won't that suggest to the jury I'm guilty?'

'There is no jury, and the judges who make the decision will not take your silence as an expression of guilt. It's not as in the UK where the case starts and moves uninterrupted to a conclusion. In Spain, cases are booked into the tribunal calendar. We will run for two or three days and then break off for a week or two until the calendar can be readjusted.'

'It could go on for weeks?' I ask incredulously.

'Months, possibly.'

I slump back in my chair. For some reason, the only cogent thought I have is the mental anguish of having to put up with the timeless sound of George Michael.

The evening before the trial she is back again.

'Things can change over the course of the judgement,' she explains, 'but here is my initial strategy.'

The witness under protection was a Ukrainian immigrant and small-time criminal named Yegor Dudik who, some months earlier, together with a compatriot and strong-arm man, Denys Hordiyenko, had held a Danish couple hostage in their holiday home near Estepona over a weekend, systematically robbing them of money and valuable possessions. Hordiyenko also gave the man a beating and sexually assaulted his wife. When both men were arrested, Dudik attempted to do a deal with the authorities, stating he had knowledge of an unsolved crime committed over twenty years earlier, shopping his accomplices and the man who originally commissioned the crime. According to the snitch, Rinat Kryvorobycho, who everybody knew as Robi, was the ringleader, and Dudik would testify that he heard him on the phone to 'Mr Gilbert' confirming the job had been done. Although Robi had since died, Dudik was convinced the other gang members would come after him to exact his silence once word got out that he has named names. Hordiyenko has already threatened to kill him.

Bella explains her tactic would be to discredit the man as a witness and, by doing so, cast serious doubts on his testimony. And so it evolved. Her questioning and persistence on the second day of the hearing was so effective that Dudik became confused, contradicting himself time after time and finally agreeing with Bella he really had no idea to whom Robi was speaking on the phone or who, if anybody, commissioned Gonzalo's murder. I was elated at her performance.

That was easy, she tells me. There is now a three-day break before the hearing resumes and Salvador is to give evidence, followed by Sikorsky. She warns they will be more difficult nuts to crack.

Her approach will be to frame her questions along the lines she considers are closer to the truth. Salvador has to substantiate why he sat in a crowded hotel bar with Gonzalo and passed over an envelope with the cash. The hotel's closed-circuit camera focused on the till operation has a panorama feature which clearly shows the two men at a table by the window. It's an exhibit in the evidence file. My grainy phone camera image proves nothing. She will question him on the blackmail scam with the task of refuting evidence asserting Gonzalo became involved solely for the money. Gonzalo's real motivation, she will claim, was well known to Salvador. Gonzalo wanted to ensure Gilbert went to jail for fraud so that he could have a free rein to be with the woman with whom he was totally infatuated and whom he believed was expecting his child. She would suggest Gonzalo became angry and threatened to expose the conspiracy in order to achieve his aim. Such a threat would have endangered Salvador and given him motive to want Gonzalo out of the picture.

I remember it all in such nitid detail as if it were happening today. We were just starting. Bella stood there in an open black gown that would have never closed around her unless she put a slit in the back. You could plainly see underneath the gown she was wearing a mohair roll-neck jumper and a pair of baggy denims with an enormous elasticated waistband.

Before the next witness can be called, she makes an application to the tribunal. In the light of the testimony of the previous witness, which has given rise to serious issues of doubt and credibility as to the Public Ministry's decision to prosecute the case, it is her submission I should be released on bail during the course of the judgement. Her intervention prompts a flurry of objections and counterarguments on flight risk, witness interference and gravity of the charges, but, to my eternal surprise, the judges rule that I am to be electronically tagged with a restriction not to move beyond a ten-kilometre radius of an apartment which Bella is to arrange for me in lodgings adjacent to her office block. My interpreter suggests that the original suggestion could well have come from the judge to Bella, in private, but I never get the opportunity to talk to her about it.

It is well into the afternoon session when Bella begins her cross-examination. I am stunned, more by Salvador's appearance than the litany of lies and manipulation of the truth coming out of his mouth. He would be in his late forties by now, but he looks and sounds like a hardened old police officer verging on retirement. He has never progressed through the ranks, ambition replaced by a pot belly and bull neck. I can only imagine he must have not only come to terms with his place in the pecking order but used his muscle and influence to taste the good life through his various scams. He speaks slowly and convincingly with the dismissive approach inherited from his father, his words chosen carefully based on years of standing exactly where he is today, giving evidence against the accused. It's a polished performance but I have faith in my lumbering giant of an attorney to find the cracks in his lies.

Five minutes into her questioning and Bella stops in mid-sentence, her head slowly moving from side to side, finally turning to look at me. Her lips part to say something but there is no sound. She turns back to face the bench and pitches forward onto the polished wooden floor like a tree sawn through at the trunk. For all the activity around her body over the next twenty minutes, my guess is she was dead before she hit the ground.

In the melee that follows, I am totally ignored. The courtroom is cleared and I end up alone in a holding room, unsure of what is to happen next. Eventually, I am returned to my cell with the ridiculous request from the guard to wait, as if I have a choice.

The next morning the anxious young woman who seemed to spend her life following Bella around, running errands and fetching coffee, arrives with a court official. He attaches the tag to my ankle as the woman watches, her eyes red and sore from crying, her thoughts far removed from what is taking place. I know how she feels. There is a hollow sensation inside me, a portent of the volatile situation I am now in and a sadness tinged with anger that my future has, once more, been cheated by death.

As I breathe in fresh air and feel the sun on my back again, the gloom lifts. For now, I am as good as a free man. Amongst my meagre possessions, the bank card still works, there is still over two thousand euros of Roger's money in my account and I am leaving Seville, the tribunal and my worries behind, albeit temporarily.

***

The second-floor apartment Bella's office organised for me in Huelva is literally two doors away from the office block from which the firm operates. It is small but serviceable and, above all, inexpensive, with the rent paid a week in advance to a grumbling old lady who lives on the ground floor. I am to report to Bella's office every weekday morning at ten and at the police station over the weekend. The electronic sensor can be activated at any time by the police to determine my location. The case will resume back in Seville in ten days' time.

At first, the novelty of freedom is enough but, after four days of aimless wandering around the streets of Huelva and hour after hour of browsing in the El Corte Inglés department store, I am bored and restless.

My punctilious attendance every day at ten has lulled my overseers into the realisation they can get on with their lives without worrying about me. The senior partner of the firm has finally been laid to rest at a funeral which, it seemed, half of Huelva attended. Bella Bastos was a prominent local figure in more ways than one, the eulogies as sincere as the tearful faces that crowd around the grave. Now, she is gone; time for her partners to dry their tears, both genuine and crocodile; time to concentrate on the struggle for rank and prestige in the new hierarchy of Bastos y Asociados – Abogados. For good or bad, nobody is paying much attention any more to their high-profile client.

As far as I can tell, for the first two days following my release the tag was activated by a flashing red light on an hourly basis to confirm my location. On subsequent days, the light comes on only once, between eight-thirty and nine in the morning, presumably when whichever policeman responsible arrives on shift or is leaving.

I am going to take a chance, a calculated risk.

I wait until the light flashes on and off before leaving the apartment. If everything goes to plan, I will clock in at the lawyers and catch the ten-thirty service. All being well, nobody will check up on me until the next morning.

The local bus snakes along the coast road towards the sprawling resort of Islantilla with its impressive hotels and apartment blocks, wide sandy beaches, bars and restaurants, now almost all closed and shuttered, hibernating until the short summer season gets underway again. Apart from a few dog walkers and elderly keep-fit enthusiasts jogging along at a snail's pace, replete with arm-mounted mobiles and headphones, the streets are deserted.

At the far end of the town, the road runs along close to the sea line, a less populated area where wooden buildings are set amongst the trees, interlaced with dirt roads threading through the undergrowth past a campsite and circling back to join the road to Sanlazer. Gonzalo lived somewhere around here. The association brings back memories of that terrible night.

The local municipality has erected a new roadside sign, ostentatious in both size and verbiage, with a digitally enhanced photograph that could easily be mistaken for a shot of the French Riviera. The greeting in Spanish is repeated in six languages, one of which in English is incorrectly spelled as 'Wellcome to Sanlazer'. I have a déjà vu moment when, in the distant past, I talked about misspelling in English and the difficulty it must give people used to pronouncing words guided by accents when trying to get their heads around the language. I assume the conversation was with Rosita. Where we were, I cannot recall, but my memory comes alive. I used the example of how, if you pronounced 'bow' slightly differently, it means different things and, more confusing still, one of the pronunciations is exactly the same as 'bough', which means something else again. I feel there is locked in my brain a sequitur to this recollection, a follow-on I struggle to grasp but which eludes me.

We arrive at Sanlazer. My heart is racing with the smell of the place.

As far as I can see, nothing much has changed in all those intervening years. There are clusters of new developments set back from the coastline, but the area around the condominium I knew so well is exactly the same. I open the back gate of one of the villas closed for the winter to reach the communal gardens and swimming pool. As I stand on the spot where I last saw Rosita, tears begin to well in my eyes. The weight of responsibility for her death lays heavily upon me.

A middle-aged woman walks towards me from the villa that once belonged to TM and his family. I guess that following the tragedy they must have sold it. The new occupant is dressed sombrely in a black skirt with a thick jumper pulled tight around her.

'Are you all right?' she asks in Spanish.

I try to choke back the sobs with gulps of air, but I can do nothing but shake my head.

Her head turns to one side, the look quizzical. 'You're Gilbert, aren't you?' she says in halting English. 'My God! You are an old man.'

I have no idea who she is.

'You don't remember me, do you?' She gives a cynical laugh. 'You had no time for me then. I guess I wasn't worth a memory, was I?'

'Isabel?' I do the calculations. She would be in her early thirties. This woman looks closer to fifty. 'I'm sorry. I can honestly say I would not have recognised you.'

'Not the voluptuous young disco queen, brash and ready to take on the world any more, am I, Gilbert? More the bitter old spinster, gone to seed with pockmarks on her cheeks, old before her time from all the drug abuse. Hardly surprising, is it?'

'You are the last person I expected to see. I assumed the villa would have been sold on. I just wanted to remember it the way it was. I mean no offence.'

She holds out her hand, encouraging me to take hold of it. The skin around her fingers is hard and brittle, freezing cold to the touch. 'Walk me back. I have some hot chocolate percolating on the stove. We can talk.'

'I don't have long.' I am suddenly nervous. This is Salvador's sister. She will tell him I have been there, what we have talked about; the man whose testimony is intended to send me to prison for murder. 'My bus is leaving soon.'

It was as if she could read my thoughts. 'I have been following the judgement, the reports on the television. You are in all the newspapers. Fame has caught up with you.'

'I think you mean infamy.'

'A crime of passion. The women's magazines love all that – partner of pregnant woman accused of hiring her lover's killers, her brother to testify against him. Don't worry, I don't talk to Salvador or his family any more. We have no time for each other.'

The sofa in the lounge is the one on which Rosita and I made love so many times. I run my hand tenderly across the frayed material, evoking memories that must have brought a smile to my lips.

'Nothing has changed,' she says, handing me a mug of thick, steaming chocolate. It tastes so comforting.

TM died within a year of the tragedy; a broken man, Isabel tells me. Romina soldiered on with the business but suffered a stroke ten years ago and failed to recover. TM's intention was that the business and two properties would be divided equally between his two remaining children, but it didn't turn out that way. Eliana produced a document, signed in Romina's shaky hand, willing the family home and business to Salvador, leaving only the villa in Sanlazer to Isabel.

'I told Salvador I would challenge the document but he knew, in the end, I would not stand up to him. He promised to share the sale proceeds from the business with me, but he lied about the amount he got and gave me barely enough on which to survive. I returned from England after another failed relationship and six years working as a hotel receptionist. All I am left with is this place, some small savings and my earnings from teaching English in Islantilla to a few students. I have not spoken to Salvador or his bitch of a wife in years. They can go to hell for all I care.'

'As I recall, you were close to Eliana. What went wrong?'

She collects my empty cup and nurses it between her bleached white fingers. 'Salvador never succeeded in getting promoted because, fundamentally, he is just a dull plodder with no initiative. Eliana was the schemer, the power behind the throne. On the face of it, he was the macho man, just like our father, but behind the scenes she controlled and manipulated everything he did. She pretended to be my friend, but it was all self-serving.'

I hesitate before posing the question, but I have to have an answer. 'Did you know about Rosita's affairs with Gonzalo and Robi?'

She smiles. Had she done so earlier I would have recognised her. It's the smile, unique and unforgettable, natural for one second, sarcastic or demeaning the next. Today, it is simply natural. 'We all knew, you silly man, but don't get all chauvinistic about it.' She saw my expression change. 'Rosita and I took after our father. Just like him, we were both highly sexed. God knows the merry dance he led Romina and how many half-brothers and sisters I must have roaming the streets of Madrid. But for us, sex and love were totally separate, one purely physical, the other, emotional and far more elusive. Countless men will tell you they love you and have no idea what they really mean by it, other than, "if I say this, it will make you want me," or, more often, "if I say it, sex will follow". You were different, and Rosita really loved you. We all did.'

I look up in shock.

'Don't look so stunned. You were different to the men Rosita had been with before.'

'I was much older.'

'That too. But you cared about what was going on in her mind, her point of view, her opinion. You never tried to dominate. You are the only man she had known who really listened to her. Most of them wanted to just get inside her knickers and then control her. She admired and respected you and I was really jealous.'

'You, Isabel? Surely you were just a kid.'

'And a really mixed-up one. My father took pride in parading me around like a doll, almost prompting me to act as some provocative sex symbol. Look what I've produced, boys? Aren't I really clever? You can look, but don't touch.'

I recall that first Christmas Eve at the disco.

'And suddenly, there you were, a combination of father figure and lover. I used to fantasise how you rejected Rosita and turned to me, but in reality you barely looked at me, and when you did, you always treated me as a spoilt little girl.'

'Which you were, as I remember.'

She shakes her head violently 'Only in the material sense. At the emotional, caring, loving level, my life was barren and has always been so.'

'I am truly sorry. I was too preoccupied with all the new things in my life to notice.'

'If I couldn't have you, I would learn to hate and despise both you and Rosita. And, as the years passed, I did, with a passion. When we arrived to spend that final summer, my life had already changed for the worst. I wished you were both dead, you pair of smug and self-satisfied hypocrites, leeching on my father's generosity. If my resolve to hate you weakened, Eliana was always there to stoke up the fires of contempt.'

'Eliana?' I always felt in many ways she was a kindred spirit. 'I thought we got on together.'

She gave me her demeaning smile. 'Eliana! You must be joking. She despised you and really loathed Rosita. You were enjoying success together whilst she was sinking in the mire with my poor brother and their offspring. She said you were weak, couldn't control Rosita, who was sleeping around behind your back. I told her that I thought you were good for Rosita. That really made her mad.'

For some obscure reason, I picture an iceberg. If you just see what is visible on the surface, you can have no idea of the scale of what exists out of sight, below the waterline. I have never once imagined my relationship with Rosita could have stirred up a maelstrom of emotions amongst the rest of the family.

'She told me not to be naïve,' Isabel continues. 'You were no different to all the rest and she would prove it by seducing you whilst I looked on. I know she led you into the backyard. I could hear everything through my window, but I just could not accept that you would give in to her. She wanted a hold over you, something more than what she claimed to have already. When it came to it, I could not let my illusions be destroyed, so I called out to her, but really I wanted to let you know I was there to save you.'

'If we are baring our souls, it would be only right to say that you did exactly that; you saved me from myself.'

She is about to say something else but checks herself and changes the subject. The moment of intimacy is lost and the conversation drifts back to the present. Isabel has been closely following the trial. As much as I want to stay and listen to her opinion, I have to bring the conversation to an end. The bus service is irregular and I have to get back to Huelva.

She is glad our paths have crossed again and hopes I am acquitted. It is a tragedy my lawyer died so suddenly before she had the chance to tear Salvador to pieces. 'I hope her successor is equally as good, but I somehow doubt it,' she says as we part.

How prophetic those words proved to be. I have paid Pedro Silva Leal no more than peripheral attention so far throughout the hearing. From time to time, Bella would look icily in the direction of her second before issuing a summons for him to join her by wiggling her index finger. He is a tall man with a scholarly appearance and looked out of place hovering alongside her, head bowed, hands behind his back as he listened intently to her instructions.

But Bella Bastos is no more. Now, it is his turn to take centre stage, to get even. In retrospect, I guess I must have been the manifestation of the end of fifteen years of anger and frustration as the whipping boy of a difficult and self-opinionated woman.

Dr Pedro Silva Leal extends me little consideration. My comments, intended to assist his otherwise inept cross-examination of my accusers, are brushed aside as irrelevant. He makes Salvador appear a paragon of righteous virtue. As for Sikorsky, now so frail and weak that he has to sit to give evidence, his haunting testimony describes me as a calculating and jealous husband who sought to involve him in the murder of his wife's lover. If Bella is turning in her ostentatious mausoleum, then, surely, my end will be in the prison cemetery.

The two judges will deliberate and give their verdict in a week's time. I will be remanded in custody. Silva Leal tells me to expect the worse.

CHAPTER THIRTY-FIVE
Huelva – 2009

The tariff is eight years, the maximum sentence, so I'm told, for the lesser charge of what, in the British courts, is termed 'a joint enterprise to procure grievous bodily harm'. The weightier charge of murder was set aside on reasonable doubt, based on Dudik's self-serving testimony that he only intended 'to rough-up the guy so he had trouble walking in the future'. Predictably, Silva Leal hails it as a victory. I could have been put away for twenty years, and he makes it sound as though I would have deserved it.

Promises of urgent action to consider grounds for an appeal evaporate like steam from a kettle, and I am left with the uncompromising reality of facing life in a prison cell until my mid seventies.

One day, Bella's flustered female assistant appears. Don't ask me when. The days and weeks have started to fuse together into one perpetual dawn-to-dusk endless routine. According to the woman, they propose to transfer me to a facility near Tarragona designed for prisoners convicted of Category One offences. I am way past reacting. Even so – 'designed' – what a strange word to use about a prison.

I have been sinking fast into profound desolation these past weeks; not eating or washing, or sleeping hours at a stretch. It all seems so pointless. I dream of death, the disorientation of stumbling around in the pitch blackness, hands out, pleading but failing, longing to cling onto something to lead me towards the pinprick of light in the distance, the pathway to an end and a release from the burden of life.

Latex-gloved hands shake me awake, dragging me roughly from my cell, tearing the clothes from my body, cursing at the stench where I have fouled myself, calling me 'filthy English whore's son' as if nationality, xenophobia or birthright fairly describe my disgraced state. The tiles feel cold against my back as I stagger to stand and fight the freezing jets of water that leave welts all over my body. My outstretched hands are useless in defence; my pleas for them to stop, a source of amusement to the guards watching me squirm under the assault.

I am given an ill-fitting tracksuit bottom and a white T-shirt that were never mine, with the curt instruction to sit upright. A guard stands in front of me, gripping my hair with one hand as he wields an electric shaver across my face. Finally, he brushes the lank strands of hair to the back of my head, standing back to admire his handiwork before pushing me towards the door.

The reason for this cursory bout of hygiene, I realise, is the presence of the couple now sitting across the table from me. The young woman appears visibly taken aback by my appearance, sufficient to warrant checking the photograph in the file in front of her. The slightly older man in the bomber jacket over a polo-neck jumper is trying to look nonplussed as the guard chains my leg to the floor-mounted restraint. It's not because I'm dangerous, he explains in halting English. He points to the fresh, jagged scars on my left wrist. Anybody on suicide watch has to be restrained for their own safety. Pens or any sharp objects must not be placed on the table. He will be directly outside the door should they need assistance.

Looking back, it was the interview with this DCI Hammond from the Newport constabulary, nervously supported by young Kate from the British Consulate in Seville, that pulled me back from a downward spiral. Like an eddy of water from the depths of despair propelling me towards the surface, I realise I cannot and must not give in to the blackness. On that day, I discovered a reason to survive. Maybe revenge, once accomplished, is never as satisfying as the prospect of revenge. But revenge unfulfilled, I believe, is one of the most powerful driving forces that motivate the urge to stay alive.

I do not acknowledge their wary greeting. I don't care why they're there. Why say anything? My silence, coupled with a vacant expression, is plainly frightening the girl. It gives me a weird sense of power, a sort of poor man's Hannibal Lecter moment.

The policeman raises a sheet of paper from which he starts to read a prepared text. His hand wavers slightly. He coughs.

I am to be formally advised that Newport constabulary is making enquiries into the death of Madeleine Forbes, pursuant to the coroner's decision to suspend the inquest. I was a friend of the deceased. This is the reason for the interview.

It's all copper-speak, preamble, so, I say nothing. Why bother to acknowledge the facts? Again, he knows I visited her on the morning I left for Portugal. The taxi driver who took me to the house waited whilst I checked around the back. My excuse was she could be in the kitchen with the radio on and not hear the front doorbell. The driver confirmed I was out of sight for about ten minutes. So what?

At last he asks a question.

'I wanted to talk about her car,' I reply. 'It was still in Portugal. I needed to make arrangements with her to get it back.'

More questions; stupid questions.

'We didn't talk about anything at all because she wasn't in. At least, if she was, she wasn't answering the door. Yes, I did notice her other car was there. That's why I persisted, called out in case she was in the bath. No. No reply, so I left. I was in a hurry. What money? She never gave me any money. I've just said, I never saw her. What is this?'

The questions become innuendos; the innuendos turn into allegations. She supposedly gave me five thousand pounds because we were in a relationship. There were hairs with my DNA on her pillow, my toothbrush in a tumbler in the bathroom. How should I know how they got there? Somebody must have planted them. Maybe it did sound incredulous, but I can't think of any other explanation. No, we were not having an affair. Yes, I do admit to having been with her in the hotel. But only in the bar. Again, no. I had not been to the hotel previously with her, as you put it, to spend several afternoons together. Why would we? We were both unattached. A hotel was a married man's province for an affair; certainly not the venue for a single pensioner on income support.

I suggest he speak with Mr Davenport. The mention of Roger's name reanimates his line of enquiry. Am I aware that Madeleine asked Mr Davenport to lend her five thousand pounds to give to me and that she told him she was afraid I would ask her for more and lose my fiery temper again if she refused? Is it not the case when she rejected my request, I was so angry I pushed her so that she tripped over the belt of her dressing gown and tumbled down the stairs to her death? The police are prepared to accept it was unintentional, a spontaneous reaction meant to frighten but with fatal consequences. I just need to come clean.

'It's a fanciful story that owes more to someone's imagination than any factual evidence.' I start to get to my feet. 'I've already told you that I did not see Madeleine on the day you are asking about, nor was I a part of her private life, and, no, I was not present when she died. In fact, this is the first I know of exactly how she met her death, and it sounds to me like a tragic accident. As to the money you keep going on about, it was a loan from Mr Davenport. Madeleine had nothing to do with it.'

Hammond is like a dog with a bone. 'Is it true at some point you asked Madeleine for money and she refused?'

'I recall telling her when we were in the hotel bar I needed some money to go to Portugal. She may have misunderstood and thought I was approaching her, but my objective was to let her know I was going to tap Roger for a loan.'

'Did you arrange the meeting at the hotel?'

'No. I found out that she was going there.'

'How?'

'I don't remember.' I do, but I am not prepared to bring my niece and her part in the plot to his attention at this time. As far as killing his line of enquiry stone dead, it is my get-out-of-jail-free card. Neither Roger nor Madeleine were aware of the connection, and I am beginning to understand this story was concocted by Roger, intended to extricate him from having to admit the affair and, at the same time, finger me as the guilty party. I will wait and see where this all leads before dropping the bombshell.

'Why was she at the hotel, if not to meet you?'

'None of my business. Maybe Mr Davenport can give you a better explanation.'

'The five thousand was never enough for you though, was it?' He reaches inside his coat pocket for a small white envelope.

'It was plenty.'

'I don't think so,' he insists, pulling out a thin gold chain which he winds around his fingers, leaving the pendant, a four-leaf clover, dangling in front of me. 'Recognise this?' he asks.

I recognise it immediately but, as the realisation sinks in, I need time to consider my reply. 'It looks like the one Madeleine used to wear. It was her grandmother's, I believe.'

'Do you know where it was found?'

I know exactly. This wasn't just of Roger's doing. Vernon was complicit in this attempt to frame me for Madeleine's death. The truthful explanation would be pointless. Both Walid and Vernon would deny any involvement. They contrived to ensure it was in my possession. I shake my head. 'I have no idea.'

'Mrs Davenport, your former wife, has confirmed the necklace was her friend's treasured memento and is missing from her jewellery collection. The Portuguese police discovered it in your dressing gown when they searched the property where you were living.' He makes it sound as though he has just hit the home run.

I try to look bemused. 'Sorry, I can't help you.'

'I suppose it was planted, just like the hairs and toothbrush.'

'I assume so.'

There is a sensation like a hot wire being drawn through my body. Under what circumstances did the necklace come into Vernon's possession in the first place? Madeleine would never have parted with it willingly. I am left in little doubt by his final question.

'Were you aware of any delivery that Mrs Forbes was expecting on the day of her death?' Did I see a motorcycle courier dressed in black leathers in the vicinity of her house as a neighbour has testified? I remembered Madeleine's comment about seeing Vernon in the car park when we were in the hotel bar.

My emphatic denial is meant to hide the dread and anger I feel. Everybody is out to get me.

CHAPTER THIRTY-SIX
Huelva – 2009

I'm back from the brink. My cell is looking reasonably clean for the first time in weeks. It's the only way I can prove to myself I have succeeded in resisting the urge to end it all.

I am still in solitary; for my own safety, the warden assures me. My status is likened to the ageing gunfighter in the Wild West with a deadly reputation, newly arrived in town. There will always be young punks keen to take on the old hand and teach him a lesson to prove their ranking in the hierarchy of the townsfolk. The warden sees me as a soft target and, as such, pending my transfer, created a myth to circulate throughout the prison grapevine. The guards who deal with me can see the funny side. Although my appearance and demeanour belie the profile, I have been branded as an evil psychopath with countless victims to my tally.

DCI Hammond ended the interview by warning there could be further questions for me at some future date. I imagine it must have been a follow-up meeting that prompted my summons to accompany the guard the next day, but I was wrong. This time, I'm led into a large room with some twenty inmates sitting across tables, talking in hushed tones to their visitors, loved ones and family members. Faces turn to look in unison, visibly curious to lay eyes at first hand on the monster from solitary. Whispered activity increases but I pay no attention.

The transformation from nondescript caterpillar to stunning butterfly is amazing. Isabel has chosen a dress to enhance her stocky figure and voluptuous bustline, discreet enough but sufficiently tantalising to cause repeated sideways glances from the other inmates. She must have spent hours at the hairdressers to achieve the look and wore just enough make-up and a hint of perfume, subtly intended, I guess, to remind me of Rosita.

'This is a lovely surprise, Isabel.' I'm genuinely delighted but taken aback to see her.

She is nervous, her hands gripping tightly at the edge of the table, her knuckles bleach white.

'Dr Silva Leal's office told me you were being transferred to another prison. I had to see you. I haven't been able to sleep.'

'Why not?'

Tears begin to cloud her eyes. 'You are not a bad person, are you?'

'Not in the way I have been made out to be. Why do you ask?'

'I am.'

'You are what?'

'A bad person. I listened in the tribunal to my brother and the other man tell lies about you and I said nothing. I could have saved you and I didn't.' She looks down at the floor, then turns her eyes towards me. 'I told your lawyer but he said it would not have made any difference. I must wait to testify when it comes to your appeal. I'm afraid.'

'Afraid of what? What are you saying to me, Isabel?' I go to take hold of her hand but the guard's rebuke is swift. She looks startled.

'Just explain it all to me, please, Isabel. I promise I won't be angry or think badly of you. Relax.'

She gulps in a mouthful of air. 'The summer it all happened, you remember?'

'Go on.'

'I told you before, I hated Rosita. She had you and you wanted her, not me. I had gone off the rails, slept around with countless creeps, done drugs, anything I could lay my hands on. Somehow, I managed to keep it all from my parents. TM would have gone mad. When I arrived at the villa, I was already sixteen weeks pregnant.'

'By whom?'

She gives a grunted laugh. 'God knows. I can't remember the faces. Some useless piece of shit, I expect. Eliana knew some woman who could help me to get rid of it. She had been a midwife and knew how to use a knitting needle. For it to happen, we had to get everyone out of the house. Eliana said that she would use Salvador's bonus to give the family a treat and send them all to Seville, including you.'

'Did Rosita know?'

'Of course. She wouldn't be able to go in her condition. Actually, she was quite supportive.'

'And Salvador?'

She looks amazed. 'Don't be silly. They both knew everything, relied on each other. I told you already. She schemed, Salvador was the muscle.'

'I'm listening.'

'We went early in the morning to the woman's house. She did it on a plastic sheet draped over the sofa. I knew something was wrong. She took ages to stop the bleeding. Eliana got me back to my bedroom. I was pale and weak through loss of blood, passing in and out of consciousness to start with. Rosita and Eliana had one argument after another. Rosita insisted I go to the hospital. Eliana refused point-blank. I could have died, but she insisted we took the risk to avoid the consequences.

'It was early afternoon when I came round. It must have been the shouting. Gonzalo was in the house. At first, he sounded hurt, pleading with Rosita to come with him. He claimed she was confused and really did love him. He would take over the family business. There was plenty of money. He would look after her much better than the tired old Englishman could.'

I feel the Adam's apple react in my throat as I listen.

She catches the look in my face. 'I'm sorry,' she says with a weak smile, 'but that's what I heard.'

'Go on.'

'She told him to go, that she had never really cared for him. His voice rose. He started to shout. She didn't know what she was saying. It didn't matter anyway, because her precious Gilbert would be going to prison. He had tipped off Salvador about the delivery someone or other was making to the business.'

'Sikorsky,' I interrupt.

She nods. 'Salvador had got fifteen thousand euros off Gil to keep quiet, but Gonzalo insisted he hadn't done it for money. Their deal was to ensure both Gil and this other man ended up in jail, but Salvador double-crossed him. Rosita must have gone to attack him, calling him all manner of things. Finally, she told him the baby wasn't his. He said she was just saying that to hurt him but he loved her and didn't believe it.'

'Was Eliana in on this conversation?'

'No. She had gone out, back to the woman to see what medicines she should buy to help my recovery. She was scared I wouldn't make it.'

'So, Rosita was alone with Gonzalo?'

'They thought I was unconscious. Rosita said she had asked to test the baby's DNA. It was not Gonzalo's child. He had gone berserk, threatening to go to the police, saying that he would be coming back when you were there to have the whole thing out. You were both going to suffer the consequences.'

She stops, memories of the pain and suffering of that day etched in her eyes, across her face. I can tell she has no intention of saying any more, but I insist. I must know.

'I don't know how to tell you this. It seems so cruel.'

'You can't hurt me any more than I have been already.'

'Rosita was on the phone, speaking loudly and in that slow, precise way so that Robi would understand. His Spanish was never that good. She said she was afraid Gonzalo would come back to the villa. I don't know what he said, but she acknowledged that he and some others would have to go away for a while. She talked about six thousand euros she could get her hands on. He had to protect her. It was their baby she was having and she wanted it to have a mother and father.'

'She said that?'

'I think she meant that you would be the father.' It's a sop to my pride, but the truth doesn't matter now.

'I don't doubt a word you say, Isabel, but I don't think it eliminates me from complicity in Gonzalo's death. After all, when we spoke on the phone I asked Rosita to get Robi to protect her.'

My reaction leaves her deflated, but I urge her to continue.

'For a while, there was silence. I must have slept again.' She fidgets in her chair, adjusting the form-fitting dress she is so obviously unused to wearing. 'Eliana had just returned after running some errand for Rosita. There had been phone calls. This time, the argument was louder than ever. Eliana was accusing Rosita of betraying the family. Rosita talked of despicable blackmail. How she would have thought her brother incapable of such evil. Wait until her parents heard. I could tell Eliana was scared. Rosita said it didn't matter what happened to her business; she would encourage Gonzalo to go to the police. She could testify that the fifteen thousand euros was missing from their savings. She would convince Gil to tell the truth.'

'Is that everything?'

She shakes her head. 'Eliana told Rosita you had tried to seduce her, but she had rejected you. Rosita shrugged it off. She already knew. It meant nothing.'

'It was a bluff. How could she know? I never told her.'

Isabel looks sheepish. 'I did,' she says. 'Rosita laughed at me, told me you would really have to be desperate to fancy Eliana.'

'Do you know who attacked' – I hesitate – 'killed Rosita?'

Again, she shakes her head violently, this time her eyes blinking rapidly, clearly alarmed at the ferocity in my voice. 'No, I honestly don't,' she says in little more than a whisper. 'The fever had started. Eliana had said she would find Salvador and get help. I could hardly take my head off the pillow. All I remember are muffled voices from the living room.'

'How many voices?'

'I couldn't say. Rosita, I could make out.'

'Did she appear to know who she was talking to?'

Isabel's weak smile is one of apology.

'You have to appreciate I was gripped by a fever that lasted for two days until it was urgent enough to hospitalise me. The day after that, they operated.' She searches for the word but gives up. 'They had to take out all my lady parts.'

'A hysterectomy?'

'Yes. I went through the change of life at twenty.' She turns her head away, staring at the dirt-ridden air conditioning unit that whirrs from the ceiling at the end of the room. 'Men say it doesn't matter, but they always find an excuse for ending the relationship soon after they discover I can't have children. They are hypocrites, but I can't blame them. I'm damaged goods; worth a screw, but no more. So I gave up relationships altogether. I don't think about it any more.'

I reach to take her hand but she withdraws it before I touch her. 'Don't pity me,' she says. 'It doesn't suit you.' She gets up to leave but something jogs her mind. 'The only other thing I remember from later that night is when Eliana was calling through the window to Salvador, who was waiting in the road for the ambulance. She asked where Rosita was, and had he seen Gil? A minute later, you rushed upstairs, calling my name and cursing, demanding to know if anybody was about. I was surprised you had not met up with Eliana.'

I thank her for her honesty.

'You will be out inside six months,' she says. 'You can buy me dinner.'

As it happened, her remark turned out to be prophetic, but not for the reasons she imagined. Her testimony was never needed.

CHAPTER THIRTY-SEVEN
Aranjuez, Spain – 2009

Five months have passed since my transfer to the jail in Aranjuez, some forty kilometres south of Madrid. As much as I originally dreaded the thought of moving from Huelva, where I had slipped into the routine of an established inmate, the move to Aranjuez stimulated me in a way I never thought possible.

The windowless prison van provided no opportunity to glimpse the city as we made our way to my new home, but the prison library has several illustrated books describing the history of what is now a UNESCO World Heritage Site, once famed as a Royal Estate where only the first family and other nobles were allowed to live. I was entranced by the photographs of impressive buildings commissioned by royal patronage, where the privileged classes existed in an exclusive social bubble for over two hundred years during an era of ostentatious Spanish heritage.

Even the prison was exceptional. I now understand why Bella's assistant described the building as 'designed'. Amongst its rambling corridors is an area of thirty-six family rooms where inmates can live with their spouse and young infants. I often hear the sound of children playing in the specially constructed playground or their excited chatter as they leave or return from a nursery outside the prison walls. It's surreal and makes me think of Francisco. I have begun to write him letters – short one-page efforts – every week, never expecting to get a reply. I end up pleasantly surprised.

The drawing shows a stickman, slightly better drawn and proportioned than his earlier efforts, with hands locked onto prison bars. A woman and child are as close to the edge of the page as he could have placed them, both blowing kisses to the man. I am really touched. The brief letter from Jasmin is polite and to the point. There has been a lot of upheaval in her family since my departure. Things will never be the same again. At first, she was angry I exposed them to investigation and incriminations, but now, she has come to realise, once everything was out in the open they could get on with living their lives without looking back. Francisco never forgets me and always talks about his *avô*. Intrigued, I reply, asking her to explain what she meant by 'upheaval'.

Although I get a new precious drawing every week from Francisco to decorate my cell wall, Jasmin has never sent another accompanying letter.

Filipe Junqueras is an apologetic-sounding young man who walks with drooping shoulders and a pronounced arm movement, giving him the appearance of a clockwork toy. He has a boyish face with a dark brown mole in the middle of his forehead that I find my eyes irresistibly drawn to as he introduces himself. He sounds out of breath, as though he has walked all the way from Jerez, but I soon ignore the repeated shuddering intake of breath as I listen to his explanation for seeking me out.

He acted as Roman Sikorsky's lawyer. Some months ago, his client was diagnosed with a particularly aggressive form of pancreatic cancer. Thankfully, he died last week after months of debilitating and painful suffering. Whilst still in command of his faculties, Sikorsky prepared a sworn statement to be submitted to the tribunal following his death.

In summary, he admitted to having lied and committing perjury at my trial. He confirmed he took the decision to kill Gonzalo from the moment he learned of the conspiracy which led to his apprehension by the policeman, Salvador Rodriguez, on the night his vehicle was stopped on the way to make a delivery to me.

When he learned from his nephew Robi of the threats made by Gonzalo to Rosita Rodriguez, with whom Robi was in a relationship and who was expecting his child, he determined to expedite the planned assassination. He claimed to have acted with Robi and two hired accomplices to kidnap and kill his victim after making him dig his own grave in the forest. He also claimed to have made two payments of fifteen thousand euros to Salvador Rodriguez, the first to avoid prosecution on the night he was stopped, and the second, many years later, when Rodriguez told him the police had damning testimony from Dudik, one of the accomplices, that would implicate Sikorsky in Gonzalo's killing. Rodriguez offered both men a way out. A sequence of events was concocted to ensure both Dudik and Sikorsky, when formally interviewed, would incriminate Hart as the instigator of the plot.

The reality was that Gilbert Hart knew nothing and had absolutely nothing to do with the disappearance and assassination of Gonzalo Ramirez.

His final words were that he wanted to die with a clear conscience, by apologising to the tribunal for misleading the judges.

'I have to give you this,' Filipe says, handing me a sealed envelope. There are six lines in a shaky hand, sadly betraying the state of Sikorsky's health when he wrote it. He asks me not to think too badly of him. He is sure I will understand his position and forgive him. Look on the bright side. My prison sentence is not an unfair price to pay for all the wrongs we have committed. His punishment is far worse.

I fold the sheet of paper and tear it into small squares, letting them filter through my fingers onto the floor.

'Have you much experience as a defence lawyer?' I ask.

He has, and I make sure when he asks Silva Leal to transfer my case files, he passes on my letter of thanks for all the incompetence displayed in securing my conviction. I tell Filipe not to wait for a reply.

My sentence is eventually expunged plus legal costs, together with the princely sum of thirteen euros per day compensation for time served, and I am a free man. My paltry belongings handed back include the photographs I borrowed from Brigitte. I figure it's time to return them.

CHAPTER THIRTY-EIGHT
Porto – 2009

Brigitte's battered visiting card is still in my wallet along with a few hundred euros, all that remains after organising a suitcase of new clothes, a ticket for a flight back to Bristol from Porto in four days' time and a kitschy bunch of red roses I feel a little embarrassed to be holding as I wait for her to answer the door to her apartment.

'You're early,' she says, accepting the flowers as if it was the least she expected. A casual glance and they are tossed onto the kitchen work surface. 'You've lost weight. It suits you. I hear you've had an interesting year.' She pecks me on the cheek.

'You could say that.' I laugh. 'Not one I want to repeat.'

I'm not sure whether I'm relieved or disappointed she doesn't enquire further. It's either tact or disinterest. I settle for the former.

'When Pedro knew you were coming, he asked if he might join us. I know he is keen to talk to you.'

My expression must register the dismay I feel. I hoped for some private time, a chance to be alone with a woman who has fascinated me and occupied many a waking hour in my thoughts since the first time we exchanged banter. Okay, maybe Borodin does deserve a bollocking for feeding me to the wolves when he was supposed to be watching my back, but time and other priorities have dulled my animosity. Anyway, his presence will definitely put the kibosh on my plans. I take a deep breath. Whatever, it's out of my control, a fait accompli. Until he arrives, let's catch up, she suggests.

Brigitte studies the photographs I hand back to her as if seeing them for the first time. She takes her time studying the images showing Hugo. 'Things have happened since you went away,' she says reflectively. 'It's been hard to take, even if you are on the periphery of the family, as I am.'

'Jasmin said as much when she wrote to me. What happened exactly?'

'Are you planning to go to Cavalla?'

'I'd like to see Francisco before I go back to the UK.'

'Best that you let Jasmin explain the developments. She can give you a more detailed account than I. To be frank, I prefer not to dwell on the past.'

She leaves me wondering what the hell had been going on, as she reacts to the sound of the intercom and Borodin's arrival.

He greets me as a long-lost friend, so happy I have been able to resolve 'my little problem in Spain', as if it was a speeding offence or something equally trivial. As Brigitte busies herself in the kitchen, preparing the finishing touches to the beef casserole in red wine she claims as a speciality and her grandmother's recipe, I launch into Borodin for leaving me exposed on the day of the ill-fated visit to the safari park. He pooh-poohs my protestations with a humour that really riles me. There was always someone watching my back, he claims. It was not possible to keep in contact on the day because he did not wish to involve Sargento Lannier in the detail of the arrangement.

'Why not?' I ask.

'Lannier was – is – of interest to us in connection with an ongoing investigation.' His mood changes from flippant to serious, a glance to check Brigitte is not within earshot. 'You deserve an explanation.' He leans closer and speaks in a low voice. 'In fact, our investigation has developed in certain areas that will be of concern to you. However, anything said here tonight must not leave this room. Is that clear?'

'Brigitte is not a party to it?'

He shakes his head. 'Absolutely not.'

I give him my word.

His preamble introduces facts I have already broadly figured out during those long months in solitary confinement. Amongst the products manufactured by SantaCavalla is a medication for ADHD, Attention Deficit Hyperactivity Disorder, mainly a methamphetamine, distributed in pill form. The product is also widely known on the recreational drug scene as ecstasy. He reminds me at our last meeting we talked about the drug carfentanil and its potency, ten thousand times that of heroin.

'Both of these drug types are synthetic, laboratory created. In the case of carfentanil, SantaCavalla is allowed to hold controlled quantities for certain veterinary uses, but it is readily available on the dark web from illicit Chinese sources.'

I reached the conclusion he is expounding a long time ago, so I interrupt. 'So, with or without corporate sanction, there is a cottage industry in Cavalla, producing and distributing the ecstasy tablets I came across in the Moroccans' warehouse. Now, you are going to tell me who is behind it.'

There is a curt nod of the head. 'We are convinced it is not an authorised sideline. The Brazilian holding company is still relatively small, but it has some interesting R&D projects and is unlikely to take the risk. We suspect there is probably a collaborator in the Brazilian set-up who is helping to source some of the raw material, but everything tells us that this is a Reyes family venture.'

'Really?'

'I hoped your annoying presence would flush them out, but your investigation into your son's death took you in other directions. These are things in which Lannier is interested, not us.' He stops, stretching over for an envelope in the inside pocket of his bomber jacket. 'That's not totally accurate. There was one aspect of your meddling we found worth investigating.'

'Which was?'

'We dropped it. I'll come back to it after dinner. It was outside our remit. As I say, we passed the detail onto Lannier.'

'But it was you who sent Lannier to the safari park?'

He shook his head then thought about it. 'Indirectly, I suppose you could say. He was never made aware of our arrangement. We suspect he is a user and sources supplies from the Moroccans. From your last call to us, it was obvious you were in danger and could achieve nothing for our cause. For two months we suppressed a request from the Spanish to act on an EAW they issued for your capture and return. We explained you were a suspect in an ongoing investigation, and tested their patience. As soon as you were no more use to us, we ordered Lannier to arrest you.'

'Great to know who your friends are when it counts.'

'What did you expect?' He seems perplexed at my reaction. 'You have information locked in your head for which somebody considers it is worth killing you ... or did. I doubt they are bothered now.' There is a sardonic laugh. 'We knew where you'd be, if we needed you back.'

My intended reply is stifled by Brigitte's entry. Dinner is great. The casserole is rich, heavy on the red wine sauce and dotted with some deliciously light dumplings Brigitte claims are a local speciality. After clearing the main course plates away, she returns from the kitchen waving my bunch of roses in front of Borodin's face. 'Glad there's at least one gentleman in this diner tonight,' she says.

At that moment, I know my fantasy dream evening with her is just that: a fantasy. There is something a lot more than just friendship in the way they look at each other. I have lost that bet with myself, but I am definitely not going to let it spoil the evening.

The conversation is animated, a lot to do with their mutual friends whom I would never get to know, peppered with funny stories about her loan clientele and their tactics for avoiding repayment arrangements. A leisurely two hours pass before Borodin offers to prepare the coffee and disappears into the kitchen, laden with more dirty crockery.

'You seem to have a new best buddy?' I venture.

'Gilbert, I can tell underneath that matter-of-fact exterior, you are really, and probably always have been, the last of the romantics. They don't exist any more. In fact, you are positively antediluvian. Pedro fits nicely into the category of keeping your friends close and your enemies closer. We are both utterly ruthless.'

'I can believe it. I must watch my back.'

She leans over, reaching to hold my face between her hands, the hint of her perfume rising into my nostrils, intoxicating, suggestive. 'It's an old saying, but there are exceptions to every rule. I heard from Jasmin how you described your set-to with Vernon. You didn't tell the authorities.'

Her fingers are massaging my temples. I'm having trouble concentrating. 'Tell them what?' I manage to say.

'Don't play games with me. That your son tried to kill you and wants you dead.'

'I haven't got it in me. He's my son, whatever his actions. Maybe he's not so misguided after all.'

'You don't really believe that. He survives by virtue of your guilt, but he will go too far. Maybe he already has; events may have already put him outside of your control.'

Something tells me this is more than just conjecture. She knows something. Hugo. She had once been his mentor, a kindred spirit. It had to be. 'Has Hugo said something?'

She looks anxiously towards the kitchen. Her hands withdraw and she leans back, slowly shaking her head as she reaches into her pocket. 'I think you should keep this one,' she says. 'After all, it is of your sons.' She hands me back the photograph of my two boys on holiday in their swimming trunks, standing in front of the beach bar.

Am I supposed to draw a conclusion from my question and her reaction? I look at the photograph. I can't see it.

'Here we are.' Borodin returns with three *café solos* and the brandy bottle. The conversation reverts to its casual superficiality, drifting into social topics and politics. Whether it's the influence of alcohol, Borodin makes his various attempts to pronounce 'ambivalent' sound like 'ambulance', eventually inciting a remark about my damn stupid language.

Brigitte is quick to react. 'It's not the grammar I find difficult or, for that matter, the pronunciation. It's the spelling most foreign nationals find difficult.' She looks straight at me. 'Don't you agree, Gilbert?'

I acknowledge the nature of the difficulty, recalling all those instruction manuals for Chinese products produced in comic English and the road sign on the way into Sanlazer that bade me 'Wellcome'.

Borodin reaches for Brigitte's hand, squeezing it tight and sending a shiver down my spine. 'If I promise to load the dishwasher, can I have another ten minutes with Gilbert before he leaves?'

In one sentence, I am being told my time is nearly up and he is staying, intending to occupy my precious final minutes with more police-speak. I could protest, claiming there is nothing further to discuss, but he's finger-drumming impatiently as if what he has to say is important.

However delicately put, her tight-lipped expression suggests Brigitte does not appreciate being summarily dismissed. I feel smugly vindicated. For now, she raises no objection other than the dishes can wait for the morning, but I hope she lets him have it with both barrels after I've left.

'I thought you would want to know where our investigation into your son's death has taken us.'

Right at that moment, as I watch her walk out of the door, I could not have cared less.

'We are convinced Lino and his brother Lourenco, the technical guy, are responsible for the production of these amphetamine pills spiked with carfentanil. Distribution is handled by his nephew, Hugo' – he nods towards the door – 'her favourite, who can do no wrong. He uses the services of the Moroccans and their transport business to move the goods. We need to catch them red-handed to make a conviction stick, but with you fishing around and the explosion still under investigation, production ceased and we are waiting for it to start up again. They must be getting desperate, but they need to change their modus operandi.'

'How come?'

'There is a black market for these recreational drugs throughout Europe. The pills were packed by Albert into the centre of the prayer cushions. What could be more innocent than using such a harmless faith item to move this deadly cargo around?'

He now has my undivided attention. 'But Jasmin and Adele were involved in producing the cushions. Are they implicated?'

'We don't think so. From what I understand, when needed they would help with cutting and sewing. Albert did the filling, and always when they were not present.'

'How does the explosion tie in to all this?'

'The current theory is that there are two motives. Firstly, Lino had organised the sale of a quantity of product that Hugo should have had but no longer possessed because he was running a secondary operation unbeknown to his uncle by syphoning off stock. Hugo was under pressure to explain the shortfall, not just from Lino but from the Moroccans who were being urged to make the outstanding deliveries. That's where you came in.

'I regret having to say this, but your son Albert was willing to go along with a plan to see you dead, presumably revenge for discarding your family when he was a boy. Together with Vernon and Hugo, he hatched a plan to invite you to the wedding, somehow immobilise you and lock you in alongside the gas boiler. As an expert in the field, their evidence would be you had offered to try and locate a gas leak, failed, and the explosion had killed you. The house would be destroyed, ostensibly along with the remaining drugs which they had, in fact, already removed, and the insurance company would deal with a claim for the damage without too many uncomfortable questions.'

'Remember, at the end my son sacrificed his life in order to save mine. As for the rest, you are either making a lot of unsubstantiated assumptions or you have inside information?'

'Educated guesses based on forensic analysis,' he parries with a dismissive smile. 'My reason for telling you how we see things goes along with a simple request.'

'The ulterior motive again.'

'Not really. We would prefer it if you returned directly to the UK, but, if you are determined to go to Cavalla, please do not get involved in any aspect of our ongoing investigation, which is reaching a very delicate stage. Take the information that I have given you in good faith, with the assurance that when the process is concluded, I will bring you up to date. On no account interfere with the status quo. Is that understood?'

'You talked about another line of enquiry?' I nod towards the bomber jacket and the envelope he returned to the inside pocket.

'Those disturbing photographs found by the police in your room prompted us to take a look at the Reyes family issues in case they had any bearing on our investigation. The autopsy report on Vicente Reyes threw up an interesting aside. On the face of it, it was an open-and-shut case of a nasty suicide. The man had blown his brains out with a shotgun, and the pathologist at the time wasn't really looking for any deeper motives. However, taking a fresh look, our guys suggested the reference to a faint trace of a garlic-like smell in the urine report indicated the presence of allin and the relevant corresponding sulphoxide in the liver.'

'You are losing me.'

'The sulphoxide compound concerned is found in a sedative known as acepromazine, available in both pill and injectable forms. It is not only a sedative, but where the subject is suffering anxiety, it can increase sensitivity.'

The technical explanation is beyond me. 'So, the man took some form of tranquiliser beforehand. So what?'

He used his fingernails on one hand to clean under the nails on the other. 'Acepromazine is a controlled substance, available only on prescription. It is used almost exclusively to sedate dogs, cats and some farm animals. Never on humans. You have to be an expert to ensure the correct dosage.'

'You're saying Jasmin ...'

He shows the palm of his hands. 'I'm saying nothing. It is true that three doses of this particular medication are shown in the veterinary practice records as having been transferred to the local pharmacy. I believe you know the pharmacist. But from there, the trail goes cold and, thankfully, it's a closed case; and with a lack of substantive proof' – he lets out a sigh – 'well, better for the local police to sort it out ... or not, as the case may be.'

I walk into the kitchen to say my goodbyes to Brigitte. Another man is staying over and the roses are back on the counter, still wrapped and cast aside.

'Try and find a vase with some water to put them in,' I say. 'If you're not interested in taking off the wrapping and giving them a chance to bloom in the right conditions, you will never appreciate their beauty.'

It's the first time I've seen her lost for words, avoiding my eyes, the flush of red wine on her cheeks.

CHAPTER THIRTY-NINE
Cavalla – 2009

The house is as I remember it, dark and sombre, hidden from the road behind a canopy of leaves of various hues of green and brown. Nobody is in. Madeleine's Astra still sits in the driveway, covered in a debris of vegetation, uncared for and probably unroadworthy. I'm surprised nobody has come to claim it but, on reflection, I have no idea who are Madeleine's next of kin and whether they have any idea of its existence. I make a mental note to deal with it when I get back to the UK.

My initial fear is that Jasmin decided to back out of our meeting. She said four and it is now closer to five. I begin to expect a no-show, but she eventually turns up looking flustered, with Francisco in his child seat, straining forward to catch a glimpse of the stranger standing in the drive.

For me, it is a joyous reunion. Francisco has gained both height and bulk in the ten months we have been apart, and his unconditional acceptance of my re-entry into his life fills my eyes. I promise him I am not sad. It's just a silly old man delighted to see his grandson once more.

After apologising for the delay – a stressful day at the clinic – Jasmin busies herself around the house, leaving Francisco to excitedly show me all his new toys and demonstrate his drawing skills using a box of crayons that must be easily two-foot square and contain every colour under the sun. Of course, I kept his drawings. They are stored in the bottom of my case, ready to take pride of place on the wall of the lounge in my apartment.

Bed is out of the question. Clad in pyjamas and a matching dressing gown adorned with a jolly snowman, who he tells me in a serious tone is Olaf from Frozen, Francisco eventually falls asleep in my lap. His little fingers grasp my hand as he purrs contentedly.

Jasmin hands me the soother, saying I probably won't need it, and sits down on a dinner chair facing me. She leans forward, elbows supported on her thighs, hands clasped under her chin.

For the first half an hour, we skirt around the topic foremost on our minds. I describe the passage of events in Spain whilst she listens almost too intently, asking pointed and pertinent questions to which, in a number of instances, I struggle to give honest answers. In retrospect, I see her probing as a means of trying to reach a decision. Can she fulfil her promise and trust me with an explanation of the truth behind her past and the circumstances that brought Albert into their lives? Originally, I was looking for motive and reason. I now know the answers, but not from her lips. For her to confide would signify acceptance of me as – how can I best describe myself? – a surrogate member of her immediate family; more importantly, a permanent appointment as Francisco's grandfather.

'Tell me, Gilbert, what was your primary motive for coming back to Cavalla: to see your grandson, or to learn of the realities now facing my family?' Her face is flushed, almost as if she is embarrassed by her own temerity, but it somehow reminds me of the attractive, self-possessed woman I met on my first day in Cavalla. I can see the traces of family similarity with Brigitte, a combative, resilient attractiveness yet an underlying mix of vulnerability and resentment when confronted with male dominance.

'Do I have to put them in order?' I smile. 'If I do, I love your son as my grandson. Unconditionally. I believe we have a relationship transcending blood and parentage and, wherever the rest of our lives lead us, I will strive to protect and nurture the development of Francisco until he is a man in his own right. He is the one person in this world who matters to me. Your family issues are very much a poor second.'

She is less tense now; I hesitate to say relaxed, but somehow satisfied a decision has been reached.

Most of the story I know or have already pieced together over the months of nothing to do but think about everything.

As a girl moving from puberty into maidenhood, she was continually abused by her father, Estevão. His twin brother, Vicente, was always around, a voyeur with a camera, as Jasmin describes him. Performing sexual acts to gratify her father progressed to rape and, when still fifteen, to pregnancy. Inés learned of the pregnancy too late to do anything about it, moving with her daughter to relatives in Spain, having spread the word to all and sundry it was she who was having the baby.

'The birth was long, complicated and extremely painful. I am told I nearly died, my young, frail form inadequate to handle the trauma. Apparently, the cord ended up around the baby's neck, starving his brain of oxygen. Forceps were used on the baby's head, causing irreparable damage.' She sits in pensive silence, reliving the experience, eyes closed as events are triggered in her mind.

I say nothing.

Eventually, her eyes open. She takes a deep breath and goes on. Inés worked it all out. To explain Jasmin's weakened state, she was presented as recovering from an appendectomy whilst Inés pretended to breastfeed the baby on milk expressed from her daughter. The baby was pretty much in a vegetative state from the start. The doctors said he could die at any moment. They hurried to have the boy christened. He passed away shortly afterwards.

'At that point, your father committed suicide?' I ask.

She hesitates, her lips pursed, eyelids fluttering slightly. 'My mother found it hard to cope. She said we were being punished by God for a terrible sin. She would nurse the baby for hour upon hour, sitting, clinging to him, muttering at the ceiling. His death came as a blessing to me and a tragedy for Inés. She has never got over him. I am certain the experience influences her attitude to Francisco. She could never let herself get close and emotionally involved again.'

'Did she know what your father and his brother were doing to you at the time?'

She looks at me and raises her shoulders. 'Some questions are best unasked. We all have to live with ourselves. I almost began to treat their despicable behaviour as a part of growing up. If she knew, maybe she conditioned herself as well.'

'How did she react to her husband's suicide?'

There is a long silence before she speaks. 'I expect you will hear anyway. Let's be kind and say, although he wanted to, my father was too weak to take his own life, so Inés helped him on his way.'

'She was there?'

'She waited until he was drowsy from the effects of the sedative she had given him and then slit his wrists as he watched her. She has made a full confession to the police.'

'Why?'

She avoids the question, opting to advance the storyline. The experience with her father instilled in Jasmin the urge to despise and distrust all men.

There were never any boyfriends. And when there was the occasional night out, sex was out of the question as both too traumatic and painful. A girlfriend had once had other ideas but Jasmin found the suggestion as unpalatable as the prospect of a heterosexual relationship. She learned to avoid any situation which might compromise her.

The world moved on. Sordid memories of the past began to blunt against the dull edge of time passing; her attitude to men and their attitudes hardened into a credo and her life became comfortably predictable. She met Hugo's partner, whom she described as a thoughtful and understanding man and whose presence was never a threat to her. Albert listened, made interesting observations and, unlike most men, did not spend most of the time talking about himself. He was somebody who she found it easy to get on with.

'Nearly five years ago, my grandparents – the old couple you met at the wedding – asked me to go to the farm to treat an ailing sow. The pig-cote is alongside the cottage in which Vicente lived. It was a chilly day with frost on the ground. He offered a cup of something hot which I gladly accepted. When I came to, I was roped to a bed, confronted by a wall filled with photographs of me that he had taken when my father was alive. I was looking at this disgusting, deranged old man, standing naked in front of me, rambling on about how this would be the finest moment of his life, a pledge to Estevão fulfilled.' She breathes in deeply to still herself at the memory. 'My uncle raped me. I discovered later I was again pregnant.'

'Did you not want to abort the foetus?'

She shakes her head. 'I could never live with myself if I countenanced such a thing. I was not that stupid though. As the pregnancy progressed, an amniocentesis test showed the baby did not display any genetic family defect.'

'Were you not afraid somebody might find out and tell?'

'Terrified. There would be too many questions, gossip and rumours, providing a link back to my father's death. I made up a story about boyfriend who lived in another country and avoided any more searching questions by spending the latter months of the pregnancy with my relatives in Spain, just as I had with Martin. Francisco was born in Granada.'

I pose the question to which I guessed the answer months ago. 'And Vicente? There was no suicide, was there?'

'Under interrogation, Inés eventually confessed to killing Vicente as well as her husband. The photographs you found are in the hands of the police. She claimed retribution for his part in my abuse by Estevão. Her defence is diminished responsibility. The lawyer thinks she will serve a short sentence in a controlled facility.'

'How did they come to suspect her?'

For the first time, she appears to relax, the burden of confession passed. 'The case of Vicente's death was never closed. Lannier was like a dog with a bone. Initially, he was prepared to treat Vicente's death as suspected suicide, a shotgun wedged under his chin, but when the medical evidence came to light that the arthritis in his hands was so advanced he could never have pulled the trigger, the case remained on file. If it was murder, the choice of suspects was limited.'

'But Inés didn't kill him alone, did she?'

Jasmin stiffens. Francisco wriggles in my lap, opens sleep-filled eyes and, reassured, closes them again.

'Why do you say that? Inés confessed.'

'It's what mothers do; protect their offspring.'

'Sorry?'

'I suspect the authorities believe it might have been a collective effort to see him off in the manner he deserved. Someone would have had to make sure he was quite receptive when the gun was placed under his chin. Someone else to help him pull the trigger. Maybe even a third, unrelated party was in on the action.'

There is a look of resignation on her face. 'And who is prepared to advance this theory?'

'Absolutely no one, I imagine. I don't see it would do any good. The circumstances won't change, and even if Inés did not pull the trigger, she was complicit.' I try to give a reassuring smile. 'You should just be aware such a theory, as you call it, does exist.' If Borodin is right, I thought to myself, she is about to face a great deal more family trauma. 'Tell me about Albert.' Time to change the subject.

'What is to tell that you probably don't already know? I was pregnant, "Who is the father?" the popular question, either spoken or inferred. The story of a missing boyfriend was wearing thin. Albert was under intense pressure from his domineering mother to find a wife and give her a grandchild. He needed a cover to carry on his affair with Hugo and, happily, we liked each other enough to spend time together. It was Hugo's suggestion. He had bought the house for them to share, but they never got to really live in it.'

'And when the baby came, with no trace of dark skin or Caribbean features?'

'It happens. Most of his antecedents are Caucasian. You have to brazen it out. People can choose to believe it or not, but it's what is now on the rectified birth certificate.'

'That's what makes me such a lucky grandfather,' I say, smiling to alleviate the tension.

'Sandra never accepted the baby was Albert's. Sly comments and innuendos were the best she could manage. She showed no affection for Francisco. I remember once when she actually said she was awaiting news of the next one to brighten the winter of her years.'

'And the day of the explosion? What do you know of that?'

'Only what Hugo told me and the information the police released. Both Albert and Hugo, to a lesser extent, lived in the shadow of Vernon's threats; not only the fear he would tell Sandra the truth about their relationship, but his generally unstable behaviour and unpredictable displays of violence if his will was challenged.' She looks at me enquiringly. 'When I accused them of cowardice, Albert said it wasn't only that. Something had happened in the past that could get them all into serious trouble. He would not say what it was. You have no idea, I suppose?'

'None at all.'

'On that morning, Albert opened up to me. Your invitation to the wedding was a sham. Their idea was to confront you, tell you just how much they hated and despised you for walking out on their mother. You were to go and stay out of their lives forever. I have to say in fairness to Albert, he had serious misgivings about such callous retribution, but he told me he could not break ranks without putting the plan at risk.'

'The plan?'

'To confront you, I assume. As tempers were likely to be lost, Albert suggested I take Francisco out for a few hours. When we returned – well, you know the rest.'

It sounded genuine. Either that or she has a degree from the Richard Burton School of Acting. I am tempted to let it go.

'And the confrontation at the safari park? Vernon's presence?'

There is a flicker of defiance in her eyes. 'You were poking around in our family's past. Disclosure could be potentially damaging for not only me and my family – it might encourage Sandra to start prying, and she could afford expensive, professional investigators. You were leaving the next day. Hugo was convinced they could persuade you to leave us in peace.'

'I bet he was.'

I have learned everything she knows or is prepared to disclose. The Reyes family is an enigma. Everything in plain sight is but nothing compared to the tangled web laying hidden from view. I wasn't going to learn any more. If my objective is to understand what prompted Albert to finally risk his life to save me, I guess I'm as close to the truth as I will ever be.

As gently as possible, I shift Francisco from my lap. 'I had best be going,' I say. There is a franchised motel at the junction to the autoroute. I intend to book in for two nights.

'Don't be silly.' The words spill out. 'He will be devastated if you are not here when he wakes up. Your room is still empty. I made up the bed when I knew you were coming.'

I gratefully accept. Even though I have left the next day free in the hope I would spend it with Francisco, the offer helps to protect my dwindling finances.

The call comes through unexpectedly the following morning. I hold on to a cheap Spanish pay-as-you-go mobile which still has credits and I keep for emergencies.

The display shows the name of Junqueras. He's relieved to hear I am still in Cavalla. Sikorsky's death-bed confession and my release have triggered significant developments. Salvador has been suspended from duty pending a disciplinary investigation, and the tribunal in Huelva has authorised a police request to exhume Rosita's remains for a new forensic examination. Whilst enhanced scientific techniques might be an argument of fact, the need for further work was substantiated on the grounds that the initial findings were inconclusive and the prime suspect was not the perpetrator of the crime.

The examination has now been concluded and the body reburied. Why, I ask, is a copy of the report and the findings in the hands of Lannier in Cavalla? What is the interest of the Portuguese police? Junqueras is adamant. It is an issue of DNA. Can I please stall my questions and speak to the local police chief, either on the telephone or, preferably, in person? If I need any further clarification, I can call him. He will be sending a detailed letter to my UK address.

As intended, I spend the day with Francisco. We walk and play as we did, as if nothing has happened, our relationship unbroken. The route is carefully planned to include an impromptu lunchtime meeting with Adele to say my goodbyes, an extended trip to the children's playground and an unseasonal ice cream in the café close to the police station.

At precisely four that afternoon, Francisco and I are seated in Lannier's office. We are both listening to what the police chief has to say. Fortunately, Francisco does not understand one word and busies himself tugging impatiently at my sleeve. Sadly, I acknowledge every single word as the truth begins to unravel in front of me.

Did I recall my son was involved in a fracas on the day I first arrived in Cavalla? As a matter of course, a swab was taken and his DNA profile posted on the Portuguese database. Although further tests will be necessary, traces of a matching DNA were exchanged through the European Prüm system which indicate Vernon was present in Sanlazer at or around the time Rosita died. Lannier needs to know his current whereabouts in order to advise the Spanish authorities.

He dials a number and hands me the phone. 'If I make the call,' he says, 'he becomes a flight risk. Whereas you can say you just want to meet up with him.'

Sandra's brittle voice is suspicious. Haven't I done enough damage? Stay out of their lives. After berating me for what seems like an hour but can only have been a minute or two, she calms down. Why do I want to speak to Vernon? He doesn't want anything to do with me. Anyway, he doesn't live with them any more. There was a misunderstanding with Roger. He moved out. After five minutes of coaxing and reassurances, and various interruptions from Francisco that she must have overheard, her mood changes. She asks if it's Albert's son I'm with. I tell her it is. Her voice shaking and full of tears, she finally gives me Vernon's number.

'I warn you. He'll just tell you to go to hell.' She slams the phone down.

'He's in the UK somewhere,' I say to Lannier. 'Is that good enough?'

'I will advise the police in Huelva. They will no doubt ask you to arrange a meeting.'

They don't need to. I am anxious to speak with Vernon. I have to understand his involvement in Rosita's death.

He answers at the first ring, his voice thick and incoherent. A female voice is singing and giggling in the background. There is no reaction when he realises it's me. I suggest the following day at my flat. He must have put his hand over the mouthpiece. There is mumbling and then raucous laughter from both of them.

'That's very convenient for us,' he says. The laughter starts up again. 'Can't wait, can we?' More laughter, and the phone goes dead.

Sleep comes in fits and starts. I'm still exhausted as the alarm sounds and I drag myself out of bed. I never appreciated what 'gut-wrenching' meant until I say goodbye to Francisco. I promise to write every week and to return very soon. He gives me a drawing of a fat stickman holding a little boy tight, with kisses all over the page. I have to turn my face away from him.

***

I have the photograph of the two boys balanced on my lap as the stewardess passes to check our safety belts are fixed for landing. She goes to say something but thinks better of it. Sad how a spontaneous reaction is stalled these days by caution and suspicion, isn't it?

Brigitte must have known all along. Maybe Hugo pointed it out to her. She dropped me enough clues but refused to get directly involved. I must have looked at that photograph a hundred times. I must have walked past that beach bar at the end of Sanlazer as you look out at the skyline of Islantilla. I may have even stood and laughed with Rosita as we considered, however logical it may sound to the foreign ear, the signwriter should have checked before painting the word 'cock-tales' on the bar wall. Mind you, if he meant it, it was genius.

I have nothing to laugh about now. Both of my sons and Hugo were in Sanlazer and implicated in Rosita's death. The thought makes me shiver.

CHAPTER FORTY
Chepstow – 2009

In the fading light of a damp autumnal day, everything seems somehow smaller, more compact than I remember. I've never really noticed how we seem to squeeze everything tightly together on this small island of ours. The rows of semi-detached houses are squatter, the tree-lined roads, narrower, yet the hustle and bustle around me, noisier and faster, mainly school children pouring out onto the road, filtering in all directions. They stride past my measured gait at lightning speed, many inadequately dressed for the weather conditions, some so untidily it looks as though their clothes have struggled through a day's learning in sympathy with their brains. Animated chattering is interspersed with the occasional whoosh of a firework from some back garden; then, momentary silence as eyes turn skyward to watch the explosion of multi-coloured lights. Tomorrow is November the fifth, the UK's annual celebration of a failed terrorist act five centuries ago.

Welcome back to Chepstow, Gil!

I check for the spare front door key in the plant tray under the ornamental bonsai tree, surprisingly still intact and looking remarkably healthy. As I anticipate, the key has gone. I use the one on my keyring.

In the hallway, I can already detect the unpleasant scent of fast food remnants, stale fat and the clawing scent of an air freshener, combining to produce a far more repulsive aroma. It appears a unilateral decision to occupy my space was taken some days before the invitation I extended and, judging by the dirty crockery in the kitchen area, a week or longer is my guess. The three pairs of skimpy female briefs soaking in the kitchen sink say he has company. No wonder their humour on the phone when I suggested we meet at my place.

I move gingerly through the apartment, expecting Vernon to rise up from some corner and assault me. It's illogical, I tell myself. There is nowhere to hide in such a small space.

A mound of post, mostly junk mail leaflets, slithers from the arm of the sofa onto the floor. I bend to pick it up. All the envelopes have been opened, the contents left untouched. The two exceptions are of immediate interest:

one, in Madeleine's writing, with the wrong flat number that somebody has crossed out and corrected; the other, stamped with the logo of Junquera's firm in Jerez. Judging by the postmark, it must have arrived this morning. Both envelopes are empty.

I eventually find the letters under the pillow in the bedroom. Both have been screwed up and then carefully folded back out again. My pulse begins to race as I read the contents.

I run out into the road. No logic, just desperation. Taxis never pass in Chepstow touting for clients. I turn back into the apartment. I find Sandra's number from the call list. No reply. Please speak after the beep. 'Sandra or Roger, call me as soon as you get this message! It is vital I speak with you. It concerns Vernon. Do not ignore this!'

Dark thoughts possess me. The only ray of hope is that he hasn't taken the letters with him. Intentional, or, in his haste, has he simply forgotten? I telephone again. And again. And again. She made the recording sound like a period TV family drama, so formal and upper crust. 'This is Sandra. None of the Davenports are in residence at the moment. We promise to check your message as soon as we are back. Don't hang up without telling why you called.' And I didn't. Should I call the police? I study the display. 999. Indecision. Should I press call?

I must have lain on the bed. I don't remember doing so, but there is that sense of foreboding as I open my eyes. It's already night. There's a shuffling noise coming from the lounge.

I use the glow from the mobile to look around. Vernon is sitting on the floor, back to the wall, knees pulled tight into his body, secured by hands gripped together, his head resting on one shoulder as if asleep. But his eyes are wide open, glazed, eyelashes encrusted with the dried seepage from blocked tear ducts. In the gloom, I can make out a heavily stained white T-shirt and a pair of denims that, by the stench, have been fouled and dried on him more than once.

His eyes follow me as I click the light switch. Nothing. I remember. I'd missed a couple of direct debit payments two years ago and the electric supplier installed a prepayment meter in the hall cupboard. Automatically, I look for the change jar on the mantlepiece. It's empty. The pair of Chinese vases I purchased at a local auction many years ago, which stood either side of the jar, are missing.

He must have read my thoughts. He speaks in a hushed, whispered tone as if it is all too much of an effort. 'Call it a delayed child maintenance payment if you like.' He waves an arm around the room. 'You don't have much shit worth selling. It's all fake, just like you.'

I fish for some coins in my pocket and make my way out to feed the meter. The light from a naked bulb does nothing to improve the shambles that was once an orderly, if somewhat sparse living area. In the attempt to feed his habit, he must have been through everything, discarding my detritus over the floor if it had no resale value.

For the first time, I notice the shattered woodwork around the small window at the back door. Before locating the spare key, he must have forced the window. Judging by the state of the rotting wood, the damage is not recent.

'Suppose you're expecting an apology for the mess?' He stands directly behind me. I didn't hear him. I wheel around. His back is propped against the kitchen wall, alongside the knife rack.

I feel behind me for the key in the back door. It is ice-cold to the touch as I turn it. The door creaks as it opens.

'Let some fresh air into the place. It stinks, and so do you. Why don't you take a shower and change those clothes?'

'I need some cash.' There is no menace in his voice.

'Take a shower and we'll talk about it. How long is it?' I mean since he washed but he assumes I must be talking about his last fix.

'Two days, but the man said he don't want no more fucking porcelain.' He laughs to himself. 'So your chamber pot's still under the bed.'

I don't have one, but it lightens the atmosphere.

'I don't need the money for skag. I have to leave, and sharpish.'

'Why? I've only just got here.'

'Now you're back, people will come looking for me.'

'Not here. Nobody knows I'm back. Whatever it is, you're safe for now. Get cleaned up and I'll see what I can do about the cash.'

To my surprise, he accepted the suggestion without question or an abusive reaction. I use the lengthy shower interlude to clear up the worst of the mess. There is the sound of my wardrobe door opening.

Vernon is significantly taller than me, and the tracksuit bottoms I used to wear for knocking around the flat finish halfway up his calves. The long-sleeve sweatshirt has frayed cuffs and 'Sanlazer' in crumbling white lettering emblazoned across the front. He has tried to look presentable by combing his matted hair but the glazed eyes and stretched, gaunt features tell their own story.

'So?' he presses.

'Answers first,' I reply with a boldness I don't feel.

He shrugs. 'They kicked me out a week ago. I was living in an old caravan parked alongside the house.'

I raise my eyebrows.

'Don't worry,' he says. 'It was hidden by the trees. The neighbours couldn't see. Mum would never put her street cred at risk.' There is a touch of bitterness in his voice. 'Entry into the house, forbidden, *verboten*. I got a bit desperate, forced the window and took his poncey cufflinks the Rotary Club had given him – supposedly gold with 'RD' engraved on them.' He shakes his head. 'Gold, my fanny! Gold-plated and worthless. The man gave them back to me just now.'

He tosses them at me.

'When I said I need answers, I wasn't talking about your living arrangements,' I say. 'I spent ten months locked up in Spain. A day never passed when I didn't imagine having this conversation with you. How it would be. What we would say to each other without provoking violence. Why was a son so desperate to see his father dead that he twice tried to kill him? Had he committed murder? Was there anything I could have said or done that could have made things right? I need to understand.'

He has the letters from the bedroom in one hand. 'You read these? Did you always know?' he asks.

I shake my head. 'Sorry. I didn't, but I'm not going to use what's in those letters as an excuse.'

His thoughts are elsewhere and he appears not to register my reply. 'And the money?' he says, eventually.

I take the bank card out of my wallet and pass it to him. He raises his eyebrows, an unspoken question.

'Just short of three hundred pounds. I'll ask the questions and you answer. When we finish, I'll give you the number. Now, why don't you tell me everything from the start?'

He moves quickly towards me. I didn't see the plastic ties in his hand until the last second.

PART THREE – VERNON – REVENGE

CHAPTER FORTY-ONE

There.

Now you know everything. No fairy story, is it?

My father! Look at you. Pitiful! If you think those tears on your cheeks, that weak, wobbling chin, are going to make any difference to the way I feel, think again, and take a hike! Accept the fact you made me what I am, no matter how you try to excuse your actions, apportion blame or look for pity in your senility. Whatever you may say, you arsehole, it's all down to you; nobody else.

What did you call it, nature versus nurture? Your favourite line was we all start off this life with a blank sheet of paper. Your parents begin by writing on it and, as you get older, others join in with their comments, but the boldest of all the words come from your dad, the man who moulds and guides you. Tell me, what guidance did I get from you?

It's no accident you've ended up a sad and lonely old man. The only thing I remember of you as a child is the man who was never there. I knew the lines on the palm of your hand as if they were my own. Not because you beat me – although a slap wasn't out of the question when you were angry or frustrated – but the palm held out in front of you was supposed to say sorry, don't come any closer, I'm just going out to work, a client, a delivery, a job, a staff problem. Always a reason for not being there, and you rarely were. The other extended palm said keep quiet, I must just read this document or take this phone call; it's important. Business is what matters. Without business, there is no family. Excuse the whimpering sound in the background – it's my son trying to get my attention. Now, what were you saying, caller?

Sound about right, Father?

You created someone who in your world had little or no value. On the contrary, you treated me as an irritant who you could fob off with the change in your pocket or the promise of a treat tomorrow. I lived my infancy in the knowledge I had no relevance, no pride or self-esteem by your standards.

How could I deal with this vacuum? Mum was always there, of course, dealing with the minutiae of family life, making sure I was all the things well-turned-out offspring should be, shielding me from the unspoken racial prejudices of the adults and trying to explain away as irrelevant the taunts so easily voiced by my peer group. Her preoccupation was to survive and then to thrive in a white man's world. She tried to give me value purely as a black person, never as an individual in my own right.

As a child, your weapons for self-defence are crude. I chose hatred. If I could identify someone to hate – black, brown or white – they would be below me and I would be above them. That was my guide to self-worth; placing a value on my status as a person in my own right. Sometimes it would be a teacher, maybe the vicar or that vile choirmaster who would squeeze your knee, the local policeman who enjoyed making fun of me, anybody in authority. I guess my naïve rationale placed such people high on the social status ladder, which meant I was worth even more if I could belittle them in some way.

If they were poofs or had feminine traits, all the better. Remember, Mum was born in Suriname, daughter of a Muslim mother and evangelical father. Apparently, although my grandmother had foregone her faith to marry her husband, many of her Sharia teachings had been passed down to Mum, above all the one that said homosexuality was a vile form of fornication and should be punishable by death. When I told her I had contrived to capture 'Bender' Benson, the biology teacher, on my Polaroid, kissing his boyfriend goodnight outside a restaurant, and I had pinned the print to the staff noticeboard, she said he got what he deserved and should be fired. He was. Even when I claimed to have accidentally slammed down the lid of my music-rest table on the choirmaster's hand, causing severe bruising, she had smiled to herself. She never punished me for my actions, never the failed disciplines you tried to impose to – what was it – 'put me on the right track'.

And then there was that psychiatrist you ashamedly referred to as a counsellor. Waste of money; better spent on a line of coke. She wouldn't see me any more when I asked her if, now she had heard all about my problems, she would be turned on if I slapped her about a bit. Remember? Of course you do. I think you fancied her.

Things might have changed you when Albert came along, but they didn't. You were still as distant and preoccupied as ever, probably more so than before. I had to take him under my wing, teach him that he did count as a person and not just somebody you could pat on the head at social occasions as part of your perfect family set-up. What do they say is the average family

– dad, mum and two-point-four children? That's exactly what we had, if you count tragic Celine as the point four. I would go regularly with Mum to visit her in the home, but by the time Albert was a toddler, if I saw her once or twice a year ... poor cow! I miss you, Celine.

I tried my best with Albert, but he eventually found a hiding place in all that Buddhism bollocks. There were times he would drive me potty with that foul-smelling incense and those ridiculous rituals. I can't imagine being alone for a whole day, let alone going to some retreat for six months to find your inner self and not being able to speak to another soul. I'm the sort who enjoys what's happening on the outside, not examining my navel to see if it suits my personality. Anyway, it was his world, so leave him to it.

Suddenly, Rosita was there. You will never meet a sexier, more promiscuous woman, and I was at the age when you are totally infatuated, without control or compromise. I was totally in love with that woman and she knew it. She caught me with a photograph of her while I was masturbating.

You didn't like the next bit, did you? I enjoyed telling you. You said I was a liar, that she wasn't like that. Believe me, old man, I regret to tell you she was – sorry about the emphasis – and I loved every minute of it. No real sex – I was too young, she insisted – though God knows I tried. She would laugh at the expressions on my face as she gave me a handjob, my eyes transfixed on her tits as she played with them. She really despised me and I knew it. I didn't care.

It wasn't difficult to see she was after you, and I recognised the exact moment when you realised and took advantage of the situation. God, I hated you. I was so jealous. I wanted her all for myself, but I knew that if I told Mum, Rosita would have to go. It was the first time that I wanted to kill you. I wish I had. She'd still be alive now.

Then, out of the blue, you go and run off with her. What a piece of work you are! Move your brain to your dick and leave us all wondering what the hell we'd done to drive you away. When Mum told us, we all stood around in silence. No one knew what to say. Albert must have been about thirteen. You would never have imagined the words coming out of his mouth. He idolised you. 'He's not my father any more. We will be better off without him.' Both Mum and I were astounded he could have spoken like that, but he was right.

Now I had someone I could really hate, for ever and a day.

Those early weeks, Mum took it really bad, though she tried to put on her 'hurt but coping' face whenever visitors came around. Amongst some really caring friends were a sprinkling of arseholes whose mouths bleated sympathetic words whilst their eyes said 'I knew it would never work. I told everybody. Now see. I was right.' One of their offspring chose to voice his opinion at school in a much cruder form. I wouldn't be surprised if there is still a bloodstain on the ground behind the science block. The assault got me excluded from school, and a police caution.

It was all your fault and, in a way, the turning point in my life that started me on this downward spiral into what you see now. Every day, I blamed you, and every day, the hatred grew stronger until it became an obsession. I planned so many ways to kill you, prolonging the pain and suffering with every new scenario.

Mum was seeing a shrink, someone Roger had recommended through contacts at the golf club. It was Roger who emerged from the pile as Mum's confidant. They had known each other for a long time and were good friends. I knew from the way he ogled her that he fancied Mum; but there again, lots of men did.

Whatever you say, I still think you must have known what had gone on.

Putting that to one side, Roger was slowly muscling in on your old turf. I'll give him credit. She needed him then and he really helped her. Mum didn't want any aggro. When she finally came to terms with the fact that you weren't coming back, she was willing to accept some deal you had proposed, but Roger convinced her to go for your jugular. She had to stand up for herself, get tougher and secure the future for the family's sake. I agreed with every word he said.

You looked a fucking sorry sight coming out of the lawyer's offices. It was the happiest I'd felt for months. Mum and Roger had stuck it to you. What a partnership!

Of course, I didn't realise at the time it was all part of his ploy to salvage the wreckage after the train crash. Marrying Mum was the next logical step, and for a few months he acted his part as the caring stepfather. But he couldn't keep it up. I accept I was a difficult case to handle, but he only paid lip-service to the paternal responsibilities and I couldn't really blame him. At the end of the day, he was only there for the sex and the kudos and security that a large chunk of money brings. We kids were part of the package he had to put up with.

For a few years everything went along without too much hassle. I was a weekly boarder at a school for kids with special needs. My special need was regularly shagging the girl who liked to cut nicks in herself with a razor blade. I made sure no cutting instruments were around when we were on the job. She's still around today. As you can see from what I'm holding in my hand, she graduated from razor blades to this beauty, a double-edge, cold steel boot knife, specially imported from the good old US of A. Mandy would have been here to meet you, but she hates people she doesn't know, unless they're into a line of coke or a hairline flick on the arm which takes over thirty seconds to bleed. She sends her apologies.

Actually, it wasn't a bad school. From the academic standpoint, I learned a lot more than I had done at the comprehensive and the teachers made the subjects interesting and topical. The other good thing is that all the pupils were troubled, so when problems did arise, the school would close ranks and sort it out with no outside intervention. It's a maxim I've always tried to follow.

Being away from home so much meant I drifted even further away from Albert. What with his Buddhism and all that, I never saw much of him, and when I did, we had little to say to each other beyond 'How's it going?'

When I left school, Roger got me a job with an electronic components firm. I was good at concentrating on detail, and soldering circuit boards was right up my street. I must have been about seventeen. Anyway, I got home from work to find Mum panicking. We were supposed to be going to the golf club for dinner. Roger was being presented with a trophy, some prick of the month prize, and Albert hadn't showed up. I was to go and find him. He must be at the library. He was; in the reference section behind the applied maths alcove, getting a blowjob from a blonde bloke who looked as though he was in training to become a piston engine.

This little incident not only explained why Albert had no girlfriends but presented me with a hold over him I had up until the day he died. He begged me not to tell Mum, but the genie was out of the bottle – I've always wondered why it wasn't the lamp – and I've got what I wanted a dozen times by suggesting if he didn't play ball, I'd drop the hint indoors he was a faggot.

Always worked a treat – at least, until … well, you know when.

As I said, things had calmed down. Mum and Roger lived their own lives, sometimes in harmony, often apart, but the arrangement seemed to work. Then one day, that prick of a solicitor who acted for you, Paul something-or-other, turned up out of the blue. I'd seen him at a couple of our house parties, where he seemed to spend his introductory greeting to Mum, Roger and any guest prepared to talk to him apologising for having represented you during the divorce proceedings. Roger said he was more than grateful for everything he'd done, but the prick still didn't get it.

Anyway, he had come round to check whether we had heard the news you and Rosita were going to have a baby. You had stupidly emailed him. Sandra told him we weren't interested in what you were doing and suggested he follow suit, but as soon as the door was shut behind him, she broke down. Talk about losing the plot; she was totally out of control. I'd never heard Mum and Madeleine lose their tempers with each other, but accusations were flying around. Madeleine must have known about the pregnancy and should have let Mum know. Madeleine said she had heard but didn't want Sandra to be upset, which sent Mum into another rage, ranting on about expecting her best friend to tell her everything. Her anger saw Roger expelled from the marital bed to the spare room, leaving him to go around mumbling something about 'men have their needs' under his breath. In the end, she went away for nearly six weeks. Roger wouldn't say where, but I saw an invoice from a special care home for a treatment called electroconvulsive therapy.

It was about then I started to put my plan together. Mum would be avenged.

I was down in Brighton when the news came. I'd gone to fetch Albert. Mum was due home and Roger felt it would be therapeutic if we were all there when she arrived. My brother was involved with some Portuguese guy who was doing a language course at the university. They had met at an anti-vivisection rally in the summer and Albert had stayed on in this Hugo's apartment. Got himself a temporary job in one of the shops in the Lanes. They were all over each other. It was sickening. Albert would have just turned seventeen. Hugo was about the same age, maybe a little older, but acted like he was the big man, worldly wise, not country bumpkins like us. I soon put that wanker in his place.

Mum was back home about a week when Celine died. I've heard your excuses but the facts are you didn't reply and you missed your daughter's funeral. There was a silver lining. It finally toughened Mum up into realising exactly what a worthless article she had married and ensured all your so-called friends recognised you for the bastard you are.

By the time spring came, I'd told my boss where he could shove his circuit boards and I was on the dole. I had a plan that needed to involve my brother and his boyfriend. I hadn't been abroad for years. By this time, the happy couple were shacked up in Cavalla. Hugo was working for his uncle and I met the whole family. Pleasant enough. I smoked a few joints with some hippy friends and told Albert what we were going to do. He said I was crazy, but when I explained if Mum found out he was a shirtlifter, she was bound to have a relapse and end up back in the asylum … Well, I ask you, what could he say?

We met up in July at Hugo's aunt's place in Porto. Strange woman: refused to answer Hugo's questions about her ex-husband and spent all day reciting poetry to the wall. Hugo said some young poet was her latest flame, though God help him, having to put up with her.

The drive down to the Costa del Sol could hardly be described as a barrel of laughs, with those two morose bitches in the back. Anyway, I did try to make it more of a holiday. We started off in Malaga, worked our way to Marbella, Torremolinos and along to Gibraltar. The other two had livened up a bit and went off to look at the apes and some caves while I shagged a barmaid from the bar we'd been in the previous night. I could have been back in Newport, it was so strangely similar.

Eventually, we made our way up to Seville and along the Costa de la Luz to Islantilla. You were right. That's where we took the photographs, in front of the beach bar with the cock-eyed English writing. But that came afterwards.

I could see you were tensing up when I said 'afterwards'. I thought then, he's going to do something stupid, so watch him.

We found your villa easily enough and watched the comings and goings for a couple of days. In the end, you drove off with suitcases, leaving Rosita and another woman to wave you goodbye. I said to my two stalwarts, 'Look, they've left me Rosita and one for you two to share.' The colour was almost drained from their faces. I told them to forget they were queers for the day and stick to the plan.

Stupidly, I must have missed seeing the young girl and this other woman – was that her mother? – leave the villa. We could have gone in then but the opportunity was lost. They came back in a taxi. The girl was as white as a sheet, leaning on the other one for support, and crying. I thought, she's going straight to bed.

You were looking anxious just now, Father dear, perched on the edge of your chair, ready to pounce. Don't think about it. If you fall on this knife, it will slit you right open.

We waited until early evening. It had started to drizzle. Albert said they had decided not to go through with it. I pushed him around a bit, forced them both to take a slug from the bottle of firewater I'd bought from the garage and told them to start working up a hard-on.

We were in luck; the other woman shot off in a car somewhere. It was time. Rosita was on her own in the lounge. The girl was, I guessed, in bed. We put on the face masks and went in.

I knew you'd do something silly. Hardly the speed of a panther, was it? You are so pathetically predictable. Now look what's happened. You've got a nasty cut on the arm and the plastic ties have made some nasty welts on your wrists. And shouting, cursing me and all the other stuff sounds more than fair in the light of current events, doesn't it, Father dear? What's more, as usual, you are jumping to conclusions. Can we calm down now?

Okay. That's better. The plan was that we would act as one, but it all went to pot. The other two had totally lost their bottle, so I said to wait by the door and let me know if anybody was coming. Rosita recognised me straight away, even with the mask on, and started laughing. The bitch! I thought, I can't have that, so I took it off and slapped her around a bit until she started to get scared. I undid my flies and told her it was about time she had a portion of black dick. Do you know what the whore did? You'd never believe it. It was just like the old days. After we'd talked a bit, she put her hand around it and said, 'We can do something about this.' I couldn't stop myself. In seconds, I must have come in her hands. She wiped them on the see-through wrapover she was wearing over her dress.

I remembered the emotion I felt when I was a kid. When she'd finished, I would look at her with those doleful eyes, full of juvenile infatuation, and crave her attention. Not now. What I saw before me was a heavily pregnant, middle-aged-looking tart with spots on her chubby face, greasy, lank hair and the unpleasant scent of impending motherhood. The disgust must have shown in my face because she started to get really scared. I told her to ring you on my pay-as-you-go and make up an excuse to get you back to the villa. She couldn't reach you at first, but she put on a good act to whomever she was talking.

Time passed and I was beginning to get impatient. Then it all happened in the space of a few seconds. I'm not sure whether it was one or two cars that pulled up outside, but it spooked my two lookouts and they disappeared out of the veranda doors. Rosita seized the opportunity, tore a gash in my arm with those ridiculously long nails of hers and made a dash to follow them. She stumbled over in the greasy, damp yard, her legs splayed apart. It was nearly dark by this time. She picked herself up, started off running as best she could, shouting something that sounded like 'ruby, ruby,' over and over again.

I followed her to the swimming pool. It was deserted. No lights. I nearly tripped over her. She must have slipped on the wet tiles, fallen badly. There was blood seeping from between her legs, one of which was bent under her. Somehow her pants were around her knees. I swear it had nothing to do with me. She was unconscious. I heard your voice approaching. There was a row of bushes nearby, so I hid.

It was bizarre, like a scene in a Greek tragedy. Right at that moment, the clouds must have parted like the curtains on a stage, giving way to a backdrop of hazy moonlight.

You knelt down alongside her, cradled her head for a minute or so, before sprinting back to the villa. As you left, another man, who I had seen earlier driving off with you but in a second car, arrived, looked down at her and spoke in Spanish to someone. The other woman I had seen earlier appeared out of the shadows and spoke softly to the man, who reacted by rushing round to the front of the villa. I could see the reflection of approaching blue flashing lights in the sky, so I guessed he must have gone to direct the emergency response when they got there.

I couldn't believe my eyes. Rosita must have regained consciousness. Her arm was raised and she was scratching at the face of the older woman who let out a stream of Spanish, took Rosita's head between her hands and forced it back onto the tiled surround. It must have nearly split her head open.

The woman was strong. She turned Rosita's body over, pulled her by the shoulders and let her slide into the pool, face down. She had her foot balanced on Rosita's back, keeping her head under water until she heard the sound of voices approaching. Why the man had led the medical team to the pool the long way round, instead of through the villa, puzzled me. He must have done it to give the woman more time, I guess, allowing her to slip away unnoticed.

Yes, she had stripped the wrapover off Rosita before she pulled her into the pool. Just as well. Most of my semen and traces of blood were all over it. She took it with her.

Anyway, you got back just before the ambulance crew arrived. The noise had drawn people from their villas and a small crowd had developed. I managed to join them and slip away to find my courageous companions. I have to say that as I left, I had a little smile to myself. Not because somebody had wanted Rosita dead; I couldn't really blame her for your failings. I wouldn't have done anything serious to her, but I wanted to really get at you. No, I smiled because you were screaming into the night sky. Your pain was gut-wrenching. It sounded like nonsense: 'Gorgonzola, I'm going to kill you,' over and over again. I thought, good, he's suffering, just like Mum is.

Give it a rest! What's the point in crying? Feeling sorry for yourself? I'll make a cup of tea for us and you can let me have your PIN number. Have to get off soon. I'll pick up Mandy and we'll be on our way.

I've put the tea down there for you to look at. You're a bit out of control, so I can't really let your hands free until I've drunk mine. No milk or sugar, I'm afraid, and we've had to share a used teabag. But never mind, it's hot, or, at least, mine is.

Why are you asking me? You know why you got the invite to the wedding. It had nothing to do with Albert wanting to rekindle your relationship. I put him up to it.

Hugo has had money problems for years. This time, it was getting serious. He was using Albert's prayer cushion business to ship amphetamines across Europe. He was in it with his uncles and some Mr Big or other who was in Brazil. Lino handled production and shipment; Hugo was responsible for distribution, working with three Moroccans. I understand you met them, so to speak. The merchandise was packed in the house you stayed in. Hugo and Albert kipped there off and on when they were busy making and stuffing cushions.

Trouble was, Hugo had been doing some private business; a few packs to start with, but it had got serious around the turn of the year and there was a big hole in the stocks. Hugo was about to front up and come clean. He would ask for six months to find the money. Albert asked me if I could tap Mum for some money to help him out. I laughed at him. I told him he would have more chance of shagging the Dalai Lama.

There were problems all around, but I thought of the solution to make everybody's wishes come true. Jasmin could resolve the questions around her boy's parentage; Albert could get Mum off of his back about settling down and producing grandchildren; Hugo could get an inflated settlement from the insurance company, pay back his aunt the money she had lent him to buy the house with enough over to clear his debts; and I would get my prize.

Why? You ask why? Wasn't Rosita's death revenge enough to satisfy my need to hate you?

It would have been, but you stupidly came back to Wales. Your presence, twenty miles from where they live, set Mum off again. She had started talking about you once more, introducing you unnecessarily into conversations with people, new bouts of nervousness and anxiety. I had to finish it once and for all. So, there you are: a sham marriage; your presence, not as the groom's father but as an inquisitive and incompetent heating engineer; a gas explosion that destroyed you and the house; and no excuses for the insurance company to wriggle out of paying up. Another plus was that Hugo could clear out whatever stocks he had and pretend they had been destroyed in the explosion.

I came round that morning to tell you what I thought of you and exactly why you had been invited. I didn't want you to die thinking we'd forgiven you. I hadn't finished before you passed out from the roofie Albert had put in your coffee.

Of course, I should have realised Albert would bottle it. The Moroccans were looking for Hugo and money. Albert calmed them down, but he'd lost the plot. I went off to a bar with Hugo to establish we were elsewhere when the bang went off. You were propped up in the meter cupboard alongside the boiler. All he had to do was walk away, but no, he decides to save you and kill himself in the process. What a waste!

There. That's the whole story. Your part of the deal now. The PIN number, please, Father dear.

Today? You want to know about what happened today? It's the full confessional, is it? What do I get when I finish; say three Hail Marys and receive complete absolution? I can't see it, somehow. All right, I'll give you another five minutes if that's what you want. I've got all the time in the world.

It's simple really. I read the two letters. Actually, it goes back to the day before you turned up at that hotel in Usk to meet Madeleine. She had been round at Mum's for their normal gin-and-gossip session. I was short of cash and knew Madeleine kept twenty quid in the glove compartment of her car for emergencies, so I decided to borrow it. There was a note in there as well, with the name of the hotel, the following day's date and a time. I thought I'd turn up and see what was going on. Lo and behold, you two are cosying it up in the bar. I took a pic with my phone with the intention of letting Mum know what you were up to, only Roger saw it first and told me to cool it. Broaching it out of the blue with Mum would upset her and set back the relationship with the only real friend she had. I couldn't argue with that. Still, there had to be an angle.

Another cash crisis and I had no option. I drove the bike round to her house and went in for a chat. She was really off with me. There would be no money. It was time for her to come clean with Sandra about the affair. She had arranged to go out and tell him – I assumed at the time the 'him' was you – her decision was final. And did I know what I was? The bitch started to call me all sorts of names. I pushed past her and made my way up to the bedroom to look for something worth taking. I desperately needed to get wasted. I took a few bits of jewellery, some cash, when she goes to hit me. We're at the top of the stairs. I push her away. I didn't mean for her to fall, tried to get hold of her dressing gown belt, but it was no good. She's lying at the bottom of the stairs in a heap, out cold; her mobile is going berserk. I panicked. I could hardly phone for an ambulance with my pockets stuffed with her trinkets, could I? So, I beat it.

Roger told me later that she was dead. I played the upset innocent, comforting Mum and thanking my lucky stars that no one suspected my involvement. Apparently, you had turned up at her house in a taxi; must have been just after I left. The police wanted to speak to you and a motorcycle courier who had earlier been seen making a delivery to her, according to some nosey neighbour. What a result!

Roger convinced me you were somehow involved and needed to be taught a serious lesson. On top of that, you owed him money and had no intention of paying it back. He knew the police wouldn't do anything without serious proof. I thought I could help that along by breaking into this place to find something to leave in her bedroom to convince the police you were involved with her. I had to smash a window, but I found some of your hairs on a comb and a toothbrush I could leave in her bathroom.

About a year ago, Roger came to me with a proposal. The coroner had left an open verdict on Madeleine's death whilst the police followed up on various lines of enquiry. They were on to you and Roger wanted to make sure it stuck. He had a pendant that had belonged to Madeleine, in the shape of a four-leaf clover. If it could be found in your possession, then, considered together with Sandra's testimony to confirm her friend had been wearing it the previous day, it would support the theory you were lying and had seen her on the day she died.

I should have twigged him then. How did he come to have the pendant she was wearing around her neck when she fell down the stairs if he hadn't been in the house that day? I was too obsessed with framing you to question the simple truth staring me in the face.

So, I went off to Portugal, ostensibly to collect Albert's personal effects and seek a reconciliatory meeting with you when I would take the opportunity to plant the pendant. I had a better idea. There was talk of visit to a safari park. What a golden opportunity to catch you by surprise and finish what the explosion should have done and what Hugo failed to do in the hospital when he changed the IV bag – finally get rid of you!

That old cottage? That was you, was it? Hugo suggested I stay there, out of view, a place to hide. He was supposed to bring me some gear. I was strung out. Thought I heard him walking about. Imagine. If I'd seen you, we could have had a nice little tête-à-tête. Yes, I saw the little child as I cycled away, didn't recognise him. The car was open. I checked to see if there was anything worth taking. The little fucker wouldn't stop crying, so I shouted at him. That shut him up.

The pendant was easy. Walid and his mate owed me a favour. The night before Albert's sham marriage there was a fight in a bar. I was with Hugo, who got into a row with the two Moroccans about money he owed them. They started to push him around. I joined in to try to stop them and ended up the worse for it. The police came, hauled us all in. Hugo told me that the police chief was after the Moroccans and it would be a bad scene if they were sent to court, so I took the blame. I said I started the fight and that it was racially motivated. Walid and his mate walked and I got a caution.

Albert told me you knew about the fight. I got Walid to give you the pendant back on the pretext I had tried to use it to buy drugs from them but it was worthless and he wanted nothing more to do with the Hart family. It worked a treat but God, I was unlucky. I nearly had you at the safari park just as the law turned up to collar you. I had to disappear before the policeman recognised me.

Good old Roger! He really set me up to do his dirty work. After all that, he kicked me out of the caravan two weeks ago. I know I wasn't supposed to have anybody staying, but Mandy's different. And why do you need two sets of golf clubs? You don't, do you? I think the set I nicked was your old one anyway. I needed the cash. He went berserk.

What did I do to him today? The blood on the knife and the stains on the T-shirt?

That letter… from Madeleine … saying she understood your motives and was planning to see Sandra the next day and confess? She would be meeting Roger at the hotel that same day to tell him her decision was final. I watched Mum's face as she listened to me. He blustered and denied everything, but she could tell it was the truth. Not a word passed between them.

I told them about your solicitor's letter from Spain. There had been a forensic examination of the skin fragments found under Rosita's fingernails, something called low template DNA, where small samples are amplified, whatever that means. As your son, our DNA would be so similar that any test at this stage would show that it was more likely your skin, not mine, under her fingernails. Not so. There was no DNA compatibility whatsoever. I loved the solicitor's professional compassion, so utterly false. 'I regret and am sorry to have to advise you that the sample taken is a match on the Europol database with that recorded in Portugal of your son, Vernon.' Not only am I now bang to rights for Rosita's death, but I find out I'm not your fucking child anyway.

Mum went white. I didn't need to ask who my father was. She blurted it out. 'Your dad was always working, never any time for me. It was one night and one night only, a golf club dinner. I was lonely and drunk. Roger was so attentive.'

If I'm shouting, I apologise. Do you know something? You can give me all that spiel about it not mattering, it's the nurture that counts. The simple fact is I'm the result of a one-night stand in the back of a three-litre Rover!

No, I didn't attack him. Do you hear that? Lot of traffic outside. What's all the commotion? Where was I? The PIN number. Your birth year? How corny! I should have guessed.

How many times do I have to say I didn't? The pompous old fart, my biological father, makes his fatal mistake. He says a worthless fuck-up like me could never be his son. Mum grabs the knife out of my hand, cuts herself in the process and stabs him in the chest. She is going berserk.

I can't have that, can I? I pull her off. He's still just about alive. She lets the knife fall. I pick it up, wipe the handle clean, grip it tight and press it down into his heart. I try and get her to listen. She has to say it was me. I tell her the same thing a dozen times. She's babbling on. Her mobile is ringing. I can't leave her like that. Best to knock her out, leave her unconscious. When she comes round, maybe she'll think it was me. She's the victim in all this, not the guilty party.

Now you know absolutely everything. You've been studying the knife. Quite something, isn't it? I guess it's time for the final act.

EPILOGUE
Madrid – 2019

Tomorrow will be Francisco's fourteenth birthday. Throughout all these years, I've kept in touch. I write religiously once a month. Jasmin replied, just once, telling me briefly what he was doing, how school was going, how he would often mention my name.

I received the first letter written by him when he was ten, a schoolboy's stuttering, irregular hand, just one paragraph in disjointed English, signed with his love. Every month came a new letter, always one paragraph, always signed with a kiss.

I used to wait anxiously for the post but as the months passed, the letters, longer in content and in improving English, started to arrive with a two-or three-month gap as his young life evolved and I became a distant memory and, maybe, an obligation, like the ageing family dog who nobody has the heart to put down.

The analogy is a little off beam in that, now at seventy-six, I still keep fit, and most of my faculties, if you ignore my deaf ear and troubled memory, are in reasonable working order. I am not yet quite ready for the knacker's yard.

Loneliness is the biggest problem and, with it, the countless hours spent living and reliving the events of the past. If only I had been this or done that. I know it's a pointless exercise but I can't help it.

I turned down the offer of a place in a geriatrics' residential home, waiting in the queue for eternity with a lot of dribbling, incontinent old farts who start every sentence with the word 'remember'. No thank you. Of course, they moved me from the place in ... Chepstow, was it? Yes, Chepstow. I couldn't have stayed there. Too many painful memories.

If I close my eyes, I can still see Vernon's face in front of me. He does not speak for five minutes, his eyes flickering, darting unseeing around the room as he relives everything he has just told me. I misjudged him. His only quest in life was to protect his mother from the suffering I brought on her. It still is. My death was always his only solution. I try to maintain my composure.

The plastic ties bite deeply into my wrists. The blood on my cheek where he barely touched me with the point of that lethal-looking knife has congealed, but I still have the taste in my mouth. Irrationally, I feel no fear. I can accept his solution. I just don't want it to hurt.

Did he realise the cars braking to a halt in the courtyard were more than likely the police? In the end, when there was no reply from Sandra, I telephoned, demanding they went to her house before something terrible happened. They must have arrived too late.

Vernon is moving the knife from one hand to another when there is a loud rap on the front door. He looks at me, at first confused, and then, the realisation he will not be escaping with his precious PIN number and my three hundred pounds. The police are announcing their presence, demanding entry. There is the sound of feet pounding on gravel, hushed voices at the back door.

I watch as his grip tightens on the knife. He starts to laugh, that laugh I recalled in the midst of my failed memory. He takes a step towards me.

'Do you know what Madeleine said to me at the funeral?' The knife is perfectly still, inches from my chest.

I shake my head.

'She suggested I take pity on you. The suffering of a parent who loses a child is worse than death itself. Do you believe that? She said the parent had to go on living with the pain; a pain that would never leave you. Do you get that?'

He stops, waiting for an answer.

'This is all your fault,' he says. 'I hope you rot in hell.'

With that, he draws the knife across his throat.

For what seems like an eternity, there is no blood, no sign of any cut. He is toying with me. His hand goes to his neck. Blood starts to course through his fingers. As he collapses to the floor, there is a smile on his lips.

The day after tomorrow, I am going to do what he hoped. I am preparing to rot in hell.

My invitation to Francisco's birthday is propped on the mantelpiece. My plane ticket, one way, is booked.

I shall look forward to renewing my acquaintance with Lino, now he has served his ten-year prison sentence. I wonder if he still has those pristine creases in his trousers, but I expect a decade of wearing baggy prison overalls has rid him of that foible.

Of course, seeing Jasmin and Francisco will be the highlight of my trip.

It's a pity I won't be able to take Sandra with me. She has been kept in a secure psychiatric facility near Bristol pretty much since the day Roger died. She was on twenty-four-hour suicide watch in the early days when I tried to see her, but now, the last I heard was she lives in a world of her own, a young girl, teacher's pet, back in the Caribbean, and recognises no one.

Jasmin told me that Madeleine's old Astra is still in working order, parked in her driveway. Francisco takes a keen interest in car mechanics and has been working on it for me. They took my licence away many years ago, but I doubt I shall have any problems with the authorities if I go for one last drive.

I've heard Madrid is very pleasant in the spring. I've kept tabs on Salvador and Eliana over the years. He somehow managed to avoid prosecution for any involvement in his sister's death and to finally secure promotion to captain shortly before his retirement from the force. As far as I know, Eliana was never implicated. I decided not to pass on the details of Vernon's testimony to the police. Hearsay from a dead murderer would carry little credibility. Besides, for Rosita's sake, it has to be me who will finally mete out the justice she deserves.

Under any circumstances, I would have waited until Salvador's three children were adults and had left home. Salvador and Eliana now live alone in the house that once belonged to his parents. That much I know from Isabel, along with the fact that most days they take a morning walk to the local pastelería for coffee.

Crossing roads in Madrid can be very dangerous, especially when an oncoming vehicle is being driven by a senile old man who has no licence. I hope they recognise me before they die.

Geoff Cook

Geoff grew up in South London, the latch-key child of a widowed mother who struggled in post war Britain to turn a place to live into a loving home. And she succeeded. Love you, Rita. RIP.

Geoff has had a varied commercial and financial career, living or working in countries with a Latin flavour, (South America, Southern Europe) as well as London and the Welsh Valleys in the UK. His experiences extend from professional accounting, investment banking and pop music management into running a ceramic tile factory and retail outlets, managing a leisure complex, operating a restaurant ship and owning and cheffing in restaurants on the Portuguese Algarve.

As a child, he opened a street lending library and developed an interest in literature and writing, turning his hand to numerous articles and projects over the years. In 2010, he published his first full-length novel as an e-book and has gone on to write a number of plays and novels, of which *Deaf Wish* is his latest offering.

Current projects include *Octogen*, a futuristic novel about life in 2060 without oil and the internet, *The Last Rights*, the story of a holocaust survivor with a dangerous secret and *Deguello*, a thriller set in Korea.
For more information, go to www.geoff-cook.com

PROLOGUE
THE LAST RIGHTS
by Geoff Cook
(Publication 2020)

ZURICH, SWITZERLAND – Last December

He walked silently on tiptoe across the darkened room, picking his way carefully between the sofas and armchairs, nearing the solitary figure sitting with her back to him, facing the bay window. The source of light was a solitary standard lamp set next to the wheelchair. Strands of frayed golden braid, partially detached from the fabric on the lampshade caused the insipid yellow glow to cast uneven fingers of light and shadow across the floor until they were absorbed into the blackness.

Closer now, he could make out the distorted reflection of her face in the window; eyes transfixed on a point in time that was not the present as she stared straight ahead at the swirling cloud of snowflakes that filled the night sky beyond the glass.

'I've been expecting you,' she said, finally. Her frail voice was laboured, the words expelled from her mouth on a current of exhaled breath.

'You have?' He sounded bemused. He was old too; – nowhere near her years – but, he ruefully accepted, still a long way past his prime.

'For the last seventy-five years.' A staccato cough growled in her throat. She was laughing. 'But we were too careful to let you catch us.'

He went to move forward, to face her, but a thin bare arm, limp, wrinkled skin hanging with barely any bone to cover, lifted to stop him. And it did.

'I have no wish to see your face.' A stuttered intake of breath. 'Do what you have to do, but I choose not to witness my executioner.'

'You mistake my intentions. My mission was simply to find you, to seek your cooperation.'

'Seek my cooperation. . .' There came another cough, a dry, jagged bark that propelled her head forward and scattered spots of blood on the handkerchief she had drawn to her mouth. 'You suggest that the assassin needs help from the victim?'

'I mean you no harm.'

She raised her hand. As she motioned for him to move nearer, he noticed fungus had blackened the nails on her fingers.

'Not a pretty sight, am I?'

He treated the question as rhetorical. There were no words of comfort.

He looked at her reflection in the window and prayed she would not catch the expression on his face.

Silence prevailed. Slowly, she raised her head to look at him. 'Do you believe in natural justice?' she asked.

Her eyes were blue and still so vital, as if the final bloom on a wilted plant. They studied him.

'I don't know.'

By her dismissive shrug it was a weak answer, not what she wanted to hear.

'It is natural justice that keeps me alive.' She stopped to regain her breath. 'It has judged me not only for all the wrongs I have done but for all the wrongs done to me that I have condoned. And its sentence' - she fought for air and inhaled afresh – 'its sentence is to keep me breathing so that I am obliged to witness this physical decay. My punishment is to survive in pain.' There was another pause. 'Yet with every passing day as the body succumbs, my mind grows stronger. Do you know what hell is? You shake your head. Then I will tell you. Hell is not being able to forget the past.' A grimace, and then, 'And now, you come.'

'Me?'

'You say you were sent to find me. Do you come to demand satisfaction or to bring absolution?'

'Absolution? Isn't that something in God's gift?'

Her hand beckoned him nearer still, her stale breath warming his cheek. 'Ah, God. I wondered when he would make an appearance.' She studied his face. 'You have a cut on your cheek. It will leave a scar.'

'I was playing with my grandchildren and got a little too over-enthusiastic. Hide and seek. Do you know the game?'

Her mouth creased into a weak smile. The giggle was no more than a rattle in her throat. 'I have been playing it all my life, but I cheated. If you want to win, you cannot expect the hunted to imagine that the hunter will wait until a hundred has been counted. One step in front is never enough. It can be a vicious game; no rules.

'Maybe God will be your arbiter.'

Her emaciated body stiffened. 'There you go again about God.' She breathed in heavily. He sensed she was angry. 'Don't you think I know? There is no God. God is an illusion, created by those who fear death; a panacea that provides a safety net for the lost souls who tip over the abyss of life into the unknown. Only the net is not really there, so you keep falling into the darkness for eternity.'

'You seem so certain. How can you know?'

'I just do. Your God is benign, all powerful? Don't nod your head. Say yes or no with conviction.'

'Yes.'

Her eyes closed. 'A lie. If a God really existed, he would not let the innocent suffer at the hands of evil.'

'Can the denial of innocence be reason enough to reject all religion?'

'You ask too many naïve questions. What is it you want of me?'

'You avoid an answer.'

There was a long pause. She appeared to be stilling herself, organising her thoughts. 'The innocents are left with no choice but to discard their faith when they realise their call for help has been ignored. Most succumb to the will of the aggressor and die in body and spirit at his hand. Those who manage to survive find their innocence is replaced by a malevolence that is as great or even greater than of those who inflict the suffering.'

'And you survived. I need you to tell me everything that happened.'

Was that an attempt at a laugh? He was not sure.

'There is not enough breath left in my body to speak of my life ... much beyond the time in my mother's womb.'

He placed his hand on hers. 'I cannot conceive that you did not make provision for this day.'

'I must sleep now. Tomorrow it will end.'

Before he had time to reply, she had closed her eyes. In sleep, her breathing was laboured and tormented; the death throes he recalled of his own father. Yet, as the minutes passed, she did not perish. Her eyes opened wide and alert, as if the sound of the trap had told her the animal had just been snared.

In her world there had been no interlude of respite in their conversation. She was giving weight to his last remark. She held his gaze once more.

'Are you certain you really wish to know? You will be signing your own death warrant.'

'I have no choice.'

She withdrew her hand from his and pointed a wavering finger. 'The cupboard. There is a file. It is all in there.' Another bout of coughing overcame her. Heavier spots of dark blood peppered the cloth.

He returned with a small leather-bound document case. She had used sheets from a writing pad, hundred upon hundred filled with small neat writing; a fine nib with black ink. There was a musty scent that told him the narrative had lain unread for many years.

'You have now been cursed with my burden and I, by the same token, relieved.'

'How come?'

'If it is not your intent to silence me, they will surely know of your coming. Death I will welcome, but no more torture. I will tell them that a man came for the file and they will seek you out. They will not stop until the truth is extinguished.'

He took the black leather gloves from his overcoat pocket and put them on, interlocking his fingers so that they fitted tightly. Two steps and he stood behind the wheelchair, his hand releasing the brake.

'I feel I am beholden to you,' he said with a smile.

Printed in Poland
by Amazon Fulfillment
Poland Sp. z o.o., Wrocław